DAPPLED LIGHT

DAPPLED LIGHT

A *novel by*

JESSICA MARKWELL

Matador
9 Priory Business Park,
Wistow Road, Kibworth Beauchamp,
Leicestershire. LE8 0RX
Tel: (+44) 116 279 2299
Fax: (+44) 116 279 2277
Email: books@troubador.co.uk
Web: www.troubador.co.uk/matador

ISBN 978 1783061 006

British Library Cataloguing in Publication Data.
A catalogue record for this book is available from the British Library.

Printed and bound in the UK by TJ International, Padstow, Cornwall
Typeset by Troubador Publishing Ltd, Leicester, UK

Matador is an imprint of Troubador Publishing Ltd

*In memory of my mother Eelin Page
who gave me DWP's box of papers
and said that I should write.*

Glory be to God for dappled things —

For skies of couple-colour as a brinded cow:

For rose-moles all in stipple upon trout that swim;

Fresh firecoal chestnut-falls; finches' wings;

Landscape plotted and pieced-fold, fallow and plough;

And all trades, their gear and tackle and trim.

All things counter, original, spare strange;

Whatever is fickle, freckled (who knows how?)

With swift, slow; sweet, sour; adazzle, dim;

He fathers-forth whose beauty is past change:

Praise him.

Gerard Manley Hopkins (1844-89)

CHAPTER ONE

January 1861

 Angus, Scotland

As she walks, Chrissy Hogarth holds her baby close, as if she would warm him. Over her shoulder is slung a sealskin bag. The day is very cold; the winter mist chills right through her cloak, jacket, camisole and linen shift. Inside her hard boots, her feet have almost ceased to feel, except for a place at the back where — with every step — the harsh leather rubs more raw the flesh of her heel. Chrissy has walked three miles from her home in Marketgait. She has chosen St Dunstan's because it is the prettiest churchyard she knows; in spring the slope is yellow with primroses and nodding cowslips, and in summer the bank grows pink with rosebay willow herb. A huge oak tree spreads its comforting arms over the little church, and a pair of elegant silver birches spring high beside the first stones. The church has an added benefit: it is isolated, separated by a narrow road, hedged with hawthorn, from the little hamlet of Constan.

She lifts the latch of the wrought-iron gate. Great flakes of white snow drift down, falling like manna from the sky. It is a sign, thinks Chrissy. A sign, if not of the Lord's outright approval, at least of His understanding. She lifts her wide blue eyes to heaven, and bows her head in gratitude. She draws the baby yet closer. She believes that God is smiling on her; he will forgive the lack of official ceremony. She pictures Jesus taking little Thomas tenderly in His arms, then leading him — now walking with sweet baby steps — to where on a pink cloud other babies play, tinkling bejewelled rattles of ivory and gold. Chrissy is suddenly overcome; Thomas will be safe with Jesus and in the company of merry playfellows, but he will no longer be with her. She has been sustained on her journey by the belief that she is doing the best she can for her child, but now selfishly, savagely, she thinks of herself. How will she live without him? What purpose will she serve, alone on God's earth? She has known her baby for only a night and a day, yet never before has she experienced such a powerful feeling of love. The love has felt like a physical blow, knocking and flooring her; for hours she has lain with him in her arms, doing nothing, incapable of sensible thought, until a stray blackbird has flown through the grating, flapping wildly and serving as a brisk reminder of life outside.

Chrissy sits herself down on the carved oak bench inside the porch and suppresses a sob. Softly, she draws back the woollen shawl to look once more at the dear small face. She marvels at the perfection of the baby's eye-lashes, she traces with her finger the sweet bow of his mouth. Then she turns her head to lay her cheek against his — it is as cold as that of the marble angel that decorates the tomb of Alfred Brownlee, and his beloved wife Jane. She lifts him away from her, cupping his little body in both her hands. His expression is serene; it is as if he has fallen asleep. Gently, she kisses his brow and soft dark hair. With infinite care, she pulls away the shawl to reveal his hands. They are a miracle of organisation: the miniature fingers appropriately proportioned, so that the third finger stretches to twice the length of the thumb. The joints — two to each digit — are just like her own, and the nails shine like mother of pearl, with — at the edge — a perfectly manicured small white moon. Chrissy feels a tightness at her full breast and a gathering in her womb. She weeps out loud, longing to feed her son. His birth had seemed a miracle. Alone in her room, she had thought when she felt the pains that her menses had come. She took laudanum, then as the pains grew worse, she took some more, her arms shaking as she lifted the vial to her lips. She took whisky too, from a bottle she was saving as a gift for the Montgomerys to be handed over on Christmas day. Unworldly with the drink, doped by the drug, lying on the thin straw mattress of her metal bed, she had felt a grinding, a pushing, and a burning. A slithering, and then her baby was there, the hair of his head slicked down with wet, his body smeared with her blood. She had dried him with her sheet, and once the afterbirth had followed, she bit through the cord with her teeth. From the first she had called him Thomas; the name came to her as if whispered. She knew he lacked strength — he never cried, as newborn babies should. Perhaps he was simply too small to survive, or perhaps his heart had found it too much of a struggle to beat. Or maybe it was the process of breathing he found impossibly difficult; his breastbone had heaved with each quick inspiration and a hollow had appeared under his ribs, as if he were being squeezed. Yet as he lay beside her, he had turned his head to study her face and it seemed that he blinked his eyes in recognition.

It grows dark; in the graveyard the snow continues to fall, ghostly against the dusk. Sometimes it drops steadily, sometimes the wind whisks it into flurries. The memorial stones are becoming topped with white, and the ground is already covered. Chrissy must wait no longer. Tenderly, she wraps again her precious bundle, taking especial care to cover the little icy feet. She places Thomas on the seat beside her, reaches for her bag, and opens it. She pulls out a freshly ironed

3

pillowcase, a lump of coal and a brass shovel. Using the edge of the shovel, she chips off a piece of the coal. For some moments, she is overcome; she would like so much to keep Thomas with her in the living world. But for his sake, she must let him go. She must give him a Christian burial so that he can live forever with the Lord, bathed by His love, and warmed by His care. Still weeping, she tucks the chip of coal inside the shawl, next to his skin, then she slides Thomas's body into the makeshift shroud. She has already chosen a spot at the bottom of the hill, near a pile of hay, scythed by the sexton on a summer's afternoon. The site is away from the main burial area, but still well inside the churchyard fence.

Stepping out, she stumbles on an unseen root. She has been sheltered under the roof of the porch, but now she shudders in the freezing air. A gust of snow blows sharp. She ducks her head, and pulls tight her cloak. She makes her way through the memorial stones and down the slope. The hay has become a covered mound. The pillowcase — when she puts it down — is camouflaged, white on white. Chrissy takes out the shovel, and attempts to dig.

But she does not even make a dent; the metal of the tool makes no impression. Angry and despairing, she beats the hard soil with her fist, making her knuckles bleed. She had thought God was looking upon her in a kindly way, but now she feels tricked and betrayed. In her zeal, she has failed to take into account the elements. All the while God has deliberately chosen not to remind her of the consequences of His seasons. He has watched with equanimity, knowing that she will be thwarted by the frozen ground. Chrissy cries out in her grief, a high-pitched howl. Exhausted, defeated, she sinks to her knees.

For a long time Chrissy remains kneeling in the bitter cold. Love has impelled her to St Dunstan's, but love has proved misleading. She is at a loss; she can formulate no plan for what to do next, because the words necessary for thought no longer seem to be there. It is as if more snow — sheer and soft — has filled her head. She is vaguely aware that she is hungry. There is a hollowness in her stomach, but the hollowness extends upwards, everything inside is cold and sheer and white.

The lurch of a branch — brought low by its load, built-up flake upon flake — startles Chrissy, and brings her to her senses. If she stays outside any longer, she will surely die. She gets slowly to her feet. What to do? She can try to hide Thomas's body without burying him, but this would seem unworthy, and there is the risk that he would be ignominiously found. She can start the long walk back to the docks, taking Thomas with her, but this would be no solution at all — she would have achieved nothing, and besides, she does not have the strength. There is a third choice; she can take cover in the church. She will be warmer there, and if she can remain there unnoticed, the weather may turn for the better. God willing, the ground will once again grow soft, allowing her to complete her task.

With Thomas tucked under her arm, and her bag slung over her shoulder, Chrissy climbs with slow steps back up the hill. Outside the ancient doorway, she pauses to ask God's mercy for the way she has railed against Him. If she is to enter His house, she must first ask His forgiveness. She offers her prayer of penance, then looks around for an indication that she has been heard. She waits, and fails to see one. But now, an instinct for preservation is waxing strong. Chrissy pushes at the heavy latch. She thinks at first that the door is locked; she cannot move it. She pushes upwards with all her strength, and finally it lifts; it is the cold that has rendered it stiff.

The church is austere — there is little in the way of decoration save for a carved rood screen, with a simple cross at the top. There are no cushions on the seats of the pews, and the baptismal font is unadorned. The high pulpit looks threateningly down. Chrissy is disturbed by a vision of the Reverend Willis, jabbing an accusatory finger. She is tempted to go back outside, but the draw of shelter is too powerful. Holding Thomas to her, she gives a kind of bobbing curtsey as she faces the altar; if she kneels on the cold tiled floor, she may never stand up again. She turns, and chooses a seat on the south side of the building, away from where the wind blows a whistling draught under the door. She settles herself under a chiselled memorial to John Harris, Fusilier of the Queen's Bays, who at the age of eighteen had lost his life at Lucknow, gallantly defending her Majesty's Empire. He would have been the same age as me, thinks Chrissy. It occurs to her that however tragic the young man's death, at least in India he would have died warm. This thought is so unworthy she hangs her head in shame.

Once more, she lays Thomas gently down, close beside her. From her bag, she takes the Holy Book. It falls open at St Luke, Chapter 12. *'For there is nothing covered,'* she reads, *'that shall not be revealed; neither hid, that shall not be known.'* She feels her heartbeat quicken, and covers her mouth with her hand. The verses are a message from God. Their undoubted meaning is this: whatever she does, Thomas's little body will be discovered. It is hopeless — she can do nothing to protect him from an eternity of limbo. Chrissy sits in the pew, her gaze transfixed. Chilled to the marrow, and too broken to cry, she longs suddenly for the oblivion of sleep. She stretches herself out, using the pew as a comfortless bed.

She is woken by the clattering of the latch and the whine of the hinges as the heavy oak door is opened. It takes a moment for her to work out where she is; when she does, her first reaction is to hide. She picks Thomas up, and as quietly as she can, she lowers herself to the floor. Shaking with cold, and with fear, she crouches between the pews. Someone walks briskly into the church — nailed boots are ringing on the hard tiled floor. She keeps her eyes tight shut, and prays that she will not be noticed.

The footsteps travel behind her, towards the reading room. The curtain is pulled back; she hears the clattering of rings on a metal pole. Someone grunts with exertion — force is being applied to some object. The wind whistles; perhaps an open window is being closed. Eventually there is a slamming sound. The person walks back into the church, and the steps turn eastwards, towards the altar. Chrissy expects that for a time there will be quiet, while prayers are said. But once again, the footsteps change direction. They are coming straight towards her. Discovery seems inevitable; she lifts herself from the floor, and slides back onto the seat.

A tall, portly man is looking at her, with his mouth hanging open in surprise. Chrissy recognises the bushy black beard and bristling eyebrows of the Reverend Willis.

'You took my breath!' he says, in accusation. 'I heard a sound, and thought I would see a rat. Not — a ...,' he pauses. 'A *woman*. What was it you thought you were doing? Appearing from nowhere, in such a way?'

'I — I was resting.' Chrissy stammers. 'I took a nap. I was waiting for the evening service.'

'Then you will wait another hour.' The Reverend mops his brow. He is clearly shaken by Chrissy's unexpected appearance. 'You say you were having a nap! Sleeping is not a respectful way to treat the House of God.'

'I am sorry sir. Truly I am sorry. I ask your forgiveness.'

'It is not *my* forgiveness you should ask. It is His.'

The big man leans forward. He is frowning and his face is close; his breath smells of fish. 'I do not know you,' he says. 'You are not of this parish. You were waiting for the evening service?'

'Yes, sir.'

'You have chosen to visit us after sundown, when the

7

weather is atrocious. It is snowing hard.' He pulls his large hands, causing his knucklebones to crack. 'And you are alone.' He moves his face yet closer. 'Tell me the truth,' he says, lowering his voice. 'Is it that you have run away? Have you nowhere else to go?'

'Indeed, sir, I have a home. I take lodgings off Marketgait.'

'Marketgait?' the Reverend repeats. 'Why, that is by the *docks*.'

Chrissy notes the emphasis on the last word, and thinks; he believes I am a person of ill repute. In as firm a voice as she can muster, she says, 'I have regular employment. I work at the Canadian Tannery.' She widens her eyes. 'I came here to pray.'

'On such a night?'

'Yes,' says Chrissy, wondering how she would begin, were she to tell the truth.

'I would prefer that you were more straightforward. Are you are in some kind of trouble? Tell me.'

'I feel God's presence strongly in this place. I have come here previously with my landlady, Mrs Montgomery. I heard you preach on All Hallows' Eve.'

The Reverend is not listening; he is eyeing the pillowcase. '*No!*' he shouts. 'I do not believe you. You did not come here to pray… I think you came here *to steal!*'

Chrissy takes up the linen bag. Tightly, she holds Thomas to her.

'You came here to steal, and you have so little shame, that you thought you would rest here till the weather improves.' The Reverend reaches out. His cheeks are flushed with anger. 'Give me that bag. Let me open it!' His fingers have closed over the cloth. 'What is it that you have taken?' Flecks of spit fly from his lips. He pulls at the bag, trying to wrest it away. 'The silver plate from the vestry?'

Chrissy pulls back. He pulls harder. Chrissy cannot easily

admit defeat; she is like a wild dog from the municipal pound defending her pup. She tries to sink her teeth into the Reverend's right hand.

'You minx!'

Chrissy feels a stinging blow to the side of her face. The shock takes her breath away; she opens her mouth for air.

The Reverend steps back. He cups his right hand in his left. To her alarm, Chrissy observes that a bruise is forming.

'Sir, I am so very sorry.' Her tears fall fast. 'I did not mean to cause you hurt. My baby. You see — my baby. My poor baby.' She can say no more; she is overcome.

'Your baby? You have a child? Where is he?' The Reverend looks around.

'He — he is here.' She indicates the pillowcase, which she still holds close.

'In there! Why, that is no way to treat a child!'

Chrissy sees with shame the mark left by her teeth. This time she offers no resistance. The Reverend seizes the bag, and pulls Thomas from it.

He draws the shawl away, and recoils. 'The child is dead.'

'Yes, sir. I know so. It is to my eternal grief.'

The Reverend gives Thomas back to Chrissy. He does so hurriedly, and with distaste, as if he is frightened of catching a disease. He shakes his wounded hand, then leaves it hanging against his coat. In silence, he turns it slowly, so that he can study the deep-red bruise on his palm. Of a sudden, he appears disassociated; it as if the hand is an exhibit, rather than a part of himself. 'You had better come with me,' he says. He speaks in a low voice — almost a whisper. Chrissy is alarmed by his tone; she would prefer his hell-fire bellow. 'I will take you to Constable Crieff,' he says. 'You will come easily? Or will I need some rope? There is some in the vestry cupboard.'

Chrissy hangs her head. She knows she must be punished. 'I will cause you no trouble.'

The Reverend continues to speak in a voice that is quiet and controlled, but his eyes burn bright with anger, under his heavy brows. 'I would be pleased for you to walk,' he says. 'However, I fear you would give me the slip.' He purses his lips, as if calculating a mathematical equation. 'It is not far to the constable's cottage. We will both travel upon my horse.'

Outside, the snow has ceased to fall. The sun is down, but the whiteness gives out a strange kind of light, as if the earth has changed places with the moon. The Reverend's large grey horse is standing by the porch. He seems so high off the ground, Chrissy wonders how she will ever manage to mount him. The Reverend tells her to use the base of the porch as a step. He hauls her up, his big fingers pressing hard into her upper arm. All the time, Chrissy somehow manages to keep hold of Thomas.

We must look a strange sight, she thinks, as she balances precariously in front of the saddle and clings to the horse's mane. It is as if we are a family — not a gaoler and a miscreant. An owl flies out from a tree in front, its eyes and beak unnervingly resembling a human face. She dips her head as she is brushed by an overhanging branch.

They travel on. Chrissy soon finds herself rocking with the horse's roll, with the Reverend's exhalations hissing rhythmically in her ear. She is preoccupied with the baby's burial. As soon as she can, she will ask the Reverend to protect Thomas from an eternity of purgatory. Surely no man of the cloth would truly want to punish an innocent child. The Reverend will show mercy. He will give Thomas a proper service; he may even allow the grave to be marked. For herself, she will explain that she is prepared to accept her punishment for assaulting him — whatever it may be. She will go to prison for ten years; she will be transported to Australia. It matters not, what happens to her, so long as Thomas is saved.

They travel on, in silence, until the Reverend halts his horse outside a grey stone cottage. He dismounts and barks at Chrissy to follow. She jumps, lands awkwardly on one foot, and stumbles, taking three quick steps. The Reverend seizes her by the scruff of the neck — pointless to repeat she has no intention of escape. He bangs noisily on the door, which is opened by a large, round woman wrapped in a Campbell tartan shawl.

'Why, Reverend,' she says. 'Do come in. Come in, out of the cold.'

The constable clatters down the narrow wooden staircase, which leads up from the freshly whitewashed hallway. He looks as if he has been asleep; he is still pulling on his jacket. A smell of cooking emanates from the kitchen. Chrissy finds herself envying the atmosphere of harmonious domesticity.

'I am sorry there is no fire at the front of the house,' says the constable, ushering them through to the back room. Two small children look up shyly from the floor, where they have been building a tower of wooden bricks. An older boy puts aside a stick he has been whittling. At a nod from his father, he places another log on the fire.

Chrissy watches as the flames leap, and the log spits sparks. Suddenly, she feels herself shoved from behind. She is propelled unceremoniously towards Constable Crieff.

'Take this woman into custody,' thunders the Reverend. 'Arrest her. She has viciously attacked me, and in that bundle, is wrapped the body of a dead child!'

 **Equatorial Africa**

Lokim digs a toe into the soft sandy soil of the dry riverbed, and feels it grow wet. He crouches down, and begins to dig with both hands. At the base of the hollow, a puddle appears.

11

He splashes his face, fetches a stick, excavates some more mud, then waits for the sediment to settle. There is a spring further up in the hills, where the water runs fresh and pure. Lokim, however, has decided not to make the trip. The night before, his manyatta riotously celebrated the wedding of his friend Niampa. The villagers danced with wild energy — far into the night — in between drinking gourd after well-filled gourd of posho. Lokim found the beer-drinking entirely pleasurable at the time, but this morning he has a fuzzy, thumping head and limbs that are heavy with lassitude. His languor is exacerbated by the heat of the day — although it is a full three hours before the sun will reach its zenith, the temperature of the arid air is already high. Sitting back on his haunches, he watches a trickle of sweat run down the decorative scars of his belly. He needs to feel more energised — while the revellers were dancing, a bush fire was observed glowing red against the darkness, snaking its way down one of the mountains north of Kidepo. For Lokim and his tribe, the crackling flames and thick smoke present an opportunity. The impala will be running hither and thither, churning the earth as they go, frantic with the need to save themselves. The tribe must put up nets to encircle the animals as they flee; Lokim, alongside the other young hunters, will dig a large hole in which to entrap them.

He scoops more water and tips it over his head, wetting his hair. Refreshed, he gets to his feet, takes his spear and walks to where — under a thorn tree — his cow Pila patiently waits. He gently pushes Pila's backside with his foot; she lumbers to her feet and he leads her to the watering hole. He watches intently as she drinks. It would be difficult for Lokim to articulate the complexity of what he feels for Pila, in the unlikely event that anyone should ask. The cow was a gift from his Uncle Atum, who had reared her from a calf. Atum bequeathed her to Lokim as he lay dying, not from some battle injury as he would have wished, but from a sickness which left him for weeks lying prone in his hut, spewing and retching until all his energy was spent and he had not the fight to carry further the burden of existence. Lokim remembers his uncle's last wretched few days with regret. He had made the mistake of listening to two toothless old women who shared a tumbledown hut just outside of the village. He believed their tale that his uncle's body had been invaded by the evil spirit of the cackling hyena which used to frighten travellers by Bakil Hill, and on this basis, he had shunned him. Yet before Atum's final illness took hold, the two were very close. Lokim was Atum's eldest nephew. Having no children of his own, it was to him that the older man chose to pass on the wisdom he had gleaned from studying the raw surroundings in which the Ik struggle to maintain life. He taught him how to read the skies, so Lokim learned the difference between clouds that would merely scud over the hills — leaving the earth still parched — and those that meant life-giving rain. He taught him which berries upset the digestion, and which are good to eat; he showed him which leaves and roots it is best to gather, and which should be left on the tree or in the ground.

Pila delicately shakes her head, eager to dislodge a couple of flies which have settled on her nose. She looks up, questioningly. Her lashes are long, like those of a Pokot girl, and her eyes are curiously light. They remind Lokim of the piece of clear orange-coloured rock, which Niampa's cousin exchanged for a goat. Everyone gathered round to see the marvel. At its centre, a powerful witchdoctor had embedded a calf-stealing cheetah, having first turned the thief into an insect, with delicate spotted wings. Lokim rubs Pila's neck with long, smooth strokes. On cold nights, he sleeps beside her, moving right up close, so that he is warmed by her heaving flank. When he goes hunting, Pila comes with him, giving both her milk and her blood for his sustenance. Her hide is pale as the creamy white kathi flower, and her pointed ears are soft as the down of a bird. They are pink on the inside — the colour of a child's tongue; on the outer side, they are the smoky shade of a grey-winged moth. Lokim watches as Pila dips her neck once more to drink. She steps backwards, replete.

Gently, Lokim taps the cow with his spear, and the two move off, rhythmically walking as they follow the track, wending their way home. Passing a collection of large grey rocks, Lokim thinks again about Atum. Just above the outcrop, tufts of long flat-leaved grass grow, and hidden amongst them is a plant whose roots can be used to rid a cow of tapeworms. Atum knew exactly how long the tubers should be boiled, and he had a way of soothing sick animals, so that once the mixture had cooled, they swallowed their medicine readily. He had tried to show Lokim how he could do the same. Lokim breaks off a slender branch from an acacia tree, and uses it as a switch, tapping Pila's back leg. Atum's death came before his greatest secret could be shared. He had promised that after the next full moon, he would trek with Lokim high into Didinga country, where they would gather the scarce leaves that he needed to brew his most special potion. This drug could be produced only rarely, because of the necessity of preserving the precious plants. The recipe had been passed down to Atum by his grandfather, a senior elder of the tribe. Lokim had been given the liquid just once — it was both to celebrate his first battle, and to take away the pain after his shoulder had been pricked and scarred to mark the occasion. A few drops had lifted him to a spinning, magical heaven, where he saw colours and shapes so beautiful he was robbed of speech by the intensity of the wonders he experienced. After the colours had subsided, he slept a wonderful, refreshing sleep, during which — and he has told no-one this — he had a mystical dream about a strange woman, not of his tribe, nor even of his kind.

The village is abuzz. The party of the night before has left

14

a euphoric glow, and now everyone is pulling together to prepare for the hunt. '*Kire ejok Akuj*' sing the women as they prepare the nets: 'Truly god is good'. The men assemble their weapons, collecting long poles, spears and bows and arrows, and placing them in a row. The children dart around like swifts; they help where they can, jostling each other and jumping with excitement. Lokim is infected by the mood; his head is clearing and his laziness has gone. Niampa emerges smiling from his marital hut and places a hand on Lokim's shoulder. '*Ida piaji,*' he says. 'Greetings.' He is the most senior of the young warriors. As leader, he explains the strategy. There is insufficient time for the women to finish mending the nets; Kokoi's *abang* – her ancestor – has reliably predicted that a wind will get up, quickly fanning the flames. The young men of the village are to divide into three parties; he has put Kadot in charge of a group to cut down brushwood, so that any gaps in the snare can be temporarily filled. Lokim is in charge of the hole-diggers and Niampa himself will lead the hunters who will drive the trapped animals forward. The older men of the village, together with the women and children, will form the two lines of a V. At the sound of a pipe, the lines will walk towards each other, closing the animals in; at the second sound of a pipe, the women will start to beat their drums, making the frenzied creatures run even faster. 'We'll have a feast,' says Niampa, showing nearly all his white teeth. 'Meat for a village ten times our size! We'll have a party, all over again!'

Lokim sharpens his spear, using the fist-shaped piece of rock that is one of the treasures of the village. The stone is valued for its hardness, and for the way it glitters with threads of silver. It was found by Amuarkar, when he was a young man, hunting up near Turkana country. Amuarkar is old now, blind in both eyes and bent with rheumatism. In exchange for use of the shining rock, the villagers ensure that – each day

— a helping of porridge is brought to his hut, together with a gourd of clear water, collected from the spring.

Lokim touches Amuarkar on the arm. He carefully replaces the stone, pressing it into his curled and crippled hand. 'Thank you,' he says, 'I'm going now.'

'Be careful,' says Amuarkar. His wrinkled, leathered face looks troubled. He lifts his head and takes a long breath in. 'I can smell the fire — and for you, I can smell something else. There is danger.'

Lokim laughs. 'There is always danger, when hunting,' he says. 'An animal does not readily allow itself to be killed.' He steps out from the gloom of the elder's hut, into the sunshine.

There are ten warriors in his party as they set out through the scrub, and they bring with them five cows. The young men sing as they walk, and they talk of the good times to be enjoyed once the hunt is complete. Koralai jokes that he will capture a leopard, and use the skin to make himself a fine apron. He will wear the hollowed head on his own, so that he appears to have four eyes; his small siblings will quake in alarm. Tinga wonders if he presents his sweetheart with a haunch of impala, who knows what she might not be prepared to do? Comically, he rolls his eyes and sticks out his tongue. The laughter subsides, and then so does the conversation. The heat is making the going difficult, and the terrain is treacherous. There are rocks which slip, and snakes lurking unseen. There are rope-like creepers to avoid, and unexpected ruts, camouflaged by vegetation. Lokim walks with Pila beside him, steadying her when their descent is steepest. Every so often, she flicks her tail in annoyance at the flies which buzz around.

They have just crossed a dry gully, when the cow trips on a fallen branch. Her leg buckles and she lands on her knees. She tries to get back to her feet and succeeds on her third attempt. There is blood coming from a gash in her shin. Lokim

16

pulls her to stand, and checks the wound. There is a lump above the bone — she is severely bruised.

'Go on!' Lokim calls to his friends, with a throw of his arm. 'Koralai knows where the trap's to be set.'

'Are you sure?' asks one of his friends.

'Quite sure!'

He has to coax Pila to continue walking. She keeps stumbling; he pulls gently at the loose skin of her neck, while singing a song of encouragement. Slowly they make their way down the hill. Lokim does not hurry. His friends are out of sight; another slope intersects, and they have dropped behind it. He blinks as beads of sweat run into his eyes. Soon he will have to find water. Pila stumbles again, and this time he lets her stay resting on the ground. He stands looking out at the parched brown countryside. In the valley below is a deserted cattle compound. It has been made by the Jie tribe; Lokim can tell by the particular shape of the tattered grass huts. He touches his shoulder, remembering the Jie warrior who had tried to spear him, before he was able to fight back. Lokim had felled him with a single blow, landed accurately with a heavy stick.

Pila rhythmically licks at her wounded leg. Lokim shades his eyes with his hand, trying to spot where the scrubby trees grow green — indicating a water source that will serve them both. Suddenly, his heart quickens. His ears strain at the sound of undergrowth being crushed. He turns and sees a large male lion.

The lion is looking straight at Pila. It opens wide its mouth, and snarls. It moves forward, intent on the cow; it can smell her blood. Lokim has a very short time in which to choose. He can leave Pila to her fate, or he can try to protect her. He positions his spear. At the movement, the lion leaps forward. Lokim's aim is good, and his arm is strong; the spear pierces the lion's flank. But that is all it does. The lion turns, enraged, and reaches out to strike out at Lokim, who leaps back, but not quite in time; the lion has drawn its huge claw down Lokim's thigh, making five red stripes. The lion claws at him again, this time ineffectively, for Lokim is just out of his reach.

Pila is on her feet. 'Move!' Lokim shouts to her. 'Go home!'

The spear is still in the lion's side. It twists, distracted and enraged by its presence. Lokim takes advantage of the delay, and starts to run. He is fit, a good athlete, and he runs swiftly. He turns his head to see the lion following him, seemingly unencumbered by the spear. Lokim continues to run, with long, headlong strides. He runs with the extreme impetus of a man chased by the possibility of immediate mortality. He runs with a wild, primitive energy, covering the rough scrubland with extraordinary speed. Turning his head, he sees that the spear has fallen out and the beast is gaining ground. A few more strides, and Lokim will be just so much flesh between those two great paws. His right foot fails to contact solid earth; he tumbles and finds himself rolling headlong down the hill.

 Glasgow, Scotland

'So, tell me Tom,' says James Stewart pleasantly, 'tell me again, who were the sons of Noah?'

Tom swings his legs, kicks out at a table leg and scowls. James smoothes his hair and waits.

'I don't know,' Tom mutters, looking at the floor.

'Oh, I'm sure you do,' says James, evenly, 'we went over this only yesterday. They were Shem, Ham and Japheth, and *"of them was the whole world overspread"*. Shem was the father of all the children of Eber — from which we get the word Hebrew. Japheth was the father of Gomer, Magog, Madai and Javan. And what about the youngest? What about Ham?'

Tom remains stubbornly silent.

18

'You remember — Ham was the father of Canaan. What happened to him?'

Tom does not answer, but he does look up.

'Well?'

'He was cursed.' Tom says sullenly.

'That's right! After the unfortunate episode with the wine — which we won't explore again as there are aspects of that incident which aren't altogether suitable for those with younger ears — Noah said, "*Cursed be Canaan; a servant of servants shall he be unto his brethren*". James regards his young pupil with sympathy. The boy looks tired, as well as bored. His mother considers him weak and she constantly frets about his welfare. 'Maybe we've done enough for this morning,' he says. 'We'll stop early, then this afternoon, we'll have another go at that Horace. If we get it finished, we can do some practical work. Shall we make a model of the ark? Would you like that, Tom?'

Tom looks troubled. 'We haven't got any wood.'

'We can beg some kindling, if I can't get hold of anything better. For glue, we'll ask cook for some bones. I'll show you how to mix the paste. We'll make the boat to scale. Let's call it a science lesson.' James studies his pocket watch. He nods at Tom. 'You can go now. We'll meet again at lunch.'

In his little upstairs room, James Stewart looks in the mirror as he splashes his face, combs his beard and reties his cravat. He is by no means a vain man, but neither is he stupid. He knows that his striking red hair, aquiline nose, and tall, athletic frame can help to get him noticed. He tips more water from the ewer into the basin, picks up a brush, and energetically scrubs an ink stain from under his nail. His physical appeal to society women is an essential part of his fund-raising: they tend to have influential husbands, with incomes large enough for a portion to be shared, provided the cause is sufficiently worthwhile. Mary has told him that a Mrs

Aitken will be attending lunch — she is married to a wealthy coal merchant. James whistles as he repositions his shirt collar and pulls down his waistcoat. He thinks about the boy. Tom is a not an easy pupil, but then what would one expect? The elder Livingstone children have had an unsettling time, what with moving from house to house and missing their father. Their father — to think! The great David Livingstone! James sometimes wants to pinch himself to confirm his presence in the real world; he considers himself extraordinarily fortunate to have found favour with Mary, wife of the celebrated author of *Missionary Travels*.

At lunch he sits at the head of the table; to his left is Mary, and to his right, Mrs Aitken. Robert occupies the other end, flanked by Tom and Agnes, with Oswell in the middle. James says grace, thanking God for what they are about to receive, and asking — as they do every day — for Him to protect and provide for the intrepid party facing the perils and privations of the Zambesi.

The meal consists of braised mutton cutlets and pigeon pie. Mary and the children eat heartily, whilst Mrs Aitken is more circumspect. 'I have to think of my digestion,' she says, modestly lowering her gaze as she refuses croquette potatoes and a spoonful of neeps. James suspects that the woman is also concerned to preserve her narrow waist; she is strikingly pretty with bright dark eyes and milk-white skin. Her hoop-skirted dress of red plaid trimmed with blue, looks very becoming. In comparison, Mary in her dun-coloured workaday clothes, looks more plain than ever. But then, Mary does not try. She is oblivious to fashion, and this, James reflects, is not to be wondered at. In London and Edinburgh, she is as out of place as a little brown sparrow in a ring of blue-winged jays. But in the heat of Africa — where Mary has spent the majority of her life — bright silks and crinolines surely serve as nothing but an encumbrance.

'How is Dr Livingstone?' Mrs Aitken asks. 'Have you heard from him?'

Mary, who has been occupied with teaching Oswell to cut up his food correctly, puts down the knife and fork, and rests her hands in her lap. 'Not lately.'

'I'm sorry. It must be a concern.'

'One does not expect to have frequent news. Africa is not like Scotland, with the convenience of the Penny Post. David has to wait for a passing trader, before his letters can be carried. I am sure matters are progressing satisfactorily.' Mary's countenance betrays her reassuring words. Her brows are knitted together, and lines have appeared around her mouth.

'I hope — when you did last hear — that the news was good?' persists Mrs Aitken.

'I believe that he is keeping physically well. There was some trouble with the boat — the *Ma Robert* — she was taking in water.'

'The *Ma Robert*! How quaint! Surely, my dear, you mean, the *Pa* Robert!'

'The boat was called after me. That is my African name. It is the tradition in that part of the continent. Robert is my firstborn and I am his "ma" — his mother.'

'How very odd!'

'You may think so.' Mary sniffs, fishes for a handkerchief, and wipes a drop from the end of her nose. 'Personally, I count it an honour to be given such a title.' She scrapes back her chair and swiftly leaves the table. 'I have to see to Baby.' She passes hurriedly out through the door.

Mrs Aitken suppresses a smile, and glances across to James. 'I didn't think I could hear Baby cry,' she says in a tone of mock mystery. 'I imagined little Anna to be perfectly content with her nursemaid.'

It occurs to James that to sophisticated women such as her

guest, Mary might appear to be little more than an amusing oddity, however famous her husband. He can't help feeling somewhat irritated at his employer's lack of decorum. It's all very well — he thinks — not bothering with smart dress, but as regards manners, Mary could perhaps try harder to fit in with the milieu. James has no wish to be disrespectful, nor does he wish for Mrs Aitken to feel cold-shouldered. He risks a conspiratorial smile, then says, 'A mother, I think, is always concerned for her child. It is the way of nature. What of you Mrs Aitken, are you blessed with any offspring?'

'Stop it!' Robert shouts suddenly.

'I beg your pardon?' James is bewildered.

'You were laughing at her. You were laughing at our mother! And *Ma Robert* is perfectly fine for a name!'

'I can assure you, I was doing nothing of the sort!' James is embarrassed. He feels — despite his protestation — that he has been caught out. He watches, helpless, as Robert rushes to follow his mother from the room.

Oswell has had his head down, pre-occupied with his food. Now he looks up, and opens wide his mouth, displaying its contents. He pushes away his plate and begins to howl. Tom looks at him, and stretches out his hand. With his lower lip wobbling, the older boy looks towards his sister for help.

'Don't be upset,' says Agnes, with sweet practicality. 'You know how troubled Ma can be, and Robert is so hot-headed. Come Oswell, sit by me. Carry on eating Tom. Have you noticed the edge of your pie? It's like a wall. Let's smash it down, like Joshua doing battle at Jericho.'

For a moment there is quiet, then Mrs Aitken says, 'As yet, Mr Stewart, I have no children. But were I to have a daughter, I would wish her to be as sweet and kind as you are, Agnes, dear.'

James is tempted to say, 'Hear! hear!' but that would be unseemly. He makes a little heap of his cutlet bones, and wonders whether he should go after the recalcitrant Robert. He is rescued from his decision-making by the reappearance of Mary, who carries in her arms the plump-wristed Anna. The child waves cheerily, and shows her new front teeth.

'Colic,' says Mary, settling herself back in her chair. 'All better now.' Anna bangs on the table and smashes her fist into a potato croquette. 'Robert's gone to his room,' says Mary. 'We'll save him some pudding. It's his favourite — apple hedgehog.' One-handedly, she heaps more buttered spinach onto her plate. A splat of green lands on the white tablecloth. 'Oswell, dear, please return to your seat. You're not a little person, like Baby.'

Everyone eats in silence, while Oswell wriggles rebelliously in his chair.

At length, Mary says, 'Please forgive Robert's rudeness. He is not used to society. His upbringing in Africa leads him to forget sometimes the conventions of good conduct.'

'Africa!' says Mrs Aitken, shaking her pretty head, 'it sounds so gloriously exotic. Tell, me Mary, where you lived, did you see ostriches? And elephants? Were there lions and leopards, and little laughing monkeys, like the ones in London Zoo?'

'All those things,' Mary says. An absent look has come into her eyes. 'I have ridden on an elephant and made a pet of a monkey.' She hands Anna a crust. 'To me, such creatures do not seem strange. Africa, to me, is home.' She sighs. 'But I am not sure I will travel there again.'

'Are you not anxious to be reunited with your husband?'

'Indeed I am. However, I fear I could not leave the children.' Her arm tightens around Anna. 'I simply could not bear it.'

'Would they not travel with you?'

'I must consider their education. And perhaps it is for others to take up the mantle; to bring civilization to those troubled lands; to end the evil trade of slavery.'

23

Mary looks abstracted, her mind traversing that faraway and unenlightened place. Please let her say something, thinks James. And dear Mary! Right on cue, she does.

'Mr Stewart is one with such an idea,' she says, her tone sharpening. Deftly, she removes a pigeon wing from Anna's hand and substitutes a carrot. 'James, tell Elizabeth of your plans.'

So James explains his dream of a Free Church settlement on the banks of the Zambesi, where cotton fields will flourish, planted and nourished by men who humbly worship the Lord, yet who stand proud, fearing no-one, whilst earning a decent wage in return for their labour. As he speaks, he feels himself grow hot; a fire blazes within him, so convinced is he both of the worthiness of his scheme and of his own suitability to lead the monumental task.

Elizabeth listens carefully. 'You will require funds,' she says. 'With your permission, I shall speak to Mr Aitken.'

 Broughty Ferry, Dundee, Scotland

'Please Miss Scrope, *please*.' Mina Stephen age thirteen clasps her hands together as if in prayer and flutters her long lashes over her clear brown eyes. 'Al says the weather's turning. If we don't go today, we may not have another chance to skate before spring!'

'It's true,' says her sister Maggie. Her manner is more level, but just as persistent. 'We only want to go to the ornamental pond on the esplanade. We won't have to ask for the carriage, and you won't have to walk far.'

Maggie is just one year older than Mina, and looks very like her — tall and slim, with chestnut hair. Maggie's hair is pinned up — unlike Mina's which flows free. Mina would like her hair to be put up, too, so that her status as the youngest in the large Stephen family would be less obvious to everyone. On the other hand, alongside the put-up hair she would have to exchange her comfortable stays for a corset, and this she is less willing to do.

'Very well,' says Miss Scrope. She nods her head, but with little enthusiasm. She looks down at the tiled schoolroom floor.

Mina drops her hands, so that they hang by her sides. The victory has been too easy. Rather than feeling triumphant, she is disconcerted. What must it be like, she wonders, to be a person like Miss Scrope? To always have to comport yourself in a manner so contained, never to express much of an opinion unless it is over a matter of etiquette, and then to go home at night to the loneliness of a rented room? A flush of generosity leads her to say, 'You can join in, too. You can borrow Helen's skates. She left them behind — they're still hanging in the boot room.'

'Thank you, Mina — I fear that would be inappropriate.'

'I don't see why!'

'Enough,' says Miss Scrope. 'We'll finish the next part of *The Pilgrim's Progress*, then we'll get ready to go out. Sit down, girls.' She sighs. 'Christian was about to struggle with the slough of despond.'

'"Here, therefore, they wallowed for a time",' reads Maggie in a loud voice, '"being grievously bedaubed with the dirt."' She pushes the book to one side. 'Sounds like one of the pigs on the McClouds' farm.'

'Or an otter,' Mina suggests. 'We saw a whole family washing in the river when we went up to Dunoon. After they were clean, the little ones got themselves dirty again, sliding down the river bank.'

Miss Scrope frowns; her spectacles have slipped down her long nose. Sensing her disapproval, Mina dips her head and tries to continue at the point where her sister has left off. She gets as far as 'Christian began to sink in the mire,' when she is interrupted by Maggie.

'Hope we don't do that, on the esplanade,' she says, with a giggle. 'If we do, perhaps "A man called Help" will come to us, disguised as a representative of the British Humane Society.'

'Enough,' repeats Miss Scrope, in a way that is not unkindly. 'Let us finish there.' She consults her timepiece. 'We'll be back by lunchtime, I'm sure. But in case of the unexpected, I'd better talk to Cook. I'll explain that we will require only a simple lunch on our return. It will be adequate for the kitchen maid to fetch us some soup.' She gathers her belongings and leaves the room, swishing black bombazine.

'In case of the unexpected!' Maggie is laughing. 'Maybe she really does think we'll need rescuing! And the pond can be nowhere more than two feet deep!'

Mina responds with a brief smile. She is thinking again about the limitations of Miss Scrope's life. The governess wears black in mourning for her father, a minister of the Presbyterian Church, whose death has occurred the previous summer. She carries with her a miniature of him; Mina has noticed that, every so often, when she thinks she is unobserved, Miss Scrope opens the enamelled cover to look − with a wistful expression − at the old man's face. Mina wonders how she would feel, if her own father were to die. It is impossible to imagine; Alexander Stephen, head of the great firm, is as solid as the timber with which he builds his stout ships.

The air outside is sharp and cold. The smoke from a hundred coal fires mingles with the sea mist, creating an ethereal haze around houses, trees and carriages. The castle − which is said to be haunted − is barely visible on its promontory. The esplanade, however, is anything but ghostly, crowded as it is with townspeople, refreshment sellers, a steam organ, and a Cossack with a dancing bear. Mina has seen the bear before. She turns away. The poor animal does not really dance, it just sways pitifully, on its tethered feet.

There are other young people from the big houses on the ice, but also — and, really, this is the thrill of skating — all sorts of other people, besides. There is young Mr Mips from the grocer's shop, and Charlie Dow, the telegraph boy. There is even an off-duty fisherman in a rough canvas coat; he weaves his way around the pond with incongruous grace.

'Please Miss Scrope, will you hold our muffs?'

Mina and Maggie strap on their skates, then push themselves off. Maggie nearly loses her footing and straightaway, an arm is stretched out to support her. The arm belongs to Robert Mudie, an apprenticed engineer, who is sporting a rather fine top hat and a starched cravat. He looks at Maggie with such frank admiration, that her sister is quite embarrassed for her, and — to be honest — a little jealous. Mina knows she is too young to have a follower, but it would be reassuring to learn that she has some appeal for the opposite sex. The four elder Stephen girls have married and moved away; matrimony is considered the natural state for a woman. Mina envies her big sisters the freedom they enjoy from running their own houses, and her mother has always stressed that a woman's true fulfilment can only result from a 'suitable' match. But, thinks Mina — as her skates skim the ice — she herself is determined never to marry simply because it is convenient and the 'done' thing to do. She will want to feel passion. She thinks of *The Taming Of The Shrew*, which she has recently read, and which she longs to see at the Theatre Royal. She would like to be to swept off her feet, like the feisty Katharina. She pictures herself thrillingly battling with a man like Petruchio, then falling prostrate into his arms.

'Careful!' says Maggie.

A shop girl has tripped in front of her and they almost

collide. The girl is pulled upright by her beau. He is the handsome young highlander from McClouds, who delivered Corona's tall spruce tree at Christmas. The girl is laughing helplessly, and her hat is askew; she exhibits an enviable abandon.

Mina and Maggie continue to circle the pond. They wave at Miss Scrope, who watches from the water's edge. Miss Scrope waves back decorously. Although there is only the slightest hint of snow, she has put up her umbrella. This has the effect of making her appear a little eccentric. Mina remembers the umbrella arriving in the post, soon after Miss Scrope had begun her employment at Corona. She said it was a present from her brother, and she grew quite pink with pleasure as she took it outside to try it out. Moira, the ladies' maid, said afterwards that she couldn't understand the fuss; it was just an old-fashioned thing, with ribs made of baleen, instead of modern steel.

Mina puts out a hand, to hold Maggie back. The fisherman is in a world of his own. He skates fast, leaving trails of churned ice in his wake, apparently oblivious to the way he is forcing people out of his path. Mina wonders what drives the man. Is it exuberance at being released to the shore, after months at sea? His red cotton neckerchief shows up bright in the mist. Is it worn for decoration, rather than for warmth? Does he perhaps have a sweetheart — the daughter of a fellow fisherman, or some woman from a far off country — and does he skate so energetically because he is fired by a love that is returned? Mina must cease her speculations — Miss Scrope has closed her umbrella and is waggling it backwards and forwards to indicate that it is time to go home.

'Goodbye,' says Robert Mudie, eyeing Maggie, as the girls fasten their boots. He bows extravagantly, nearly slips up, and is quickly supported by one of the red-headed Connell boys, who grins at his friend's discomfort.

They walk back in silence, listening to the rhythmic roar of the sea. Mina would prefer to chatter, but is restrained by the presence of the chaperone. Gossip is a pleasure to be enjoyed untrammelled; the joy is lost, when constantly frustrated by reminders of propriety. Miss Scrope walks between the girls — literally a dark presence, engulfed, as she is, in her black woollen cape.

Entering Corona's wide front door, Mina inhales the aroma of roasting beef and realises how hungry she is. The gong in the hallway is sounding for lunch in the dining room; the girls would have been in time to eat with the rest of the family, but Cook's orders cannot be countermanded, and so they must make do with soup.

And the soup, when they sit down to it in the school room, is really rather unpleasant, made as it is by Katie, the new kitchen maid, from gristly gobbets of pink lamb, diced carrot, and congealed lumps of pearl barley. Mina swallows as much as she can, before pushing the bowl aside.

'Could we please have some more bread?' she asks the maid.

The governess has been staring morosely into her own empty bowl. She looks up, suddenly energised. 'Finish your soup,' she says. 'Mina, it ill becomes you to be so particular!' A solitary whisker sprouts from her narrow, jutting chin. 'Your careless attitude should be a source of shame to you! You have grown up in a world of plenty, but a person of sensitivity would not be so cavalier about such privilege. There are many who would fall on their knees in gratitude for such a meal.' Her shoulders rise and drop, in time with her quick breaths.

Mina places the soup bowl back in front of her, and swallows a mouthful of carrot. 'I do know we are blessed to live the life we do,' she says, with genuine humility. She is thinking of the Cossack, and his miserable bear. The man's cheeks are hollow, his once fine coat threadbare.

'Who knows what the Almighty has planned?' says Miss Scrope, sounding mollified. 'One day, you may find yourself in altogether different circumstances. Perhaps, then, you will look back with longing, at the good life you enjoyed, here at Corona.'

CHAPTER TWO

February 1861

 Bridewell Gaol, Dundee, Scotland

Chrissy lifts another coil of ships' rope onto her lap, and begins to untwist it. Black dust from the loosened tar makes her cough, and the harsh strands cut at her blistered hands. There is a clang as the hatch to the left of the cell's metal door is opened and a tin plate, together with a mug, is pushed onto the shelf inside her cell. She adds the fibre to her already unravelled pile, which lies in a round heap beside her. She gets up, straightens her aching back, and goes to fetch her breakfast. She swallows the bread hurriedly, trying to ignore the specks of dirt that discolour the crust. Slowly, she raises the mug to her lips. She has learned to drink her water carefully, in order to savour it fully. She shuts her eyes as she swallows, and tries to transport herself to a simpler time. She pictures a young child in Kirriemuir, playing with her brothers beside the clear free-flowing stream that ran down to feed the River Tilt. She experiences the thrill of ice-cold water as a small hand reaches down for a smooth white pebble, she watches freckled brown trout flick their tails as they swim through fronded weed.

She finishes eating, straddles her pot, then returns to her

oakum picking. It is an empty, mindless task, which leaves space for her imagination to run wild and dark. She has to shepherd her thoughts constantly, as if they were horned Highland sheep. Despite all her best efforts, the grimmest of images sometimes enters her head. She sees the judge don his black cap; she is held up by the warders, one on each arm. 'Take her down,' she hears him say. Chrissy shudders; such imaginings are the devil's work. She is innocent; no jury will believe she has killed her child. The rope is harsh in her hands — blood is caked under her nails. She ignores the pain and continues to separate the strands, then roll them on her lap. Her fingers move faster and faster. It is a month since she has been brought to Bridewell. If she stays longer, and does her work well, she may progress to sewing, or sorting rags.

She pauses to cough, picks up another rope, and then another; repeatedly, her torn hands fly. No-one she knows has visited her in prison, with the exception of George Montgomery, who came but once. He was so dismayed to find himself in such surroundings that his speech developed an unaccustomed stutter. When the door clanged shut behind him, he had jumped like a startled rabbit. He was dressed in his Sunday best, which made Chrissy want to weep; she felt such shame that a decent man had been made to enter such a place. He stayed for a short time only — he came only to bring the news that an attorney had been assigned to her case, after Frank Barton had intervened.

He had turned and said, 'I don't know why it is that Mr Barton does not come himself!' His face had reddened, and his voice was sharp. Then he had banged on the door to be let out.

Afterwards, Chrissy wondered about the visit, and about Mr Montgomery's anger. The truth of Thomas's parenthood was extraordinary, perplexing and wonderful. But was her landlord under the misapprehension that Frank was the baby's father? The thought was distressing. Not for herself, but for dear, good-hearted Frank, who — since their first meeting — had behaved so generously towards her. She had been treated with nothing but courtesy and respect, whenever she was in his company. What of Frank's mother? Was the old woman thinking the same? Chrissy stands up and brushes an accumulation of tar from her grey prison apron. The dust gets everywhere. It is in her nostrils and ears, she can smell it in her hair. 'You are contributing to the supremacy of Her Majesty's Navy,' the Governor had said on a tour of inspection. He had stood with his arms folded, as he watched her work. Chrissy wants very much to believe this is true. Sometimes she tries to cheer herself with the image of a sailor in his black-ribboned hat, sealing his ship safe from leaks with the caulking she has prepared. If thoughts of Thomas come to mind, she tries to hold for a moment the image of his sweet face, then, quickly, she must turn her mind elsewhere before she starts to cry. Peters — the pock-faced warder — has said that the baby's little body still lies unburied in the deadhouse, up at Maryfield.

Footsteps in the corridor, followed by the sound of bolts being drawn back. The door opens and in walks the warder clanking her heavy keys.

'Someone to see you,' she says. She sniffs, then turns away.

Hugh Proudie, the young advocate, steps into the room. His shirt is freshly laundered, his shoes newly polished, and his pink cheeks smoothly shaved. He has white-blond hair and a bright cherubic smile. He reminds Chrissy of the picture of the Angel Gabriel that used to hang in the chapel schoolroom in Kirriemuir. She is hot with shame; she has no means of hiding her piss pot.

'Well, Chrissy,' he says, 'I hope you're ready?'

'Ready sir?'

'Why, did they not tell you? The inquest — it is today!' He taps the basket of papers that he carries.

Chrissy's head spins; she feels she can barely stand.

'I thought it was next week. Next Tuesday.'

'The day was changed. The Procurator — Mr Croall — he has business in Edinburgh. From tomorrow, he will no longer be in Dundee.'

Chrissy sits back down on her stool. Strange and comfortless as her present life is, she has grown used to it. So many hours spent alone have left her with the sense that she has lost the ability to converse; she feels she would be unfit to be received in the most mellow of company. The prospect of being put on trial — the business of being publicly questioned, mocked, disbelieved and exhibited — seems unendurable.

'Can it not be delayed?' she asks. 'Can the hearing not wait till the Procurator returns?'

'Why, no. Nor would we want it to be.' Mr Proudie is smiling. 'I have good news. I have read the doctor's confidential report. As it is a legal document, it was sent out to be copied. I know the young clerk at Murdochs who usually does these things. For three shillings he made me a copy, too.'

Chrissy does not speak. She stares ahead of her, at a point in the wall.

'It is good news,' repeats Proudie. 'The doctor's examination has led him to conclude that your baby died of natural causes. The jury will not convict you of murder.'

'What of the other charges?' Chrissy asks. 'I cannot deny the physical harm I caused the Reverend.'

'Trust me,' says Proudie, stepping to the door. He knocks, to signal that he is ready to leave. 'Just read out what we have prepared. All will be well.'

In less than an hour, Chrissy is handcuffed by Peters, and led from her cell. It is a dank, sunless day, but Chrissy finds herself blinking at the comparative brightness of the light outside. Waiting in the prison yard, there is a covered cart. The driver is a squat man with a red face. He gives Chrissy a slow wink, as she climbs inside. She ignores him, trying not to let her face betray the trepidation that she feels.

'Think you're too good for the likes of me?' the driver says, turning towards her. He narrows his eyes and adds, 'Coming from this place, you're not fit to clean my boots.'

Chrissy wants to kick out and howl. She thinks of her gentle father. His heart would have broken, to see her in such a situation. She thinks, too, of her mother, whose temper was so often frayed by poverty and want, but who nevertheless took pride in her five children. She would boast to the neighbours of their quickness with letters. For the sake of her parents, and for her own survival, she must not add to the humiliation that has been visited upon her. 'Be an example to me,' she whispers to Jesus, remembering the courage He displayed in the Garden.

The cart comes to a halt. 'Get up,' says Peters. 'We're here. This is where the inquest is to be held.'

They have stopped outside a public house called the Drum and Monkey. Peters pushes Chrissy ahead of her. It is strange to be in a warm, carpeted building, which smells of tobacco and beer. Chrissy catches a glimpse of herself in a fish-eye mirror; her head looks tiny and her brown prison gown billows out in the convex glass. From somewhere, Constable Crieff appears. 'This way,' he says, indicating an arrowed sign which reads, 'To the saloon.'

On a long wide table in the centre of the room stands a wooden box. Around the table are gathered a dozen men of differing ages and varied dress. Are these the jury? At the head sits a grey-haired man with a sheaf of papers; he must be the Procurator. Other people stand and sit — every possible space is filled with people chatting and laughing, as if they are there to celebrate a happy social occasion. Chrissy looks around for anyone she can recognise. Two girls from the Tannery are sharing a settle by the fireplace. One of them, Susanna, smiles in greeting. The other girl, Rose, is too busy chatting to look up. Chrissy sees the Montgomerys, standing together behind a backgammon table looking ill at ease. There is no sign of Frank Barton.

Hugh Proudie hurries into the room, followed by the Reverend Willis. They are a contrasting pair — the first fresh-faced and blond, the latter with his brows knitted together above his thick dark beard. The Reverend darts a look at Chrissy, causing her heart to pump even harder. She feels she can scarcely breathe. She prays again for strength. Someone says in a loud whisper: 'She doesn't look like the Lamp Girl.' The woman adds, 'she's far too pale.' With an odd kind of start, Chrissy realises that there are people at the hearing who have been drawn to attend by the Tannery's advertisement. They are curious to compare the broken reality with the pink-cheeked image. The more disparity between the two, the more satisfaction she will provide. She pulls herself up, forcing herself to stand tall. Proudie smiles and makes his way to stand beside her; from his presence, she gains some strength. Of Thomas she does not — she dare not — think.

The Procurator bangs the table with the flat of his hand and the hubbub subsides. 'Let us proceed,' he says. 'I am here to convene an inquest as to the cause of death of an infant child of Chrissy Hogarth of Marketgait. Miss Hogarth was found with the infant on the 8th January at St Dunstan's Church Constan by the Reverend Aiden Willis.' He puts down his papers. 'Reverend Willis, will you please read your statement.'

The Reverend's statement is short and factual:

'On the afternoon of January 8th I called into St Dunstan's Church. I was on my way back from giving a sermon in Downfeld. I called into the Church to check the vestry window. There is a loose catch, and a blizzard was blowing. I found the young woman — Miss Hogarth — lying in one of the pews. It seemed she had been trying to conceal herself. I felt that she was not to be trusted. I tried to seize the bag she carried, thinking it contained goods which had been stolen. Miss Hogarth tried to prevent me from doing so, and bit me viciously on the hand. The bag contained the body of a young infant, together with a shawl and a piece of coal. I then took Miss Hogarth to the cottage of Constable Creiff, where I asked the constable to arrest her.'

There is a general murmuring and buzz of noise, while the Reverend's words are discussed.

The Procurator again bangs the table. It is Chrissy's turn to speak. Proudie hands her the sheet that he helped her to write, using as a table the floor of her cell.

'My name is Chrissy Hogarth,' she reads in a shaking voice. 'I live at Marketgait, and work as a seamstress at the Canadian Tannery. On the 6th January I gave birth to an infant son. He was weak and lived but a few hours. I wanted him to be buried in consecrated ground and so I took him to St Dunstan's Church. The ground was too frozen for me to bury him, and so I took shelter in the church. I was surprised by the Reverend and upset when he accused me of being a thief. It is true that I bit the Reverend, and I am very sorry for this.'

The Procurator puts down his quill pen.

'Miss Hogarth,' he says. 'I am curious as to why you did not ask for your child to be buried in a private service.' He looks round the room, and adds, 'You would not be the first young woman from the docks to give birth out of wedlock.' This last comment is followed by laughter.

'I was concerned that the Reverend might refuse. And then my baby would have been left in purgatory, unable to ever find peace.'

'Purgatory, Miss Hogarth? Are you a Roman Catholic?'

'No sir. My mother was. She was a Catholic from the Highlands. It was her who told me about Limbo.'

'I'm sure the Reverend will confirm that this is not a

concept to which the Presbyterian Church subscribes. Do you count yourself a Presbyterian?'

Chrissy nods, to the sound of more muffled laughter.

'Miss Hogarth, it is fortunate that we are not here to discuss the variations of religious belief. We might otherwise be here for a very long time. There is one point about which I am curious — why, in the wrappings, was there found a piece of coal?'

'To bring luck, sir.'

'I see,' says the Procurator. 'You wanted — as it were — to cover all possibilities. You bring ideas borrowed from the Catholic faith to a Presbyterian church, and for good measure, you throw in a piece of superstition.' Now the laughter is raucous. Chrissy wants to cover her ears with her hands.

'I was trying to do the best for my baby.'

'The best thing would have been to be honest and direct. I know Aiden Willis. He would not deny an innocent child the chance of a Christian burial.' He pauses, and taps together his fingers before continuing: 'Miss Hogarth, I am sure that the jury are keen to get on with their business, having first made use of the excellent facilities provided by Mr Jenks, the landlord of this establishment. I will not waste their time further, nor that of the company gathered here to witness the proceedings. Where is Dr Davy?'

A portly man in a check coat steps forward.

'Dr Davy, I will not ask you to read out your report since medical details must always be considered private. However, I would ask you to confirm your conclusion that the child died of natural causes?'

'That is so.'

'In which case, the business of this inquest is concluded.' The Procurator pushes the wooden box in the direction of the Reverend Willis. 'I am sure a discreet burial can be arranged.'

It had not occurred to Chrissy that the wooden box contains

Thomas's remains. Now the proximity of her son causes her to be seized by a violent longing to hold him. Reason swiftly tells her that — after a month — the corpse will be in a state of putrefaction, and will have become a thing of horror. She realises that the sweet odour — which she had identified as a leakage of gas from an unlit pipe — is the smell of decay. She can stand no more and begins to sway on her feet.

'A chair!' says someone. 'Miss Hogarth is about to faint!'

As Chrissy sinks down, the significance of the Procurator's words reaches her. Little Thomas is to be properly buried. The Procurator has put the Reverend in such a position that he cannot refuse. The child's rotting physical body is an irrelevance. Thomas will exist in a state of perfection for all eternity. She covers her face to hide her tears of happiness. In her mind's eye, she sees her baby once again romping blissfully on his pink cloud, bathed in the glowing love of Jesus.

She remains seated on a dining chair, quietly sobbing with relief. As if from far away, she hears Proudie saying something about the other matters — about the assault, and the concealment of her pregnancy. He is saying there is no need for these charges to be considered — he is asking for a new witness to be called. Soon, thinks Chrissy, she will be back at her work table, sewing tippets at the Tannery. She is suffused by a feeling of wellbeing. Everything is turning out for the best.

The witness is Peters. The warder reads hesitantly. Nevertheless her voice is loud.

'The accused has been in Bridewell for thirty one days. I have oversight of the women in her Corridor, which is Corridor C. I work a fifteen hour day, and during that time I have had one day off, so I have had many opportunities to observe Miss Hogarth. She is a woman of strange and violent moods. Sometimes she is very still. She sits on her stool and looks into the distance as if she is seeing visions. When she drinks water she does so slowly, as if she imagines herself to be imbibing alcohol. Then, when she works at the oakum, she pulls the fibres very fast, as if she thinks she will be whipped, but there is no-one there. I believe that Miss Hogarth has been driven to lunacy.'

'Dr Davy, would you agree?' asks the Procurator.

'I would, sir. It is not uncommon, when consequential to the loss of a child.'

'Reverend Willis, would you object to the charge of assault being dropped?'

The Reverend sounds weary, as if he has grown tired of the episode. 'I would not object, so long as the woman is detained.'

'That settles it then. Dr Davy, can the necessary paperwork be completed immediately, so that arrangements can be made for Miss Hogarth to be removed from the prison? It would seem compassionate for Miss Hogarth to be transferred to the Public Lunatic Asylum as soon as possible.'

Hugh Proudie walks over to Chrissy. 'There,' he says. 'I told you it would be all right. All the charges have been dismissed. Isn't that splendid?'

 **Equatorial Africa**

Lokim has been dreaming that he is in a dark cave. There is a glimmer of light that he is trying to reach, but when he walks towards it, his feet sink into mud. A rock has rolled loose, and is nudging at his side. He opens his eyes, to find that the rock is Makot's foot. The sun is already up and Makot is telling him that it is time to move on.

He touches the scar on his head, making a circular movement in the coils of his hair. The moon has gone through a whole cycle since he set off with his friends from the village, but on some mornings, his head still throbs. When he fell down the hill his skull hit a stone, which cut at his scalp, and made him go into a deep sleep. And when he woke up, the sun had moved right down in the sky. He remembers his first unsettling sight of Makot. His companion had a missing front tooth, and his face was painted red and white from some witchdoctor medicine. He had the markings of a seven-times killer, which alarmed Lokim — having lost his spear, he had nothing with which he could defend himself. But when Makot saw that Lokim had woken, he brought him precious water to drink, stored in a hollow shell of an ostrich egg. The body of the lion lay nearby, already skinned. Vultures circled and descended to feed. Lokim remembers with a shudder how one grey-feathered bird stood near him, hunched like the malicious elder from a marauding tribe. The bird had peered at his flesh as if he was longing for death to render it palatable.

Lokim rises slowly, stretching his long limbs. He kicks open the protective enclosure of thorn branches — which he built with Makot the night before — and lopes off to empty his bladder. He returns to find that Makot has covered the embers of the fire, and is already milking one of the cows. Lokim watches the young warrior as he kneels on one leg, squirting the white fluid into his calabash. Makot has saved his life, not once but twice. In return, he has demanded Lokim's loyalty and in gratitude, Lokim has given it. But Lokim sometimes finds his companion a harsh taskmaster — not so much towards himself, which he could forgive — but in the way he treats his two fine cows. The terrain through which they are travelling is stony and often steep. The poor animals sometimes fall to their knees from exhaustion and lack of water. Then Makot hits them with a stick that is three fingers thick. Lokim thinks of Pila. He never used more than a light switch on his own cow. And he never did so to cause hurt —

rather the action was a way of communicating the bond that bound the two of them.

'Here,' says Makot, offering the filled calabash. 'Have some breakfast. Yesterday was long,' he continues, kneeling again to get milk for himself. 'Today should be easier; for most of the way, we can follow the riverbed.'

Lokim lifts the gourd to his lips and begins to drink the creamy milk. He should not be critical of his friend, he has so much to thank him for. Makot has told him how he was stalking an impala— with his spear already raised — when he saw Lokim tumbling and falling. The lion followed swiftly. The great beast was bleeding from his side, but was energised by the chase. Makot waited behind a bush, then sprang out. He had further weakened the animal with one well-placed thrust to the neck, then he used a large stone to smash into his skull.

When Lokim recovered consciousness and saw that the lion was dead, his first thought was that he must rejoin his companions. But the head injury had affected his balance; his legs were unsteady. He lay back down. Makot cared for him, bringing him cooked meat, as well as water. Then Lokim's body was gripped by a violent fever. He felt as if his blood boiled inside him, and he sweated so much that the dry dust grew wet where he lay. He saw things that were not there. He looked at the thin trunk of the acacia tree and it seemed that it was peopled with tiny moving figures, and disturbing, grimacing faces. One of his ancestors appeared, an old woman called Dola. She looked at him hard and long, before invoking the spirit of the elephant grass. She rocked on her heels, asking the spirit to sing him back to sleep. Lokim fought to stay awake. Dola had been a bad wife. She was said to have been unfaithful to her husband, and when he found out and beat her, she talked with a viper and arranged for the snake to bite him on the heel. Lokim felt so wretched, he feared that the fever would kill him. His eyes burned inside his head and his limbs shook. Then it was that Makot saved his life for a second time. From a pouch, he brought out the bark of a special tree. He soaked the bark to make a medicine, which he made Lokim drink, forcing him to swallow while he raved. The fever subsided, and from that point, Lokim's weakened body began to grow well.

For a few days the two young men had stayed where they were, in their makeshift camp. When Lokim announced that he was strong enough to go home, Makot pleaded with him not to do so. He suggested instead that they should travel south together, to Rotoma. He said there was a trader in town — from a foreign land — who was prepared to exchange animal hides for handfuls of brightly coloured beads. Makot would take the lion skin to barter with. He would give some of the beads to Lokim, so that when the time came for him to return to his village, he would not arrive back empty-handed.

'Please,' Makot repeated. 'Come with me. It is much safer to travel with a companion than to journey alone.' Lokim had felt he was not in a position to argue. Besides, apart from Amuarkar and Niampa — who had his new wife to distract him — no-one from his village would miss him much.

Lokim finishes his milk, and wipes his mouth. The calabash has two holes bored into it, through which a rope has been threaded. He slings the rope over his shoulder and follows Makot, who has hoisted the rolled lion skin on his back, and is pulling his cows, one by one, through a particularly dense scrub of thorns.

They continue their journey, mostly in silence. Makot leads, Lokim follows. At midday, when the sun is high, they stop at a watering hole to rest. Beside the dried up river, old men sit in a semi-circle on two-legged stools. They watch impassively as children press their feet and hands into the riverbed, then shriek with delight as they splatter one another with mud.

Women collect water, scoop by scoop. One woman uses a container that Lokim has never seen before. He frowns in confusion, trying to make sense of the thing. It has four corners, which is odd in itself — nearly everything in Karamoja is round. It glitters in the most mysterious way, and it reflects like water — Lokim can see the green of a nearby tree, shining back at him. It is not made of stone — the woman lifts it easily, and its walls are thin as the shell of a snail. It is a strange and magical thing, which Lokim longs to own, but he has nothing with which to barter.

Lokim thinks about the beads he will possess. He imagines them, round and rolling in his palm, red, blue and green. He wonders how large his share will be, and if he will have a sufficient quantity to buy a goat, or even a calf. He thinks of Pila, and wonders again if she is safe.

'Would you like some?'

Lost in thought, Lokim does not at first respond. When he does look up, a girl wearing a scrap of torn cloth is holding out a block of baked sorghum.

Her plump friend propels the girl forward with a little shove. 'It is sweetened with honey,' she says.

Lokim is aware that Makot is watching, with an expression that is hard to read. The young man lies with his hands behind his head; his body marks looking very prominent on his naked torso. 'Thank you,' he says. 'But what of my companion — is there some for him too?'

'Our gift is for you alone.' The girls exchange glances, simultaneously cover their mouths with their hands, and giggle . 'Your friend is not handsome, like you.'

'With pleasure, I will accept your cake,' Lokim says, with a smile. 'But I will share it. My friend and I have travelled far together.'

When the sun is lower in the sky, and the cows are rested and have drunk their fill, Lokim and Makot continue their journey. After a little, Lokim finds that his left foot hurts whenever he takes a step; the sole has been pierced by a needle of gorse. He reaches down, but cannot remove it. He tries conversation, to take his mind off the pain.

'I hope the people of Rotoma will be as welcoming as those villagers,' he says.

Makot hits the backside of the leading cow. 'If not,' he says, 'I have my spear.'

Lokim hobbles quickly, to keep up with Makot. He has the opportunity to mention something which has been preoccupying him. 'I have nothing with which to fight. If we find the right sort of stone, and a straight strong stick, we could make me a spear, so that I too, am armed.'

'Be patient,' says Makot. He pulls a thick branch out of the way of the cows. 'When we have exchanged the lion skin, you can have the finest weapon that beads can buy.'

'Until then?'

Makot shoves at the branch with his foot, pushing it into the undergrowth. Disturbing a large beetle, he pauses to watch the insect as it lifts its dazzling wings, then takes flight. 'It is not worth stopping.' The beetle lands on a thick blade of grass and disappears against the green. 'Another night, another day's travel, and we will have arrived.'

They make good time. The next day, after an early start, they reach Rotoma when the sun is still high in the sky. Lokim looks around in amazement. He cannot believe the size of the place. He has never seen such a large confusion of huts gathered together in one place, nor so many people. Old toothless women watch from doorways as they pass, wide-eyed children smile and follow in their footsteps, before turning away and disappearing down one of the tracks that snakes between the buildings. Everywhere chickens scratch at the earth and luxuriate in the dust, spreading and flapping their brown-black wings. Young goats with clean white pelts seek out their mothers with bleating cries, then butt contentedly at their full pink udders. Rotoma is a wealthy place. As well as the profusion of animals, Lokim is struck by the amount of cloth both men and women are flaunting. Lokim catches the eye of a young girl carrying on her head a round load of plantain. She resembles an exotic flower. He averts his gaze and looks down at the worn and dusty piece of hide which he himself wears to cover his nakedness. In Karamoja, cloth is rarely seen; the tribesmen have only animal skins or leaves with which to cover themselves.

Makot is walking purposefully beside him, ignoring all distractions. He pushes and prods at his cows to keep them moving. He has told Lokim that the visiting trader is a man called Santos. For safety, they must go straight to his hut. Santos, being rich and powerful, can offer protection against the young warriors who will be returning to the town once they have finished the day's hunting.

Lokim feels a tap on his arm. Makot is indicating a path off to the left.

'It is this way,' he says, with a jerk of his head. 'I remember from before.'

They come to a rectangular hut, with a strange undulating roof made of something other than leaves. Makot brings the cows to a halt. He beckons to a young boy and indicates that he is to guard the animals, miming with a hand movement that the child will be rewarded for his labour.

'Come.' he says. Lokim is still gazing puzzled at the mysterious roof. Makot prods at him, then leads him inside.

It is some moments before Lokim can adjust to the darkness. He blinks, several times. When he finally opens his eyes, he is looking at a thin-lipped, narrow-nosed man, who is seated on several rolls of cloth, piled up one upon another. The man has a striped cloth wound around his head, and more cloths encase his body.

On his left hand, he wears a thick bracelet of beaten silver. Santos is clearly a man of considerable substance.

'So,' he says to Makot, 'you are here once more — you have returned.' The trader's voice is strange, high and fluting. He speaks haltingly, in the Acholi language — it is sufficiently like Karamajong for Lokim to make sense of the words. 'Let me see your specimen.'

Lokim is puzzled. Makot makes no effort to off load the lion's skin from his back and unroll it. Instead he takes Lokim's arm and pushes him forward. Santos gets to his feet. He is tall-framed, with a soft, rounded belly. He steps up close. Cupping his long, tapering fingers under his chin, he pulls open Lokim's jaw. He does so with gentleness; the movement feels almost seductive. Lokim does not think to protest.

Santos is looking into his mouth. 'Good,' he says, with an approving nod.

Realisation hits Lokim like a blow to the stomach. He has been betrayed. Every fibre of muscle in his body tightens. He wants to grab Makot's neck, he wants to crush his windpipe. But when he turns, Makot is not there, and when he heads for the doorway he sees that it is blocked by two warriors armed with spears and bows and arrows. He tries — against the odds — to fight. He kicks out until a sharp flashing wrist knife is produced, and the blade is put to his throat. His arms are seized and roughly wrenched behind him. His hands are viciously tied with rope.

And so begins Lokim's life as a slave.

 Glasgow, Scotland

James and Mary are seated in the front parlour of the grey stone house. It is evening; the servants have been dismissed from their daily duties, and at last the children are abed.

Robert went unwillingly, complaining of being treated as someone far younger than his fourteen years. Mary eventually compromised by allowing him the bright oil lamp from the study, so that he could better enjoy the latest instalment of *Great Expectations*, from *All The Year Round*. Robert went to fetch the lamp, and returned to say a curt goodnight. But James heard the boy cursing under his breath, as soon as he was out of the room.

Mary shakes her head as her son's footsteps sound heavy on the stair.

'He needs his father,' she says, flatly. 'I fear he is out of control.'

James does not know how best to respond. Robert can be a difficult, surly youth, but there is also a sensitive, caring side to his nature. It is true that the boy would benefit from more contact with Livingstone — James thinks back to his own father, who provided for him a model of godliness and propriety — but Livingstone's work is of such value and importance that it surely must take precedence over all other duties, including that of protective patriarch. James has a notion that this is not what Mary wants to hear. He stretches his long legs, rises to his feet, and moves to put more wood on the fire.

'You are thinking that I am inconsiderate,' says Mary, without rancour. 'That it is my duty to care for the children alone, while David carries out his work.'

'No-one, Mary, could call you inconsiderate.' James speaks with genuine warmth. Mary is the kindest woman he has ever known, aside from his stepmother. He kicks at the log, causing flames to leap and sparks to fly. He swallows, as he remembers how bereft he felt after the other woman's death.

Mary has noticed his changed demeanour and is looking at him with concern.

James sits himself down. 'Sorry. In some ways you remind

me of my stepmother. She was very dear to me.' He pauses. 'And I to her, I think.'

'Was?' Mary speaks softly.

'She died two years ago, while I was still a student at St Andrew's. For a while afterwards I hardly functioned. I found myself at such a loss.'

'I am sorry to hear that she died, and more, that you have suffered so.' Mary moves over to James, and rests her hand on his. 'She was blessed to be so cherished by you.'

James wonders at the propriety of Mary's touch. But her hand is a comfort and it leads him to speak aloud thoughts which he holds private. 'My mother had faith in me. As well as love, she gave me self belief. She encouraged me to become ordained, and shared my dreams of Africa; she made me feel that I could truly bring about a change in those benighted lands.'

Mary withdraws her hand and moves back to her chair. 'Benighted?' she asks. Her tone is light, but a tiny ripple of criticism has washed into her voice.

James runs the thumb of his hand down over his beard. He has noticed this before about Mary; she can be illogically defensive of Africa and the ways of its people. Illogical, because her entire life has been dedicated to bringing Christianity and civilisation to that dark continent. James finds Mary's inconsistencies irritating, but also intriguing. He longs above all to see Africa for himself, and to meet its people, so that he can decide for himself what is worthy and what is to be abhorred.

'Surely it is right to bring Christ's teaching to those who have not yet had the privilege of hearing it? Love thy neighbour as thyself, for example — if that commandment were obeyed, there would be no slavery.'

'Slavery is unquestionably wrong.' In the candlelight Mary's features appear softer, so that James finds himself wondering how she would look if her hair were dressed in a more becoming style. 'But if our African brothers sell one another, it is because the white man foments that dreadful trade. And while slavery may have been abolished in Britain, there are plenty of British prepared to do business with the Portuguese, who continue to bring thousands of men, women and children from the interior to the coast.'

'The Portuguese are to be reviled for what they do.'

'Yet they are not all bad. And David himself has sometimes befriended the traders, when he has been in need of food, or protection. Not all British men are good. And not all Africans crave enlightenment, though it suits the missionaries to believe otherwise.'

'Mary! How can you say such a thing. You yourself are of missionary stock — a Moffat, born and bred at Kuruman — and you are married to the greatest missionary of them all.'

'David is not primarily a missionary. He is a gifted explorer. He is like a genius wandering child with all the enthusiasms, energy and tantrums of an infant as yet untamed by the world.' Mary is looking fondly into the fire. James finds himself pierced by a niggle of envy for the famous man who holds her love.

'You were speaking of Enlightenment. It must always be a blessing for a man — whatever his colour — to receive the gift of God's word.'

Mary sits back and smoothes her grey flannel skirt. Her hands are unadorned, save for a single gold band. The only other jewellery she wears is tied with a ribbon around her neck; it is an enamelled miniature of her husband. 'The word God can mean different things to different people', she says carefully. 'I think that we all hold a different image of Him in our hearts. It cannot be otherwise, for no man can look directly into other man's soul. The tribes of Africa may not believe in a Christian deity as we do, but I have seen cave paintings in the Drakensberg that depict a spiritual life of marvellous depth and complexity. What is more, the paintings are of considerable skill and refinement.'

James remains silent. He dislikes being at a loss in an argument, but Mary is speaking of things of which he has no knowledge. A worm of doubt wriggles into him. He has been so sure of his destiny, but such conversations lead him to think that his ignorance will be a severe impediment to the task ahead. From out of the miniature, Livingstone gazes at him with an expression that appears both challenging and pugnacious.

He gets to his feet. 'I'll go to Robert — I'll wish him goodnight. I hope to find the boy in a mood that is more congenial.'

No gas has been installed in the terraced house so James takes a candle from the mantelpiece to light his way. In the hallway, a cold winter draught blows from under the front door, causing the flame to flicker and bend. Robert sleeps alone in what is little more than a box room; he has grudgingly agreed that the privacy it provides is compensation for its small size. James listens at the door. He can hear no sound, so he opens the door softly, thinking that — despite his protestations — the boy may already be asleep. The room is in darkness. James listens again, thinking to hear the sound of regular breathing, but he hears only silence. Bringing his candle to the bed, he finds a bolster where Robert's head should be. He wonders if Robert has taken himself off to the water closet. It is then that he notices that Robert's clothes have gone, and that his shoes are absent too.

When James tells Mary that he cannot find her son, she remains oddly sanguine. Together they search the house, and when they find no trace of the boy, she merely lifts her shoulders and repeats, 'I told you — Robert needs his father.'

James is alarmed. 'Where can he be?'

'Playing dice, I expect. He has done this before — he takes himself out through the back staircase and goes out into the town. There is a game called hazard that he enjoys.'

'He goes out at night to play hazard! Why, Robert is only fourteen!'

'He — he has difficulties. He has never adjusted to life in Scotland. I'll wake Isabel, the maid. Her brother brought him back when it happened last time. She will know where to find him.'

James wonders at Mary's sangfroid as he hurries from the house. She is a conundrum to him; calm in circumstances which would have any other woman reaching for their smelling salts, but capable of over-reacting and taking to her bed when pricked in some unexpectedly sensitive spot. He remembers an occasion when she became completely overwrought over an advertisement for Barrel and Funk's baby food. The wording made her so cross that she rammed on her bonnet and stomped off for a walk down the Byers Road in order to work off her anger. The memory of her frankness still makes James blush; 'a mother's breast is best for a newborn babe,' she had expostulated, pulling her cloak around her. 'It is wicked to suggest otherwise.'

The cold is bitter. He shivers and thinks wistfully of a thick felt coat, lined with silk of kingfisher blue, that he has seen in the window of a tailor's shop in Sauchiehall Street. Such an indulgence is far beyond his purse; he is saving hard for his forthcoming adventure. After a discourse with his conscience, he has even sold his inheritance of family silver to give ballast to the fund. He turns into Lawrence Street, praying that Isabel's supposition is right, and that Robert will be found in one of the back rooms of the Red Lion. Street lighting gives the terraced houses a dingy, yellow hue and the wind whips at his ears. In his haste, he has not thought to put on a hat.

He hurries into the tavern. The games room is so thick and

fuggy that for a few moments, it is hard to make anything out. Nearly every customer is enjoying a tobacco pipe, and the wind whistles down the chimney, billowing out more smoke, together with particles of black soot. A lamp in the centre of the room is emitting a smell of paraffin so strong that James feels quite light-headed. Once his vision has adjusted, he sees a group of men gathered round a green baize table. The caster is a florid-looking man with a missing front tooth. He guffaws in satisfaction when he sees what he has thrown. Robert is standing away from the group. He looks hunched and defeated, and in his hands he cradles a glass of stout. James pauses to consider the lad. Unlike Mary, Robert is tall; in height he could pass for a man. Like Mary, his hair is dark, and he has a prominent, well-shaped nose. His eyes are lowered, and as James watches, he uses the palm of his hand to wipe away a tear. James has planned to remonstrate with the boy, but he is disarmed by compassion.

'Robert!' he calls, feigning surprise. 'Your mother and I thought you were at home, enjoying the latest delights of Mr Dickens. Let us find ourselves a seat — we can have a talk, before we return.'

They move to the snuggery; the room is snug in name only. The fire has been left unattended, and the few glowing embers in the grate give out scant heat. Away from the older men, Robert's tears fall fast, so that James sees him once again as the child that he is. 'I owe money,' he says. 'The dice did not roll in my favour.'

'How much?'

'Four shillings. Not too much. But I haven't got it.' He covers his face with his hands.

'I'll settle your debt.' James thinks sadly of the depletion to his precious fund. 'But Robert, this must not happen again. Tell me, what is it that causes you to behave in such a way? Think of the disgrace that you could bring upon your father, were it known that David Livingstone's son is a drinker and a gambler.'

'I do not see why I should be careful of my father's reputation.'

'He is a great man.'

'Maybe, but he cares little for his family. He has a need to keep travelling, to keep finding things out and to record what he has learned. I worked it out — first on the boat to England, then afterwards, at Kendal, when I was in the dormitory and all the other the boys around me were asleep. It's like a disease. His need to keep moving comes before anything.' Robert puts his glass back down with such force that James is concerned that it will crack. 'There was a time in the Kalahari when we nearly died because we had no water. I was just five, Agnes was four. I remember crawling under the wagon, trying to keep cool, and crying myself to sleep with this terrible, desperate thirst. Then he sent us away with Mama, as if we were nothing. He is a careless person. Careless of those that love him, and careless of himself.' Robert finishes his drink. 'He is not deserving of my mother's devotion.'

 Broughty Ferry, Scotland

At Corona, Mina Stephen brushes her long hair with a silver-backed brush. She does so because Miss Scrope has told her not to bother coming back downstairs until she looks more presentable. Mina is at a loss to know what it is about her appearance that has annoyed the governess; the grey-sprigged dress that she wears is suitably modest, with a wide white collar that is freshly starched and scrupulously clean. Mina suspects that Miss Scrope's fault-finding is simply the result of a fit of irrational bad temper, but she has no desire to provoke the teacher further. So she obediently brushes her hair, again and again, until it is as smooth as silk and shines like satin.

Mina is in the bedroom which she used to share with Maggie, and which — since Helen's marriage — is now entirely her own. It is a beautiful room, with elaborate plasterwork on the white ceiling, a marble fireplace, and a large bow window above the formal flower garden. Looking out, Mina sees that the snowdrops on either side of the walkway have formed abundant white drifts. When she has finished her piano practice, she will gather a posy of the delicate flowers to sketch, under the tutorship of Mr Rimes, the drawing master.

First, however, she must return to the schoolroom. With light feet, she descends the wide staircase. She asks permission to re-enter, then sits herself down on her chair next to Maggie. The governess's mood seems to have lifted; she makes no further negative comment. As it is a Wednesday, Miss Scrope is attempting to teach the girls Italian. Today, rather than returning to Baedeker's grammar, she brings out a faded copy of Petrarch's sonnets, the relevant pages carefully marked with embroidery wool. She seems particularly affected by the Italian poet; when she reads out his poems, she adopts a strange monotone, and at the end of each line, she pauses and lowers her eyes. She suggests that Mina and Maggie should try setting one of the poems to music, for performance at a public party. Mina's Italian is not fluent and she thinks that this is an aspiration too far. Nevertheless, as Miss Scrope reads out 'soleasi nel mio cor…' she finds herself moved by the beauty of the flowing words. She is touched to learn of Petrarch's intense and tender love for Laura — a love which could never be returned because Laura was already married to a French count. When Miss Scrope recounts this tale of thwarted passion, she puts her hand to her chest, and there is a catch to her voice, which Mina finds hard to interpret.

Maggie is absent from afternoon lessons; she has a dress fitting, because she has persuaded Mama that a new outfit is essential if she is not to be humiliated when she goes to stay with the Camerons at Easter. Judith Cameron is Maggie's best friend; they are the same age, with birthdays just three days apart.

Judith's father is a jute merchant, who has recently opened a new factory in India. The processing equipment was carried over the ocean in one of the Stephens' ships. For a short time, the easy alliance that had always existed between the two families was severely strained, because a suitable price for transporting the machinery proved difficult to negotiate. Both men remained polite in their dealings with one another, but neither James Cameron nor Alexander Stephen could countenance losing money on account of an expected flexibility due to the presumed ties of friendship.

The Camerons live nearby, in a large, turreted house near the sea front. Their holiday home is in Braemar, not far from Balmoral. The Stephens have speculated on the possibility that while Maggie is out walking or riding, she will meet with the Queen and the Prince Consort, and will fall into conversation with the royal pair. Rumour has it that Victoria and Albert like to play at being commoners; the couple are said to go about daringly unaccompanied by servants or guards, whilst enjoying their highland retreat.

Mina usually likes her drawing lessons, but today Mr Rimes is late, and when he does arrive, he is clearly out of sorts. His pale complexion contrasts starkly with the black velvet jacket he wears, and with the Spanish black hat — like a tam o' shanter without a pompom — that is crammed on his head. Seeing the snowdrops that Mina has placed on the table, he lowers his dark eyes.

'Such beauty…' he shudders. 'Such beauty… and yet so ephemeral. I can't endure it. Within the hour, these flowers will droop. Soon they will wither, by tomorrow their white petals will be brown and touched with decay...' When the tutor covers his eyes with his long fingers, Mina notices that his nails are bitten down to the quick. He begins to cough. 'I can't endure it!' He removes a large yellow handkerchief from his upper pocket. 'Take them away.'

Mina carries the rejected posy to the kitchen, where Katie leaves off peeling potatoes to supply a little glass jar, which she fills with water. 'You can keep them,' Mina tells Katie, 'They will brighten the windowsill.'

From a faded carpet bag, Mr Rimes produces a roll of canvas, paper, pastels, pens and charcoal. He has ceased to cough, but underneath the Spanish hat, his brow is wet, and the whites of his eyes are shot with red. Mina thinks he would be better off at home, tucked up in bed with a hot water bottle. She knows that in reality, there is little comfort to be had for Rimes, at his house in Dundee. Mina has overheard Mama discussing with Miss Scrope whether the drawing master should be allowed to keep his position, given the scandalous behaviour of his wife. Mrs Rimes is reputed to model half-naked for two other artists. She keeps a slovenly house, and takes excessive amounts of laudanum. Mina was impressed at the way Miss Scrope defended the tutor; with unusual directness, the governess told Mama she thought it would be unfair to condemn a man for his wife's indiscretions.

Mr Rimes hands Mina a sheet of paper, ink and an old toothbrush. He moves his tapering fingers to and fro across his forehead. 'I can't do much today... I am too tired for creativity. Fetch fern leaves from the conservatory — make spatter pictures. Look in your fern book — identify the subtle differences between each sample. Add the pictures to your album, the specimens correctly named. I will offer guidance, if you should so require...'

But when Mina returns from the conservatory, Mr Rimes

does not bother looking at the leaves she has brought. Instead, he continues to stare at the canvas which he has unrolled. 'What do you think?' he says. 'It is this that has exhausted me... . I completed it three days ago, but since then, I seem unable to find rest...'

Mina is taken aback by the picture. Rimes has painted a shepherd and a shepherdess lying together in a field, surrounded by lambs. Their posture and proximity are shocking, but it is the expression on the woman's face that is most disturbing. Her eyes are drooping, and her jaw is slack; it is as if she has been satisfied by some food or drink — yet there is no sign of either in the picture — the woman looks instead at the young man. The woman's naked feet peep from under her skirt, the toes are spread apart, as if to indicate a state of utter relaxation.

There is a pause; Rimes's breath sounds loud and quick. Mina tries to find something to say; she is too shocked to comment on the shameless couple. 'I — I like the lambs,' she says eventually. 'They are extremely realistic. She waves a frond of fern. 'I have brought this. Could I draw it? The leaves are very fine. It is a type of maidenhair, I think.'

'Maidenhair,' Rimes gives a high-pitched laugh. '*Maidenhair*. Very fine. Yes indeed, very fine.' He laughs again. 'Let me present you with a pencil Miss Stephen.' He laughs again; it is a harsh, rasping sound. 'I think this one has plenty of lead.' Abruptly, he falls silent. Beads of sweat glisten above his beard. He looks so ill and exhausted that Mina wishes there were something she could do, that would make him feel better. She would like to offer comfort — to make Rimes well again. Mina feels suddenly cross with the faithless Mrs Rimes who is so careless of her husband's welfare. The woman should show proper concern and Rimes should be encouraged to take advice from a doctor.

CHAPTER THREE

March 1861

 Royal Lunatic Asylum, Dundee, Scotland

Chrissy is lying on her mattress on the floor of the dormitory which she shares with forty-seven other women. On the front wall of the Asylum, an inscription declares that its purpose is 'To restore the use of reason, to alleviate suffering and to lessen peril where reason cannot be restored.' Forty years have passed since this stone was unveiled; the building, intended for fifty, now holds upwards of two hundred troubled souls.

She wakes reluctantly. She has been dreaming that she is in Kirriemuir. In her mind, she has been playing five stones with her brothers, as her mother prepares the midday meal and her father works the shuttle of the household loom. She pulls her blanket around herself and tries to hold onto the comforting aura created by her imaginings. The fragile images of her childhood home dissolve and break, ethereal as gossamer. Unwillingly, she opens her eyes, and is suffused with dismay at the full and harsh realisation of her current situation. It is not the discomfort of her life which she finds hard to bear, but the lack of privacy. The inmates are watched intently twenty-four hours a day. In order to ensure that they can make no escape, the building is surrounded by high walls, capped with broken glass.

Chrissy waits for her turn in the washrooms. The women are mostly silent as they queue. Sometimes their minds are filled with sorrows that are too private to share. Sometimes, it is the fear of being reported that robs the women of speech; the attendants keep notebooks in which to record any words or behaviours that are considered outlandish, and will require — after discussion with the doctors — to be challenged. The attendants expect to be addressed as 'Nurse', but Chrissy thinks it unfair on Miss Nightingale to give any of them such a title. Apart from their sailcloth aprons, there is little to differentiate them from the female gaolers who bullied her in prison. Since arriving at the asylum, she has observed that of the staff it is Mr Connor who displays most compassion. As an indication of his progressive views, the superintendant has banned the use of scolds, straight-waistcoats and fetters. However, Chrissy has heard of other 'treatments' which she is equally anxious to avoid. Everyone dreads the isolation of the padded cell, and one young girl who was admitted to hospital for rebelliousness, having twice tried running away from home, has told Chrissy that she was given such an overdose of purgatives that her life was only saved by a dangerous procedure which involved a filtration of liquid to her stomach. A sad woman, who had fallen on hard times after the death of her curate husband, has whispered to Chrissy of 'the bath of surprise'. She was made to walk along a corridor, thinking she was being taken to chapel by a different route. Suddenly, the floor gave way, and she found herself plunged into a deep trough of icy water. The widow had screamed out in terror, believing that she would drown.

Prayers before breakfast are led by Mr Connor. The women sit at long tables in the middle of the dormitory and are served with porridge from a huge metal pot. The servings are not small, but the gruel is thin and without salt to give it flavour. Breakfast at Albert Street is the most Spartan meal of the day. Lunch is a thick soup with bread, and supper is a positively generous repast, consisting as it does of meat, potato and a kind of vegetable stew. Chrissy tries to comfort herself with the thought that conditions in the asylum are a great deal better than those she would experience, were she still in Bridewell Gaol.

Mr Connor is a firm believer in the healing virtues of industry, so after the meal the women are set to work, sweeping and scrubbing, before being allocated their individual tasks. Chrissy would like to be sent to the sewing room. Using her skills would restore a sense of normality to the daily rhythm of her life. But it would be unthinkable for her to request such a move. When the attendant reads out 'Miss Hogarth, today you will be counting beads, under the supervision of Mr Horrocks,' she bows her head in acquiescence.

Bead-counting takes place in a cold, square room with windows so high that it is impossible to see anything more than a glimpse of the dark winter sky. The space has been designed to provide the minimum of distraction. The aim of the process is therapeutic. It is hoped that the concentration required in numbering and sorting, will so totally occupy the women that all unhelpful thoughts will be banished from their minds. Chrissy takes her seat on the wooden bench, next to an older woman who wears a wreath of dried rosebuds in the grey curls of her hair.

Horrocks is a young man with a large white face that is pocked like a grubby piece of lard. He owes his position to being the son of Mrs Horrocks, one of the senior nurses; his mother has persuaded the superintendant that the presence of a male attendant in the enclosed asylum would make the inmates' environment more like the outside world, and would thus improve their wellbeing. But young Horrocks has little interest in management, and seemingly no interest in the inmates' welfare. Whenever he can, he finds errands to run, that necessitate his leaving the building. He often shouts at his charges, but Chrissy has observed that he takes no particular pleasure in exercising the power that he has been given. He is not malicious; his bad-temper results simply from his wish to be elsewhere. Now he carries into the room two rush baskets full of glass beads that are variously coloured red, green, yellow and blue. He places the baskets on the deal table, distributes to each woman four smaller baskets, then gives each of them an abacus. He retires to the corner of the room, settles himself down, and is soon lost in the reading of a ghoulishly illustrated penny dreadful.

Chrissy picks up the beads between her thumb and forefinger, collecting five together in her palm, before dropping the group into the appropriate basket. She has tried different ways of working, on different days. Sometimes she collects just one colour at a time, and will not begin on red beads until all the yellow ones are gathered; on other days, she scoops up five of each colour in turn. Whichever way she works, time passes with infinite slowness. Horrocks is supposed to check the women's counting from time to time, to ensure that the shifted beads on the abacus correspond with the counted beads in the baskets. He rarely does this, knowing, as he does — and as the women do — that his final duty will be to tip all the sorted beads back into the big baskets ready to start the whole process again on the following day. As there is no incentive for her to apply herself to the accuracy of her task, Chrissy allows her actions to become so automatic that her mind is able to both count and think at the same time. Always her thoughts turn to Thomas. She wonders if she had behaved differently she might have been able to preserve his life. She would like to know of his life in heaven, and who is with him in paradise.

After an hour, Horrocks stands up and tosses aside his magazine. 'Tell anyone that I've left you alone, and I'll have you sent stone-breaking at the work-house.' He glowers, then leaves the room.

For a time the inmates remain dutifully silent. Chrissy continues counting, until she is nudged on the arm by her neighbour. 'Give yourself a bit of a rest, dear,' she says. 'We get little enough respite, in this place.'

The woman looks at her kindly. When she smiles, Chrissy realises that she is younger than her grey hair would suggest. Her name, which Chrissy has learned at roll-call, is Deborah Buchanan. 'What was it that brought you here?' Deborah continues. 'You don't mind if I ask? You're not an imbecile like Betty, and you don't hear voices, like Jane.'

Chrissy reflects that Betty and Jane are the exceptions. Most women in the asylum would be considered unremarkable were they out and about in the town. It is poverty that has brought some to the place, the relentless want of food and pleasure has reduced them to despair. Others have been admitted because of their failure to conform. She knows of two women who are in the hospital because they petitioned their husbands for divorce. She hesitates before replying, 'I had a baby. Then afterwards, he died, and I did something foolish.' Anxious to take the focus from herself, she plucks courage and asks, 'and what of you Deborah? What was it that brought you here?'

'Vanity,' she whispers. 'I suffer from vanity.'

The woman's once-pretty face is shadowed with bewilderment. Chrissy is moved to say, 'It seems harsh to be deprived of your liberty for an affliction so commonly suffered by women, and indeed, by some men, too.'

'My vanity was overweening.' Deborah touches her dusty coronet.

She looks so sad that Chrissy feels disposed to turn the

conversation by speaking of herself. 'Bead-counting is not a productive pastime. I would prefer to do mending. Do you know the Canadian Tannery? I used to work there, making tippets and muffs — I hope one day to return.'

Deborah brightens. 'A tannery sounds a rough kind of place. Was there not a fearful odour?'

'I soon got used to the smell. And our room was a happy place in which to work. The manager — Frank Barton — was a true gentleman. We were brought tea in the afternoons, which we didn't have to pay for, and on Fridays, we were all given a piece of fish.'

'You speak of this man Frank with warmth.' Deborah looks up knowingly. 'Did he favour you?'

'Mr Barton tried to get help for me, before I came here. He always acted as a gentleman should.' Chrissy does not want to boast, but there is such pleasure to be had in speaking of her previous life, that after a brief hesitation, she goes on: 'It is true that he thought I was pretty. In another part of the factory, whale oil is processed. He arranged to have my picture painted, so that it could be used to advertise the oil they use for lamps. I sat for a Mr Watt while he painted my portrait, and now my picture is on all the Tannery's products.'

Deborah looks away. 'I would have loved that, to have been painted. I would have worn my green taffeta dress.' She turns back. 'But tell me? Do you not miss your husband? Does he not wish for another child?'

'I have no husband.'

'Oh.'

Chrissy bridles at the familiar tone of disapproval. She resolves to keep silent no more. 'Thomas was a gift to me, from Jesus.' she says. Her voice is quiet, but she speaks with firm deliberation. 'He did not have an earthly father, for I was never with a man.'

Deborah looks at her, open-mouthed. But there is no time

to respond verbally, for at that moment, Horrocks comes hurrying back into the room. The women swiftly fall silent, bow their heads and mechanically resume counting. Deborah's movements are too slow. Horrocks seizes her basket of yellow beads, and shakes it under her nose, as if she were a horse, and the beads were oats. 'Is this all you've done!' he shouts. 'You dozy old baggage!' He cuffs her lightly on the side of the head, knocking her crown askew. Deborah puts up a hand to straighten her wreath and looks with appalled dismay at the scattering of papery petals which have fallen to the floor.

For the rest of the morning, Chrissy feels wretchedly responsible for the broken flowers. At lunchtime, she tries to talk to Deborah, but her friend appears lost in a world of her own. After they have eaten, the women are sent in groups of four to visit the privies, and when they return, they are made to assemble in single file. 'Quickly,' barks Biggins, the oldest of the attendants, as they march down the corridor, for religious instruction. Biggins's voice is deep because she smokes a pipe whenever she gets the opportunity; tobacco has streaked her white hair with yellow strands. In the chapel, Chrissy manages to catch Deborah's eye, but Deborah turns away. Chrissy is troubled by the expression she has fleetingly caught on the other woman's face. She has recognised a look of pity, mingled with embarrassment.

Chrissy's heart beats hard inside the bodice of her thick linen dress. It is painful to speculate that her account of Thomas's miraculous arrival might not have been believed.

Mr Connor leads a lesson on the Parable of the Sower. He delivers his teachings theatrically and it is clear he enjoys the sound of his own rich voice. He asks the women to ensure that they are fertile ground for the Lord, which leaves Chrissy pondering. Opportunities for doing good — or for doing anything other than bead-counting — are so limited at the asylum. 'Today,' Connor's voice continues to boom, 'we are privileged to have with us a special guest. The Reverend James Stewart intends to work with the great missionary, David Livingstone, bringing light to darkest Africa. He will speak today on the Gospel of Saint Luke, following which he will give you a brief outline of his plans.' Mr Connor throws open a side door and ushers in a tall man with red hair. James Stewart strides to the lectern, smiles, finds the right page, then opens the asylum's large leather-bound bible. The presence of the striking young preacher is both thrilling and unexpected and there follows an electric buzz of excitement. The women cannot keep silent. They gasp and titter, and although the chapel is so cold that Chrissy can see her own breath, Betty enthusiastically flaps at her face with an imaginary fan.

 Equatorial Africa

From behind him, Lokim hears a sudden high-pitched wail. He wants to turn his head in response, but cannot do so since such movement has been made impossible by the weight that bears down on his shoulders and chafes at the skin behind his ears. The weight makes him ache with a splitting pain that is almost too much to endure. Around his neck, Sadeen, the pock-faced trader, has tied a goree — a heavy-branched sapling, used by the slaver as a cumbersome form of control. The shaft of the tree has been tied to the trunk of the goree of the man behind, so that they resemble an ungainly four-legged animal.

Through necessity, the two men have learned to walk in step with one another. They do not otherwise communicate, and at nightfall when the caravan stops Lokim avoids eye contact with the thin Bugandan to whom he is by day attached. Early on, when they had travelled for two days from Rotoma and were stopped by a waterhole, his co-captive told Lokim that his name was Beccalo. But any further attempts at conversation were halted by two sharp lashes of Sadeen's whip. Then Hosne — the other trader — had touched his dreadful stick in a special way, making a loud bang. The stick sent something deadly into a young goat, tethered nearby, so that in an instant the animal lay lifeless, with a spreading red stain spoiling the white of its pelt. Hosne had pointed at the goat, and then mimed a jabbering mouth with his hand. Fixing Lokim with his eyes, he had drawn his hand across his throat to indicate that this would be Lokim's fate, too, were he to keep on talking.

Lokim lives in fear of the stick. He knows for certain that its evil magic works on people as well as animals because two days after the goat incident, one of the group had tried to escape. He was a young warrior and Lokim had felt a strong sense of identity with him, because both men had been delivered to Santos's rectangular hut on the same day. During the night, the warrior had secretly cut through the rope that tied him, by rubbing it against a sharp stone. He was spotted by Hosne as he silently made his way towards the shelter of the undergrowth, where the forest bordered the clearing. Lokim had been unable to sleep because of hunger and the mosquitoes which buzzed around his ears and bit into his flesh. By the light of the moon, he saw the creeping man, and willed him to be free. But Hosne was also awake. He lifted the stick and there was a burst of fire, the man jerked wildly, tried to move forward and then lay dead. Lokim had watched as Hosne and Sadeen tied his remains to a tree as a warning to the rest of the group. By morning, the hanging, lifeless body was already attracting flies, and the man's eyes were being pecked by vultures. When the caravan moved on, the warrior's body was left behind, to be eaten by hyenas and other animals.

Since then, around thirty days have passed. Each day

follows the same wretched pattern. Hosne and Sadeen use their kicking feet and buffalo whips to force their captives to walk, hobble and stumble through the bush. The group sets out soon after sunrise, and continues to travel right through the midday heat, until it is evening, and even the well-nourished traders are forced to give up from exhaustion. The coffle now consists of eleven people — five men, five women and a child. They walk in single file, all roped together. When stopped, the slaves are never allowed to be alone; even the act of defecation has to be performed when linked and under guard. For Lokim and Beccalo the humiliation they endure at these times is intense, joined together as they are, by the rigid gorees.

Food is distributed three times a day. It consists of cassava or sorghum, purchased by Hosne from local villagers in exchange for bolts of calico cloth. There are no pack animals to help with the carriage of these supplies so everything is carried on the heads of the captives. Lokim is sick of the bland food — he longs for meat or the sweet flesh of a mango — but what he craves most is the purity of the clear water which bubbles from the spring above his village in Karamoja. Instead, he has to satisfy his thirst with scoops of muddy liquid, scrabbled from the riverbed when permission has been given for the caravan to halt.

When Lokim was first captured, he burned with a rage that was so intense it felt like a fire, coiling inside him, with darting flames that were so hot his throat grew tight, making it hard to breathe. He still wants revenge, but more than anything, he wants to survive, and he has learned that anger takes up energy which he can ill afford to waste. Now as he walks, he forces himself to think back to the good times of his childhood, when the rains made the valley green for five seasons in a row, and during the long summer days he would play with the other children of the manyatta, making toy cows from the clay in of the riverbank, and miniature shelters made from straw. He tries to summon the figure of Atum, always so wise and generous with his knowledge — but the thought of Atum is bittersweet, because of his uncle's lonely death. Behind him, Beccalo is trying to sing, a high-pitched eerie sound like the cry of an injured bird. Mostly, Beccalo does not sing. He moans and sometimes, when he cannot help himself, Lokim hears his unseen partner sob, then weep.

The path dips down a steep hill. As a result, the weight of the gorees shifts forward, so that Lokim is carrying what feels like a double load. The wood puts extra pressure on his knees and the balls of his feet so that he finds it hard to keep his balance, but he knows that he will be lashed if he falls. He tries to put aside all other thoughts, in order to concentrate intently on keeping upright, but he is distracted by the sound of wailing. It is the same high pitched cry that he heard previously, but now the sound is even more acute. Lokim is surprised. He has recognised the voice of Luma, a tall Turkana woman, whom he has learned to admire for her stoicism and grace. Wearing a leather apron, and a necklace of brass, she walks with dignity, seemingly unencumbered by the weight of her young child, who babbles and reaches out, but has not yet learned to walk.

The terrain flattens out, making travelling easier, but Luma's cries have begun to irritate Hosne, who strides up and down the line, frowning. He gets out his whip then appears to change his mind. He signals to the caravan to stop. The slaves drop quickly to the floor of the forest, wanting instant rest for their aching limbs. Lokim wonders if Hosne has been moved by uncharacteristic compassion; he thinks it possible that even the trader has noticed and been touched by the selfless way Luma cares for her little girl, whose innocent smiles bring rare joy to the travellers. For the first time, Lokim looks at the trader not as an oppressor, but as a fellow man. He sees a squat figure, with a dirty, once-white cloth, wrapped around his plump midriff. Hosne is dark-skinned, but his nose is not wide like an African's but pointed, like a worked piece of flint. His lips are thin, not full, and his teeth have been darkened by something that he reaches from a pouch to chew. Hosne puts down his whip and wipes at the sweat that glistens on his face. His eyes are bloodshot — Lokim realises that the trader is touched by fever. He finds himself wondering about Hosne: what impels the man to be a slaver, to live a life of discomfort that entails travelling constantly, without cows to tend, and a settled home? Are he and Sadeen well-rewarded for their miserable work, or does Santos have some other hold over the two men?

Luma points to her daughter. The infant's head droops forward and when she tries to look up, she scarcely has the energy to open her sunken eyes. Luma raises begging hands towards Hosne. She takes the baby from her back, slings her forward, places a hand on her chest, then shakes it, miming that the baby's flesh is burning to the touch. 'Please,' she says, in Acholi.

'I can do nothing,' Hosne replies slowly, in the same language. He looks at the child with his wild red eyes.

Luma pulls herself to her full height; she stands tall and straight as a coconut palm. 'Untie me,' she says, speaking carefully. 'I could find leaves to heal her sickness. Wait half a day, then I will come back to you.'

'No,' says Hosne. He looks exhausted. He has seated himself on the ground, and is using a large grey rock as a backrest.

'Please,' Luma repeats.

Hosne's face is running with sweat. Suddenly, he gets to his feet. His eyes are blazing. With fevered energy he seizes the baby from Luma's arms. In front of them all, he dashes the little girl's head against the rock.

He tosses the child into the undergrowth, where she lies, broken and lifeless. Lokim sees that her skull has been flattened on one side. Hosne picks up his whip.

'Move,' he says. He lashes the ground. 'Move, or you'll feel this on you.'

Lokim feels a dreadful sense of despair; a world in which his keeper can cruelly and casually destroy the life of a child lacks all savour. He wants to give in to exhaustion, he wants to cease the struggle for survival, on which he has been so intent. With dismay, he realises that what he feels is of no relevance. He cannot escape, he cannot end his misery, he can only do as he is told. Alongside the rest of the slaves, and being careful to move in unison with Beccalo, he gets to his feet. But Luma looks at Hosne with an expression that is hard to interpret. Then, slowly, she sits herself down, cross-legged.

'Get up,' says Hosne.

Luma says nothing. She eyes the trader defiantly.

Fearing what may happen, Lokim would like to look away, but he is mesmerised by Luma's courage.

Hosne moves closer. He has put down his whip and picked up the stick. 'Get up,' he repeats.

Luma does not wail or call out in grief. She looks straight at the trader, her lip curled in contempt. It is as if their roles have been reversed, and she is the one who holds all the power. For a few moments, Hosne hesitates. Then he shakes his head. He raises his dreadful stick, a loud sound follows, and Luma slumps forward, blood streaming from her chest. Hosne gestures to Sadeen, who unties her body, then Sadeen reties the rope, so there is no break in the caravan.

'Move,' Hosne repeats.

Along with the rest of the slaves, Lokim begins to walk.

'Move quicker,' Hosne says again.

Lokim sees that the trader's expression is deranged; the fever has affected the man's brain. He quickens his step, and

71

the caravan shuffles on. His heart beats rapidly, his adrenalin roused by the shock of what he has seen.

After a time, when his pulse has settled to a more normal pace, he thinks about Luma and the love she bore for her daughter. He wonders how he would feel, were he to find freedom, and were he ever to become a father. He wonders how protective a parent he would be, and who might be the mother of his child. For some reason, he thinks of the woman he saw when he had taken the magical drug given him by Atum. As he walks, tied with rope and weighed down by the heavy goree, the image gives him comfort.

 Glasgow, Scotland

The sun gives the day an unseasonable warmth, adding to James's sense of wellbeing. He whistles as he walks down the street. His inner voice — which is usually so persistently critical — has quietened, freeing him to enjoy some rare moments of self-congratulation. Money is still short, but otherwise plans for his great undertaking are progressing well. Mary has been generous in her support. She has sent letters to Livingstone recommending him for his industry, knowledge and application. Livingstone's replies have been accepting and encouraging. James steps to one side, out of the way of a uniformed nursemaid, who is pushing a large-wheeled perambulator. The maid gives him a quizzical look and he realises he must appear an incongruous character — soberly dressed, bible in hand — and promptly ceases to whistle. The bible weighs heavy; he has been giving a lecture on St Paul at the Academy School. His afternoon will be refreshingly free of ministerial duties. After finding some lunch, he intends to continue his medical studies at the Infirmary.

James notices two large ceramic pots filled with purple

crocuses; their yellow stamens are glinting in the sunlight. He reflects with satisfaction that his committee has grown to an influential group of twenty men. Some of the industrialists could have been more generous financially, but all have expressed enthusiasm for the Scheme. He is in demand as a preacher, travelling around Scotland by horseback, coach and train. He has addressed rich merchants, radical students, gentlewomen, shipyard workers, asylum inmates, apprentice boys and hospital patients, and at every opportunity he has spoken not only of God, but also of his proposed work in Africa.

He pays sixpence to enter an oak-panelled coffee house and orders himself some eggs and bacon. A young waiter in a striped waistcoat holds out a box of cigars. James politely refuses, but accepts a copy of *The Times*. He is keen to keep up with the swiftly changing events from across the Atlantic. There is a direct link between the Civil War and the Scheme since the Unionists are blockading the ships that bring America's cotton across the ocean to be worked in Lancashire. So far, the blockade has not been catastrophic, but — once any hoarded supplies have been used up, and if it is not lifted — the mills will fall silent and hundreds of thousands of workers will endure the despair of the unemployed. As James drinks his coffee, he thinks again how much Britain would benefit if she could obtain an alternative source of good quality cotton, a source that was secure, reliable and not the product of slavery. So much of Britain's wealth is dependent on cotton… the northern towns of England are literally synonymous with the trade — in Australia, cotton sheeting is known as 'Manchester'. The Civil War is a wretched and bloody business and James sincerely wishes that it was at an end. However, the longer the fighting lasts, and Atlantic trade disrupted, the keener mill owners will be to obtain alternative supplies from Central Africa.

He smoothes out the paper, and reads of Abraham Lincoln's inauguration; he wonders what sort of a president the lawyer is likely to be, and how history will rate him. Lincoln seems to be a man of courage, and he has a direct turn of speech: 'In *your* hands' James reads, 'my dissatisfied countrymen, and not in *mine*, is the momentous issue of civil war. You can have no conflict without yourselves being the aggressors.'

'Excuse me, sir.' James looks up; he has not noticed the waiter. He folds away his paper and settles down to eat.

The bacon is delicious, and so are the eggs. He mops his plate with a piece of soft new bread. He pays for his food, then sets off briskly towards the hospital. Not even the stench and squalor of the narrow High Street can lower his spirits. When a man pisses onto the paving stones just in front of him he strides right over the puddle, as if nothing were amiss. When heavy drips plop onto his head, from a line of wet washing strung between the shabby houses, he ignores the drops of cold water. He is looking forward to the afternoon; he is to assist at an amputation, before attending a lecture on anatomy to be given by Lister, the newly appointed Professor of Surgery.

It is the example set by Livingstone that has led James to study medicine. Having read and re-read *Missionary Travels*, he has come to the conclusion that Livingstone's reputation amongst the Africans owes as much to his medicinal skills as it does to his conveyance of the word of God. Livingstone is given protection, and his teachings seem the more attractive, because he practises arts which are seemingly magical. It is unsurprising that to the untutored, the advances of modern medicine — for example the pain relief brought by opiates — appear not only astounding, but also miraculous. And in a way — James reasons — they *are* miraculous, for they are part of Creation.

There is another reason for training as a doctor. In Africa, such knowledge could be important for his own self-preservation, and therefore important to the continuation of the Scheme. Also, and this is an area where James only rarely allows his mind to venture, he would like one day to have a wife and children and in a crisis, he would want to be able to provide his family with appropriate medical care. As yet, he has not met any woman he would wish to marry. Secretly, he longs for a soulmate — a woman who would share his life and dreams, someone beautiful, someone courageous, someone who would combine a practical outlook with being romantic and loving... His high spirits lower, he feels he wants too much.

He consults his pocket watch, and increases the length of his strides; the operation is to start at two o'clock, and it is already a quarter to the hour. Reaching the grey-walled infirmary, he practically runs up the steps to the fourth floor. The operating room is circular with a domed glass ceiling, and tiered seating. Already, members of the public have congregated, ready for the show.

Joseph Lister is at work, checking an assortment of knives, saws and clamps which are laid out on a trestle table, next to a jar of liquid labelled 'chloroform' and a pile of soft cloths. James is to act as a dresser, handing over instruments and if necessary, holding down the patient. Joseph greets James with a brief handshake. He is a gentle, serious-faced man in his thirties. James feels awed and rather disadvantaged in his presence. Although Lister is only three years his senior, the other man's knowledge is formidable, his intellect sharp as one of his cutting knives.

The patient is a baker's boy who, having fallen under a cart, has suffered a severe injury to his right leg. He is supported into the arena by John Cowie, another of the Infirmary's students. John is kindly and fun-loving; he jokes that the amputation will be so quick and painless that the boy will afterwards be expected to entertain the audience by singing a rousing ditty. The boy attempts to smile, but his face is white; he has seen the blood-stained table on which he is to lie. The crutch he leans on offers insufficient support; John just manages to catch him before he falls to the ground.

James expects Lister to begin operating as soon as the boy is lying prone and without his checked trousers. Instead, he takes advantage of the chloroform's effects to thoroughly examine the shattered limb.

He looks up. 'The patient's life will be much enhanced if we can preserve his leg.' He speaks loudly to make himself heard by those at the back. 'The patella — the knee cap — is broken in three places. I will wire it together — a technique I have learned from Professor Syme, who practises in Edinburgh. The femur can then be fixed, and provided no infection sets in, the boy should be walking in a matter of weeks.' The applause from the audience is lukewarm. They have come for the drama of seeing a severed and bloody limb sawn off and dropped in sawdust and have been cheated of the spectacle by the surgeon's skill.

The operation takes a long time. The baker's lad awakes from his anaesthetic-induced sleep and starts to fight. Lister puts down his pliers. 'More chloroform, please. But not too much. Like ether, the vapour can be dangerous if administered in too large a quantity.'

Once the procedure is over, two waiting porters lift the drowsy boy onto a stretcher. 'Put him in a side ward,' Lister instructs. 'Please arrange for extra meat and beer at my personal expense. I want the patient to have every chance.' He hurries off. A nurse has called him to another part of the hospital, where a pregnant woman is haemorrhaging dangerously. The anatomy lecture will have to wait.

'How are you?' John asks. 'I hear that you have been busy

preaching, and tutoring. I am impressed that you also find time for your medical studies. Tell me, what's Livingstone's wife like? My sister met her somewhere — she said she's a bit of an odd fish, and has no manners.'

'It is wrong to say such a thing.' James feels himself flush. 'Mary is an exceptional woman. She has such knowledge of Africa, and has endured such privations… She should not be judged by those who have no understanding.'

'Are you insulting my sister? I think you may be. Sir, I think you should say sorry!'

Still angry, James begins to stammer an apology. Then, realising that John is laughing at his discomposure, he falls silent.

'It's all right. My sister's opinion is not to be valued. She's completely superficial and interested in nothing but clothes. You do look cross, though. If I didn't know better, I would think that you and Mrs Livingstone were sweet on one another, and that the two of you had been billing and cooing in her intrepid husband's absence.'

 Broughty Ferry, Scotland

'All done,' says Moira, the ladies' maid. She hands Mina a mirror. 'You look bonny as a briar rose. See how the chignon looks at the back?' Moira is from the east side of Glasgow. She pronounces the 'chig' of chignon so that it rhymes with 'wig'.

Mina considers the new style. She looks older, with her hair pinned up. 'Thank you.' She smiles at the maid, and hands back the glass. Putting her hands over her ribcage, she draws in her breath, then laughs at her own discomfort.

'A corset does feel strange, at first.' Moira nods. 'But you'll get used to it.'

'Perhaps you could loosen the laces, just a little? I don't think I'll be able to eat!'

'No,' says Moira. 'We want you looking at your best, at least when the guests arrive. Now let's sort out that skirt.' She bustles round, lifting petticoats to adjust the ribbons that hold up the sprung hoops of Mina's brand new crinoline. 'Come into the hallway so you can look at yourself properly.'

Mina's brother John has recently been made a partner in the firm of Alexander Stephen. The occasion is to be marked with a grand dinner, and Mama has agreed that all her unmarried daughters can have new dresses for the event. Mina has chosen a wide, full gown of the palest yellow silk, with flounced sleeves, several underskirts and an embroidered panel at the front, adorned with satin bows. When she looks at her image in the huge gilt mirror at the top of the staircase, a part of her wants to skip with delight. It is a fairytale dress and, even to her own critical eye, she looks lovely. But another part of her feels no such happiness. As the youngest of the Stephen children, she and Maggie spend their days in the schoolroom, and are chaperoned by Miss Scrope; for the most part, they are isolated from the goings-on in the rest of the house. As a result, Mina is protected from the hurts and taunts that characterise the relationships between some of her older siblings and Papa. But on social occasions, it is impossible to ignore the fact that of Alexander's sixteen living children, he favours some more than others. Especially, he likes Hannah — for her beauty — and Al — for his business skills. Especially, he disfavours poor good-hearted Sam, who wants so much to please, and he is unkind to Janet, who shares the same desire. As Mina enters the oak-panelled library, she can hear Papa shouting out above the general chatter.

'Fetch me something to write on!' Papa demands, 'Come on — make yourself useful! There's an equation I want to show John.'

Mina is about to respond, when Janet hurries forward. She extracts a notebook from the top drawer of a Wellington chest, and presents it to Papa, with a deferential curtsey. She wears a black-and-white striped dress, and frowns in concern, so that she looks older than her twenty-two years. Papa takes the book without acknowledgement, and Janet turns away, crestfallen.

When she was eighteen, Janet declared that she was in love with John Beattie the haberdasher's son. She tried without success to get permission for John to court her. John's charms were hard to determine. Mina remembers a smooth-faced young man who opened drawers and boxes when the girls went to Beattie's for their ribbons and trims. Soon after, John left Broughty Ferry, and from that point on, Janet seemed to lose all confidence in herself. The shame of the episode still clings to her like an invisible cloak. It seems to Mina that Janet is forever to be punished for her past.

Mina looks around. The drawing room, which normally looks rather sombre, has been transformed. Mama has ordered hot-house flowers from the early-morning market and the housekeeper has decorated the room with large vases brimming with creamy white lilies, larkspur and jasmine. Mina's two eldest siblings have not made the journey from their homes in Aberdeen, but the rest of the family are present, except — of course — for Andrew. Mina dutifully greets Anne, who is on the arm of her solicitor husband Duncan Wilkie Paterson. There is something about DWP, as he is called, which makes Mina uneasy. It is not simply that he teases Sam, it is rather that he addresses the servants in a manner that is unnecessarily abrupt. Mina looks around at the company. It seems that the girls from Corona are being rivalled by the other Stephen women in the extravagance of their dress. Marjory — who at twenty-one still lives at home — is looking lovely in plum-coloured silk, but Mary looks even more dazzling. She wears a jade-green dress, with skirts that are swagged and frilled. Above her tiny waist, her bodice is decorated with more frills, and at her neck, she wears a necklace bright with large diamonds and emeralds. She looks appreciatively up at her husband, John Templeton. The Templetons manufacture carpets, and the business is doing well; John is telling Al that President Lincoln's wife has recently ordered an elaborate new carpet for the drawing room of the White House.

When Mina's brother James makes an entry, the hubbub in the room dies down. This is partly because even to his siblings James's appearance is striking. He is tall, with thick black hair and a full black beard. But the main reason everyone quietens is the presence of his new wife Eliza, who gave birth to their son just a month after the death of his first wife, who shared Mina's name. James seems not at all embarrassed at this unusual order of events; he introduces Eliza with pride, and Mina, in return, does her best to be polite. James moves on, and goes to greet Al. Mina watches, as Al turns away. She knows that Al is owed money by James — she has overheard Al say that James cashed something called a promissory note, when he was away in America. Now he claims he does not have the resources to settle the debt.

The dinner gong sounds, and the party moves into the long dining room, which is ablaze with the light from a dozen silver candelabras. The silver was fashioned in Edinburgh, having been brought back brought from Burma, where the firm have a large teak plantation. Mama — or Elspeth, as she is called — sits at one end of the table, while Papa — Alexander — presides at the head, with Hannah on his right. Her off-the-shoulder dress is of peach-coloured satin, decorated with gem stones. The colour compliments her perfect, warm complexion and rich brown hair, but she is distracted — her smiles look forced and insincere. Papa turns to Hannah frequently, and sometimes takes her hand.

Service is *a la français*; the table is already laden with a dozen dishes, including two types of soup, two types of fish, pasties, patties, jellied hams, eight roast fowl, six rounds of beef and four saddles of lamb. Alexander says a brief grace, then the meal begins. Inevitably, the talk turns to business.

'How is William Street working out?' Al asks John Templeton. 'Have you enough space there?'

'It is big enough, though only just. In hindsight, it would have been preferable to rebuild the factory from scratch, rather than take over that old cotton mill. We've had to use the attic space for our special commissions.'

'We'll need to expand soon, too,' says Al, with satisfaction. 'We're running out of room at Kelvinhaugh. We're building a new composite ship. I hope it will be the first of many.' Al's face is animated and his eyes sparkle. Mary says that Al loves ships, as some men love horses, and other men delight in exquisite paintings.

'Composed of what?' John looks perplexed.

Al laughs good naturedly. 'Oyster shells and mermaids' scales. Or maybe we'll just use those for decoration. Seriously, it's good news for the firm. I've been granted a patent. The Admiralty are interested, and we've had a visit from the Under Secretary of State. The *John Lidgett* is nearly complete — she's neither wood, nor iron, but composed of both.'

'What's the advantage of that?'

'On a long voyage, iron will foul on the bottom with barnacles, and a wooden vessel will be weakened by worm in the planking. A composite ship has a wooden bottom, protected by copper, which is poisonous to barnacles. With a smooth base, a ship will travel more swiftly. We've started building a tea-clipper for the Robertsons on the same lines. She's named the *Sea King*, but I think they plan to sell her on to the Confederates, who will — of course — change her name. The Robertsons will have to hand her over in secret, though the government has relaxed its position a bit recently. As you know, officially, Britain is now "even-handed".'

James looks up : 'So events in America are proving good for business?' There is no mistaking the sharp edge to his tone. Eliza gives him a warning look.

'Now, now,' says Alexander from the top of the table. For a man in his sixties, his ears are still sharp. 'If you're after more money, forget it, James. You've had your due.'

James and Andrew were bought out of the business two years previously. Mina is aware that that both men persist in considering themselves hard done by. Constrained by her corset, she gives a little sigh. The ill-feeling aroused between Al and the pair has reached such a pitch that Andrew has been banned from the house. Of all her brothers, Mina enjoys Andrew's company the best. He is passionate and witty and fun, but she has not seen him for a year. Andrew never wanted the rugged life of a seafarer, or the responsibilities of a large work force. He chose medicine as a career, and now practises as a doctor in London.

'I'll say no more,' says James, smoothing his waistcoat. He flashes a smile at his father, his perfect white teeth contrasting with the black of his beard. 'Because I am considerate of your feelings, Papa. And moreover, I am solicitous for the sensitivities of my dear Mama.'

Sam half stands up, then sits back down again. He is only just eighteen, and has no head for alcohol. 'You don't know anything about sensitivity!' He is flushed from the French wine, which flows freely at the table.

'I trust that you do not refer to my recent marriage.' James touches the wedding ring, on Eliza's hand.

'Of course not.' Sam is unexpectedly near to tears. 'You know what I'm talking about. It's nothing to do with Eliza, as well you know! What happened — it was wrong! You seem to have no conscience!' Unlike the rest of the family, Sam is fair-skinned and lightly-built. He looks frail as a gillyflower as he glares at James. Mina looks to Mama, hoping that she will intervene.

Elspeth says nothing; she seems unconcerned by Sam's discomfort. She inspects her plate, and pokes a brawn patty with her fork. It is Alexander who addresses Sam. 'Be quiet,' he says sharply, as if he were talking to a dog. 'Behave properly when you're in company. Or perhaps that is too much to ask?'

Sam opens his mouth to reply, then changes his mind and closes it.

'And stop gulping like that! You look like a toad, catching flies.'

Mina wants to cover her hands with her ears; she hates the way Sam is treated. Papa seems to find his very existence an irritation. She wonders if this is because Papa dislikes Sam's appearance, or because he is intolerant of Sam's slowness with the mathematical calculations which his brothers find so easy. Or maybe Papa has no patience because Sam is, by so many years, his youngest son — but then, she is the youngest girl, and she isn't badly treated. Whatever the reason for Papa's cruelty, it is simply not fair. Mina looks across the table, trying to catch Sam's eye.

'Oh, I don't think he looks like a toad.' James's manner is seductively pleasant. 'He's more like a spiteful little adder, wanting to turn you all against me.'

This is too much. Sam gets up to leave.

 Unexpectedly, it is Hannah who next speaks. 'Sit down,' she says, gently. 'Stay with us.' She turns to James. 'Your jokes can be unkind. They ill become your good nature.' Then she addresses Alexander: 'I think you should apologise, dear Papa. It is unseemly to speak sharply at the dinner table.' She playfully touches his chest and adds, 'It is bad for your digestion.'

The moment is saved. The men move on to a discussion

about the best site for a new shipyard, while the women gossip about Mary Livingstone, wife of the explorer, who has moved to Scotland and is reported to have simply no idea how to dress. Hannah takes no part in the conversation. Mina thinks again how beautiful her sister is, but Hannah's beauty cannot hide her unhappiness. Her expression is bleak, and there is a degree of desperation in her sister's eyes, which is — to Mina — completely unaccountable.

CHAPTER FOUR

May 1861

 Royal Lunatic Asylum, Dundee, Scotland

Chrissy counts out ten beads at a time, separates them by colour, then puts them in her baskets. When she has got to fifty, she slides her abacus across. She picks up another handful and picks out first the yellow beads, then the green and then the blue. Outside the walls of the lunatic asylum, the sun must be shining, for despite its high ceilings and lack of sunlight, the air in the counting room is very warm. Chrissy fights to stop her eyelids drooping in the stuffy atmosphere brought on by the early summer's day. A blue bottle buzzes, then bangs itself against one of the high windows. It is joined by a companion and the two flies intermittently hit at the glass. Chrissy observes that Horrocks is also having trouble staying awake. He is sitting in his chair, his penny dreadful has fallen unnoticed to the floor, his arms hang loose and his head nods forward. He pulls himself up, but his mouth falls open and before long, he has fallen fast asleep.

The women watch Horrocks, as field mice in barley might anxiously observe a predatory stoat. Once they can hear that his snores have fallen into a rhythm, they relax. They cease bothering to count properly, they begin to whisper to one

85

another, and then they get to talking in low, urgent voices. Most of them savour the experience of being unsupervised, finding it a rare and enjoyable treat. Betty is an exception. She has to be gently restrained from waking the warder; today she believes that she is Mary Magdalene and she thinks that Horrocks may perhaps tell her the whereabouts of her vessel of nard. Jane takes her hand and leads her to sit back down. The two women sit side by side, speaking of life in Galilee.

'How are you, dear?' It is Deborah, who asks. She smiles at Chrissy, while she adjusts what's left of her faded coronet. 'We haven't spoken for a while.'

'I am well, thank you. I trust you are well, also?'

'As well as one can be, in this place. I have written again to my husband. I am hoping he might secure my release — I do so long to see shops, and to wear pretty dresses, and to read *Household Words*.'

'I am sure that he is doing his best — he must wish very much to have you home.'

Deborah looks wistful. 'I wish I could believe that were so. You do not yourself have a husband, I am right in saying?'

'No,' says Chrissy, wondering if Deborah is making a veiled reference to Thomas's birth. 'I do not.'

'A husband is only to be considered a blessing if he behaves as a husband should.' Deborah speaks without guile. 'Handsome is as handsome does.' For a moment she looks sorrowful, then she perks up: 'Tell me, did you ever have a suitor? You told me about a man named Frank, but if I remember rightly, he was your employer. Was there anyone else? Did you go ever go out to the theatre? Did you go to dances? Tell me — you were a seamstress — did you sew fine dresses for yourself?'

Deborah looks searchingly at Chrissy, hungry for her mind to be transported elsewhere.

It is a few moments before Chrissy speaks. 'I did have an

admirer.' The memory is painful, but she continues, nevertheless. 'He was the son of a wealthy shipbuilder. We met by chance — when it was raining, and he offered me a lift in his cab. He told me that despite being the daughter of a cottage weaver, I could hold my head as high as any woman. He gave me embroidered silks that his family's ships had brought back from India, and rare feathers from the giant moa bird, all the way from New Zealand. He sent me love letters, and said he would marry me.' She stops. It is hard to recall the magic, confusion and eventual hurt of those few early summer weeks.

'Did he mean it? Did he really want to marry you?' Deborah is agog.

'I think he did, in a way. But in another way, it was all fantastical. Andrew said that I should change my name — he wanted me to call myself Mary Dundas, after the city of Dundee. He wanted everything I understood and held dear to be wiped away, like chalk from a board. He introduced me to his brothers — we took tea at the George Hotel — but I was not allowed to say that I worked at the Tannery. Andrew told them I was employed as a governess. He tried to turn me into something I was not, and could never be.'

'And then what happened?'

'He must have realised that you can't do that. You can't change who a person is, just by wishing. He broke away from me — he said he still loved me, but I must no longer consider myself engaged. He came to my lodgings to say goodbye. I never saw him, afterwards.'

'What of your virtue? Did he treat you with respect?'

'Oh yes. He never did more than hold my hand, and — just once — he kissed my lips. He said that they were irresistible, like candied cherries.' Chrissy wipes a tear from the corner of her eye.

'You were badly used.'

'Andrew came spinning into my life, like a whirling

sycamore seed. Then he was taken away, as if by a gust of wind.' Recklessly, she adds, 'When my son was born, I felt that God had taken pity on my unhappiness.' Straightaway, she regrets having mentioned Thomas.

Whether it is from tact or because of her overwhelming interest in the frivolities of dress, Deborah mercifully changes the subject. 'Tell me,' she asks, 'did you make yourself a fine outfit, from the Indian silk?'

'The silk stayed in a box, then after a time, I sold it. The money went to pay my rent.'

'What of the feathers — from the moa bird?'

'I gave them to my landlady — to Mrs Montgomery — to be a trim for her hat. As for Andrew's letters, I burned them in the grate.'

'So you have nothing to remember him by. No jewellery. No keepsake.'

The two women fall silent. Deborah raises her arm and smoothes a petal between her thumb and forefinger. 'I would be lost without my crown. It is a reminder of better days. I wore it to a ball. I was dressed as Titania, from *A Midsummer Night's Dream.*'

Chrissy pictures Deborah laughing and dancing, surrounded by friendship and good cheer. 'Better days,' she says.

'Do you have any possessions with you? Mr Connor says it is good for us each to have with us something that is special. The object should bring comfort.'

'I have only a sealskin bag, a bible, and a piece of coal.' Chrissy thinks back to the churchyard, and to the time when her presence in the church was discovered by the Reverend Willis. The brass shovel had belonged to the Montgomerys and was returned to them by Constable Crieff.

'Your coal — is it to bring you luck?'

'In a way. A shepherd brought it to my parents' cottage,

when I was a child. It is to me a precious thing, for on its surface, God has clearly engraved the image of a fern.'

Absorbed in their conversation, Deborah and Chrissy have failed to notice that the rest of the women at the tables have ceased their chatter, and are once more counting beads. When they glance up, they find that they are being observed by Horrocks.

'Shut your mouths,' he says, without much conviction. He yawns. 'Get on with your baskets. Mr Connor says you have to fill at least three each, or we'll all be for the high jump.' He leans back in his chair, rubs his eyes, scoops his magazine up, then settles back down to read.

Chrissy carries on counting. She places ten blue beads, ten yellow beads and then ten red beads, in separate piles. She repeats the process five times. When she has collected fifty beads of each colour, she slides her abacus across. Next to her, Deborah is doing the same. Betty has a different system: she is making a whirling pattern of blue beads only, that trails in a line off to the left, so that it looks like a snail. Jane has begun to spell out her name in capitals, using beads of yellow and red. Horrocks seems unaware. He is reading a crime story. The illustration shows a barber chasing a running man, with a razor in his hand.

Chrissy continues to count. The sound of gently clattering beads is soothing to her. Her actions once more become mechanical, and soon her mind is floating free. As always, she thinks of Thomas. She recalls again the perfection of his newborn body. She remembers his little feet that were not yet arched, and his hands that — though they were so tiny — were able to reach out and grasp. She remembers her son's expression, as he held her gaze — he had furrowed his brow, and pursed his lips and then had given a half-smile, as if he had worked out a puzzle and were pleased to have found the solution. She pictures Thomas grown bigger and rounder, though still very much a baby. She sees him with the wings of an angel, she hears him laugh with delight as he soars high into a brilliant blue sky. Now Thomas has been joined by other winged babies; together they play hide and seek amongst pearly white clouds, until they are stilled by the presence of Jesus, who appears on a hill of shining green grass. Jesus walks forwards, holding out His arms in welcome; the babies gather round, with folded wings.

'Suffer little children to come unto me.' As she scoops and counts, Chrissy thinks of the verses of St Luke, and of the sermon that was given by the minister with red hair. The visit of the Reverend Stewart had lit the chapel, as a shooting star might brighten the night. His good looks and energy, but — most of all — the way he had listened to the questions that followed his talk, and the respectful way he gave his answers — these things had caused a continuing agitation in the inmates' beating hearts.

Horrocks looks up. Chrissy speeds her sorting, pushing the beads of her abacus without bothering to be accurate when totalling the numbers. She relaxes when she sees that Horrocks has looked back down; he is scrutinising a picture of a gun-toting highwayman. The Reverend had spoken passionately of the need to bring Christianity to Africa. He had talked of cotton-growing as a means to end slavery, emphasising the suitability of the land for growing such a crop, and the economic benefits for Britain. More importantly, he had stressed that Africans were no less deserving of God's grace; they were as entitled as white men to the gift of eternal life. In some ways — such as having so little in the way of worldly goods, they were even more entitled. Stewart had quoted Our Lord: 'For it is easier for a camel to go through a needle's eye, than for a rich man to enter into the kingdom of God.' The tribes of Africa — he had concluded — were more than ripe for conversion. Unencumbered by the trappings of wealth, innocent of the venalities that characterised some aspects of so-called civilised society, they needed only for the Word to be brought to them in order to enjoy the benefits of salvation. Chrissy weighs in her hand a mixture of blue and yellow beads. She knows for certain that Thomas's soul is saved; she has been assured by Mr Connor that his body lies buried in consecrated ground. She thinks now of innocent children dying in Africa, who — pure as they have been in life — are barred from entering paradise, because their parents — through no fault of their own — have no knowledge of Jesus. In her mind's eye, she sees a group of black children eagerly gather at the gates of heaven, only to be turned away. The children plead with St Peter who sorrowfully shakes his head. Hand in hand, they walk back along a path, weeping tears of bitter disappointment. Chrissy is distressed by these imaginings. She would like very much to help James Stewart with his work. But confined inside the asylum, there is nothing she can do or give. She drops her beads uncounted back into the basket. With an audible sigh, she slams back her abacus.

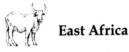 **East Africa**

Lokim cannot sleep. He cannot get comfortable — he has chosen a bed where the dried-up grass is soft, but a rock lies just under the soil and because he has grown so thin, it presses into his jutting hip bone. He lies awake and considers the events that have resulted in him being no longer enslaved, and yet not free.

After he had killed Luma, Hosne walked on briskly, and used his whip to force the slaves to keep up with his quick pace. But it was mania that drove him for the fever had seized his mind and body and soon his quaking legs rebelled. He came to a halt when he stumbled then fell to the ground, where he lay moaning. He struggled to his feet, then tottered towards the scrub. But before he could reach any cover, he had to lift up his cloth and open his bowels. The bouts of dysentery racked him again and again. He was beyond bothering with modesty, he did not care who saw him as he squatted to defecate or lay in his own stinking brown stench. The caravan came to a halt, and for two days and three nights the slaves rested under the spreading shade of a baobab tree, while Sadeen kept guard with the fire stick, and Hosne struggled against those of his ancestors who were pulling him towards his death. On the third day, when the group had nearly run out of water, Lokim felt almost sorry for Sadeen. Without Hosne, he was at a loss as to know what to do next.

Sadeen crouched beside Hosne, fanning him sometimes with a dried banana leaf, willing him to stay alive. As Lokim watched the drivers, he tried to use the wretched goree as a kind of neck rest. His hands were tied behind his back and he was roped to the rest of the slaves, but he no longer suffered the further discomfort of being directly attached to Beccalo. Sadeen had separated the two men. He had tethered the Bugandan to a gorse bush, apart from the rest of them because he, too, was suffering from severe dysentery. Two more of the slaves were — to a lesser extent - afflicted. Lokim prayed that he might stay healthy, until either he was released or — and this sometimes seemed simpler and therefore preferable — he painlessly dropped down dead.

Sadeen stayed awake as long as possible, so that he could remain on guard. When he finally succumbed to sleep, Lokim — who headed the line — tried to encourage the rest of the group to get up and move forwards. He thought he could perhaps use his feet to overcome Sadeen, but the men and women to whom he was roped lay in a kind of torpor, and refused to be roused. Thirst and hunger had drained them of all energy to resist.

A young herd boy saved the caravan. He was returning to his village with a goat that had strayed. Sadeen seized him by the arm. He indicated to the boy that he wanted to drink, then let off his stick to demonstrate its power. He pointed and walked with his fingers, to show that he wanted to be led to a watering hole. The boy nodded in assent, and even offered his goat to be milked, so that Hosne could be revived. Sadeen gestured to the slaves, who lumbered to their feet, and hoisted what remained of the supplies on their heads. Sadeen ordered Lokim to carry Hosne on his back. He loosened the ropes that attached the goree and for a short time untied Lokim's hands. Temporarily unencumbered, he enjoyed a peculiar sensation of weightlessness. With difficulty, Lokim managed to lift Hosne up; he staggered at first, under the bulk of the slaver. The group walked on. Beccalo remained tethered and Lokim realised with a sense first of shock, and then of resignation, that the man — for so many weeks his walking partner — was being abandoned to endure a lonely death.

The youth led them to a riverbed, and showed them the best place to dig. Having done so, he turned to leave, then set off back to his village, with his goat ambling beside him. Lokim watched enviously. The boy could have been himself in a different time. For the rest of the day, the caravan refreshed themselves, taking turns to dig handfuls of the muddy water. That night, they all slept well. Too well, as it turned out. For the boy must have returned with his friends. When the slaves awoke, half their precious supplies had gone.

They moved on, following the meandering path of the dried up river. Sadeen walked alongside, keeping control with his fire stick. Lokim sweated under the weight of Hosne, who put his arms around his neck, and clung to him, as if he were an infant child. But the day after that, Hosne would not wake; his ancestors had taken him to their world. In this way, Lokim was relieved of his burden, and Sadeen was left in sole charge of the caravan. The next day a male slave died, his body broken by dysentery and fever. A woman died the day after. Both were left unburied.

And now there came a shift in the relationship between Lokim and his captor. Sadeen looked to Lokim for support and would ask him to convey messages to the six remaining slaves. Speaking in halting Acholi, he told Lokim that he believed Hosne had been cursed: he had been unable to withstand the fever because he was being tormented by the spirit of Luma's child. He thought that the other three deaths were also the result of a curse and he was being punished for not defending Luma. She had been a strong, healthy woman, and would have fetched a good price. They were to meet up with Santos at a place called Eldoret and Sadeen feared that Santos would punish him when he saw how many slaves had been lost.

Lokim did not know how to respond to Sadeen's familiarity. He could not help feeling flattered that he had been chosen to receive such confidence, but at the same time he despised the trader for being prepared to do the base job that he did. He was unequivocally pleased with one aspect of his new status: he no longer had to wear the goree. In comparison, the rope that attached him to his companions was easy to tolerate. But the caravan's supplies — much depleted by the theft — were running low. Soon, the slaves' rations were reduced to a handful of meal a day. Their bodies grew weak from hunger, they swayed on their dragging feet, and sometimes fell. Lokim could see that on either side of the riverbed, the bush had shrivelled from lack of rain. They came to an area of cultivated land where villagers had planted fields of maize, but the cobs had failed to grow, and the relentless sun had turned the leaves brown instead of green. Sadeen began to look as gaunt as the rest of them. Fearfully, he told Lokim that he did not know how he could face Santos, were more of the slaves to die. Lokim no longer thought much about escape. While he stayed with the group, he was at least fed — albeit sparsely. And the riverbed slaked his thirst, though it was sometimes necessary to dig down deep, and to wait a long time for the soil to become wet.

One morning, when he awoke, Lokim saw an eland snaffling at their water hole. He reached across to touch Sadeen on the arm. He pointed, first at the animal, and then at the fire stick. The eland, though bony, would have provided food for a week. But Sadeen shrugged and shook his head. The eland looked him in the eye, then shambled off.

Lokim thought about the beast for the rest of the day. He imagined how sweet the juices would have tasted, and how much stronger he would have felt had he been able to eat its meat. He imagined his teeth tearing at the muscle, and the satisfaction he would have gained from chewing the fibrous flesh. As he walked, he considered why Sadeen had failed to kill the eland, when the trader was himself as hungry as the rest of them. He thought about the stick, recollecting the times when it had been used. Hosne, then Sadeen, had made the thing work by tipping black soot into its hollow centre, then they had used a metal rod to push a hard round stone down into its middle. The traders clicked a hook at its base, and it seemed that it was this click that ignited the fire that threw the stone that killed. But, thinking about it, the click only worked because of the special soot, and the right-shaped missile. A supply of stones had been kept separate from the stick, in a leopard skin pouch. Lokim realised that he had not seen the pouch for some time — not, in fact, since the robbery. The stick could not work without the contents of the pouch — and in all likelihood, the pouch had been stolen by the boy. So the reason why Sadeen had not killed the eland was that the stick had lost its magic. And without its magic, Lokim reasoned, Sadeen had no power.

Behind him a women called Auma had fallen, saying that

she was too weak to continue. Sadeen argued with her, while the rest of the caravan listlessly waited. Lokim was angry with himself for not having realised earlier that the weapon had been rendered useless. Eventually, Auma was persuaded to get up, and the caravan shuffled slowly on. Auma fell several times more, before Sadeen agreed they could stop and rest. Each time, she was bullied and cajoled by the trader. He clenched his hands as he pleaded with her and explained that if she was left behind, she would surely die.

Lokim sat in the line, roped to the other slaves, eating his meal. He watched as Sadeen lay down exhausted, having first fetched water for Auma, and brought it to her in a hollow gourd. 'He is not a bad man,' Lokim thought. 'He is a good man, doing bad work.' He told Sadeen that the following day he would carry Auma on his back, as he had previously carried Hosne. It would be much easier for him to do this, if he were untied. He said that Sadeen should not fear that he would escape since it was not in his interests to do so. The fields and the bush were barren, anything green had shrivelled in the drought and the only living creatures they saw were birds. The vultures had grown fat on the carcasses of animals and the bodies of men.

When morning came, as agreed Sadeen unknotted the ropes which bound Lokim's wrists. As soon as he had done so, Lokim told Sadeen that he knew that the stick had lost its magic. Then he calmly untied the rest of the slaves. Too exhausted to run away, they looked to Lokim to be their leader, and Sadeen for his part was content to do the same. Emaciated and hollow-eyed, the trader seemed relieved to hand over all responsibility to the man whom — for months — he had held captive.

Lokim tried to formulate a plan. The caravan's most pressing need was for food; without it, they would die. They could continue the journey to Eldoret, in the hope that Santos would at least feed them, whatever else he might do. But, on reflection, Lokim would prefer not to willingly hand himself over to the thin-lipped trader with the fine clothes bought from the proceeds of his horrible trade. Three days back, Lokim had noticed some white birds with black-tipped wings flying high in the sky. The birds had legs like saplings, as if they were made for wading, and long stout bills as if for reaching deep into water or mud. Lokim decided to lead the group in the direction that the birds had been heading. He thought they might have been returning to a big river or lake. If the group rationed their supplies even further, and were able to carry with them some water, they could perhaps make it to a place where water was abundant and the grass once more grew green.

For two days, the travellers retraced their steps along the riverbed, with Lokim carrying Auma whenever she felt too weak to walk. On the third day, when they saw several tall anthills, they stopped to forage for termites. One of the men made fire using a rubbed stick and dried grass, so that they were able roast the little creatures. They winnowed off the insects' wings by tossing them in the air. As he crunched the protein-rich food, Lokim thought he had never tasted anything so delicious. The same day they had another piece of luck — one of the women found the abandoned eggs of an ostrich. Painstakingly, two holes were made in each of the six eggs. Laboriously, they were blown empty of the yolk and whites, each person taking a turn. Then the woman who had found the eggs pushed dried grass down into a hole she had dug in the mud of the riverbed. Using a hollow reed, she sucked the water which had collected in the grass up with her mouth then she used the reed to transfer the water into the hollow shells, so that it could be stored for the journey. The travellers' mood improved. They gathered round the fire and, for the first time in months, Lokim heard the sound of laughter. But Sadeen did not laugh. He was frightened to eat the termites. He said that, like Hosne, he had been bewitched. He looked longingly at the food, but when Lokim tried to give him a handful of the treats, he shook his head in terror, and said he would turn into weevil. Despite the heat, he seemed to shudder with cold. He crossed his arms and held his body close, in an effort to comfort himself. At one point he weakened, and put out his hand, then he vehemently shook his head, saying that he would have to live in darkness, under the ground. Lokim saw that the whites of Sadeen's eyes were blazing red, and when they lay down to rest, he was kept awake by the sound of the trader's coughing.

When Sadeen died, Lokim felt no triumph at the death of the man who had controlled him with the humiliation of the goree and the threat of execution. It was as if the previous months spent as a slave were no longer relevant. He simply regretted the loss of another member of the group. But without Sadeen, he felt more keenly the loneliness of leadership. He was not close to any of the other former slaves. Since the first death, that of the warrior from Rotoma who had been killed by Hosne, he had deliberately distanced himself from the rest of the caravan. He could not help grieving for the death of Luma, because of the woman's remarkable courage. But Lokim had come to believe that if he were to survive, he would have to do so alone, without the encumbrance of friendship or the luxury of emotion. In the days before his capture, when he used to go out from his manyatta on long hunting trips, he had experienced a trance-like state of focused attention. Everything extraneous, such as the emptiness of his belly or changes in the weather, he had excluded from awareness, as he followed the tracks and signs of his prey. He had tried, while a prisoner, to replicate that state of other-worldly calm.

But as leader, the escape of mental isolation was no longer available to him. He had to keep his companions motivated, especially Auma, who still said sometimes that she had not the strength to walk. He had to settle the squabbles and bickering that followed the distribution of rations. It was up to him to decide when it was time to stop, and when it was right to move on. It was also his decision to choose the right path.

Now, as he lies under the stars, the burden of so much responsibility robs Lokim of rest. He wonders how the caravan would have been treated by Santos, if everything had happened differently and if, as planned, the group had been handed over at the place called Eldoret. He thinks about Hosne and Sadeen, wondering again how they came to be doing the work that they did. He considers his present situation and concludes that while it is awful to be roped and tied and treated as another man's possession, it is also terrible to be thin and hungry to a point when any movement is an effort. He shifts his body again, and rubs at a sore place, where a stone has been pressing into his thigh. He hopes that he has acted sensibly in changing direction and that his instinct to follow the long-legged birds will prove correct. He moves onto his back. Looking up at the moon, he thinks how it is shaped like the claw of a beast. He asks himself where he will be, when the white light shines fat again, and he wonders if each member of the caravan will still be alive. The rock feels so hard underneath him, pressing into his shoulders and spine.

Deliberately, he slows his breathing, trying to invoke a sense of calm. After a while, an image comes to him of the strange woman he saw, when he took the magic drink. He sees her close her eyes, tilt her face to the sun, and smile. Ignoring his physical discomfort, Lokim drifts at last into a peaceful sleep.

 Glasgow, Scotland

'Tom's woken up, so I've brought him down for a lesson. He'll only get bored, with nothing to do.' Agnes Livingstone lets go of Tom's hand. She gives a little push, propelling her brother into the room.

James Stewart gets to his feet, and holds out an arm in welcome. 'Thank you,' he says, with a nod to Agnes. He cannot help noticing the fact that the girl is growing into a woman. In looks, Agnes resembles her brother Robert — tall and dark, with pleasing, regular features. 'I appreciate your thoughtfulness.' Agnes gives a mock curtsey and bobs out through the door.

James pulls out a chair. They are in the front parlour, which doubles as a place of study. 'Sit down, Tom. Shall we soldier on? We've got your entrance exam to prepare for, haven't we, old chap?'

Tom looks down at his boots. 'My head still hurts,' he says.

James is never sure about Tom's headaches. The boy's delicate health is the reason that he has not yet been sent away to school, but the aches and pains from which he suffers often disappear if he can be distracted by something pleasurable. James suspects that the pains are real but they are engendered by anxiety, rather than having a true organic basis. He wonders again about the Livingstone children's itinerant upbringing; he finds himself thinking that were he to ever have children of his own, he would try to ensure that they grew up in one settled home. But first, he would need to find himself a wife...

Tom is sullenly kicking a table leg. He looks up at the tutor. 'Can I go back upstairs?'

'Not yet. Get out your pens and paper, and we'll carry on with that botany lesson. We were learning about the vegetable kingdom.' James looks directly at his pupil, willing him to pay attention. 'Which,' he continues, 'is so vast and various, that for simplicity, we characterise plants into higher and lower series. Higher plants — which come from seeds and bear fruits — we call phanerogams. Do you remember the name for less complex groups — like mosses and moulds?'

'No.'

'We call them cryptogams. They reproduce through spores, rather than seeds. Lichens and fungi fall into this second category...' James stops and strokes his beard. Tom appears not to be listening. The boy is kicking again at the table leg. His expression is rebellious.

There is a pause while Tom continues to drum. Eventually, James says, 'All right. Let us try a different method of study. We'll collect some lichen from the garden and we'll see what it looks like under the lens of my microscope. And we'll start by studying some slides from my collection.'

James's slides were given to him by his stepmother, in the year before she died. For this reason alone, he would have valued them. As it is, they are a source of such intense pleasure that their provenance can add but little. They enable him to minutely examine the natural world so that he can enjoy its colours, patterns and symmetry in dazzling detail. The blaze of a butterfly wing, the rainbow of colours from a sample of crystallised salicine — such wonders make him tingle with delight.

Tom kneels on a chair so that he can bend his head to look down the brass column of the microscope. 'Look carefully,' James says, 'and tell me what you can see. Remember that the image has been made much, much bigger.'

'Feathers...' Tom says, after a while. 'I can see feathers.'

'Good try, but remember that things look different when they have been enlarged. Those aren't feathers. You're looking at the fibres on the antennae of the head of a mosquito.'

Despite himself, Tom is impressed. 'Mosquitoes are horrible. This looks nice.'

'Everything in the natural world is wonderful, when you consider it carefully. Now look at this...' James deftly removes one slide, and replaces it with another. 'It is a shape made up of individual algae. The mounter has had to use a hog's hair to push the pieces into place.'

'It looks pretty, like a lady's brooch.'

'I'll take it away from the lens... Now, what can you see?'

'Just a speck. No more than a dot.'

'Think of the skill of the man who put it together. And the patience. He has made the pattern because it is his way of celebrating the beauty that surrounds us. It is his way of glorifying God. ' James replaces the last slide in a mahogany box and helps Tom down from the chair. 'We are lucky Tom. We are lucky to be alive in a world that is so varied and dazzling in its creation.'

They go outside. The west-facing garden of the rented townhouse is bathed in afternoon sunshine. Mary does not employ a gardener and the area has become overgrown in the weeks that the family have been in residence, but between the weeds, fat heads of purple lavender buzz with bees, and sweet-smelling roses scramble up the stone walls. By the gate, a bush froths with early elderflowers, fizzing with scent. Growing on a post, they find some cream-coloured lichen. They scrape off some samples and James stores them carefully in the folds of a clean white handkerchief. Tom's headache seems forgotten.

But when they are back inside, the boy's expression is troubled. 'Do you think I'll really be able to pass the entrance exam for the academy?' he asks suddenly. 'I know my Latin isn't good, compared to other boys.'

'You're a clever lad. You may not have been formally educated, but your mother has taught you well. You can pass, if you study.'

'Did you like school?'

'Oh yes,' says James, holding open the parlour door. 'I loved learning. Still do, actually. And school's a great place to nurture friendships.'

'You have to do games, like cricket and rugby. I won't play well, so no-one will like me. And I won't be able to come home...' Tom's lower lip trembles.

James wants to take the child in his arms; he guesses that distraction will be a kinder comfort. 'Look. Here are two pieces of glass. Try squashing a piece of lichen between them,' he unfolds the handkerchief, 'and we'll see what it looks like, when magnified. I think you'll enjoy school, once you're there. And you won't have time to get homesick. You'll see your mother and Agnes on exeat weekends, as well as during the holidays.'

At tea-time, Tom happily tells Mary about his researches, as she spoons leaves from the caddy into a silver pot. 'Perhaps you'll be a scientist, when you grow up, at a famous university.' Mary looks fondly at her son. 'Would you like that? You don't have to be a missionary, like your father.' She cuts a slice of seed cake for James, and passes it to him on a small porcelain plate. The plate is delicately decorated with exotic fruit; it is part of a set given to Mary by one of her husband's admirers. 'Now eat up, James. We mustn't be late for the coach.'

James obediently does so, although the cake is dry, and not really to his liking. He goes upstairs to change, and finds himself wishing that the elbows of his jacket were less worn. He wants to look smart. Mr Peel, from the Dumbarton Emancipation Society has organised for him to give a talk to a group of influential industrialists at the Quaker Meeting House which he attends.

James hopes to persuade the mill owners that if a ready supply of African cotton could be imported, the shortages caused by the war in America would be resolved. Mary has kindly agreed to come with him, to lend the considerable support of the Livingstone name.

As the coach bowls along the road, both James and Mary are in good spirits. James is excited because he has secured a passage to Africa, and it is only two months until he travels, while Mary expresses her pleasure at the sight of green oat

103

fields, rippling in the evening light. Her whole demeanour is relaxed. For once, she has removed the bulky little portrait of David that she usually wears around her neck. Instead she wears a string of simple pearls, which glisten above the neckline of her flowered muslin dress. Observing Mary's gentle smile, as she gazes out at the Scottish countryside, James reflects once again upon the complexities and contradictions of his companion. On the one hand, Mary can seem puritanical — she is impervious to luxurious furnishings and the allure of social status, on the other, she freely enjoys good food and wine. She appears to be a devoted wife: she obediently allows David the freedom to continue his travels and does not begrudge him the limelight, never mentioning her own considerable achievements, or the debt owed by David to her father, Robert Moffat. At the same time, she can be privately acerbic about her husband's activities, even — on occasions — suggesting that he has not done anyone a particular favour by trekking across Africa. Her courage is boundless, and her stoicism extraordinary. The game hunter Oswell, who was travelling with the Livingstones on the night when his namesake was born, reported that she gave birth in complete silence. Yet sometimes Mary can present as the very picture of female frailty, crying uncontrollably, wringing her hands and needing the reassurance of his own presence and the oblivion of laudanum to relieve her desperation.

There are three other passengers on the coach: a middle-aged seamstress who tells Mary that she has taken her dresses to Wylie and Lockheed, the big department store in Buchanan street, a weather-beaten sailor who sits with his bag protectively under his feet and an apple-cheeked bootblack boy. The seamstress says that she had worked far into the night in order to finish the last of her samples. She looks exhausted and apologises as she pulls herself from sleep. The sailor offers to swap places with her, so that she can lean against the side of the coach. Just as she stands up, the carriage wheels hit a pot hole, so that her plump posterior nearly lands James's lap. Everyone joins the woman in laughter, as she regains her balance, then sits herself back down.

'It's a beautiful evening,' remarks the sailor. 'Scotland is looking at her best. I dinnae want to leave...'

'Going far?' James asks.

'I have a passage on a steamship. She sails the day after tomorrow, for the Cape of Good Hope.'

James cannot resist telling of his own forthcoming adventure. 'I too, am travelling to Africa.' He cannot keep the pride from his voice. 'I am to join David Livingstone on his explorations of the Zambesi basin.'

'Oh, aye.' The seaman is unimpressed. 'I have a cousin who travelled with the Doctor a couple of years ago. He crewed a screw steamer — the *Pearl*, I think she was called — to the Zambesi mouth. Good luck to you — my cousin was glad to get away. He says that the doctor can be a difficult man.'

James looks first at Mary, and then at the sailor. 'Let me introduce to you Mrs Mary Livingstone, Dr Livingstone's wife.'

'Oh, aye,' says the sailor, unembarrassed by his social gaffe. He shakes Mary's hand with no pretence of enthusiasm.

They reach College Street. With a shout of 'Whoa!' the coachman pulls the horses to a stop. James helps Mary down from the carriage. They go through engraved glass doors into the red-painted lobby of the Thistle Hotel, and make their way to the marble front desk. A uniformed bellboy is promptly dispatched to show them to their rooms.

* * *

At the Quaker meeting house, Mary is greeted almost

reverentially by William Peel and his daughter, Jane. Having worked tirelessly for many years promoting the world-wide emancipation of slaves, they have been delighted by the additional publicity given to their cause by David's Livingstone's book. The much-feted Livingstone's simple assertion that he counted the tribal leader Sebetwane as a good friend and as an equal, has done more for their cause than a thousand pious sermons could ever have achieved. Jane Peel shows Mary to her seat, and brings her a glass of cordial. She is a thin, straight-backed woman, who reminds James of the peg dolls his little cousin used to play with. Her sweet-natured and altogether admirable father has surmounted considerable personal adversity. As a young man, his face was bitten by a cousin's pet otter. The wounds on his cheeks healed, but gangrene set in, and after much pain and suffering, his nose was surgically removed. Now he slots a piece of clay piping into the flap of flesh, which is all the protuberance he has left. James does his best to overlook the effect but Peel's appearance, however much one tries to make the best of it, is completely bizarre.

As usual, when James speaks, his words go down well. He gives his well-honed speech about the high suitability for cotton growing in the verdant lands that surround the Shire River, and builds for his listeners a vision of an industrious, harmonious, God-fearing country, which will provide a bustling template for other parts of Africa. Heathen tribes, he explains, will soon wish to emulate a society that so clearly benefits from the worship of a Christian God and the adoption of a Protestant work ethic. James lavishly praises the Peels and other abolitionists who have fought so hard to end the vile trade that treats men, women and children as if they are commodities but, he says, the time has come to build on the achievements of those indefatigable campaigners. It is time to move forwards. Ultimately, commerce in legitimate trade will prove the undoing of slavery. Once proper trade routes have been established, emancipation will follow, as surely as summer follows spring, as certainly as seedlings seek the sun. He reads out a passage from *Missionary Travels* that references the intellect and sophistication of the Makololo people. With a flourish, he unfurls a banner with Josiah Wedgwood's famous image of a chained and kneeling negro. Passionately, he reads out the emblazoned words, 'Am I not a man and a brother?' He ends his speech by himself answering the rhetorical question: 'Ladies and gentlemen, unquestionably, the African is a man. Unquestionably, he is a brother.' He bows his head in acknowledgement of the applause that follows.

Concluding the meeting, Peel thanks James for his address and says that refreshment will be offered, should anyone wish to honour himself and Jane by joining them at their humble home. The home, James happens to know, is anything but humble. The admirable Peel combines his campaigning with being a highly successful tea merchant. His house is four-storied, he has a heated greenhouse and keeps a carriage and pair with two uniformed footman.

* * *

In Peel's large and elegant drawing room, James settles himself on a Sheraton settee, and accepts a third glass of port. Normally, he consumes little or no alcohol, but he has decided to make the evening an exception. If Peel, who is a Quaker, has no problem with drinking, it seems churlish to refuse his hospitality. Mary has returned to the hotel, saying that she has letters to write.

'May I congratulate you, sir. Your address was both well-attended and well-received.'

James sees a stocky man in a rough tweed coat, looking at him askance, in a way that does not fit with the civility of his words. His expression is both dour and quizzical. James stands up, and shakes the stranger's hand. The man's palm is rough and callused. 'To whom do I have the pleasure of speaking?' James asks.

'George Rae, ship's engineer. I have returned from the Livingstone expedition, having been charged by the Doctor with the procurement of a new steamer. I thought we might have met earlier — I believe we're staying at the same hotel. I have been curious to learn for myself what you are like. On the Zambesi, we live in close proximity with one another, in circumstances that are often harsh.' Rae's eyes sweep James, taking in his slim frame, and tall physique. 'A degree of stamina is required, and a fortitude of spirit.'

'I feel flattered that you took the trouble to come here, so that you could make a personal assessment of me. I hope that you are not disappointed, and that I will not be found wanting.'

'With respect, you flatter yourself too much. I came to the meeting, because I have invested two hundred pounds of my own money, in Livingstone's boat, the *Lady Nyassa*. Like these gentlemen around us,' he indicates with a wave of the arm, 'I hope that money can be made from trade with the Dark Continent.'

James tries to conceal his surprise that one of Livingstone's closest associates should so freely admit that he aims to make a personal profit from the expedition. The desire seems at odds with Livingstone's high ideals. And yet, what moral difference is there between an individual such as Rae, and the captains of industry whose favour and support James has himself been courting? He pauses, trying to formulate a suitable response.

He is saved when the delightful Elizabeth Aitken steps forward, looking lovely in dove-grey silk. Beside her is an effete-looking man, in a sand-coloured coat. 'Reverend Stewart, may I introduce my husband, Archie? I believe that he has donated to your fund, but so far, he has not had the pleasure of meeting you.'

Rae turns away and bears down on a plump man in a yellow silk waistcoat. He looks, thinks James watching from the corner of his eye, like a wind-battered kestrel, approaching a caged canary.

The wealthy coal merchant, Archie Aitken, limply shakes James's hand. They discuss James's forthcoming trip. He promises that any donated funds will be put to good use and goes on to say how honoured he feels to be joining the Livingstone expedition.

'Will you not be fearful?' Elizabeth lowers her gaze, then raises her eyes. 'I believe there are diseases, wild animals and murderous tribes to be encountered.'

Looking down, James wishes that he was not so aware of Elizabeth's powdered, well-shaped bosom, which strains becomingly inside her bodice; her breasts nestle like two nectarines inside the confines of her dress. A part of him is indeed fearful. Usually, these fears are effortlessly subsumed by his thirst for adventure and the rightness of his cause, but just now, he cannot help thinking that it will be a severe wrench to move away from the comforts of society and the delights of drawing rooms such as Peel's. His head swims with the wine he has drunk. 'God will protect me,' he replies, with more solemnity than he intends. Immediately, he is concerned that this response has made him sound unduly arrogant, as if he believes himself to be specially chosen and therefore inviolable. 'Well, I hope He will, anyway.' He guffaws foolishly, and sits back down on the settee with more briskness than he has intended.

Murmuring that there is an official from the Corporation he should meet, Archie takes his wife by the arm and steers her to another part of the room. Looking back over her shoulder, Elizabeth gives a little wave of farewell. James drains his glass as he watches her flutter a feathered fan, while her husband languidly addresses the official. When a manservant appears, bearing a decanter on a silver salver, he nods an acceptance. The manservant is followed by Peel. James gets to his feet and accompanies his host, who generously introduces him to various influential stalwarts from the manufacturing community.

Walking back to the Thistle Hotel, James reflects on another successful evening's work. The meeting has further convinced him that once he has returned from his researches around the Zambesi it will be relatively easy to establish robust trading links. Despite his earlier moments of trepidation, he remains eager to experience the reality of Africa. The weeks before he leaves will be very busy. He wants to undertake more medical studies: he especially needs to improve his obstetric skills. He plans a railway trip to Manchester, so that he can investigate a special type of small-scale steam-powered mill and he has an appointment in London, where members of the Geographical Society have promised to supply their most up-to-date information and maps. There are some more things he is supposed to do, but he cannot for the moment think what they are.

On the way up to his room, he stumbles on the stairs and is reminded that while preoccupied with talking, he has eaten very little. His head spins. An image of Elizabeth's straining bodice romps unbidden into his mind. He does his best to suppress the thought, but an inappropriate envy of her husband Archie lingers inside him like a trail of river mist. He lies fully clothed on his bed and pictures himself having a physical fight with Archie. He jabs at him, bare-knuckled, then wrestles him to the floor. In his mind's eye, he is watched by Elizabeth. She holds a hand to her white throat — she flutters her eyelids in admiration at his all-conquering physical prowess.

He is startled by a tapping at the door. He is about to get up when the door is opened and, without waiting for a response, Mary lets herself into the room. Shockingly, she is wearing nothing more than a cotton robe and matching gown. Her hair is loose, so that she looks years younger. Behaving as if her actions are entirely normal, she walks over to the bed, and sits down. James is not at all sure how he should respond. He lies rigid as an anchovy encased in a jar, and wonders if he is dreaming.

'I wrote my letters — I have had to request an enhancement of funds from Tidman. Then I tried to sleep,' Mary starts to cry, 'but I couldn't. I was thinking about what that man said, the engineer on the coach. I get so used to people saying how marvellous David is, but the truth is, my husband is a difficult man. He ignores my requests for him to come home, yet I find it so hard to manage without him... I am not good at budgeting or making financial arrangements. The landlord is demanding a higher rent, and I simply do not have the money...' She sobs loudly, so that James feels he has no choice but to offer comfort. He puts his arm around her shoulders, and with his other hand, he strokes her soft, unbraided hair. Mary nestles against him, and after a little, she ceases to cry. She slips off her gown, and gives a little sigh.

James is suddenly aroused. In the sound Mary has made, he has heard an unmistakable tone. He has recognised in her utterance not an exhalation of despair, but the expression of its complete reverse. Mary groans again and she is clearly very much contented. And now, so is James. He has never before been in so intimate a position with a woman. It is a situation he has craved, although, at the same time, he has often prayed for help in suppressing his physical desires. His swimming head pulses with tumbling peaches and luscious melons. He sees Elizabeth's smiling lips and his mouth grows moist with the imagined taste of honey. Inside his trousers, he strains to be touched. He tells himself to remain content, that such release is beyond possibility, let alone propriety…

But Mary has grown up with the impossible. Did not the Moffats cause the desert to bloom? And she has never bothered with propriety. Deftly, she unbuttons him. Swiftly, she unties his drawers.

James scarcely dares to breathe. So much of him wants what seems to be about to happen; at the same time he is almost fainting with apprehension. Mary is a married woman, and he — James — will afterwards have to suffer the conscience of having cuckolded Scotland's greatest hero. More pressingly, he is ashamed of his ignorance. He understands from his anatomy lessons the mechanics of intercourse, but the subtleties, such as what, exactly, one is supposed to do, and how much energy it is considered appropriate to expend whilst doing it — these details are beyond him. He fears that Mary will find him wanting in a way that touches the very kernel of his being. If he fails to perform, he will be diminished as a man.

Such concerns prove unnecessary. The redoubtable Mary — experienced as she is, and seemingly untrammelled by any notions of female subjugation — has climbed on top. In a trice, she has ensured that she has been entered. They roll over — James works to quickly dispel the image of puppies in a basket at his father's farm. He soon discovers that, as well as being exquisitely pleasurable, it is really quite straightforward. He finds it easy to rock to and fro, which is all that Mary seems to require. Judging by her gasps of delight, she seems to be enjoying herself very much. At a point when he fears he can contain himself no longer, he feels Mary's whole body quake beneath him, and she exhales with a strange kind of growling sound. James is briefly concerned that he has done damage and that, in consequence, Mary is having some kind of fit. Such thoughts are interrupted when he finds himself soaring into unstoppable throes of delight. Afterwards, when he sees that Mary is smiling beatifically, it occurs to him that women are probably no different from men —for both sexes, the experience of climax is accompanied by a blissful shudder of physical relief.

James and Mary lie side by side, with Mary's head cradled in the crook of James's arm. James knows that he should feel guilty, and he does. A bit. But the alcohol has clouded his head, so that his most predominant emotion is happiness. He rejoices because his virility has been proved beyond doubt. Then he is gripped by a sudden panic — why did he not think of such a thing before?

'Mary,' he says, 'we didn't... We should have... Supposing you...?'

'Are you worrying that I might be with child?'

'Yes.'

'Don't be. I am forty-one years old. My menses are irregular — I think I am beyond my fertile years... But if you are concerned — next time, we can use a prophylaxis.'

'Next time..? I don't think...'

'Let's get some rest.'

James sleeps fitfully until sunrise, then wakes with his head thumping, to find Mary snoring peacefully beside him. In a way, he is pleased by what has happened, but at the same time, he is appalled by what he has done. He tries again to rest, but sleep evades him. The more he thinks, the more he laments that his relationship with Mary has changed irrevocably, and the worse the possible ramifications seem. He gets out of bed, and dresses himself as quietly as possible, planning to go outside for some fresh air. It is no good — he will have to empty his bladder. Mary awakes at the thud of the chamber pot as he replaces it in the nightstand.

'Where are you going?' she asks blearily.

'Out for a walk. I couldn't sleep.'

'I had better go back.' Mary throws off the bedclothes and makes her way to the door, her eyes still half-closed. 'I'll see you at breakfast.'

James opens the door to let Mary out, then feeling that some gallantry is required, he kisses her clumsily on the cheek. For a few moments, she clutches him tightly in return, then she steps out into the corridor. James follows her with his eyes, wanting to be sure that she can gain access to her room. Then, to his utter dismay, he notices that another door is already open and he sees that he is being observed: someone is standing in the doorway. With a visceral wrench, he recognises that the watcher is Livingstone's engineer, George Rae.

James retreats inside his own room. He puts his head in his hands, and several times, he curses out loud.

He cannot face breakfast with Mary. He leaves her a note to say that he is going straight back to Glasgow — Professor Lister is giving a lecture it would be beneficial to attend. He signs himself simply 'James'. He wishes that he did not have to return to Mary's rented house, but his belongings are there and besides, there is Tom to think of, and the rest of the children.

* * *

In the lecture hall, he finds it impossible to concentrate. Lister is presenting a paper on the theories of Louis Pasteur. It would all be most interesting, if only he could follow the professor's words, but they clatter around like pebbles, randomly tossed by an erratic sea. His head hurts, and while he lacks energy, at the same time, he feels restless. It is as if wherever he were to find himself, he would wish his legs to carry him elsewhere.

Before returning to Mary's house, he takes a detour to The Green, where walking beside the River Clyde, he attempts to clarify his thoughts. He will have to explain to Mary that what has occurred, can never, ever, happen again. He dreads that the engineer will tell of what he has seen, but concludes that he will have to work on the assumption that the man has better things to do than gossip. There is no way he can back out of the Scheme — he has involved too many people, some of whom have sponsored him with money. So he will have to come face to face with Livingstone, knowing that he has betrayed him in the most shameful way. He cannot come clean with the explorer — that would be doing a grave disservice to Mary. There is no way out. There is nothing that can undo what has been done. But at least, with so much yet to do before he leaves, there will be fewer occasions when he will be in Mary's company. Then once he has set off, she will be out of sight, if not out of mind.

* * *

He opens the front door with his key, and Mary comes down the stairs to greet him. He observes that under her ridiculous, old-fashioned cap, which flaps around her head like a pair of poodles' ears, there is an elation to her gentle face — a transforming happiness, for which he knows he is responsible. He cannot help himself — he is touched, and feels a stirring of desire. At the same time, he is burningly angry, because his beloved Scheme has been placed in such jeopardy — yet whatever anger he feels towards Mary, he rains ten times more wrath upon himself. He should never have drunk so much... he should never have allowed himself to be flattered by Mary's attentions. He smiles and does his best to look unconcerned. He endeavours to give the impression that nothing much has changed.

'Successful morning?' he asks. Mary had been due to visit a friend in Dumbarton.

'Oh yes!' Mary sounds quite breathless. 'And when I got

back, there was a bundle of mail for me. A ship has just arrived from Mozambique — and the captain gave instruction that I was not to be kept waiting. He straightaway sent one of his officers in a cab. David has written me so many letters!'

So David is the cause of Mary's elation. Despite everything, James is piqued. 'I hope all is well?'

'Oh yes! And do you know, he has sent for me! He has asked me to join him!'

James is stunned. It is some moments before he speaks. 'But... Mary... the — the children?'

'My first duty must be to my husband. So... I've been thinking — we can travel together! It is quite decided — I will come with you, when you sail aboard the *Celt.*'

 Broughty Ferry, Scotland

Mina waits expectantly with Maggie, while Mama finishes her breakfast muffin, wipes her mouth, then carefully folds her napkin.

'Very well,' she says at last. 'As it is a Saturday, you may ride, but I would prefer for you to do so with a purpose.' She slides her napkin through its ivory ring. 'I hear that Mrs McGovan's son has again called out Dr Scrivens, and that as a result of her illness, she no longer ventures from her cottage. Please ask Cook to make up a basket, containing whatever can be easily spared — provided that you behave responsibly, and that Winshaw is available, you may take the basket over to her.'

'Thank you Mama!' Mina would like to throw her arms around her mother in gratitude, but Elspeth has never welcomed displays of affection. 'With your permission, we will leave the table straightaway, so that we may prepare ourselves.'

Upstairs, the girls do not wait for the services of Moira. They seek each other's assistance in unfastening their day dresses, and in donning their cumbersome habits.

Maggie straightens her thickly starched petticoat, and adjusts her trailing skirt. 'It's all wrong!' she complains, as she buttons her jacket. 'The fashion this summer is for a shorter bodice, and a longer peplum. I hope we don't see the Mudie girls — I would be mortified!'

Mina looks at her reflection in the mirror, as she pins on her pork-pie hat. She does not mind whom they might meet; she cares only that the sun is shining, and she is about to enjoy the pleasure of riding along the beach to the village of Bly.

In the walled kitchen garden, Belton leans on his hoe and lifts his cap. He has been clearing the weeds between serried rows of lettuces, and red-topped radishes. 'Good morning to you!' he says. He eyes the basket. 'Are you young ladies off to enjoy a picnic? I believe that you'll find Winshaw in the yard.'

'Not a picnic,' Maggie replies. 'An errand of mercy — we're taking some provisions to Mrs McGovan.'

'Please give her my regards. She was a fine housekeeper in her day — we servants thought the world of her.' Belton sniffs, then quickly bows his head and continues to hoe.

Mina has been thinking of the visit only as a treat, but Belton's concern has reminded her that Corona's old housekeeper is suffering the misery of dropsy, and might well soon die. She walks over to the gardener, and touches him gently on the arm so that she can look him in the eye. 'I will give Mrs McGovan your very good wishes.'

Winshaw, the groom, is polishing the brass work on the carriage. It is a fine, five-glass landau, bought by Alexander earlier in the year after the firm had launched four great ships in the period of just one month. Inside, the cushioned seats are covered in the softest leather and the woodwork is inlaid with mother of pearl.

Winshaw turns to greet the girls. 'What can I do for you, young ladies? Looking at your clothes, I don't suppose you want to go out in this.' He sounds disappointed; the new coach is a source of considerable pride.

Maggie smiles appealingly. 'We would like help in saddling the horses. Then — if you have no more pressing duties — we would like you to come with us to Bly. We are to visit Mrs McGovan.'

'We are sorry to trouble you,' Mina adds. 'We don't really need an escort. But Mama doesn't see matters quite like that.'

'I have no prior commitments, and will be pleased to be of service.' Winshaw gives the carriage a final flourish, then disappears into the workshop with his duster and can. He emerges with Ben, the stable boy. 'The lad will saddle the horses for you. You can decide between you who'll take Midnight and who'll ride Dancer. I'll fetch Punch.'

He sets off, at a brisk pace, down the lane. Punch, the piebald gelding, is kept in a neighbouring yard.

Mina finds it a little strange that Winshaw refers to Ben as 'the lad.' They are the same age, both men are in their late twenties.

'Hector could do with a run!' Ben calls out, to Winshaw's disappearing figure. 'Maybe I could bring him, and come too?'

'Maybe you could,' Winshaw says, without turning round. 'I'll fetch both horses. You get those saddles on.'

Dancer is restless, and has to be held steady, while Maggie climbs the mounting block, and twists herself into her saddle. Mina is quicker to seat. She is lighter, more agile, and less preoccupied with preserving her modesty.

The four of them set out along the road, the girls out in front, the two servants behind. To Maggie's dismay, they do see the Mudies; the sisters are walking along the esplanade, arm in arm, wearing identical dresses of sugar-bag blue, together with matching hats.

Although she is the youngest, Mina is the more competent horsewoman, so when they reach the bridleway, it is she who takes the lead. She is riding Midnight — a black gelding with a white star above his eyes, who responds readily to a slight touch of the reins. The path is steep, and wet with mud, so that Midnight slips a little. Not for the first time, Mina reflects how foolish it is for women to be expected to stay on a horse while encumbered by skirts that are both very full and very long. She remembers how a friend of Mary's was killed after she had fallen, because her trailing skirts had got caught in the pommel of her side-saddle. The accident happened when Mina was twelve years old. She can clearly recall the shocked silence that ensued at the dinner table when, having absorbed the tragic news she asked, in all innocence, why women were not allowed to wear shorter, trimmer dresses, or even breeches, while out riding, if this would help to preserve their lives.

Down on the beach, Mina leads Midnight to the water's edge. The glittering waves lap at his hooves and he trots obediently, seemingly enjoying the paddle. She slows him to a walk, and directs him out of the way of a fishing boat and its crew. The men are landing baskets of haddock. She is dismayed to see that some of the silver-backed fish are still alive; they gulp, eyes staring, then flip themselves sporadically into the air. The fishermen load the heaving panniers onto the back of a donkey. One of them slaps the donkey's rump with the flat of his hand and the animal lumbers her way up the beach to a smokehouse. The stone building's chimney puffs a column of white into the blue of the sky. Midnight moves his head from side to side, as if sniffing the air; the breakfast aroma of kippers mingles with the smell of seaweed and essence of the pine needles, shed by the trees which edge the sand.

Past another couple of boats, past an outcrop of rocks, then Midnight's way is clear. Mina leans forward and gives him rein — she has to hold onto her hat, as he breaks first into a canter, and then into a gallop. The speeding horse swiftly carries her alongside the beating sea; she feels as light and free as one of the gulls, which caw and wheel in the sky above.

'Careful, lass!' Winshaw's words are at first lost in the wind. He draws alongside her and his face looks angry. 'Not too fast! There's driftwood in places, under the sand. If he trips, he'll throw you.'

Normally, it would be against Mina's nature to be rebellious, but she is enjoying herself too much to slow down. Her face is aglow; her heart beats fast with the thrill of the ride.

The two horses keep pace alongside one another, for a short distance.

Winshaw shouts loudly, 'It is not safe for you to be so quick!'

Mina is angry with the groom but at the same time, she knows that it is not Winshaw's fault that he feels it his duty to control her. She slows Midnight right down, wanting to weep with frustration. It is her lot — it is the lot of all women — to be constantly shepherded and curtailed. Mina longs to ride wildly on her horse, safely astride him wearing breeches, like a man.

The day, which had felt so carefree, is spoilt, and the weather too, has changed for the worse. From somewhere, a black cloud has appeared, and a breeze is shaking the trees. Winshaw has become an unfriendly presence — his eyes are focused straight ahead, his jaw is set. It is a relief when Maggie, who had been left far behind, catches up, with Ben beside her.

'This is a shorter way,' says Winshaw, turning his horse. 'We should not take too long — I believe it will rain.'

They follow the groom down a woodland path, which leads to a macadamised road. Soon the four horses are clip-clopping into Bly, where the little cottage is to be found, leaning haphazardly against the smithy. Mina realises that it has been a long time since she has seen the retired housekeeper. Before her illness, Mrs McGovan was invited back to Corona every year, in order to share the household festivities at Easter, Christmas and harvest time. Mina remembers a neat woman in a white cap, with a wrinkled face, like a winter pippin. It is a shock when her son has ushered the little party inside to see how much Mrs McGovan has changed. A bed has been made up, in the front room and all that can be seen is the old lady's head and a mound of bedclothes. Her face is unrecognisable. It looks grey and bloated, as if she is waterlogged. Worse, the old servant appears to have no knowledge of who her visitors are. Certainly, she has no desire to be friendly.

'I don't know them!' she rasps. 'Tell them to go!' The effort proves too much; she coughs, then falls back on her pillow. Hastily, the basket of gifts is passed from Ben to Maggie, then handed over to Mr McGovan. The young man murmurs a brief 'thank you'. When his half-hearted offer of refreshment is politely declined, he is noticeably relieved.

'We should return,' Maggie explains. 'Mr Winshaw fears that the weather will change, and we would not wish to cause our mother undue concern.'

They set off back. Mina rides at a gentle pace, side by side with Maggie. The visit has proved more than a little sobering. She had pictured Mrs McGovan looking pale and weak, but otherwise just the same. The very different reality has served as an abrupt reminder that old age can be ruthless and unforgiving, robbing individuals of their personality, as well as their wellbeing. They journey on. On reflection, Mina regrets that she and Maggie have made such a swift departure from the cottage. It would have been preferable to have stayed and to have asked what more could be done. Does young McGovan have anyone to help him with the nursing of his mother? Thinking about it, the patchwork quilt on the bed could have done with a good wash, and there was no cover on the bedside jug. Mina gives thanks for her good fortune in being both young, and in possession of the gift of health. She feels ashamed of her earlier truculence; she should be satisfied with the privilege of riding dear Midnight. In future — she resolves — she will be content to travel at whatever speed Winshaw deems fit.

Mina has hardly noticed the worsening weather. She sees now that the sea is agitated and the waves are bigger, they crash and roar against the shore. A flash lights the darkened sky, it is swiftly followed by a loud rumble of thunder. Almost simultaneously, the rain starts, first in single ominous drops. Then a deluge descends, so that in less than a minute, she is soaked through. Her starched petticoat clings to her legs like wet cardboard, and when she lowers her head to protect her face, a rivulet — which has collected in the brim of her hat — pours like a tumbling waterfall before her eyes.

Maggie is having trouble controlling Dancer who, scared by the noise and lightning is living up to her name. Winshaw dismounts, takes Dancer's rein, then turns to Ben. 'Get down, Lad, and help the young ladies dismount. We shall seek shelter at the smokery. We'll tie up the horses and leave them where they can shelter.' He has to shout to make himself heard.

The smokehouse when they reach it is a strange place. In a room at the front, knife-wielding fishwives split and gut herrings at an accelerated speed. The women's aprons are smeared with blood and there is an awful stench coming from the vat into which they hurl the fishes' discarded entrails. Looking through into the back room, Mina can see that every space is festooned with dangling kippers. The rain drums on the iron roof. Spats of rain hurl down the chimney, causing the wood in the kiln to sizzle and steam.

The women smile shyly whilst continuing their work. The foreman, a big man in a blue gansey, clears a tarpaulin from the top of a barrel, then offers it as a seat to Maggie and Mina.

At his bidding, one of the women fetches a blackened canteen. She sets about making sweetened tea, which she ladles into tin mugs. To Mina, chilled as she is by the wet, the tea is delicious — even if it does taste of kipper.

They leave, as soon as the rain has eased. The horses are calm now, as if they are in tune with the changing elements. Their hooves sink into the rain-soaked sand, as they make their way back to the town.

'I must look awful!' wails Maggie as they ride along the esplanade. 'I'm sure my hat has completely lost its shape!'

'Because mine has?'

'Yes,' says Maggie. 'It's like a coal sack.' The girls are still laughing when they reach Corona.

At the stables, they give apples to Midnight and Dancer, before leaving them in Winshaw's care. Going into the garden, they find Miss Scrope waiting for them, perched in the gazebo, on a wicker seat. She is always concerned when the girls are out riding. She is too fearful to mount a horse herself — she still suffers the consequences of a fall she had, when she was a child.

Miss Scrope tucks her book under her arm, and flaps around, like an anxious blackbird. 'Go in the side door!' she commands. 'Change your clothing, at once! You are not fit to be seen! And — good heavens! You smell of fish!'

The gong sounds. Hair combed, faces washed, and wearing clean dresses, Maggie and Mina come down the stairs for lunch.

Papa frowns as he says grace, and when he looks up, Mina's heart sinks. His expression is thunderous. He turns to Al. 'You saw him?' he says. 'Andrew had come all the way up from London? He hadn't just paid someone to lead the walkers?'

'Oh, I saw him.' says Al, dryly. 'He blew me a kiss. It was definitely Andrew.'

Mina puts down her soup spoon, her sharp appetite dulled. Andrew — her bright, loving brother — has been causing trouble again, and now the whole family will suffer from Papa's wrath. She knows what Andrew has done, for he has done it several times before. In order to cause havoc, he has got together a crowd of townspeople to walk the ancient right of way that runs along the river's edge at the shipyard. In consequence, all the boardwalks around the sterns of the ships will have had to have been dismantled, and then replaced. The carpenters will have been prevented from getting on with their proper work, with a resultant loss of income to the firm.

For a while, the meal continues in silence. Then Mama turns to Maggie. 'I have not asked — how was Mrs McGovan?'

'Her health is failing. But I think her son appreciated the basket. It was an adventure, riding back. We got caught in the storm.'

'I saw the lightning. I had thought you were sheltering safely in Mrs McGovan's cottage.'

'We had a fine time,' interrupts Mina. 'Winshaw and Ben took us to the smokery. The women made us hot tea.' Mina had wanted to say something cheerful, but she can tell from father's reddening face that she has said the wrong thing. She pinches her finger and thumb, wishing that she had kept silent.

'Winshaw took you to the smokery? You drank tea with common fishwives? And the stable lad was with you, so that you were a foursome? What madness were you thinking of?'

'My horse was frightened,' says Maggie.

'Winshaw just wanted to look after us,' says Mina, pressing her fingers harder. Father's ill-temper is causing a knot in her stomach.

'I'll have him sacked... seducing my daughters — behaving as though they are rough girls from the town.'

Hannah, seated, as usual, at Alexander's side, has been silent — a beautiful, self-contained presence. Now she speaks. 'No, you won't,' she says. 'You will do no such thing. You will treat Winshaw with the respect that is due to him. He will keep his employment.' Her voice is icily calm. 'Otherwise, father, I will take it upon myself to tell the world that the things that Andrew says of you, are no less than the truth.'

CHAPTER FIVE

August 1861

 Royal Lunatic Asylum, Dundee, Scotland

Life has improved for Chrissy. Her days are no longer taken up with counting beads — instead, her skills as a seamstress are being utilised. The Duke of Dunoon is due to visit the Asylum, on the 24th of August, and in order to give the best possible impression, Mr Connor has arranged for a gala ball to be held on the appointed day. A band of musicians has been organised, and tickets are to be made available for purchase in the town. All the inmates — both men and women — are to attend, each kitted out in an individual costume. The theme is to be 'Our Glorious Empire', all the various peoples ruled over by Her Majesty Queen Victoria are to be represented, and the main hall is to be strung with patriotic bunting. Chrissy has already helped in the laborious construction of over a thousand Union Jacks.

Deborah is beside herself with excitement. She intends to come dressed as a maharani. She believes that her husband will respond positively to the invitation — she says he will shake his head in wonder when he walks into the ballroom and realises that the lady in the beautiful Indian dress is none other than his own familiar wife.

Chrissy is concerned. Deborah's waist has slimmed to the span of a man's hand, and there is a hectic look in her eye. Chrissy thinks that Deborah may be investing too much in the forthcoming party and fears that if her friend is disappointed, her fragile health will break.

'There may be pressing business matters, to which your husband must attend,' she whispers. 'He may find it impossible to spare the time.' The two women are sitting side by side in the counting room, which now has a screen across, so that a part of it can be used for sewing. Their heads are bent over their work undoing the stitches of colourful clothes and curtains donated by Friends of the Asylum to be taken apart, cut up and remade as fancy dress. The process of unpicking is slow as they are allowed to use needles, but not scissors; the sharp implements are considered too much of a risk.

'He will come,' says Deborah. Her voice trembles with joyful certainty. She looks up, and her eyes flit across the room. She smiles, as if she can already see a familiar figure entering through the door. 'He will come,' she continues. 'When he sees me, he will hold me in his arms. We will dance, then he will call for a carriage, and together we will return to our home.'

'Hush,' whispers Chrissy. In her exhilaration, Deborah has made the mistake of raising her voice. In so doing, she has drawn to herself the undesirable attention of Biggins.

'Silence!' orders the nurse, who has been sitting on a stool with her hands on her thighs, her thumbs resting on her hips. She plucks from the floor a switch of hazel, then lumbers to her feet. She advances forwards, swishing the stick so that it hums in the air. She brings the switch down across Deborah's hands. 'Remember your purpose! You are here for the distraction of work, not for the pleasure of idle chit chat!' She uses the switch again and again.

'I beg your forgiveness... it is just that I am... so very much looking forward to the ball!' Deborah begins to rock, forward and back. 'I feel the anticipation with such intensity.' Her words are gasped, rather than spoken. 'I cannot sleep... I cannot rest... my heart is all a-flutter...' She crosses her arms, and tucks her wounded hands under her sleeves.

Chrissy watches in alarm, as Deborah rocks ever more wildly. Biggins moves towards her, as she crashes forward. There is a bang as her head collides with the table. The other women in the room cease their work and stare at her slumped and lifeless figure. Biggins appears rooted to where she stands. Chrissy thinks that the wardress must be wondering if she will be in trouble for using the switch. Officially, Mr Connor has banned all forms of corporal punishment.

Biggins glares at the onlookers. 'Think you're at the circus?' she asks, pulling herself to her full height. Her voice sounds like the wheels of a heavy cart, rumbling on gravel. She turns to a pale-haired girl called Ellen. 'Get to the infirmary and fetch Dr Perry! Tell him to come at once. One of the inmates has had a fainting fit — tell him to bring his lance — the woman will need to be bled.'

It is some time before Ellen returns with the doctor. Deborah, meanwhile, has opened her eyes. She has been moved from the bench to a Windsor chair, fetched from the visitors' room. Leaning back in it, with her coronet tipped to one side, she resembles a fading dowager queen. There is a bruise on her forehead. She complains that her heart is thumping too quickly — she finds it hard to breathe.

When Dr Perry arrives, he tips his top hat at Biggins, who turns away, flummoxed at this unexpected recognition. Dr Perry is a person of high status; he works at the asylum only two days a week — the rest of the time, he runs a successful practice in the town. 'I beg your pardon, for the delay,' he says. 'I was occupied in treating one of the cooks for the itch — I use a solution of acid, and it is essential that I supervise the application; too high a concentration can prove fatal.'

'She is overwrought,' says Biggins, jabbing at Deborah. 'She needs bleeding, or a sedative to calm her nerves.'

'I am the physician,' Dr Perry says, without rancour. 'I believe it is my place, rather than yours, to decide upon a course of treatment.' He lays his forefinger on Deborah's wrist. 'Her pulse is indeed considerably faster than one would consider desirable. Has anything happened to cause alarm?' He looks around, questioningly.

Chrissy had wanted to remain at Deborah's side, but was told by Biggins that she must carry on with her work. Now she puts down her needle. 'Deborah is keen to attend the Ball,' she says. 'She is very much looking forward to it.'

'I cannot sleep for the anticipation...' Deborah says. 'I can find no rest... I do so long to dance again...'

'Then we must ensure you enjoy that pleasure.' Dr Perry looks inside his black bag. He pauses a moment. 'I could prescribe digitalis,' he muses. 'That would regulate the heart rate. But it can prove hard to ascertain a therapeutic dose... the drug can cause delirium.' With a decisive snap, he closes the bag. 'I will treat the patient conservatively. She should be removed to a place of complete quiet, where there is nothing to distract or excite her. In two or three weeks, she should be symptom free.' He turns to the wardress. 'Tell me, is Room Four available?'

'It has remained empty since Jane was brought out.'

'Take the patient there. The more tranquillity she enjoys, the better she will feel.'

Chrissy cannot see how Deborah's health can possibly be improved by such banishment. She knows the room, having spent a long, wretched week there, after Biggins had caught her sobbing to herself one night. (She had been lying with her head under her blanket — grieving for Thomas — thinking that, as it was dark, she could do so unobserved.) Her heart sinks into her boots. Room Four is no more than a cell. In addition to being cramped, it is very dark. The only light filters in through four slats in the metal door. In order to stop patients from self-harming, the walls are padded with straw, encased in ticking. Chrissy remembers with dismay the sensation of being shut away with nothing to do and no-one to talk to; the isolation left her feeling that she had become a thing of less consequence than the rat which darted out each evening to share her bread. Worse than the isolation, was the choking stench of urine and faeces, which filled every square inch of the air. Previous inmates had freely relieved themselves onto the mattressing, causing an accumulation of bodily fluids to fester in the straw.

Another nurse is summoned; she leads Deborah away. Deborah walks unsteadily; her whole body shakes. She seems uncomprehending of her fate — she puts up no resistance. Or perhaps the over-beating of her heart is too much of a distraction; she puts a hand to her chest — her face is pale, and she gasps, raising her head and tilting it back. Chrissy tries to catch her eye; she wants to indicate her support, but Deborah does not acknowledge her.

Chrissy watches Deborah go. She sighs as she pricks her finger, and a drop of red blood spills across the seam of a yellow silk gown.

It is just two weeks until the Ball. In the following days, Chrissy and the other needlewomen must work hard if all the costumes are to be ready in time. They start work as soon as breakfast is over, and continue to sew by candlelight, until long after the sun has gone down. Chrissy does not mind the toil. She feels that a normality has been restored to her life. Unlike bead-counting, the work has a definite purpose. As she sews a plume of feathers onto a mock Indian turban, or turns a set of curtains into matching cloaks for a pair of Pacific Islanders, she makes believe that she is employed by a dressmaker, back in the town. She tries to forget that her only access to the outside world is the sky she can see from the exercise yard; she imagines that the Ball will be a true celebration, not an occasion for the Asylum inmates to be put on public show. She goes further. She invents a world in which instead of abandoning her, Andrew has fulfilled his promise. She pictures herself as Andrew's wife — she sees them waltzing together, in full public view, his hand on her waist, his arm on her shoulder. She pretends that afterwards, they go home to a little house, which they share with Thomas, who has not died, and who has instead grown to be a chubby and contented child. She makes believe that following the example of Joseph the Carpenter, Andrew has accepted Thomas's divine conception. Without argument, and with simple grace, he is happy to play the part of devoted father.

Chrissy enjoys these imaginary scenes, but sometimes reality blows into her mind, like a chill wind, so that she shudders as she sews. She knows that in truth, Thomas lies buried, she knows that her unshakable conviction that he was miraculously conceived causes her to be ridiculed by the staff of the asylum. She knows too, that Andrew, with his elegant clothes and expensive education, would never have gone through with his offer of marriage. He would not have wanted to be cast out from his sphere of society, nor would he have wished to be further estranged from his family. He had quarrelled with his father over money (he claimed to have been cheated out of his inheritance) but he spoke respectfully of his mother and referred to his younger sisters with especial warmth. There was one brother, called Al, whom he talked of with a dislike that bordered on hatred. He believed that Al had plotted to turn his father against him. However, he valued the friendship and approval of James and Sam — the two brothers she had met when they all took tea together at the George Hotel. But close as he was to these two brothers, Andrew could not bring himself to be truthful to them, about her own background and employment. Chrissy wishes that she had found the courage to be honest, and had spoken to correct Andrew, when he said she was a governess. Her god-fearing parents brought her up to be uncomfortable with any form of deceit.

Chrissy turns her attention to a brown flannel blanket, which she cuts into semi-circles, ready to sew into cones for Hottentot hats. The Hottentot outfits have been agreed upon after Mr Connor was summoned to the sewing room to arbitrate. Young Horrocks had said that for the outfits to be authentic, it would be necessary to expose a large amount of naked flesh. After some argument, a compromise was reached and it was settled that loose chemises and skirts should be provided for the women, and short baggy breeches for the men, finished with beads, spears, feathered capes, all topped off with the conical hats.

She folds the flannel that is left and puts it to one side; it can be used later to make headbands for Pacific Islanders. She threads her needle and begins to sew, using a circular movement to form swift, even stitches. As she does so, she thinks about an image she has seen in a book Mr Connor borrowed from the Town Lending Library. He had shared it with the sewing group, to offer them inspiration for their costume-making. The book was entitled *Principal Peoples of the World*, and the frontispiece showed a large handsome Englishman wearing a scarlet jacket and white pith helmet, surrounded by men from a dozen different races, who all knelt before the soldier. Chrissy had found the frontispiece unsettling. It seemed wrong, somehow, as if the Englishman were being represented as Jesus, surrounded by His disciples. But inside, was an illustration which unnerved her in a completely different way. The image showed a tall male Hottentot, with a sensitive face and high cheek bones, wearing nothing but a loin cloth, a hat and a goatskin cloak. The

African's nakedness should have been an affront, but instead of being appalled, Chrissy had found herself fascinated by the man's muscular limbs and firm brown torso. As she finishes her line of sewing and turns the seam, she wonders how she would behave were she ever to come face to face with a real-life African, especially one showing such a quantity of bare brown flesh. She remembers the inspiring words of James Stewart, when he visited the Asylum. Once more, she regrets her powerlessness and inability to help with the missionary's worthy Scheme, which would bring much-needed enlightenment to the people of Africa.

In the following days, Chrissy turns a pair of moth-eaten, buffalo-hide rugs into four Eskimo jackets, and plucks the feathers from a discarded stuffed eagle to make a set of Maori head-dresses. She turns a dozen linen sheets into wide-legged trousers, gathered at the ankle and trimmed with beads. She turns green wall hangings into Irish dresses, and paisley-patterned cotton into West African robes. At the end of each day, when her other tasks are finished, she carefully lifts from her basket a silken tunic fit for a maharani, sewn with a myriad of sequins and discarded gems. Chrissy is making Deborah's costume from a glittering ball-gown. She wants the outfit to be as beautiful as possible. She wants to be sure that if her friend is pronounced well enough to attend the dance, she will look as lovely as she did when she waltzed with her husband dressed as a fairy queen.

Chrissy has no friends or family to invite to the dance. Frank Barton had come, once, to see her in the asylum, but he never came again. Biggins had escorted her to the visitors' room, where he stood waiting, looking strained. 'I am sorry,' he had said. 'I hope you will soon be released from here, but in the meantime, I cannot hold your job open. I am sure you will understand.' She had said that, of course, she quite understood. There was a silence, which she tried to fill by asking about life at the Tannery, but a conversation about the other girls, whom she could picture joking and laughing with one another, in between working at their machines, had proved too difficult to achieve. Her tongue had felt too large inside her mouth, and tears had prickled her eyes. It had been a relief when Biggins rattled her keys to signify that the meeting was at an end. The Montgomerys had never visited. They had sent a letter to say that her room had been re-let and that they would keep her possessions in a box. She could collect them on her release, and in the meantime she would remain in their prayers.

And so Chrissy takes little interest in what she herself will wear, for she has no-one in particular to impress. She knows, too, that the ball is to take place more for the satisfaction of the Asylum's sponsors than for the benefit of its troubled inmates. There is a third reason why she does not sew something special for herself. She is ambivalent about the effect of her appearance. In the days when she was free to go about the town, she was sometimes pleased to be considered beautiful. She had enjoyed the stillness of sitting quietly while Mr Watt scrutinised her features, lifted his brush then lowered it — just so — onto his stretched canvas. However, her natural modesty meant that more often, she was uncomfortable with admiration. She would have preferred not to possess the kind of looks that turned men's heads. And inevitably, Andrew's betrayal had made her distrustful. Now, although she knows she would enjoy the sensation of wearing a dress of fine fabric, she does not wish to add anything to her appearance that might further enhance her appeal.

When the appointed day of the ball arrives, rather than showing excitement, the inmates appear subdued. It has been heavily impressed on each individual that any misbehaviour will result not only in a ban from attendance, but also in further unspecified punishments. After breakfast, Chrissy and the rest of the team put the finishing touches to the male inmates' costumes, sort them into bundles and load them into large wheeled baskets to be trundled to the men's quarters, across the yard.

At the afternoon service, a special prayer is said, asking for God's blessing upon the visiting Duke. Then the women are escorted back to the long ward and ordered by Mrs Horrocks to stand beside their beds. The nurse tells the seamstresses to distribute their handiwork; she sucks on a pencil and ticks from a list while Chrissy goes back and forth delivering the prepared clothes. The women accept their outfits cautiously; they are unaccustomed to any form of change. When Betty is handed a feathered cloak, she breaks the silence with a wail. She says she will be mistaken for a chicken; she is frightened her neck will be wrung. She is hushed by Jane, who asks permission to exchange the cloak for the plaid shawl, with which she has herself been issued. Mrs Horrocks frowns, and opens her mouth to object, then changes her mind, and nods her head. Betty is quaking with terror, and Mr Connor will disapprove if there is an unnecessary disruption to proceedings. At the morning meeting, the superintendant has insisted that the Duke should experience the atmosphere of the asylum as being as harmonious as that of a well-run family home.

It is with a heavy heart that Chrissy places the maharani outfit on Deborah's empty bed. Her friend remains in the isolation room, and Chrissy has no means of knowing how she fares. Tentatively, she has asked Biggins if Deborah will be considered well enough to join the festivities, but the nurse has scowled and said how should she know? She is not a doctor. Chrissy thinks that the maharani costume may be wasted, then changes her mind; a labour of love can never be a waste, because it has provided the worker with the gift of a period of pleasurable anticipation. She sighs as she puts on her own costume. She is not looking forward to the ball, but even more, she dreads it being over, for afterwards, there will be no more sewing to do. From tomorrow, she will once more be employed in the futile task of bead counting, while young Mr Horrocks reads his magazine and snores in his chair. Her fervent hope is that she will be transferred to the mending room.

Chrissy regrets her choice of costume, as soon as she has put it on. She is dressed as an Eskimo, from the north of Canada, in a jacket and skirt cut from two moleskin blankets. There is nothing remotely smart about the shape of the jacket — it is a kind of square. The skirt is cut on the bias, and because of an insufficiency of material, it falls wrongly, bunched to one side. But it is not her lack of elegance that Chrissy regrets. The problem is that it is a warm summer's evening, and already, she is far too hot.

The inmates shuffle and cough, as they wait to be summoned to the Great Hall. Through an open window, Chrissy can hear the band playing. She recognises — with a wistful mix of pain and pleasure — the familiar melodies of 'Molly do you love me?' and 'Nelly Bly'. Looking around her she thinks that, standing still and silent in their colourful outfits, the women resemble nothing so much as waxen dolls, on display in a giant's bazaar. She pictures an enormous hand bursting through the ceiling and a huge finger and thumb trying to create order, so that the feathered Maoris are put in one group, and the Africans are placed on another shelf. She imagines the giant shopkeeper, whose hand it is, growing impatient, so that he gives up, and knocks the women-dolls into a heap. She pictures agitated faces and flailing limbs emerging from a pile of fur, silk, satin and flannel, and then worries that her mind has become tainted by the Asylum. Surely, these are the imaginings of a mad woman?

Chrissy is saved from these ponderings by the arrival of

Mr Connor, snappily dressed as an Admiral, in a bright red coat with gilded epaulettes. He holds himself erect, and strides forward in his dark blue trousers, as if he has assumed the persona — as well as the dress — of a senior officer in Her Majesty's Fleet.

'Ladies,' he says, 'I find myself quite bedazzled.' He stands to attention and clicks his heels. 'I would consider it an honour, if you would agree to accompany me to our Gala Ball.' He gives a smile, and bows low, giving an elaborate sweep of his cocked hat. In doing so, he directs his eyes to the floor. Thus, he fails to notice that Dr Perry has entered the room, with Deborah at his side.

'Cured in the nick of time!' the doctor declares, and the superintendant looks up, startled. 'After fourteen days of tranquil rest, the patient is now well enough to fulfil her wish. Mr Connor, Mrs Horrocks' — he nods to each in turn — 'Mrs Buchanan is well enough to attend the dance.'

Chrissy thinks that Deborah's cheeks have grown more hollow, and her yellowing eyes seem larger. Chrissy's heart goes out to her — she thinks that sometimes, clever people like the doctor can suffer a strange kind of stupidity that results from a willingness to self-deceive. Anyone can see that Deborah's health has not improved, and that she has, in fact, grown more unwell whilst undergoing her so-called treatment. Chrissy cannot bear to think how much her friend must have suffered in the isolated squalor of the padded cell.

Without asking permission, she takes Deborah's hand, leads her to her bed, and shows her the glittering costume.

'Can all this be for me?' Deborah says. Her voice crackles from a lack of use. She fingers the silken pantaloons. 'They are beautiful.' She touches the gems that decorate the gilded veil. 'Such richness. So much work.' She sinks onto the bed and cups a shaking hand to her breast. 'Thank you. Oh, thank you.'

'We must be quick,' Chrissy says, as she helps Deborah

dress. 'The others have gone.' It is true — the rest of the inmates have followed Mr Connor out of the dormitory. Only Mrs Horrocks remains; she is busy donning her own costume. Over a plain cotton shift, she is tying a skirt of green paper leaves; around her neck, she places a necklace of pink paper flowers.

Once Deborah is wearing her tunic, pantaloons, veil and headdress, Mrs Horrocks and Chrissy lead her along the passageway, that goes to the hall. 'Will he come?' she whispers. 'Oh, I do so want him to come.' She walks with urgency, but sometimes stumbles, so that she leans for support on Chrissy's arm.

The Great Hall has been transformed beyond recognition. Bedecked with zigzags of bunting, and with the band on the platform playing cheerful tunes, the hall has all the gaiety of a public Assembly Room. Chrissy is fascinated by the dancers who crowd the floor. With some exceptions, such as the thin doleful man who rotates in solitary circles, it is impossible to tell which of them are the lunatics, and which are the townspeople. All whirl and twirl with equal energy and enthusiasm, if not with equal skill.

'And now!' roars the band master, 'ladies and gentlemen, will you please join me for 'The Dashing White Sergeant!'

Chrissy, Mrs Horrocks and Deborah are swiftly partnered off. Chrissy has to concentrate hard, as she dances anticlockwise for eight counts, and clockwise for three, before being turned, and stamping her feet. Deborah dances beside her; the gems of her headdress and the braid of her veil sparkle in the evening light as she is spun around, on her slippered feet. She looks as if she has been transported to an ethereal place — her whole face is lit with a beatific smile — but her eyes are restless, as they endlessly seek. 'He will come,' she mouths to Chrissy, as they join together and raise their arms. 'He will come. Surely he will come.'

'Perhaps he is already here,' says Chrissy. 'There are so many people...' In her moleskin jacket and skirt, she is getting hotter and hotter. Through an archway of arms, she comes face to face with a new partner — a black-bearded man. She tells herself that is just the heat that causes the rising panic that chokes her throat. But when the bearded man touches her arm, she feels she cannot stand it. 'I am sorry,' she says. 'I feel I must withdraw. I fear I am unwell.'

The man smiles, showing an impressive set of white teeth. 'I pray that you will feel better soon. I would like to sit it out with you, but I fear that Mr Connor expects more action of his chief guest and patron. With regret, I must remain on the floor.'

Chrissy sits, observing the dancers. So the black-bearded man is the Duke of Dunoon. He does not appear threatening or unpleasant — in fact, he is causing much hilarity by sportingly attempting to dance unpartnered. No, the Duke is alarming because he reminds her of someone. Not the Reverend Willis — although the two men do bear a passing resemblance to one another. Chrissy swallows as, like a bobbing branch submerged in a bog, some other memory almost surfaces. There was a different person ... someone who also had black hair... someone who ill-used her...

'Bring smelling salts,' calls a voice, above the music. 'A woman has fainted!'

Chrissy looks in the direction of the voice and sees to her dismay, that the woman is Deborah. She must have been trying to leave the room; she has collapsed in the doorway. Chrissy gets to her feet, but before she can reach her, Deborah has been lifted up by the doleful man, who had earlier been dancing by himself. The man seems to have acted from the desire to remove an obstruction, rather than having been moved by compassion. He holds his burden clumsily, as if carrying a rolled up piece of carpet; he looks unsure of what he should do next. Deborah opens her eyes, and smiles up at the lunatic, who stares ahead, all unaware.

Chrissy pushes aside a man draped in yards of bright cotton, in order to take Deborah's hand. Despite the warmth of the evening, her friend feels icy cold.

'He came,' Deborah says. 'I told you he would come.' She tries once more to smile, but a sudden pain causes her to place her arms protectively across her chest. Her mouth opens, her whole body stiffens, and she lies dead in the madman's arms.

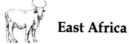 **East Africa**

Lokim sits on a large piece of driftwood and wriggles his toes. During the long walk to find water, he had been cut by stones, pierced by thorns and burned by the baking earth. Weakened by starvation, his body had offered little resistance to the infections that invaded his feet. By the time they reached the Huge Pool, each slow step had caused excruciating pain. Every day, despite his suffering, he had carried Auma on his back, until her weight had made the pain impossible to bear, at which point Lojeri or Longoli had carried her instead. There had been enough death. Without the words having to be spoken, they agreed that however ill she became, Auma would not be abandoned.

Lokim grasps his ankle and rests his lower leg on his thigh, so that he can examine his right foot. Then he repeats the process to examine his left. His soles had swelled and a sore on his ankle had dripped with pus, like sap from a rubber tree. Now the pink flesh, though still blistered, looks clean. He tests his feet by pushing them down on the sand. His footprints look reassuringly normal in size and shape.

'I am grateful to you, Bila,' he calls across, to where the women are chatting under the shelter of a wide-spreading tree.

'You make good medicine.' Bila, a woman originally from Sorito, had wrapped his feet in clay mixed with special leaves, bound with grass.

From the people who had made up the coffle, there are three men and four women left. Lokim no longer holds himself separate from the rest of the party; Longoli, Lojeri, Bila, Nangoli, Lono, and Auma, have become his friends.

Nearly one whole phase of the moon has passed since Lokim had heard Lojeri cry out in joy as he pushed aside a heavy branch, to clear a way in front. Lokim, hobbling behind, had hurried to see the source of such delight. When he saw a stretch of wide blue water, glinting and sparkling in the sun, he did not at first believe his eyes. He thought he must be suffering the consequence of having eaten some husks of mildewed grain; his Uncle Atum had taught him that a certain type of mould could make things that were not actually there appear real.

Lokim only believed that the Huge Pool truly existed once he had waded in, cupped his hands and splashed his face. He wanted to weep with relief; he had not misled his companions, he had been right to change course, in order to follow the flight path of the long-legged birds. Around the shore he saw coconut palms and mango trees: looking down he saw that the water teemed with darting fish.

Nangoli lit a fire using a rubbed stick. The group kept the fire alight day and night, partly as a protection from animals, but also because the smell of the smoke reminded each of them of home. They made shelters out of bent sticks covered with palm leaves. For Auma they built a platform on which she could lie, made soft with gathered moss. They had carried with them two small bolts of calico, all that remained of Sadeen's trading supplies. On the fourth day, when he had partly recovered his strength, Lokim took one of bolts, and went in search of the nearest village. Not far from the shore, he found a collection of mud huts inside a grass palisade. The people were curious but not hostile and afterwards, Lokim reasoned that the villagers' proximity to the Pool meant that they were used to strangers. They traded with men who came by boat from different settlements around the shore. Using sign language, he negotiated with one of the elders, and the next day he joyfully returned, having exchanged the cloth for two fishing nets and a skilfully-fashioned axe.

The next task was to find a suitable tree. It was Bila who located a well-grown palm; the trunk had grown thick and straight before it toppled under its own weight and fell horizontally across the sand. The men cut it free, and stripped off its bark. They used stones to stop the log from rolling, then the men took turns with the axe to hollow out the inside, chipping out the wood in segments. It was long slow work, and after two days they had made only a shallow impression.

'This is taking too long,' said Lokim, as he picked at a splinter in his forefinger, then rubbed a blister on his palm. 'And I am hungry for one of those big fish.' Far out in the water, he had seen a grey fish the size of a hyena, looping itself into the air. 'We will try a different way.'

They placed three piles of grass and twigs inside the slight dent in the tree trunk, and lit them from the main fire. After a day, when the fire had done its work, they used scoops of water to extinguish the flames. Then Lokim and Lojeri climbed inside, to test the space for size. They dragged the log to the Pool, climbed back in, signalled for the women to give a push, and whooped in celebration as they floated off in their rough canoe.

They made paddles from two thick branches, and soon became skilful at powering the dugout across the water. They found it easy to catch the fish that swam so plentifully. They cooked the fish on flat stones, which they had heated in the fire, served them on palm leaves and flavoured them with coconut. They told each other they were feasting like the ancestors, as they lay with full stomachs in the shade of a wide-spreading tree. Longoli speared a load of the pink, round-bellied fish onto a long cane, which he took with a small piece of cloth to a further settlement, where he received in exchange some big brown bats. For the first time in months, the group tasted fresh meat. Lokim made another expedition; he traded a length of cloth for a healthy she-goat, who provided white milk, which they fed to Auma, from a gourd.

The goat is now tethered to a nearby tree; she is bleating because she wants to eat some tufts of green grass which are just out of reach. Lokim gets up and ties her to a different tree, she butts her head and begins to chew. He sits back down, and resumes the contemplation of his toes. He moves them up and down then he stretches out his long legs. He looks down at his belly and smoothes his hands over his torso. A month of plentiful food and rest, and his ribs no longer stick out like the bones of a too-thin cow. The thought of cows in general leads him to think specifically about Pila; he wonders whether or not she ever found her way home.

He asks himself how long it will be, before he once again steps through the small gap in the fence, that surrounds his manyatta. He counts on his fingers, trying to work out how many cycles of the moon have passed since he left to go hunting and was chased by the lion. He considers how things might have changed in his village since he was betrayed by Makot. He thinks about the suffering he has witnessed, and the cruelty, so casually inflicted. He remembers the love that Luma bore for her child, and the courage she displayed before she died. That memory is too painful; he takes his mind elsewhere. Has Niampa settled down with his pretty wife, or does he continue to drink far into the night, laughing and singing with his unmarried friends? Is old Amuarkar still able to walk unaided, or has his rheumatism worsened? Who ensures that the blind man is brought porridge and fresh water now that he, Lokim, is no longer there? He thinks of Amuarkar's beautiful sharpening stone, and longs to hold the familiar object in his hand.

'Ready for some fishing?' Lojeri is standing beside him; he holds one of the nets in his hand.

Lokim looks out towards the horizon, as he paddles away from the shore. He cannot believe the size of the Huge Pool. One of the elders in the village used to speak of a stretch of water that was so vast, it had no end; the elder had not himself experienced such a thing, but he had met a Dodoth man, who knew someone who said he had sailed in it, to a far-off land. Lokim thinks that the Pool looks Endless, but he is puzzled: the man had said that the Endless Water beat like the wings of a flying bird, and that it tasted of salt.

It is a perfect day, the sun is warm but not too hot and the air is still, but not too humid. Lokim and Lojeri decide to row further along the shoreline — not because there is any shortage of fish around their camp, but simply because they are curious. As Lokim rhythmically lifts his paddle and hears a soothing splash as it descends, he exults in his restored health and his new-found sense of wellbeing. Soon, he will start the long trek back to Karamoja, using the sun and stars to guide him. But for now, he will live in the present, rejoicing in his freedom and in the comfort he has found.

With Lojeri in front, they move through the water until they go round a strip of land like a pointing finger, where the black roots of forest trees grow in tangles, like knotted hair. A flock of green birds lift themselves into the sky, calling to each other in alarm. Ahead of them protruding from the mud Lokim sees what he at first takes to be a collection of glistening rocks. Then one of the rocks opens wide a huge pink mouth and displays a set of enormous, tusk-like teeth. More mouths open, and Lokim sees that each rock has a set of round ears, that looks disproportionately small. His mouth feels dry as he realises that he is looking at a pod of hippos. The animals are rarely seen in Karamoja — the area is too dry.

Lojeri rests his paddle inside the canoe. 'They probably won't eat us,' he says, observing Lokim's alarm. 'They like flesh to be already dead. And they prefer to eat grass.'

'So we're safe? They won't attack?'

'They can get angry, especially if they have young to protect. They have strong sharp teeth. We should go back.'

Dipping their paddles slowly, so as to make as little disturbance as possible, they return to the safer waters around their camp.

That afternoon, Lokim chooses the best of the catch for drying. Since Lokim and Longoli's first trips, the freed slaves have regularly trekked inland from the lake. They have found another friendly village, where they can trade fish for wrappings of medicine for Auma. To the dismay of her companions, who not only value the Teso woman for herself but who would also count her recovery as an indication of good fortune, Auma's health has failed to improve. Every day, Lono gathers quantities of moss and fern from the rain forest, to keep her bed soft and fragrant. Nangoli tries to cool her fever with a palm leaf fan, whilst singing songs of plentiful rain and golden maize. But Auma becomes ever thinner; it seems that her body is unable to process the nourishment she is offered. Lokim has come to think that the village medicine offers little or no benefit, but does not say so. The herbs do, at least, appear to do no harm.

Lokim uses the point of an aloe to pierce first a pink fish, and then a silver one. He strings the fish in a line. He ties the rope between two trees, and is just standing back to admire his handiwork, when Bila comes hurtling from the forest, screaming out in alarm. In her agitation, she runs hither and thither, using both hands to keep on her head a pile of firewood.

'Crocodile!' she shrieks. 'A crocodile! Lying in the mud!'

She lowers her burden to the ground, and breathlessly recounts her tale — of how she was reaching for a fallen branch when a big male crocodile lifted himself from the narrow creek where he had been lurking. He snapped his great jaws, looked her in the eye, and then for some reason, he sank himself back into the mud.

In the dark of evening, while Lokim watches the fire leap and spark, he thinks that although crocodiles and hippos are dangerous, they are not devious in the way that men can be. He shudders, remembering Santos, who bought him from Makot and turned him into a slave. He goes to sleep feeling grateful to have found a place where it is animals, rather than people that are to be feared.

But the next day, Lokim sees that a strange boat has arrived in the night, which has been dragged up onto the sand. The boat is much bigger than a dugout and has a tall stick rising from it, with big sheets of white cloth tied around. He can see no sign of the men who have brought it. Feeling a sense of foreboding, he wakes Longoli who lies beside him, and points to where the boat lies beached, further along the shore.

'I think we should leave,' he says. 'I do not trust the men who own such a thing.'

Longoli uses his hands to pull open his bleary eyes. 'I expect they're just fishermen — and they've gone to the village to get supplies.'

'Ordinary fishermen — in something that size? No. We should go.'

Lokim goes to talk to the women. They are in their shelter, which they have made comfortable with a floor of reeds and woven mats. 'We like it here,' says Nangoli. She points to Auma. 'And how will we care for her, if we leave the Pool?'

146

'We can take dried fish with us… we can fill coconut shells with water…' Even as he speaks, Lokim realises that his words are pointless. His companions can see no immediate danger, while their recollections of being starving and thirsty are all too sharp.

'Auma is not well enough to be moved,' says Lono. 'And I'm not leaving her.' She picks up the empty gourd, and goes to fetch milk from the goat.

Lokim leaves the shelter, and chooses a ripe mango for his breakfast. The sweet juices run down, tickling his chin. He goes to the Pool to wash his face. As he walks, his feet sink into the soft, warm sand and the blue waters glint and sparkle in the sun. 'Maybe I'm wrong,' he tells himself. 'Please, let me be wrong.'

 Aboard the *Mail Ship Celt*

As the *Celt* nears the West Coast, the steamer pitches alarmingly. James hangs onto the deck rail, hoping for a first sighting of land. His foot slips; the lashing waves have greased the boards with foam. He looks down at the swirling sea, trying to protect his face from the wind, and when he looks up, his eyes are blinded by spray.

'Get below!' The shout is from Captain Riley, dressed in an oilskin and sou'wester, so that he is indistinguishable from one of the crew. The captain uncoils a rope, and passes it to one of the men, who works swiftly to secure the dinghy. He waves an arm. 'Go back under. I can't be answerable for your safety.'

James feels that he has been scolded like a schoolboy. He makes his way across the treacherous deck, and descends the narrow ladder. At first, he thinks that his cabin door is jammed but it flies open suddenly as the ship rights itself with a jolt. He picks up Pope's *Essays*, but when he lies on his bed, the sea-sawing motion makes it impossible to concentrate on the rules of poetry. He tries to make himself more comfortable, but the bed is little more than a shelf on top of a cupboard — the dimensions are two foot by five foot eight, and James is six foot two. He gets a notebook out of his box, and begins to plan the next day's sermon. On each day of the voyage, barring two occasions when he was ill, he has held a service for the sailors and passengers. These services have been poorly attended, and sometimes mocked, but James has persevered; if he is to be successful as a missionary, he must not be deterred, however stony the ground.

The lack of air in the cramped cabin, coupled with all the rolling and tipping, is making him nauseous. He rejects a theme of suffering — based on a verse from Lamentations — in favour of something more uplifting. He settles on Psalm 97: *Sing to the Lord a new song, because he has done marvellous things.* As the ship gives another huge lurch, James puts down his pencil, lies back, and shuts his eyes. Again, the ship lifts violently. James is beginning to reflect that if the *Celt* does succeed in making it safely through the bucketing waves, the Good Lord — aided by Captain Riley — will indeed have achieved something truly marvellous, when he is interrupted by an urgent knocking.

He opens the door in his stockinged feet to find a breathless Lily-May. She is the young servant of Mrs Sidders, another of the paying passengers.

'It's Mrs Livingstone!' Lily-May cries, twisting her apron in her hands. 'Come quick! She's screaming something dreadful!'

'Give me one minute,' says James, tying his bootlaces, then putting on his jacket. 'I'll bring some medicine.'

As he makes his way to the women's quarters, James tries to quell his irritation. During the six-week voyage, he has often been called upon to attend to Mary, and he is all-too aware that his frequent visits to her cabin have gone neither unnoticed, nor unremarked. On one occasion — after they had spent a whole afternoon together — Bates, the First Officer, had taken him aside and advised him that while he, Bates, knew that there was absolutely no impropriety involved, it was only right that James should realise that the womenfolk 'could not be prevented from wagging their tongues.' Going past the ship's galley, James puts out a hand to steady himself. He very much wishes that he could agree that nothing improper had ever taken place on the voyage. But Mary has a way with her — she knows how to gain his sympathy, and once — when the ship neared Madeira — she had succeeded in bending him to her will... and there was another time off the coast of Upper Guinea... it was just as it had been in the Thistle hotel. James grows hot with shame — and worse — with the thrill of remembered pleasure. The only way he can cope is by disassociation. He conducts himself as if the man who from time to time shares Mary's bed, is altogether a different person. He cannot be honest, even to himself — every night, he keeps a meticulous journal, but on the occasions when he and Mary have been lovers, he writes in the diary nothing at all, except the two words *dies non*. He tries to eradicate the entire day, with a simple stroke of the pen.

Mary, when he finds her, is crying hysterically. She has left her cabin window partially open and through her tears, she points wordlessly to her second day dress, which is soaking wet.

'It doesn't matter,' says James, feeling the cloth. 'It'll soon dry out. I think we're all feeling overwrought because of the way the boat's been shifting. But the weather seems to be improving.' It is true; the wind has lessened, and the *Celt* no longer heaves as she did.

'I don't care about the dress!' Mary shrieks. 'Of course I don't! It's just that everything — *everything* is wrong!'

'Hush,' says James. 'Shhhh!' And then, because he knows how much Mary craves the reassurance of physical contact, and also because it seems the natural thing to do, he takes her hand. Mary rests her head against his chest.

'Do you want some laudanum?' James asks. 'I have some, here.'

Mary leans more heavily against him. 'No I just want...' The tears begin anew. 'I just want — *I do so much want my children!*' She is convulsed with grief.

James has heard this refrain many times before. Usually, he responds with sympathy to Mary's distress, but today his seasickness leads him to be less tolerant. Mary is so knowledgeable, she can teach him so much, and there is no doubting that the name of Livingstone can open doors, but as they near their destination and are set to reach Cape Town together, he cannot but think how much simpler it would be, and how much better he would feel, were he to be arriving on his own.

'Sometimes in life, we are forced to make difficult choices,' he says, sanctimoniously. 'You felt it was right to join your husband, and that decision will reap its own reward.' He can hear the insincerity in his own voice, and dislikes himself for it.

'What of Robert, Agnes, Oswell and Tom? And I do so long to hold little Anna in my arms! How will she manage without me?'

James struggles not to sound irritated. In his own view, it is the boys who will suffer most from their mother's departure. Poor troubled Robert — who will keep him from the taverns, to which he seems irresistibly drawn? And what of Tom, who dreads the rough and tumble of public school? 'Agnes will look after Anna,' he says, shortly.

That evening, there is a strange atmosphere on board. Although everyone is glad that the journey is nearly over, the passengers experience a kind of wistfulness; they have grown accustomed to one another and to the ship's routine.

'Tell me,' says Mrs Sidders, when they assemble at the Captain's table for dinner. 'What do your family feel about your intention to join the Livingstone Expedition? Are they encouraging,' she smiles in a genial way, 'or do they perhaps think you rather hot-headed?'

James is in the process of eating a mouthful of braised mutton and boiled potato. He swallows, and pauses before replying. Ridiculously, he feels embarrassed. 'There are few left in my family, who might show concern.'

'No?' says Mrs Sidders.

'My father died of consumption, and my stepmother too. Two of my brothers now run the family firm. But my youngest brother, William, was never strong. As an infant he suffered the summer plague, with a resulting weakness.' James tries not to betray how very much alone he feels. He had held his devout father in great respect, he had revered his loving stepmother, he had rejoiced in the companionship of his cheerful, younger brother. For years when they were children he had carried the paralysed William to school, lifting him onto his back, playing the same familiar game every day — he, James, would act the willing work horse and William his omnipotent rider. He continues in a small voice, 'William died of a poisoned thorn.' Suddenly he wants to weep. He is homesick for his childhood, and for Scotland. Now that his adventure is about to truly begin, he feels woefully inadequate. A snake-like whisper reminds him that he is also a carnal sinner.

James is rescued by Captain Riley, who remarks that although it is a sadness to be without family, he can vouch from his own experience that the absence of dear-ones can make it easier for a man to face the dangers that shipboard life can sometimes bring. He proceeds to recount a tale of derring-do: earlier in the year — before he had been lucky enough to obtain his present position — he, Riley, had been employed to deliver a full-rigged screw steamer to the Unionists across the Atlantic. The ship was commandeered by a wild rabble of Confederates, and he had to run a man through with a cutlass before jumping into the sea and swimming to a small outcrop of rocks. There he remained for a week, living on shellfish and drinking rain water, until he was saved by a tea-clipper running the blockade with a cargo of cotton.

A general discussion ensues about the American War: the toll in bloodshed it has taken, and the comparative wealth of the Southern States, the character of Abraham Lincoln — whether he is sufficiently canny as a president, and his rightmindedness in opposing the expansion of slavery. There is talk of whether or not Britain should do more to help Lincoln, followed by exclamations of satisfaction that the British have led the world in the campaign for emancipation. When Bates proposes a toast to Parliament, for having had the foresight to bring in the Slavery Abolition Act, thirty years before, the group raise their glasses. Mary has remained silent for much of the conversation, but now she proposes another toast, this time to William Wilberforce. 'To Wilberforce!' the Captain, First Officer, Second Officer and paying passengers, all voice together. Mary suggests a third toast, this time to acknowledge God's mercy in allowing Wilberforce to extend his life long enough for him to learn that the Act for which he had so long campaigned had finally been passed. The Captain recalls how his father had occasion to meet with Wilberforce, not for any political purpose, but in order to deliver a box of pineapples to the campaigner's family home.

It is time to retire. Good nights are said, hands shaken, then James descends to his cabin. He says his prayers and hoists himself into bed. He folds his long limbs to fit into the too-short space. He moves his head carefully lest it collide with the ceiling. He torments himself by thinking that after all his efforts — the studying, lobbying and fund-raising — he has cuckolded David Livingstone, and has spent more than forty days in continuous motion, but he has achieved little else. James wonders if the letter of introduction he has sent to Livingstone has ever been received. James thinks about Mary. He wishes — yet does not wish — that his relationship with her were not so close. Mary herself seems completely untroubled by their liaison. Somehow, she manages to imply that while she likes him, James, very much — and would be only too happy to bed him more often — her heart remains with David, and her conscience is therefore crystal clear. Eventually, James falls into an uneasy sleep. He dreams of fermented pineapple juice, frothing high in an enamelled glass.

In the morning, James is the first passenger to be up on deck. Ahead of him, he can see Table Mountain; it resembles not so much a table, more a great granite wall. He feels this should be a red letter day but mixed with excitement, there is within him a kind of lethargy engendered by the monotony of the voyage. Each day has followed the same routine of prayer, meals, conversing with Mary and reading books. He has consumed French and English literature, he has amassed facts on theology and travel and he has studied the self-supporting missions of the Moravian Church.

Land draws closer. James has his back knocked by a midshipman, hurrying to hurl a rope to land. There is a shudder as the *Celt* bumps into the wall of the wharf. James anticipates an announcement from the Captain, followed by an orderly disembarkation. However, as soon as the ship has docked, a crowd of people assembled on the jetty begin pushing themselves over the bridging planks and onto the deck. James's foot is trampled by someone with a hand cart, piled high with melons. Boys offer to bear parcels and packages, pigtailed Chinese offer pomegranates, paper sellers wave their broadsheets and bellow out news of the latest hangings. James looks in amazement at the different types of humanity represented and realises how limited his experiences have been. There are white men, black men, brown men and men who are a mixture of races. He casts around for Mary. Somehow, she has already found her way ashore and is chatting animatedly in the centre of a group of women. James catches her eye, lifts his hat and nods to indicate his independence.

Mary is going to stay with missionary friends but James has no-one to whom he can turn for hospitality. He takes a cab to the Rathfelder, recommended to him by Captain Riley, who says the hotel is situated in the healthiest part of the town. Friends have told James that he will not survive the hardships of Africa, and on the whole he would prefer to prove them wrong.

The Rathfelder is owned by a short, barrel-chested man called Thomas Krebs. Krebs is originally from Germany, but Cape Town has been his home for over twenty years, and he seems to know all there is to know about the city. 'You'll have to be an accurate shot, if you're going into the interior,' he tells James, as he serves him a supper of spiced minced beef with a strange kind of custard on top. You'll have to kill your own game — there won't be anyone else to do it. I'd book yourself some sessions at the firing range. And the Botanic Gardens are worth exploring. They've been established for a long time — they began as a vegetable patch for the East India Company. The man who keeps the library is very knowledgeable, if you want to learn about the plant life here.'

James, having followed Krebs' suggestion, sits in the Company gardens and watches a squirrel nibble a nut, holding it in its two front paws. The little animal is fearless — it darts near his feet, looking as if it would be entirely at home in an Edinburgh park, except that it is a cinnamon colour instead of red and it has a white stripe on either side. The rose beds look similarly British, except for the border at the back, which sprouts tall cacti and exotic ferns.

The library is housed in a square white building with a tiled roof. James knocks, and the door is opened by an elderly man, who wears an orchid pinned to his lapel. The pink-spotted petals contrast exotically with the grey of his jacket.

'You're admiring my buttonhole,' the old man says. *Corycium dracomontana*. I wear something different every day. Our flora is rich — we have much to enjoy.'

They shake hands, as James introduces himself. 'You're not the James Stewart who wrote this, are you?' The librarian goes to a shelf and, after a short search, produces a slim, leather-bound volume.

James is astonished. The book is a guide to botany, which he wrote while a student. A friend called Reynolds said it should not be wasted and had arranged to have it printed and circulated by his father's firm. James had taken a copy with him, when he was seeking to become Tom's tutor. He had wanted to demonstrate to Mary that he was more than just a man of the cloth. Well. He had achieved that, though not through the means of a slim volume on botany.

He takes the book, looks for but fails to find an inscription. 'How did it come to be here?'

'Someone must have donated it, and we are pleased to possess it. The descriptions are accurate, the language concise and the illustrations well-executed.'

James spends the next two days visiting the hospital, arranging to preach at a couple of local churches and improving his skill with a rifle. After an absorbing afternoon at the shooting range, he returns to the Rathfelder and goes to ask for his key. He finds Krebs in the hotel bar, filling a decanter with wine.

'You've had a visitor,' Krebs says, giving James an odd

look. Mrs Livingstone was here. I recognised her straight away, from her picture in the newspaper. She tells me that you are awaiting the arrival of some more missionaries – and you will all sail together to Durban, then onwards, to the Zambesi.' Krebs looks as if he is about to say something more, then stays silent.

But in the evening after dinner, James is reading a newspaper when Krebs says to him, 'I would like to speak with you "man to man", I think that it is the expression.' The hotelier goes over to the bar and returns with two tots of whisky. He pushes one of the glasses towards James. 'I do not wish you to take offence – please believe me, when I say this. But I must speak out, to protect the reputation of my hotel. The community here is small, and there are people who enjoy nothing better than to talk. Mrs Livingstone came here alone – she has a strangely free way of conducting herself. She said you have been "very bad" not to have come to see her. Her manner is not what you would expect of a missionary wife. Mr Stewart, I am sure you are an honourable man, and I value your custom, but I must ask you to give my word that you will not receive Mrs Livingstone in your room, without a chaperone.'

'You have my word. Such behaviour would be entirely inappropriate.' The whisky burns James's throat. He coughs, reaches for a handkerchief and is glad to cover his face.

He takes himself outside, and studies the configuration of the stars. It is embarrassing and humiliating that Krebs should feel it necessary to tell him how to behave. What is far worse, thinks James, is that in denying his relationship with Mary, he is no better than a common liar. Fixing his eye on the Southern Cross, he wonders how ever he has succeeded in getting himself in such a mess. He toys with the idea of abandoning the expedition and all his dreams, and going home, at the first opportunity. But what explanation would he give? He would like to confess all, to come clean, especially to Livingstone, but even on a practical level, such a confession would be impossible. He would have to write a letter to the explorer, and ask Mary to deliver it. And what purpose would it serve, to come between a man and his wife? More pertinently, what is the small matter of his own conscience, set against the vast amounts of good that the Scheme has the potential to achieve?

James sleeps uneasily, until just before dawn. There is a sour smell in the room — it seems to come from the furniture, which is hewn from unseasoned stinkwood. He gives up and reads a Sechwana grammar, prepared by Mary's father, Robert Moffat. He falls back to sleep with the book in his hand. He is late for breakfast, and when he does get downstairs, he finds that on the mahogany side table, the coddled eggs have grown cold.

'I'll tell the cook to make you some fresh,' says Krebs.

'Please, do not take the trouble,' says James, waving him away, whilst thinking wistfully of omelettes.

Anxious to avoid Krebs, he quickly finishes eating and goes back up to his room. He has arranged to volunteer in the hospital dispensary, and is putting his notebooks and stethoscope into a leather satchel, when he is interrupted by a brisk knocking. He opens the door to find a boy standing in front of him, wearing a well-pressed pair of white linen trousers. The boy gives a kind of military salute, and says, 'Sah! There is a man here! He wishes to see you!'

The man turns out to be a Portuguese trader, called Jose Diabilo. James observes that the trader has allowed the nail of the little finger of his right hand to grow enormously long, so that it curls like a coiled whip. James has seen in the town that some of the Portuguese adopt this foolish affectation. It is a way for a man to indicate that he is of sufficient status not to do any manual work.

'I hear that you pretend to be a missionary,' Diabilo says,

tapping his twisted nail on the stinkwood table, 'but your real intention is to trade. I must warn you. Don't try taking over any of our routes — if you do, you will suffer the consequences.'

James is at first too angry to speak. He very much desires to punch Diabilo in his smooth-fleshed face. He contains himself enough to ask, 'And why do you think this is the case? What evidence do you have?'

'I have heard that you have brought many boxes of beads, which you intend to exchange for ivory, and for West African gold.'

James picks up the one small box of beads that he does possess, and flings it at the wall, narrowly missing Diabilo's head. A dozen small beads skitter across the floor.

'This is my fabled wealth!' he shouts, 'now get out of here, before I really lose my temper!'

He is still seething, as he goes down to the lobby. He is turning away from the counter, having handed over his key, when from behind him, he hears a familiar voice.

'Cooee! I'm glad to have caught you! You've been so naughty, keeping away, but I forgive you. It's too nice a day — we must make the most of it!'

James does not at first acknowledge Mary. He cannot formulate the necessary words; he feels ready to explode with frustration, so that his tongue sticks to the roof of his mouth. Eventually he shakes his head and says curtly: 'I'm on my way to the hospital.' He cannot bring himself to be polite. He feels that Mary's easy conduct will prove to be his undoing, and that somehow, their too-close friendship has contributed to the rumour that he is a profiteer, masquerading as a religious man.

But Mary appears oblivious to his discomfiture. Serenely, she prattles on; 'I've borrowed a pony and trap, and have a picnic, all made up. I've brought a nice bottle of wine to drink. We'll call into the hospital, and tell them you're not coming. It'll be lovely! We can go — just the two of us — to the seaside!'

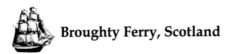 **Broughty Ferry, Scotland**

Mina and Maggie are seated in the schoolroom, making presents for the church bazaar. Mina is embroidering a pincushion for a Christening gift, under the supervision of Miss Scrope, who has suggested that she use carefully placed steel pins to form the words 'Welcome little stranger,' in the centre, before creating a border of appliqué daisies, with a beaded fringe.

Mina looks across to where Maggie is painting a paper fan using a set of watercolours passed onto her by Helen. Maggie has drawn a riverside scene with fluttering swans and a weeping willow, and is now mixing blue and yellow to make leaf green. Her sister is good at art; Mina would love to share the gift of such effortless skill. She stops herself from envy by thinking of Maggie's tears of frustration during their last piano lesson. When it was her own turn to play the piece, she did so without fault, so that Monsieur Legart stood back, clapped his hands and said 'Bravo!' Mina had not been sure how best to respond — she wondered at first if the teacher was being sincere. Monsieur Legart is a new person in their lives, recently arrived from Paris. As he frequently reminds the girls, he has known more prosperous circumstances.

She shifts her chair nearer the window, where there is more light. The pins have to be placed just so otherwise the look of the thing is spoiled, and once they are positioned, the background must be filled with a complex pattern of tiny stitches. Mina is not at all sure that anyone will want to buy her offering, however conscientiously she has worked upon it. 'Welcome little stranger' seems so impersonal. Hesitantly, she has suggested to Miss Scrope that the pincushion might be improved with some different wording, such as 'Blessings upon you, sweetest babe', but the governess has frowned, and has said that such a phrase would be over-familiar, and therefore quite improper.

Mina would have liked to have opened a discussion on the subject of propriety. She would like to know why the birth of a baby, which is such a commonplace happening, should be surrounded by so much mystery. She would like to ask why women's health in general should be shrouded in a mist of silence. She thinks, as she forms her second letter t, that it can sometimes profit a woman to have a private illness that is vague and ill-defined. Mama has a pink-cheeked friend who, on the basis that she is permanently unwell, lies in bed until midday. She studies the lives of the great composers, then gets up to eat a hearty meal, before being visited every afternoon by a young musician, who plays tender melodies on his violin, whilst singing sweet songs of love and longing. Her poor husband is banished to another part of the house, and receives a lashing from his wife's sharp tongue if he dares to enquire how long it will be necessary for these arrangements to continue before the desired cure can be achieved.

But mama's pink-cheeked friend is an exception. More often, women are disadvantaged by the fog of secrecy that descends, wherever matters of their physical wellbeing are concerned. Mina is glad that she has older sisters. When she had her first monthly visitation, she was thoroughly alarmed. In terror, she had sought advice from Miss Scrope, but the governess had been no help at all. She had flushed with embarrassment, muttered something about all women being cursed, and had told Mina that she must on no account wash her hair, before finding an excuse to leave the room. It was Helen who took Mina to the special cupboard in the laundry room, showed her where the linen rags were kept, and told her what to do.

Maggie has spread out her finished fan and is working on the next one, with an illustration of ribbons and roses. A smile lifts her lips, as she tucks some stray strands of hair behind her ear. She is clearly enjoying her work, but Mina suspects that there is an added cause for her sister's happiness. At the Diocesan picnic the week before, the young Mudies had been present. It had been clear to everyone, except perhaps to the couple themselves, that Robert had eyes only for Maggie, and that she, in return, had eyes only for him. Mina likes Robert, and can imagine that Maggie could, one day, be very happy as the younger Mrs Mudie. Mina hopes that if and when her own turn comes to find a partner, she will have the sense to choose wisely. She thinks of Janet who wanted to marry the haberdasher's son, and who has, as a result, become the object of Papa's continuing ridicule. Poor Janet — in wanting to break with convention and seeking to follow her heart, she had been admirable. Her sorrow was that John Beattie had proved to be a vessel unworthy of her devotion. The precious nectar of her love had been tasted then carelessly tipped out, as if it were so much rancid wine.

Mina continues working with her pins. She has completed the first rounded curve of the letter s, when Mama appears in the doorway. Elspeth Stephen rarely visits the schoolroom, and her unexpected presence causes Miss Scrope to become quite agitated. She gets to her feet, hastily pushing back her chair. The chair's legs scrape along the floor, making a sharp squeak. Mama frowns at the sound — her ears are sensitive and her nerves troublesome. Recently, she has spent increasing amounts of time resting on the chaise longue in the drawing room, and she has cut down on the number of calls that she makes. Moira says that Mama is entitled to rest, given her age, and the large number of fine children that she has brought into the world.

Mama does not interest herself in the girls' handiwork . She gives but the briefest nod to acknowledge her daughters. Directly, she addresses Miss Scrope, 'I would be obliged,' she says, 'if you would take supper with the family tonight, before returning to your lodgings. A cousin of Mr Stephen's will be

161

coming to eat with us — a retired clergyman. His mind wanders, as a result of a brainstorm he has suffered. I know that your father was a clergyman — I thought you could converse with our guest — and smooth out any difficulties that might arise.'

Mina expects the governess to quickly acquiesce. Instead, she stands upright with her hands firmly interlaced and says, 'It is kind of you to think of me, Mrs Stephen, but with regret, I must decline your offer. You see, I have a prior engagement.'

'A prior engagement! Why, whatever could that be?' Mama peers closely at the other woman. 'You do not have a suitor do you? If so, I must consider your position.'

Miss Scrope reddens. It is ridiculous of Mama to imagine that she could have an admirer — she is simply not that sort of a person. Mina cannot tell if her tutor is angry, embarrassed or both. 'I was employed as a single woman, and I do not foresee that my status will change. I am not wishing to cultivate any unsuitable friendships, nor do I wish to spend my time in a frivolous manner. No. I simply wish to attend a meeting.'

'Of the church?'

'No. I wish to attend a meeting of the Emancipation Society. I have been invited by Mrs Salmon to join the membership, and I have said that I shall be pleased to do so.'

It is Mama's turn to redden. She is firmly of the belief that a woman's place is in the home, and is much opposed to women doing anything that smacks of the political. She has stressed to all her daughters that there can be no higher achievement than the running of an efficient household. A month before, when she found Hannah reading the works of Mary Wollstonecraft, she had furiously tossed the book into the library fire.

'Don't you think that kind of thing is best left to the gentlemen?' Mama's words are polite, but her tone is sharp.

'I believe that there can be nothing of more importance than the alleviation of a fellow man's suffering, and I wish to play my part.'

Dear brave Miss Scrope! Mina would like to applaud her courage out loud. She knows how much the governess risks, in standing up to Mama. If she loses her position, she will be forced to live in penury, for Miss Scrope's father has left her with nothing but his little portrait. Any money that remained after the funeral expenses, went to an elder brother, who with his wife and seven children, promptly left Scotland, to start again in Canada.

Mama is clearly annoyed — she is holding onto the back of a chair, and her hand is tightly clenched so that the whites of her knuckles show. Mina wonders why she does not feel more sympathy — but then, Mama is clearly in the wrong. Also, she and Elspeth never have been close. Perhaps it is understandable that in giving birth so many times, her mother grew tired of creating new life, so that by the time that she — the youngest — was born, the wellspring of maternal love had slowed from a fountain to a trickle. But, Mina thinks as she lowers her head and pretends to get on with her pin work, if ever she has children of her own, she will love them all equally and she will tell them often how very much beloved they are.

There is a long silence, then Mama gives a loud sniff. 'Very well,' she says. 'I see that you are not to be persuaded. I trust that next time I make a request, you will find it in your capability to be more accommodating.' She sweeps from the room. Despite Elspeth's regal manner, there can be no doubting that Miss Scrope has triumphed.

The governess stands erect. She looks across to a printed map of the world, which hangs on the wall opposite. Her eyes rove from the Americas to Asia, flicking over Europe in between. 'Enough girls! Enough craft work for today! Let us re-order our timetable, so we can enjoy the sunshine. We will take the main road, then walk along the lane. Although the season is past its best, there are still wild flowers we can collect, to add to your nature notes.' She claps together her hands. 'Come on! Tidy away your things. Fetch your hats and shawls, and put on your walking shoes. We will meet in ten minutes, outside the main front door.'

There is a spring in Miss Scrope's step, as she sets off with her charges. In an unusual display of camaraderie, she links arms with the girls. Maggie looks a little sullen. Mina thinks that her sister is longing for the day when she is free of the schoolroom, and would in the meantime prefer not to be so closely associated with her governess. But Mina walks in time with Miss Scrope, enjoying and sharing her teacher's rare high spirits. She would like to talk about the Emancipation Society. What, exactly, are its aims, and what do its members actually do? But she refrains from asking — her interest would displease Mama, and would further compromise the governess.

An emerald-necked pheasant appears suddenly from the undergrowth, and flies chirrucking into the sky. Already, there are glistening blackberries in the hedgerows. The sun is warm, but not hot — the full heat of summer has passed. There is a gentle mellowness to the afternoon, which adds to the pleasure of the unexpected outing.

'Oh look!' Miss Scrope breaks free and scuttles forward to collect a tall stem, with serrated leaves. 'Wild angelica!' She hands the plant to Maggie. 'You can press this, and add it to your book. A marvellous herb. According to legend, its virtues were revealed by an angel to a monk during a terrible plague. Hence the name.'

The milk cart rumbles by. Jim the carter lifts his hat as he passes, and Mina waves in response. The cart is followed by a swift-moving Hansom cab. The driver wields a whip and sounds a horn; the girls and their governess scramble out of the way and onto the verge. Mina turns to watch, as the cab continues at the same fast pace, forcing Jim to steer his dray into the side of the road. She sees the cab's seated occupant look back at her, out of the window, and cries out in surprise.

'That was Andrew! Whatever is he doing here?'

Maggie shakes her head. 'It can't have been him,' she says, practically. 'The only reason he would be in Broughty would be to come to Corona, and he knows he's not welcome at the house. It must have been someone else.'

'You're right, I suppose' says Mina, 'Andrew is in London.' She is not altogether convinced. There had been something very familiar about the traveller. She wonders if she had maybe seen one of her other brothers, William, perhaps, come to see father about a ship, or John, wanting to discuss the yard at Kelvinhaugh.

They turn off the road and into the green lane, where the girls pick posies of mixed grasses and flowers.

'This one's wormwood,' says Miss Scrope, fingering a yellow flower head. 'The leaves are bitter, but a tincture can be made that is healing to the digestion. Take heed; sometimes those experiences which are most unpleasant to us, can prove in the long term, to be the most beneficial.'

Beside the lane, a farmer and his three sons are cutting hay, moving their scythes in rhythmic wide sweeps.

'Look!' says Miss Scrope. 'One, two, three, four — four peacocks and a red admiral!'

The girls stop to admire the butterflies, as the insects settle on a hawthorn bush, close their wings, then once more take flight. The sun casts a warm glow over the field, and lights a white check cloth, that covers a wicker basket. Under the yellowing leaves of an oak tree, twelve empty beer bottles are neatly stacked.

Miss Scrope eyes the bottles. 'Harvesting is — I am sure — the kind of work that engenders a considerable thirst. We will not begrudge the men folk their drink. But I think that we, too, deserve refreshment. We will go back — we should not be late for afternoon tea.'

As Mina walks up to the front door, she pinches her thumb and forefinger. She can hear Papa shouting — the words travel out from the window of his open study, which is next to the drawing room, on the upper floor.

It is not unusual for Papa to shout — he often raises his voice at Janet and the servants — but now he is shouting like a man possessed, using words that Mina has never heard. 'You screeving blaggard! Get out of here, or I'll have you slammed in the saltbox!'

There is a thud, followed by a shout. 'There are medical men who can provide treatments for such perversions as you are gripped by!' Mina recognises Andrew's voice — so it was him, after all. Whatever can he mean by such strange words? There is another thud and a crash, followed by the sound of splintering glass.

The girls look to Miss Scrope, seeking guidance. Mina expects that the governess will suggest they retreat back down the front path, to continue with their nature study. But Miss Scrope thinks differently; she holds open the door, and indicates to the girls that they should come inside. Her face is expressionless; she adopts the pretence that nothing untoward is taking place. Nervously, the girls step over the threshold. Mina removes her hat and shawl, and tries to shut her ears, but now the whole house is alert to the commotion. Parsons the butler coming from the dining room nearly collides with Neil the footman as he rushes from the servants' quarters. Both men hurtle up the staircase, and are nearly at the top when Andrew comes out onto the landing, looking dishevelled, and clutching a bloody nose.

He puts his free hand up into the air. 'Enough! There is no need for you to eject me from what is — after all — my own home. I am leaving of my own volition.' He starts to make his way down the stairs, when Neil seizes him by the collar.

'Where shall I take him?' the footman calls to Parsons, while Andrew struggles to break free. 'Should we call the police?'

Parsons is banging on the study door. 'Sir! Mr Stephen! Are you all right?'

The door flies open, nearly knocking the butler off his feet. 'Of course I'm all right!' Papa strides onto the landing, red in the face, and with the sleeve of his coat hanging off, but otherwise unharmed. He gesticulates towards the footman, who now has his arm braced against Andrew's neck. 'Let him go, will you! The begging muck snipe! Get him out of here!'

Released, Andrew makes his way downstairs. His nose drips blood; there is a stain on the front of his white shirt. He holds onto the banister for support.

But in the hallway, he turns back and looks straight up at Papa. 'Father', he says, 'You know as well as I, you may have swindled me of my inheritance, but I did not come here to beg. I want only to help you. If you change your mind…'

He gets no further. Papa is hurtling down the stairs: he charges like an angry bull.

Andrew does not wait. 'Goodbye, sweet sisters!' He touches Maggie lightly on the arm, then presses Mina's hand. 'You are both very dear to me.'

The front door closes, and Andrew is gone.

CHAPTER SIX

January 1862

 Royal Asylum, Dundee, Scotland

Over four months have passed since the ball, and Chrissy is still haunted by the image of Deborah, as she collapsed and died in the thin man's arms. She thinks often of her friend's final words, and hopes very much that in Deborah's last moments, her happiness was sustained by the belief that her husband had come — at last — to take her home. She hopes that Deborah is with Jesus, and is enjoying not only His love, but the love of people who were dear to her, such as her mother, who had died the month before she was admitted, and a beloved sister, who was carried up to heaven when Deborah was still a child.

The funeral service took place not in the asylum chapel, but in the Steeple Church. Chrissy was not invited to the ceremony — nor were any of the inmates. Mr Connor went, of course, and so did Mrs Horrocks. Chrissy heard the attendant tell her son that the service had been a fine affair. A long procession of pallbearers, feathermen and mutes had accompanied the hearse to the church, and a large choir had led the singing. The coffin had been heaped with an elaborate arrangement of white lilies which contrasted with the forest of black ostrich feathers that was on display. Chrissy cannot help reflecting how much Deborah would have enjoyed the show.

She misses her friend very much, especially as she had confided to her about Andrew, and there is no one else in the asylum with whom she has shared such intimacy. It is as if with Deborah's passing, a part of herself has also been lost.

Christmas at the asylum had passed miserably. The dining hall was decorated with branches of holly and — thanks to the beneficence of the Duke — the inmates sat down to a proper meal of roast goose followed by plum pudding. But throughout the festivities, Chrissy had felt separate and very much alone. She had been seated next to Jane (who had been deliberately separated from Betty, to stop the two women from whispering to one another and stroking each other's hair). Jane had done her best; she had tried to make conversation, but she had asked odd questions, such as 'What colour is your favourite watering can?' and 'Can a daisy be a bridesmaid?' Chrissy had been perplexed as to how best to respond, and when she did not immediately answer, poor Jane had burst into tears.

After the ball, Chrissy was not made to return to the tedium of bead-counting. Her skills at costume design and deftness with the needle had impressed Mr Connor, who judged her to be to be an intelligent and reliable worker. He wanted Chrissy transferred to the mending room, but was told there were no vacancies, so he approached the manageress of the laundry, who found work for her there. Now Chrissy's days are both purposeful and exhausting. At night, she is blessed with oblivion for hours at a time. In sleep, she can escape from her loneliness, her grief at Deborah's passing and the physical ache that she still feels for her infant son. Never, in her waking hours, does she forget Thomas. She remembers the beauty of his sweet face, and the perfection of his soft hands; her recollection has a vividness that is almost terrible in its clarity.

She distracts herself by applying herself zealously to any task that she is given. When it is her turn to use the dolly, she plunges and pounds it until the foam flies, and when asked to clean the wringer, she rubs it until the drum shines bright as a new shilling piece. She becomes an expert in the management of stains. When she applies lemon juice to ink, and turpentine to grease, she does so with such efficacy that she is told she will soon be able to make soot disappear from snow.

The manageress is called Mrs MacAleavy. She has a round face, and a complexion that shines clear from exposure to constant steam. She is basically good-hearted, but is subject to wild changes of mood. One minute, she can be heard cheerfully singing hymns while she sorts out the linen. The next moment, she can be seen to plunge her face into her white apron and weep copiously at the memory of some slight or hurt inflicted on herself or on someone that she cares about. She is particularly sensitive to any insults directed towards Chicago, her pet mastiff. Chicago is a free spirit, and in consequence, he constantly gets into scrapes; the manageress worries that that there are people in the town who would put a permanent end to the dog's adventures. As a result of the manageress's mood swings, a tension constantly bubbles in the laundry, alongside the cauldrons of hot suds. Sometimes Chrissy cannot help reflecting how odd it is that Mrs MacAleavy should be in a position of authority, employed on a salary, and should be free to come and go, when all the time her behaviour is so much more variable than the rest of the workers who have been deprived of their liberty, having been categorised as mad.

But no-one can accuse MacAleavy of not working hard.

Every morning, she is at her post by five o'clock, ready to supervise the fetching of the coal and the stoking of the fires that heat the coppers. On some days, she brings Chicago with her on a length of rope, or rather he brings her, for he pulls and strains on the leash, forcing her to quicken her step. The dog spends his time tied up in the drying yard, barking and whining, and trying to bite the workers, as they peg out the sheets. If they come too close, he succeeds. Chrissy has recently had to comfort a girl called Sylvia, who received a nasty nip on her calf. No-one reported the incident — no-one wanted to cause trouble.

* * *

The weather outside is bleak, and the asylum dormitory is chillingly cold. Chrissy arises as soon as the bell sounds, and gets dressed quickly, so as to spend as little time as possible shivering in her gown. The ice has to be broken in the basins that are lined up on trestles outside the latrines, and the wind whistles — sharp as razor — through the long tiled corridors as she makes her way to work. In contrast, the steaming laundry is welcomingly warm, and next to it is the ironing room, made hot by the large range that fills one wall.

The inmates' bedding is changed fortnightly. Cleanliness is next to Godliness, Mr Connor says. Chrissy remembers the filth of the padded cell where Deborah spent her last days; she thinks it is a pity this motto is not more consistently applied.

Chrissy puts on her heavy sailcloth apron, shuts her eyes and says a little prayer, asking for God's assistance in her tasks. Given the large numbers of inmates, there is an enormous amount of washing to be done. Chrissy begins the heavy work of lifting and rinsing the score of sheets that she has left soaking in a trough overnight. When the rinsing is done, she fetches a bar of Hudson's soap, shaves it into flakes, tips the

171

flakes into a tub of hot water and swills them round until they have melted to a jelly. She lifts each sheet, and rubs the entire surface with the jelly mixture, painstakingly inspecting every inch of fabric, looking for undetected stains. She frowns at a particular spot: a blob of candle wax will require the application of a hot piece of coal, wrapped in a paper twist.

'Chrissy Hogarth! Please cease your work! Mr Connor is here to see you!'

Chrissy gets to her feet and is in the process of curtseying to the director, when Mrs MacAleavy shoves at her with her elbow. 'Take off your apron,' she hisses. 'It is soaking wet!' Chrissy dutifully removes the offending garment.

'I would be grateful, Miss Hogarth, if you would accompany me to my office.' Chrissy is not sure what to make of this. She wonders if she is about to be accused of something, but Mr Connor's tone is polite, and almost friendly. She fights to remain calm; she fears being removed from the laundry.

They go to the main part of the building, where the director's office can be found, near to the main entrance. The front door has been left open, a capped delivery boy goes backwards and forwards carrying crates of cabbages, which sparkle with frost. Chrissy catches a tantalising glimpse of people going about their ordinary business in the open street.

'Take a seat,' says Mr Connor, and Chrissy sits herself down on a little button-back chair. She looks around the room; a fire burns brightly in the grate; she sees an aspidistra in a pot, velvet curtains and a daguerreotype of a woman and child above the mantelpiece. 'I have brought you here,' the director continues, 'because I have had good reports of your industry and, if possible, I would like to help you move on from our care. Our dormitories are ever more crowded and every day we are having to turn away cases — some of whom are in desperate need. There is a laundry locally, where I believe you could obtain employment. But before I can recommend your release, I understand from Mrs Biggins and Mrs Horrocks that you persist in a strange delusion.'

He eyes Chrissy severely, and she bites her lip.

'Miss Hogarth,' the director continues, 'the circumstances of your admission were these: You were found in the village of Constan, at St Dunstan's Church, carrying a dead infant. Subsequently, it was established that the child died of natural causes. However, you maintained you had no knowledge of who the father might be. Is this still the case?'

'Indeed, sir, it is.'

'You are not covering up for someone — trying to protect some married man?'

'No!' Chrissy shakes her head. She thinks of her perfect son, whom anyone would have been proud to acknowledge as their own. 'I am not. It is wrong of you to say such a thing.'

'So you still maintain that the child you bore was the result of an immaculate conception. Do you not realise that this is not only nonsense, but also a kind of blasphemy?'

Chrissy fights back her tears. She has nothing on which to blow her nose, and will not use her sleeve.

'Miss Hogarth, please believe me, when I say I wish to help you.' The director sighs. 'I have had good reports of your conduct, and I have seen for myself the results of your industry. It would be a shame for you to be detained here unnecessarily. There is a mesmerist — a Dr Cunliffe — who has offered his services to the asylum. I would like him to see you, in the hope that he can effect a cure.'

The next day when Chrissy is in the drying yard, she is summoned to the treatment room. The mesmerist is a slight, serious-looking man with button lips and round spectacles — he has a habit of pushing them back with his third finger. Chrissy has no desire to be cured, and is firmly of the belief that no cure is necessary, but she dare not make herself open to an accusation of disobedience. A straitjacket hangs by a hook on the wall; it serves as a warning of what can happen if an inmate is considered uncooperative. Mr Connor is seated on a chair in the corner. He says he has asked to be present at the session, as he would like a greater understanding of Dr Cunliffe's methods. Chrissy is relieved that there is another female present — Mrs Horrocks comes to stand beside her, to act as a chaperone.

Dr Cunliffe asks Chrissy to get up onto the couch, and then he adjusts the backrest, until she is comfortable. All the time, he talks in a slow, monotonous voice, explaining that Chrissy should feel free to express herself as she wishes. No judgements will be made; he desires only to understand more of her situation. Despite her reservations, Chrissy feels herself beginning to relax. The room is above the director's office — it is warmed by the chimney that rises from the fireplace. It is pleasant to lie still, instead of doing washing.

Dr Cunliffe gets out his fob watch and swings it rhythmically, in front of her. 'I would like you to follow this with your eyes, and while you do so, please picture yourself in a situation where you have felt contented and safe... think back, perhaps to a time when you were a child... when you were carefree and untroubled.'

Chrissy sees herself playing by the stream near her childhood home in Kirriemuir. She knows that she is still in the treatment room, but somehow, the reality of her physical situation no longer seems particularly relevant. She forgets the presence of Mrs Horrocks and Mr Connor: a pleasant lethargy steals over her — her eyelids grow heavy, and her breath slows.

'With each swing of my fob watch, you will find yourself relaxing further... now tell me, what do you see?'

'I see a child, playing with her brothers, using sticks to dam in a stream...'

There is a pause. After a time the doctor says, 'And where are they now, the members of your family?'

'They all died in the cholera epidemic, except for my eldest brother, who went to America.' It is an odd feeling, the memory of the death — within weeks of each other — of her parents and siblings is normally associated with almost intolerable grief but now, although she feels sad, she is able to distance herself from that great sorrow.

The session continues. Dr Cunliffe asks Chrissy how she came to be in Dundee, how she found work in the Tannery, where she lodged, which church she attended, what she did on a Sunday, who her friends were… and in between some of the questions, he reminds Chrissy of a time she paddled barefoot, on a summer's day.

'Did you have an admirer? A gentleman friend? Someone you were courting?' Dr Cunliffe swings the fob. He speaks without inflection, in the same monotonous tone.

'He was called Andrew. He said he would marry me… He introduced me to his brothers, but then he thought better of our alliance.'

'And was Andrew the father of your child?'

'No. He only ever kissed me once.'

'Now think back… see yourself again, as a small child, playing in the stream… There is nothing to fear… no-one can harm you… no-one can hurt you… did someone else ever kiss you, touch you, have physical relations with you?'

Chrissy swallows. She sees a fair-skinned boy, and a black-bearded man. 'I think perhaps someone did.' She feels herself grow tense.

'You are a little girl again… happy and carefree… feel protected by the peace you felt then. Gather that peacefulness around you, and feel yourself protected.' Dr Cunliffe continues to rhythmically swing his fob. 'Now tell me what happened. Take your time… there is no hurry.'

Chrissy's heart is beating fast. The sense of peace is deserting her, as memories surface that have been long suppressed. But she carries on — the words tumble out in a rush. 'Andrew took me to have tea with his brothers — he wanted to introduce me to them. At the time, they behaved like gentlemen, but in the evening they came to my lodging house. They must have followed our cab, to see where I lived. I think they knew I was not a governess, as Andrew had said.'

'Please continue… You will feel better once you have faced the truth. You are not at fault. Remember — you are safe here.'

'Andrew's brother James came to the door. He said that Andrew had been taken suddenly ill and was asking for me, so I went with him and got into the cab. Sam, his youngest brother, was there smelling of drink. It was a lie — Andrew was not ill — it was just a pretence to get me out of the house. They took to me to a rented room, and gave me a glass of gin. I said I did not want to drink it, but James said I should accept their hospitality, or they would not feel disposed to take me home. James laughed and told Sam that he would be the butt of jokes, if he went to sea and had not yet been with a woman.' Now Chrissy has begun, she cannot stop, and the words tumble like a rushing river. 'I remember that afterwards I tried to get up — but I could not stand. I remember feeling very sick, and I remember James's face being very close to mine.'

Chrissy breaks off. She looks up; the tears run freely down her face. For a time, no-one says anything. It is Mr Connor, who breaks the silence.

He moves in his chair and emits a sigh. 'So this is the explanation for your immaculate conception. The episode you describe is sordid and regrettable, but it is far from being extraordinary.'

Chrissy sees Mr Connor's expression, serious and troubled, and the pity on the face of Dr. Cunliffe. Mrs Horrocks is frowning, and her mouth has fallen open. Chrissy remembers a hand, small and soft as a rose petal, and perfect little feet, with toenails that shone like mother of pearl.

A shout comes out of her. It is as if the sound has been wrenched from the very core of her being. *'He was still beautiful! He was still precious. He was still mine!'*

Unexpectedly, Mrs Horrocks steps forward. Ignoring the two men, she takes Chrissy in her arms. 'Bless, you dearie,' she says. 'Of course... Of course he was.'

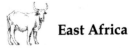 **East Africa**

The tropical downpour falls on Lokim in heavy drops, making runnels on his unprotected body. He would like to raise his knees and curl himself into a ball, but he cannot do so. He has to keep his legs straight because his ankles have been fitted to circlets of iron, and chained to a heavy stone. His wrists have been fettered to a plank of wood, which is attached to a post, and his arms ache painfully from being held outstretched. He is hollow with hunger and his mouth is dry with thirst. Raising his head, he holds out his tongue in an effort to catch some of the rain. Around him, the market sellers move quickly to protect their goods; lids are slammed on pots of colourful spices, bolts of cloth are pushed under tables, open sacks of maize are hastily tied closed and someone throws a cover over a cage of brightly-feathered birds.

Lokim hears a loud clap of thunder and a sizzle of light splits the sky. The storm that follows energises him. He straightens his arms and tries to slide his hands through the metal rings that encircle his wrists. He kicks out at the stone to which his feet are chained — he has a vague idea that if he could make the stone roll, the weight of it might separate the chain from his ankle cuffs. He stops, having realised after a moment's reflection that rolling the stone would simply cause the chain to tighten. He forces himself to breathe slowly, as the thunder rolls overhead. He distracts himself by watching the child who plays in front of him — she must be the daughter of the trader who sells leather from the stall directly opposite. The girl is naked, save for a string of beads around her middle. Oblivious to the thunder and lightning, she dances in the rods of rain. She splashes and stamps in the accumulating puddles; she is carefree and happy, as if she has never known hunger, anger, sickness or pain. She ignores Lokim's watching eye — he might be a heap of cassava, for all the notice she takes.

The storm abates and soon the sun comes out, heating Lokim's skin, and filling the air with the scent of damp earth. The leather trader has returned to his stall. When a customer offers too low a price for a finely wrought belt, he expresses mock outrage, vigorously shaking his head. Then when the man eventually walks away the trader runs after him, begging him to come back. His daughter runs along beside, watching her father, and copying his every move.

Lokim can no longer take any interest; his arms are aching almost insupportably. He shuts his eyes, seeking but failing to find the solace of sleep. He wonders how long it will be before his keeper returns and if, when he does, the man will bring water and food. He thinks back to the easy life that he and his companions enjoyed on the shores of the Huge Pool, before they were recaptured. He wishes, as he has done over and over again, that he had trusted his instincts when he saw the strange boat. At first, he had believed that he had been wrong, and that all was well. He had been using a chip of metal he had found to carve a piece of wood into the shape of a cow, when a young boy came from the direction of the boat, to ask — by gesture — the way to the village. Lokim had pointed to the path, and the boy went on his way. They saw nothing more of the strangers and for the rest of that day, Lokim had felt a sense of relief, thinking that the others in the group were right, and that the boatmen meant no harm. But at night time, when the former slaves were settling down to sleep, they were surprised by three men, who came with chains and fire sticks. Longoli shouted out and tried to defend himself with a stone. They killed him with a fireball. When Bila tried to fight, they flogged her and raped her, then flogged her again. When she still resisted, the youngest man used his stick to hit her very hard, until he broke her neck. Auma they killed as soon as they went to her bed, felt her limbs and realised they were little more than bone.

Although Lokim had raged inside, he had put up no resistance as he was roped to his companions and made to walk away from the camp. On board the boat, they were trussed and tied, and were made to lie on the deck motionless, like four sacks of grain. By the light of the moon, Lokim could see that a load of ivory also lay on the deck. The elephants must have been young when slaughtered, for the tusks were small. Lokim could hear the sailors talking and strained to understand the meaning of their words. He thought he heard the name 'Santos' but he could have been mistaken. The men did resemble the trader; they had the same straight noses, with small, soft mouths, and like Santos, they wore fine clothes. Two of them fetched a lamp, and got out a board with pits of sunken wood. Lokim was kept awake by the clicking of stones as their game progressed. The men cursed when the lamp went out. They refilled it, then cursed some more as some of the oil was spilt.

In the morning, Lokim turned his head as far as he could, searching for something that might provide a means of escape. To his left, he could see the oil container. Stuck to the front, and peeling off in one corner like a piece of bark was a picture, which had been painted in extraordinary detail. The image was of a white woman, with blue eyes and red hair, and in her hand she held a flame. He blinked in disbelief, then relaxed. He ceased to struggle. The image that had come to him when he had drunk Atum's potion had been vague. From now on, whenever he summoned the healing woman, he would clearly see her face.

The youngest man kept pointing to the ivory. There seemed to be an argument going on about its ownership. Eventually the leader of the group lost patience. He raised his hands and seizing two of the tusks, he pushed them at the younger man, causing him to almost lose his balance. Then he pointed to his fire stick. The young man had at first hesitated. Then he threw the tusks out onto the shore, before he went below and climbed back up with his own fire stick and a bag of belongings. He pointed towards the captives, and the leader made another gesture of impatience. Suddenly, he kicked Lokim — who happened to be nearest — then he bent down and rolled him off the side of the boat. Lokim fell heavily into the shallow water. The young man — they called him Abu — scrambled down, and pulled him onto the sand.

And so Lokim became Abu's bearer, carrying the ivory on his shoulders, as they trekked back along the shoreline of the pool. After two days of travel, Abu indicated that they should stop and make camp. They waited, and in another two days, they met up with a long caravan with scores of slaves, who carried lines and lines of elephant tusks. The traders greeted Abu as a friend, and Abu joined them in prayer, kneeling, swaying and lowering his head to the ground. Lokim wondered in the following weeks if Abu and his companions prayed so often because they were desperate for rain. The drought had not lifted, and the parched ground caused everyone to go hungry. When the slaves fell as they walked, they were thrashed for doing so and if they did not immediately stand up, they were thrashed some more, then left behind. When given his sparse rations, Lokim showed restraint. The slave roped next to him in the line had tried to seize an extra portion, and had been punished in the most terrible way. A kind of cage had been fastened over his face and head, and a metal stopper fitted into his mouth. Lokim would always be haunted by the desperate plea in the other man's eyes.

The caravan travelled onwards through the vast bush, passing carcasses of animals and the skeletons of men. As the slaves died, some of the ivory was abandoned. It was buried in the ground: the traders hoped they would be able to return at some later time to collect it. After three cycles of the moon, they came to a place where the path rose steeply. From the top of the hill, Lokim could see before him the straight criss-crossing roads of a large town. By now, the rains had come, but half the traders were too weary to continue walking. They chose to sell their tusks in the square of the marketplace, where they were given glinting silver in exchange. Lokim was stripped naked and crammed into a pen with around fifty others. He was bought by a pale-skinned man, who took him to his house. Lokim hoped that he was to become a cook or a gardener, but instead, he was taken into a backyard and chained inside a hut. Three times a day, he was fed maize porridge through a hatch, so that the flesh returned to his body. Gradually, he came to realise that he was being fattened for resale. Now, here he is, back in the market place. He has been pinned down like a hide that has been put out to dry.

The sun beats down. He is prodded and kicked by prospective purchasers and his eyes are forcibly opened wide. One man puts two fingers up his nose and peers intently inside his nostrils; Lokim cannot imagine what the man thinks he might find. His keeper returns, but without food or water. He brings another man with him and they squat on the ground, chatting and joking with one another. Both men chew the kind of nut that Hosne used. When they open their mouths, Lokim can see that their teeth and spittle are stained deep red.

The ache in Lokim's shoulders intensifies. How is it

possible, Lokim wonders, for one man to inflict such cruelty upon another? His keeper had no reason to pin his arms when he was already firmly chained. It is as if there is a sickness that can steal men's minds, making them want to deliver unnecessary suffering. Life in Karamoja was harsh — food was often scarce, and cattle raids meant killing — but he cannot remember anyone in the manyatta causing another man pain, just for the sake of it. Lokim has found that the only way to cope — the only way to survive as a captive — is to force himself to engender within himself a kind of calm. Then he takes his mind elsewhere. The best times are when he escapes to the magical world he found, when he swallowed Atum's potion.

A pale-skinned man approaches. He walks up to Lokim and feels his outstretched upper arm, then he inserts his fingers between Lokim's front teeth and forces down his jaw. The keeper gets to his feet and the two men begin to barter. The keeper points to Lokim's long limbs, the other man points to an unhealed sore on Lokim's wrist. Eventually, they come to an agreement, and in exchange for two ivory bracelets, Lokim changes hands.

 **The Zambesi**

The *Pioneer* tugs its way slowly up the river. The boat is ridiculously overcrowded. A lot of space is taken up by the small exploratory steamer — commissioned by Livingstone and optimistically named the *Lady Nyassa* — which has been upturned on the front deck, and is now being utilised as a temporary home for the two mission ladies and their housekeeper. Mrs Burrup has cut up her thick petticoats to use as curtains, both for the preservation of modesty and also to keep out the innumerable flies. The expedition's coal supplies have long since run out, but quantities of wood have been gathered to fuel the engine. The logs have not been secured and from time to time one rolls across the boards and hits one of the crates of specimens that have been haphazardly collected by Livingstone's brother Charles. Another clangs into the piles of canned food that lie heaped beside the funnel. Containers of supplies jostle for space alongside a farm cart, two mules, a pony trap, Miss Mackenzie's many boxes, her large mahogany wardrobe and her pet donkey, Kate.

Miss Mackenzie is the sister of Bishop Mackenzie, who runs the mission station at Magomero. She has journeyed out to be a support to her brother, but James wonders how the presence of anyone so singularly unprepared to make any concessions towards the difference between industrial Scotland and the steaming African jungle, could ever be considered an asset.

Mrs Burrup is the wife of the Bishop's aide. James, like everyone else, finds the pretty young woman charming. She is good-natured and brims with vitality. But there is an open antagonism between himself and Miss Mackenzie. The elderly woman seizes every opportunity to express her outrage at his close relationship with Mary, and she has declared James to be downright mistaken in his allegiance to the Free Church. In Durban, she tried to persuade the captain of the *Hetty Ellen* — the little steamer which transported the party from Cape Town — to leave him behind. She nearly got her way, as it was elders from her mission who had chartered the boat. But Mary would not countenance James being abandoned — she insisted that she would never leave without him, and eventually, it was Mary's will that prevailed.

James has fetched a chair from the galley and has set up a plank as a table, in a small space between the dinghy and a barrel of engine oil. He is occupying himself by sketching a finch which has been shot and stuffed by Charles. The bird is a wonderful creature – its chest and head are a brilliant red, with a matching red beak and sand-coloured wings. Absorbed in his work, he is almost able to ignore the heat and humidity of the air, the flies that buzz and settle all around, and the mosquitoes that come drilling into earshot, then bite his face and hands. He is just making some finishing touches to the bird's head – he is shaping the eye, ready for painting – when the *Pioneer* comes to a sudden halt. His pencil slips, so that a random line besmirches his drawing. The mules clatter their hooves, and heehaw in alarm. The boat judders, moves a little, and there is an ominous scraping sound. One of the sailors gives a loud curse. For the umpteenth time, the boat's keel has caught in the sand.

James puts down his pencil. The problem is that the steamer is not only overloaded – Livingstone should never have allowed so much unnecessary baggage on board – but there is a more basic difficulty: she is inherently unfit for purpose. Livingstone's previous boat, the *Ma Robert*, had been slow and inefficient. She had been nicknamed 'The Asthmatic', before she wheezed her last, and sank near Chemba. No expense had been spared in procuring her replacement. The design of the *Pioneer* is advanced – indeed, she is a copy of one of Her Majesty's latest yachts. But in order to keep her stable on the voyage out from England, it was deemed necessary for her to carry a large amount of ballast, and so she was built to ship five feet of water. The Zambesi is, in many places, only two foot deep.

Livingstone does not admit that there is any inherent problem – he continues to insist that Providence will resolve any trifling difficulties. On the occasions when he temporarily loses faith in the reliability of Providence, he blames the sailors for not applying themselves more diligently and especially, he blames Hardisty, the ships engineer, for running the boat underpowered. Hardisty responds to Livingstone's criticism by becoming belligerent, then stealing from the wine store. On two occasions, James has found the engineer insensible on the galley floor. Missionaries and sailors are alike indebted to Gunner Young, an unflappable man from Kent, who calmly takes over whenever Hardisty suffers one of his spells. George Rae, who should take charge, has rendered himself unavailable. Having quarrelled with Charles, he refuses to set foot on the *Pioneer*. The Glaswegian has taken himself off — with a supply of tinned food — to live in a small whaler, which is towed behind the main boat.

As James carefully wraps the stuffed bird in a cloth and puts it away in a box, he thinks back to when he first arrived at the Zambesi. Everything had seemed so hopeful then. The last stage of the *Hetty Ellen*'s journey had been eased by Wilson, the urbane commander of HMS *Gorgon*. The naval ship had been patrolling the coast when someone caught sight of the missionaries' little steamer. As soon as he heard that Mrs Livingstone was on board, the captain offered to tow the other boat to the mouth of the great river. The *Gorgon* was plentifully supplied, and once they were anchored, Wilson invited the missionary party to a delicious supper of roast meat, served on bone china plates. The ship even had a phonograph, which had been cranked by a smartly uniformed officer. The machine played 'Home Sweet Home' to the guests, while they drank after-dinner port, poured from a crystal decanter.

James had been waiting with Mary on the deck, when the *Pioneer* came up the river, then drew alongside the *Hetty Ellen*. Livingstone, dressed in white trousers and a black frock coat, had lifted his gold-trimmed cap, and waved it in salute.

'He looks a great swell,' James had said, and Mary had clapped him on the back.

James did not resent the joy that shone in Mary's face, when Livingstone took her in his arms. For all the confusion, he was pleased to be at last in the presence of his hero.

However, the next morning, when he was breakfasting with the reunited couple, he observed that Mary was pink-cheeked and euphoric in a way that was all too familiar. He found himself wishing that he had refused Wilson's hospitality, and had stayed on the other boat.

Wilson seemed dazzled by the explorer's celebrity. Keen to help Livingstone in any way he could, he offered fifty sailors to crew the *Pioneer*, and said that he would himself come on board, to ensure the ladies' safe delivery at Magomero. But during the weeks that followed, the naval captain grew disillusioned. Like the rest of them, he was dismayed at Livingstone's lack of organisation, and he became more and more frustrated by the constant delays. He told James that he wished he had stayed on his own ship. He said he should have left Livingstone to his own devices.

Shouted orders are given, and a group of naval ratings loosen a rowing boat, and lower it into the water. Every time the *Pioneer* gets stuck, the same ritual has to be observed. A party has to go ahead with ropes, then pull hard until the yacht shifts. James watches, sweating in the heat and resting his arms on the railing, while the flies cluster and circle around his head.

John Kirk comes up on deck. The two men have much in common. They come from similar backgrounds, they share a keen interest in botany and both have trained as medical doctors. James admires John for his plain-speaking pragmatism. He would like to count him as a friend — he would like to talk with him privately about Livingstone. Having spent four years on the expedition, the botanist must know the contradictory nature of the missionary's character far better than most. But to James's dismay, Kirk — though polite — carefully avoids any situation where the two of them might be alone.

'I'll go to help,' says James. 'I feel useless, just standing here.'

'Quite so,' says John, and moves away.

Thinking that the sailors might benefit from the use of an extra rope, James goes searching through the chaos on the deck. There is a storage area beside the paddle, with a canvas sheet across. He pulls it back, and is appalled to come face to face with Mrs Burrup. She is at her ablutions, and wears nothing but her shift and drawers.

He reddens, averts his eyes, and replaces the canvas. 'Madam! Forgive me! I do most sincerely beg your pardon!'

'I am the person at fault.' The now unseen Mrs Burrup sounds skittish, rather than put out. 'I had no business to be washing here. But our little shelter gets so unbearably hot and airless, I could abide it for not one minute more.' She pokes her head around the side of her makeshift curtain and regards him with mock severity. 'But I am surprised at your blushes, Reverend Stewart. I understand that although unmarried, you are well-acquainted with the female form.'

James says nothing. He turns away, his face burning. Everything is wrong. His relationship with Mary is such open knowledge that other men avoid him, and amongst the women he is an open joke. He pokes amongst the stores, half-heartedly continuing his search. David Livingstone, a man he had worshipped, is an inadequate and sometimes vituperative leader. Worst of all, and this is almost unbearable because of its ramifications, looking out at the savannah, he can see no cotton. Contrary to what he has told his sponsors, it appears that alongside the Zambesi, no cotton grows at all. He — James — had ingested everything Livingstone wrote. He had swallowed it all, with the naive gullibility of a farmer's boy. Particularly, when Livingstone said that the crop grew plentifully — and that the trade simply needed organising — he had believed every word. As a result, he will suffer a public humiliation. But he himself is of little consequence. What feels awful, is the knowledge that he has misled others. If cotton

187

does not currently flourish, there is no reason to suppose that it ever will. James thinks back to the talks he gave, the hopes he engendered and the donations he accrued. He heartily wishes that he had never heard of Livingstone and had never picked up the explorer's wretched book.

The boat remains stranded for the next hour. Mary suggests brightly that virtue should be made of necessity. She encourages everyone to disembark, so that they may enjoy a leisurely walk on the bank. She and David stand by a baobab tree, holding hands. They look into each other's eyes and appear as besotted as two young lovers who have only recently met.

'Come and join us!' Mary calls out to James. 'It's cooler down here.'

Is Mary flaunting her uxorial happiness, in order to make him jealous? Is Livingstone aware of the rumours and deliberately putting on a show of domestic bliss? 'Thank you,' James says stiffly. 'But I have work to do.'

He goes below, and crouched in his tiny cabin, he shuffles through his boxes of books, seeking to distract himself. But nothing appeals and soon the air is too hot to bear. He goes back up on deck and finds Kate looking disconsolate, standing beside an empty water bucket. He refills the bucket with brown river water and is suddenly overwhelmed with pity for the beast. The donkey should be munching sweet green grass in the broad space of an open field, she should be able to drink from the clear water of a Scottish burn. She should never have been transported away from home to the sweltering heat of this inhospitable land. James puts his arms around Kate's neck and remains motionless, his head resting upon her mane.

'It's just too hot, isn't it?' The sympathetic voice is that of Horace Waller, a young Londoner who holds the title of the Lay Superintendant to the Mission. 'And it's frustrating for all of us, not being able to get a move on. Looks to me you might be going down with the fever. Wait there, while I get you some rum. I'll be back in a jiffy.'

* * *

James climbs down the ladder, across the planks that have been laid over the mud, and goes to join the ratings. His spirits have been lifted by the alcohol — and even more so, by Waller's tactful kindness.

The sailors are standing on a spit of mud that reaches into the centre of the river. They are separated into two teams. The two stoutest sailors are positioned at the back, with ropes wrapped round their waists, as if they are taking part in a village tug of war. James inserts himself into the middle of one of the lines.

'One two three, *heave*,' commands Wilson, from the *Pioneer*'s stern. 'And again, one two three *heave*.'

'Come on!' says Mrs Burrup gaily. 'You can do it!' She is standing on the bank, flanked by Miss Mackenzie and Horace. Playfully, the superintendant uses his umbrella as a sunshade. He holds it first over one lady, gives a little bow, then moves round to shade the other. He does this often, and with increasing speed — he assumes the mannerisms of a player in a music hall farce.

'Sorry I can't be of assistance,' he calls out breathlessly. 'Have to look after the ladies!' He mops his brow, and frowns theatrically as he moves faster and faster, spinning the umbrella as he goes. Mrs Burrup laughs helplessly, and even Miss Mackenzie's dry old face cracks into a smile.

The *Pioneer* slides forward in the sand. The ratings give a cheer, just as Mrs Burrup lets out a scream.

'There,' she cries. 'In the swamp! I thought I could smell something horrible.'

James leaves the sailors and goes with Waller to investigate. Amongst the mangrove roots, the distended corpse of a man lies half-submerged in the stinking water. James covers his mouth and nose with his handkerchief. But Waller regards the body with steady compassion. 'Poor chap,' he says quietly. 'I wonder what happened to him? We'd better give him a Christian send-off. You fetch your prayer book — and I'll find a spade.'

The corpse is not the first they have come across. There are crocodiles in the river, waiting to prey on unsuspecting fishermen, and a feud between two tribes called the Yao, and the Manganja, has resulted in scores of bodies being unceremoniously dumped. James had been stunned and appalled to learn that in the previous year Miss Mackenzie's esteemed brother involved himself in the war. With a crucifix in one hand, and a musket in the other, the Bishop had led a thousand Manganja in a bloody battle against the Yao.

The unscheduled burial service does nothing to dampen the jollity that results from the *Pioneer*'s release. A point has been reached where the river runs deep; the steamer's paddle churns steadily through the water. A game of charades is organised, to pass the time till supper. An elated Livingstone is suddenly all action. He announces that on the following day, he will lead a walking party to survey the plateau they can see ahead. In the meantime, he will make an inventory of food supplies. He leaps about the deck like an agitated grasshopper, picking up boxes and tins and putting them down randomly, creating even more disorder.

James does not play charades. He watches the game progress, while he sits on a bale of straw and draws a new type of reed he has found. Horace is once again acting the clown: miming the word cup-board, he is pretending to drink tea in the manner of an effete young lady. He lowers his head and looks up with his eyes, while crooking his finger and pretending to drink. James envies Waller his gaiety. He has a sudden longing to be more like the other man, and less like himself. If ever I do marry — he tells himself — and have a child, I will gift my firstborn with Horace's name.

 Broughty Ferry, Scotland

'He's gone too far! I'll have him strung from the yardarm of one of Connell's clippers!'

Mina has gone to fetch a book, but hearing Papa's angry words, she has remained immobile outside the library door. She knows that it is rude to eavesdrop on other people's conversations, but she would like to know both who it is that has gone too far, and what it is that they have done. Papa's moods dictate the way the whole house operates. She would like reassurance that Papa does not mean what he says and she would like to be sure that by the time lunchtime comes, his temper will have improved.

'Tell me Elspeth,' Papa is saying, 'How do we stop him? My own son — he will be the ruin of me.' Mina pinches together her thumb and forefinger. It must be Andrew who has angered him — or Sam. But Sam is away. He is finishing his studies in Edinburgh, before setting off back to sea.

'There is no point in empty threats, Alexander.' Mama's tone is icy. 'Such talk of stringing up — it simply is not useful... You must not be seen to over-react. You should appear to feel concern for Andrew — you should imply that he must be deranged to make such allegations... you should say they are the ramblings of a greedy mind, unbalanced by venality.'

'But he is not mad, is he? He has a successful practice in London. By all accounts, he has won considerable respect for his work at the Middlesex.'

'I'm trying to help you, Alexander!' Mama's voice is suddenly shrill. 'I'm trying to help us! I don't know the truth!'

'What do you mean, you don't know the truth! Do you not believe your own husband when I tell you that Andrew's claims are completely without ground?'

'I know this. Anne told me she had her reasons for wanting to leave home. Hers was not a love match, when she married Duncan Wilkie. As for your other daughters... I simply do not know. But I can do my best to protect the youngest two. I have asked Miss Scrope to be vigilant in her duties as chaperone.'

'Elspeth! Surely you cannot believe that I am guilty of these vile charges! What are you saying? Do you not believe in my innocence? How could you think I could do such things? I am an elder of the church!' Papa sounds dazed — more hurt, than angry.

'Let us put aside the issues of your guilt or innocence, and think what we are to do... Did Andrew say how many billboards he'd put up?'

'Here's the letter. He just says that the notices have gone up all over town.'

'To be read by anyone who passes by.' Mama's voice falters. 'Any of our acquaintances, people from the church, the wives of the men from the shipyard... the humiliation... to be pitied and reviled by such people... it is too much! Can we not pay him, as he wants?'

'But he wants thousands of pounds. And then, as Al says, there is no guarantee that he would be content with only one such payment.'

'You've talked to Al!'

'I had to. This is not just a family matter... there are business issues as well. Andrew still maintains that he and James were insufficiently compensated when they were bought out. And anyway, I need Al's support. I want him on my side.'

'Ask Winshaw and Belton to go round and take down all the posters they can find. Promise to pay them three shillings for each one they bring to you, and impress on them they must speak to no-one about what is alleged. I'll write to John and Eliza, to ask if Maggie and Mina can stay with them until things have settled... We want to avoid them hearing any of this, from the servants. Hannah can stay longer with Helen in Arbroath. And Janet? Janet can stay here.'

'Three shillings!'

'You need to give them a powerful incentive to collect each billboard. If necessary they will have to purchase the notices from others — they will require the means to do so.'

Mina tiptoes back upstairs to her bedroom, and sits for a long time at her dressing table. She tries to make sense of her parents' conversation. She looks at her image and wonders what sort of a family she has come from. She thinks about Hannah and the way Papa behaves as if they share some special intimacy. She thinks about Janet and the way she is treated as a person of lesser value. For some time, she thinks about Miss Scrope and her solicitous care. Then she takes herself back downstairs and goes to the music room.

Seated at the piano she plays — over and over again — a sonata by Liszt, that Monsieur Legart has asked her to perfect. In music, she can lose herself.

She feels a tap on her shoulder. It is Maggie. 'Coming for a walk?' she asks. 'We'll need to wrap up. It's chilly out there.'

But when they go to ask permission of Miss Scrope, the governess says that the weather is too inclement — they must remain indoors — even though the sun shines, so that the outside world sparkles delightfully in the frost.

CHAPTER SEVEN

April 1862

 The Hygienic Laundry, Dundee, Scotland

'Will you come with us Chrissy? You can if you want to.'

'I don't think so,' says Chrissy. 'But it is kind of you to ask.'
It is lunchtime at Mr Galloway's Hygienic Laundry, and Jessie
and Maddie are planning to go cowslip picking on the
following Sunday. A large benefit of being employed by Mr
Galloway is that his business is closed on the Day of Rest.
Being a devout man, he believes that it is against Scripture to
work on the Sabbath. His intention is that his employees
should spend the day studying the Good Book, in between
attending church services. But Jessie and Maddie have other
ideas. They are much more interested in having fun, and in
acquiring husbands, than in the preservation of their souls.

Chrissy, Maddie and Jessie are seated on the low wall
which separates their employer's business premises from his
private garden. The three girls are eating threepenny pies from
the butcher's opposite. Chrissy savours the gravy-rich meat.
The butcher has a justifiably good reputation in the town:
jellied mutton spills from flakes of golden-crusted pastry. She

looks at the blossom on Mr Galloway's apple trees, and gives thanks both to the Lord and to Mr Connor.

For after Chrissy had ceased to maintain that Thomas had come directly from God, Mr Connor kept his word. He had asked Dr Perry to declare her sane. The very next week, she was released from the asylum. Mr Connor even arranged lodgings for her — with a cousin of Mrs Horrocks. She would not have wanted to go back to the Montgomerys, and anyway, there was no space for her there. They had re-let her room to a bearded young man who wore a weaver's apron. When she went to collect her belongings, the man had called out for Mrs Montgomery who said she was very sorry, but Chrissy's things had been disposed of. They had thought she would never be coming back. George Montgomery had also come to the door. He had shaken her hand, but had avoided looking her in the eyes. She left the house realising that all she had in the world was her sealskin bag, her bible, and her piece of coal.

She explained the situation to Mr Connor, who talked to the trustees, and it was agreed she could have two print dresses from the donations box. She could pay for them in a year, with money from her wages.

On her first day of freedom, she went straight to Thomas's grave. After the inquest, the Reverend Willis had taken the little coffin back to Constan, where he had conducted a simple service. He reported to Mr Connor that a space had been found near to the Brownlee family tomb and he had marked the place with a simple wooden cross.

Chrissy had found the grave with ease. She wept tears of gratitude, as she gave thanks to the Procurator, who had understood her concern for Thomas's soul. She gave thanks to the Reverend, who had agreed to bury her son in consecrated ground. She spent a long time on her knees, while the wind blew around her and the frost nipped at her toes. She exulted in knowing that Thomas would remain forever in Heaven, basking in God's love. She saw him holding hands with Jesus, while looking up to Him with a confident smile. She saw him laughing, as he ran into the arms of a sweet-faced angel, with shining, widespread wings.

But re-entering Dundee, she found herself also thinking that God must have had a purpose in giving Thomas to her, then taking him back for Himself. She thought about the Reverend Stewart, and the speech that he gave in the asylum chapel. She pictured again the bitter disappointment of the children of Africa, turned away at Heaven's Gate. She wondered if — by some unknown means — God's intention was for her to help James Stewart with his work.

Walking through the city's wide streets, she chose not to dwell on the circumstances of Thomas's conception. The calm conditions in which she had recalled the assault served to lessen her outrage. Perhaps, too, a part of her had always been aware of what had happened, so that the realisation that she had been violated was not as shocking as it might have been. She had no expectation that James and Sam could ever be brought to justice. As the sons of the great shipbuilder Alexander Stephen, they would have found many protectors. It was probably for this reason that Mr Connor had refrained from suggesting the involvement of the police or a Court of Law. Besides — she thought — if the brothers had never ill-used her, she would never have known Thomas. But she believed that as a result of their action, no decent man would want her. She would remain celibate for the rest of her days.

A blackbird is singing in one of the apple trees. Chrissy watches, as a bold robin flies from the garden and lands on a gate post. Maddie throws a crumb onto the flagstones, and Chrissy does the same. The robin seems to lose all fear, as he pecks at the food.

'They're special birds, aren't they?' says Chrissy, wanting to say something, for the sake of appearing friendly.

'Why's that?' asks Jessie.

'Well — you know. Because of Jesus. The robin's red breast comes from trying to lift the Crown of Thorns, from the head of Our Saviour.'

To Chrissy's dismay, Jessie gives a hoot of mirth. 'You're daft if you really believe that,' she says. 'Doesn't make sense. That robin is one of this year's fledglings, and Jesus died hundreds of years ago.'

Chrissy swallows. 'Died and was resurrected,' she finds the courage to say.

Jessie gives her an odd look, and changes the subject. 'You know, you look ever so familiar. There's a picture on the oil cans we buy from the grocer's. It's of a girl, holding a lamp. You look just like her.'

Chrissy says nothing. She has been told by Mr Connor to say as little as possible about her past. At his suggestion, she has told the other girls that she has come straight from another laundry, where she was employed by a cousin of her landlady. It is an approximation of the truth.

But Jessie persists. 'You must know the picture. As well as on the cans, it's on a big advertising hoarding, down by the station. You've got the same eyes... the same hair colour... I could swear you're the girl.'

'Yes,' says Maddie. 'I've been thinking the same. It's an advert for the Canadian Tannery... it says something like ... *Where The Best Arctic Oil Is Refined.*'

Both girls look directly at Chrissy. 'I worked there,' she says. She is unable when directly confronted to tell a lie. 'The manager — Mr Barton — he was asked to find someone to be a model. He chose me.'

'Oooooh!' says Maddie. 'Sweet on you was he?' She gives a knowing wink, then adds generously, 'I'm not surprised, you're very pretty.'

'Frank Barton!' Jessie laughs, shortly. 'My brother works in the refinery, at the Tannery. Frank Barton's a mandrake. Everyone in the town knows that.'

A whistle sounds. It is Mr Galloway, summoning them back to work. The laundry is a small business, employing just seven people — the three girls, three older women and a driver who collects and delivers from around the town. Custom comes mainly from the proprietors of boarding houses, whose kitchens and sheds are too small to cope with the large amount of washing required by the frequency of their turnover.

Chrissy works the dolly, twisting, turning and pounding, just as she did in the asylum. She hauls wet sheets into the great copper, which takes central place in the room. As she prods the bubbling fabric with a stick, to keep it simmering under the boiling water, she thinks about Frank, and Jessie's off-hand declaration. Chrissy is not exactly sure what a mandrake is, but she knows it is something to do with preferring male to female company. The notion she had held, that the Montgomerys and others might have considered Frank to have been her sweetheart, was wide of the mark. She feels foolish, for ever having entertained such an idea.

Later in the afternoon, she is called over to the ironing room by Mrs Morrell. A widow from Fife, she is the oldest and the most senior of Galloway's employees; as such, she has the responsibility of allocating the workload. 'It is time,' says the widow, 'that you learned the proper art of ironing and starching. I can't imagine what sort of a place it was, that you worked in before. How was it that they didn't teach you?'

Fortunately, Mrs Morrell does not expect an answer to her question. She is too busy lining up the necessary equipment. Three flat irons, a box iron and goffering irons of assorted sizes are placed in an orderly row, along the top of the range.

'First, it is essential that you keep your equipment scrupulously clean. See this?' She picks up the box iron. 'Look at the base. What do you see?'

'It looks… perfectly flat.'

'It may be flat, you goose! But it is dirty! There is an area here that is discoloured by soot. If I were to place this iron, without cleaning it, upon a lady's nightdress or a baby's gown… Well…' She shakes her head and says no more. She implies that the possible consequences are too awful to be spoken of. 'It needs a thorough clean, with kerosene.'

She shows Chrissy a series of canisters, all neatly labelled in a scratchy, copperplate hand. 'Can you read?' asks Mrs Morrell.

'Of course,' says Chrissy. 'Borax. Isinglass. Potato flour. Glue.'

'I will show you how to make mixtures suitable for different fabrics and garments. A napkin, for example, will take a strong starch such as can be obtained from a thick rice flour. Let us use this pillowcase, to demonstrate…'

When Chrissy leaves work that evening, she is feeling happy and contented with her day. She had thought she knew from her mother how to iron and starch — but Mrs Morrell's techniques are infinitely more elaborate. She has been a patient teacher, ensuring that Chrissy has memorised the formula for each appropriate mixture, and Chrissy has proved to be a quick learner, so that she feels she has won the older woman's acceptance. If she is honest with herself, she is also pleased that Jessie and Maddie have recognised her as The Lamp Girl. The picture does give her a kind of status, and it is pleasant to be reminded of those serene afternoons, when she sat for Mr Watt. She wonders what has become of Mr Watt, and if he is still painting people's portraits.

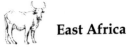 **East Africa**

Lokim is woken from sleep by a stinging sensation on his upper arm. For a moment he believes himself to be back in

Karamoja, and thinking he has been bitten by a poisonous snake, he instinctively reaches for his spear. His hand touches the arm of another man. He wonders why he is lying so close; the weather is warm — hunters usually only huddle together when the air is crisp and the ground is cold.

As he opens his eyes, he becomes aware of a heavy weight around his neck and a wash of dread sweeps his body. He wishes he could recapture the illusion of freedom that he had experienced when he first awoke. He lifts his head, and turns it from side to side, trying to shift the heavy iron circlet that is pressing onto his collar bone. He rubs a sharp pain on his thigh. It is time for the line to move on and the driver is lashing out with his whip.

Lokim is part of a long coffle of slaves, who are all heading for a far-off island, called Zanzibar. The strongest young men like Lokim carry ivory. But mostly, the men, women and children who make up the line are transporting nothing but their naked selves. The captives must walk for many days, and several cycles of the moon, until they arrive at the Endless Water, at which point they will be taken to Zanzibar on a big boat. When they get there, they will be declared free, and set to work as farmers.

Lokim knows this, because he has been told so, by a driver who spoke Acholi. Lokim feels bad that soon after this conversation, the man was punished for being too lax in his duties. He was stripped naked, smeared with honey and tied for a day to a post, to be feasted upon by swarms of mosquitoes and flies. A week later, he sickened, and was left to die.

Lokim stands up. The chain that runs through the ring on his collar is pulled taut, as the slave in front crouches down to reach out for a tiny yellow berry, which is low on the branch of a prickly plant. The man gives up and stands erect, as the whip hits the side of his face. The slave behind picks up the point of the tusk, which they carry together, and nudges Lokim with his foot, prompting him to pick up his end, too. They wait for the signal to move. A horn sounds; the drivers distribute themselves along the line. '*Moja mbili tatu!*' they chant, in Swahili. It is the language they share; the slaves have learned to understand some words, too.

With one united step, the coffle shuffles forward. The long day's walking has begun. Lokim tries to ignore his physical discomforts: the insects that crawl on his body, the thorns that pierce his feet, the hunger that makes him weak, the relentless sun that strains his eyes. He wonders if it is really so, that when they reach the place called Zanzibar, he and the other slaves will be set free. He shifts the heavy tusk; the weight of it has caused a blister to form on his shoulder. He resolves to believe that it is true, because a life with hope is easier to endure than a life without. He tries to picture himself as a farmer, in a better, future world. He sees himself planting maize and harvesting corn. He imagines having a safe place to sleep, enough food to eat and a wrap of clean cloth to wear.

But as he walks, his mind is invaded by images from the accumulation of suffering he has witnessed, since Makot betrayed him and sold him to Santos. His carefree life by the Huge Pool seems unreal. It seems improbable now, that they eased Auma's thirst with milk from the white-skinned goat and gathered moss to soften her bed. Vividly, he remembers the ailing woman's brutal execution at the hands of the men from the strange boat, and the casual rape of Bila, before she was killed. The cruelty on the long walk with Abu had been unremitting; it was followed by the squalor and darkness of the nut-chewer's hut. And after the nut-chewer had sold him in the market place, he had been kept penned for days, in a high-sided compound, with no food, and filthy water, before being sold on again.

The ivory on his shoulder weighs more and more heavily,

and a sharp little stone has inserted itself between two of his toes. Lokim longs to remove the stone, but he cannot do so. If he stops walking, even for a moment, he will cause a commotion in the line, and will suffer a beating. The coffle is like a great, slow, multi-legged insect; in order to proceed, all its legs have to act together.

They have reached an open plain. Taking one monotonous step after another, Lokim watches the line, as it turns to follow the path. He looks forward to the time when the order is given to stop. He pictures the insect/coffle coming to rest. He sees it suspended in time, like a chrysalis. He watches the spirit of the individual slaves unite together and soar free, like a huge and glorious butterfly. He imagines that he has taken a sip of Atum's potion, and despite all his suffering, he smiles. The dream-woman has touched his cheek, she has caressed him, with her soft, pale hand.

 **The Zambesi**

James is racked with fever; every time his body judders, his spine is racked with pain. When he was six years old, an aunt had given him a small suede bag, which contained a collection of marbles. He had carried the bag in his pocket and as the marbles ground and knocked together, he had been bothered by an irrational fear that the glass spheres might break. Now, lying on a rough frame bed in the house at Shupanga (which was built, then abandoned, by the Portuguese) he is reminded of those marbles. For as he shakes, he fears that his vertebrae will shatter.

From being burningly hot, he is suddenly intensely cold. His teeth chatter so hard that his ears are filled with the sound of knocking and the sound is almost deafening. He tries to keep warm, by curling himself round. He holds onto his knees with his hands, so that his body becomes a question mark. He hears himself laughing; it seems suddenly funny that his physical position should so aptly reflect his state of mind.

The questions that make his head pound, range from the broad to the particular. In no special order, he wonders whether or not he will survive, why the rats which scuttle across the room seem to travel in one direction only, how much Livingstone knows of his affair with Mary and why people describe time as being something that moves forwards.

The effort of wondering so many complex things leaves him utterly exhausted: he plunges into a deep sleep.

In the morning, the fever has, at last, abated. He wakes up feeling ravenously hungry, but the only food that is left in the house, is the remains of a packet of oats. He would like to make porridge but he lacks a fire. He eats a few of the grains, trying as he chews, to ignore their dryness. The remainder of the expedition's supplies have disappeared down the Zambesi, along with the *Pioneer*, the Livingstones and the rest of the party.

'You are too ill to travel with us,' David had said, in his abrupt manner. 'You are better off resting here.'

James steps out of bed, but he is too dizzy to walk. He goes back to lie down.

As he looks at the bats which hang from a rafter above his head, he tries to work out how many days it has been, since the *Pioneer* steamed out of sight. Just before the boat turned a corner, Young had sounded the siren in farewell. To James — ill as he was — the signal had sounded like a last post. He believes now that he will live and he gives thanks that he has not suffered the fate of Bishop Mackenzie, and his aide, Mr Burrup.

For both men are dead, having succumbed to the marsh sickness. Wilson was the first to find this out. Feeling that he could no longer stand the expedition's slow progress, he took the women up the Shire River in a rowing boat, so that they could be more swiftly reunited with their men folk. He found the mission buildings abandoned and derelict. The bodies of the two clergymen lay nearby, in shallow, scarcely covered, graves.

When the naval captain brought his charges back to Shupanga, he looked thin and drawn. Miss Mackenzie had appeared almost lifeless, and Mrs Burrup was suffering from an eruption of boils. Mary had done what she could to offer comfort, but it was agreed by everyone that the sooner the grief-stricken women — together with Kate and the innumerable pieces of luggage — were on their way back to Scotland, the better for all it would be. So the *Pioneer* had chugged off, back up to the mouth of the Zambesi, leaving James behind.

One of the bats drops suddenly; it emits a high squeak, as it spreads its hooked wings. James ducks his head as it brushes past his face. The Shupanga mission house is built of stone, with two small windows, so that even at midday, it is cheerless and dark. The roof is tiled, but in places the tiles have come adrift, and been replaced with palm leaves, which have — in turn — fallen to the ground. They lie rotting on the floor, coated in droppings.

James makes himself get up, and staggers outside. He shades his eyes with his hands, dazzled by the brightness.

The next day, just before sun down, his heart lifts at the familiar sound of the *Pioneer*'s horn. He walks unsteadily to the jetty and waits for the boat to arrive. He sees Mary standing next to Gunner Young, who mans the wheel. She lifts her scarf in greeting. James cannot help himself: he sobs in relief. Only now, can he admit just how lonely he has been.

At the Zambesi mouth, the expedition has been re-supplied by the *Gorgon*, so that the *Pioneer*'s decks are once more cluttered with tinned meat, sacks of flour and bags of rice. Wilson, having rejoined his ship, is on his way back to the

Cape and it is soon apparent just how much the captain's steadying presence will be missed. Waller, as ever, is in good spirits, and cannot find an unkind word to say about anyone. But as for the others, Hardisty is drinking heavily, the Livingstone brothers are not on speaking terms and Kirk is openly angry at the absence of any cohesive plans. Rae has left the whaler and rejoined the company, but he is monosyllabic and surly. As for Mary, she is unwell. She complains of a headache, and her abdomen looks swollen. At supper time, she eats little. She says she has no appetite, then goes to lie down.

Livingstone gets up from the table, to follow her. 'I'll fetch some of my rousers,' he says. 'She'll be better soon.' 'Rousers' are the pills he makes, to his own special recipe; their good effect seems to result from the quinine they contain.

'She's probably with child,' Kirk mutters acerbically, once he is out of earshot. 'They've been rutting like rabbits, ever since she got here.'

James is glad of the darkness, which conceals the flush that rises from his neck. All logic tells him that it is entirely appropriate for Mary and David to share conjugal relations, but where Mary is concerned, logic — like a superior friend who chooses better company — seems to leave him.

In the following days, Mary stays in her tent. Livingstone looks distracted. He says he has given her more rousers, but they are not working. He says that she is jaundiced and is concerned that her liver is affected.

'Would Mary not be better in the house?' asks James. 'It is cooler, there. I should be happy to give up my room.'

'Talk to Mary yourself,' says Livingstone. 'I am sure she would be pleased to see you.' His eyes focus on a heron, which is lifting itself from the water, flapping its large black wings. 'Now, if you will excuse me, I have work to do. I must make some additions to my charts.'

It is very hot inside the tent, but the canvas is damp, and there is an overpowering smell of mildew. James is shocked at Mary's changed appearance. Her hair is matted, her skin is sallow and the distension of her abdomen has become more pronounced. It is obvious from the condition of the bucket beside her head, that she has been vomiting. She lies quiet, hardly moving.

He takes her hand. 'Mary?'

She opens her eyes, and when she smiles, she is, for a moment, her old, gay self. James remembers an open coach, bowling along and a field of green oats, rippling in the evening light. 'I came to say that you will be more comfortable in the house.'

'You will have to carry me.'

The significance of these words silences him.

When Mary turns to face him, he sees that the whites of her eyes are yellow. 'I am truly unwell.'

'I am sure that in a few days, you will be back in service — doing all those things you do — organising our laundry, planning meals, acting as an interpreter, writing letters, attending to the sick ... I could go on...'

'I shall be doing none of it.' Her voice is little more than a whisper.

'Of course you will. We all get fever at times — that's how life is here. Why — a few days ago, I couldn't get up. Now, I am almost strong again. You will get better, too.'

'No.'

James reaches out for Mary's other hand. He cannot help himself. He weeps. He tries to do so silently, but the tears stream down his face, and drop freely onto the sleeve of her gown. Mary has by turns, charmed, seduced, infuriated and embarrassed him. She has been a giver of delight and a source of shame, but mostly, she has been a loyal and good-hearted friend.

He stays with Mary until she has fallen back to sleep. Then he goes to the house, clears his possessions and carries them to the boat. He fetches a broom and begins to sweep the leaves from the floor. He looks up, as a shadow fills the doorway.

'We should get the roof mended,' Kirk says. 'I'll ask a couple of the sailors to help. We must make the place as comfortable as possible. I was wrong about Mary. She needs proper care.'

James has been sleeping on two packing cases. He asks Reid, the carpenter, to put together a platform bed, then goes to find Livingstone. But Livingstone has taken his gun and is out on the savannah, hunting antelope.

'Don't think badly of him,' says Waller. 'He wants distraction and time to think. He is finding Mary's illness very hard. She is a part of him — he always refers to her as his rib.' James wonders briefly if Horace — having heard the gossip — is making an implicit criticism of himself, but looking in the other man's face, he sees only sorrow, and a gentle sympathy.

The mildew-smelling tent is hotter than ever. But Mary herself looks brighter. She puts her arms around James's neck as he carries her to the mission. He empties the bucket, brings fresh water and finds in the store a sheet left behind by Miss Mackenzie, which is more or less clean.

'I think you would breathe more easily, were you to sit up.' He fetches his own pillow from the boat, and asks Reid to surrender his, too. He would like to comb Mary's hair, but — perhaps ridiculously — he is concerned that Livingstone would consider this too intimate an act.

Mary smiles. 'You would make a good nurse. Miss Nightingale would be proud to count you as one of her own.'

He smoothes the creases from the sheet. 'I hope to be a good doctor, rather than a nurse. But first, I must finish my studies in Glasgow.'

'And then you will come back.' Mary's voice, though weak,

acquires a sudden urgency. 'James — don't be put off by the disappointments you have suffered. You could achieve so much... But always remember — Africa does not belong to the British — or to the Dutch — or the Portuguese. Africa belongs to the Africans.' Worn out by the effort of speaking, she closes her eyes.

James holds Mary's hand, and waits until she is asleep. He stays at her side, thinking of her words, and thinking that it is a tragedy that Mary is to be taken so young from the world, when she has so much left to do. All of a sudden, she lifts her head: 'Agnes! I must go to her! She has fallen down a ravine!'

'No, Mary, Agnes is safe. It was just a bad dream.' James strokes her forehead, and she settles. After a little, he says, 'would you like me to say a prayer, before I leave?'

'All that — it is a waste of time...'

James sees that Mary's yellowing cheeks are wet. 'Do not cry because you doubt God's love.'

'A waste of time... I care not for God. I do not believe there is a heaven. I weep for my children. I should never have left them.'

James can think of no words to say in response. He kisses her softly, on the forehead. Once she lies still and her breathing is regular, he goes back to the boat. He feels aimless, and exhausted. He pulls from his box a Portuguese dictionary — he is teaching himself the language, so that he can talk directly with the traders — but the words dance before his eyes. He leaves the boat, and goes onto the shore, where he tries to read the more familiar words of St Matthew, in the shade of the baobab tree.

He looks up, to see Livingstone walking along the shore. The explorer is lost in thought. His gun is slung over his shoulder, but there is no sign of any game. He nods when he sees James, and calls out: 'how is Mary?'

'More comfortable I think. The room is cooler than the tent.'

'I regret that I had to leave her, but I thought we would all benefit from some fresh meat. I am afraid I have been unsuccessful...'

That night, James cannot sleep. The air is too humid and he is eaten by mosquitoes, as he lies on the open deck. He is troubled by images of Mary; he sees her in Glasgow, surrounded by her elder children, with Anna on her knee; he sees her beckoning him to her bed, with her long hair loose and her gown slipped down, he sees her in Cape Town, drinking wine on the beach; he sees her looking joyful, in Livingstone's arms.

In the morning, he goes straight to the house. Livingstone comes to the door, looking haggard. He says that Mary is in a coma; he and Kirk have been putting poultices on her limbs, with no remedial effect. James bites his tongue. He has no faith in the haphazard application of poultices; he believes, with Lister, that medicine is best practised scientifically. He thinks it would be better to concentrate on making Mary comfortable — and not to treat her with quack cures.

'I have to make her better,' Livingstone says, as if reading his thoughts. 'She has recently expressed Doubts. It is vital that she repents, before she ascends to meet her Maker.'

James turns away. For the rest of the day, he avoids the house. He tries to pray for Mary, but he finds that he, too, is assailed by Doubts. It is pointless to ask God — if he exists — to make Mary well again; that is clearly not going to happen. And how can his silent incantations influence how Mary is received in the afterlife? If, indeed, there is an afterlife. Back in Scotland, it had seemed easy to dismiss religious uncertainties; they could all be swept aside, with a brisk avowal of the necessity for a 'leap of faith'. James looks out on the steaming swamps that edge the Zambesi; he hears a splash, and sees a large crocodile submerge itself in the water. Doctrines which were easy to accept in Glasgow, St Andrew's and Edinburgh, seem bizarre in these very different surroundings. He will miss Mary deeply. She is the only person to whom he could confess such thoughts.

He shuffles through his botany notes, and puts his collection of dried grasses and flowers in alphabetical order. He picks up a book on astronomy, and Taylor's *History of Enthusiasm*, but his mind is elsewhere. In the afternoon, he gets off the boat, and walks aimlessly up and down the shore.

He stops and looks out across the wide river. There is no doubting its beauty. Looking back, towards Sena, he sees that the sun is beginning to set. The water reflects an orange-red glow. He remembers a picture he once saw, of the Thames, all lit up by the great Fire of London. He thinks of Livingstone's hollow assertion that the Zambesi could be a gateway to civilisation and commerce. The shallowness of the river and, further inland — according to Kirk, who has visited the place — the obstruction of the Kebrabasa rapids, will always form a block to serious shipping. Livingstone will never admit to being wrong. But now, instead of going west, he is planning to go north.

James wonders about his own role in Africa. At some point, he will have to go back to Britain, and suffer the embarrassment of explaining that he has had to abandon his Scheme. But it will be good to see his friends at the infirmary, and to walk in the green hills above Loch Lomond. His thoughts turn again to Mary, so far from Scotland, and so far from her beloved children. He wonders how Robert is faring and if he has stayed away from the dice.

The heat has made him thirsty. He goes to the galley, to get water. Without Mary to supervise, no-one has swept the floor or wiped the shelves; as a result, the little room is crawling with ants and flies. He goes up on deck, to fetch a mop and bucket. He stops, as someone shouts his name.

'Stewart!' Then, more loudly: 'Stewart!' It is Livingstone, calling to him from the shore.

James quickly crosses the gangplank.

'Mary has little time left,' says Livingstone, wiping tears from his eyes. 'I think she would want you near.' James has no time to think through the implications of this statement; he is too distracted by Livingstone's appearance. Gone is the dapper figure, who — just a few weeks before — had waved his gold cap in greeting. David is unshaven, his clothes are dirty, the buttons of his shirt have been done up askew and his face is swollen from crying. He resembles an infant, who lacks a mother's care. James remembers Mary's fond description, when they sat together in her rented house: she had called her husband 'a genius, wandering child.' James suddenly understands how deep a love match, the Livingstones' marriage truly is. The long periods of separation have been an irrelevance. Mary's dalliance with himself has been inconsequential; this is why David can be generous, in Mary's last hours. The Livingstones are intertwined, as surely and stoutly as the weft and the warp of a length of Scottish tweed. James sees that without Mary, David will be lost.

Walking in step, the two men hurry to Mary's bedside.

Livingstone kisses his wife's face, tenderly, again and again. James had presumed her to be unconscious and so beyond suffering, but almost unbearably, Mary puckers her lips, and tries to respond. But soon, her colour changes and it becomes clear that her time is very short indeed.

When Mary dies, Livingstone cries inconsolably. 'I am crushed,' he sobs. 'I feel my heart has been taken from me. I don't know how I will be able to carry on. She was everything to me. She was a good person, James… She was my strength… Above all, she was a good person. She was central to my being. She was the main spoke in my wheel.'

James wipes the tears from his own eyes. He does not know who he weeps for, whether it is for Mary, for Livingstone or for himself. Livingstone continues to cry. He becomes so hysterical that James does not feel that is safe to leave him, so he stays in the room, an unwilling witness to the appalling depth of the other man's grief. He goes back to the boat once Kirk has given Livingstone a dose of opium and has agreed to take over his care.

James goes to Rae, who agrees to put together a coffin and then he asks the sailors to dig a grave. Four of them volunteer. He shows them the place under the baobab tree; Livingstone has nodded agreement to the site, in between his tears. The sailors set to work straight away, by the light of the moon. Mary must be buried as soon as possible, before her body decays in the heat. The grave must be deep, to protect her body from marauding beasts.

James goes back on deck, and writes his journal by candlelight. He is aware that he has witnessed a small piece of history, and that at some future point, other people will want to read his account. So he records what has happened as dispassionately as possible, carefully describing Mary's symptoms and the progression of her disease. He desires to protect both Mary's good name, and his own.

He tries to sleep, but as well as having much to think about, he is disturbed by the sounds of Rae's hammering, and the clink of the sailors' spades. A flock of wild geese have gathered to feed by the river. They scream and loudly beat their wings. Hours later, he is still awake. He listens to the howling of a hyena; from time to time, another one howls in response. He thinks about Mary, and his own recent brush with mortality and then his thoughts turn to his position on the expedition. From a difficult beginning — when Miss Mackenzie and Rae were doing all they could do destroy his reputation — he has gradually earned his place as an accepted member of the team. But suppose that Livingstone, having overcome his initial grief, should want to talk openly about his wife? Suppose that Livingstone suspected a liaison, but that these suspicions were never confirmed by Mary? Suppose the explorer should ask him frankly, if the rumours were based in truth? He would have to be honest. And then there might be no limit to Livingstone's anger, and his desire to punish.

When Baines, the expedition artist, had failed to keep track of the stores, Livingstone had accused him of being a common thief. Baines had been sent back to Cape Town in disgrace. He had similarly ill-treated Thornton, the expedition geologist. He had dismissed the young man for 'inveterate idleness', when by all accounts, his only crime was to have been laid low by fever. Livingstone had himself, in a rage, beaten one of the stokers, until the blood ran red and the poor fellow could hardly walk. How then, might Livingstone react to the confirmation of the news he had been cuckolded?

With little respect for their work, the sailors are singing a shanty as they dig: 'Boney was a warrior, way hay ya! Boney was a warrior, Jean Francois!'

James wishes that he could set sail with the men on the next ship home. But instead, he must justify to his sponsors the faith they have shown in him. The quick establishment of a cotton-growing industry is a pipe-dream. He must do some further exploration, to find out what can be achieved in reality. He still has some rolls of calico, which he can use for trade. Around the camp, some young Makololo men have gathered; they do odd jobs, in exchange for meat. He will recruit half a dozen of them, as paddlers; he will travel with them in a dugout, up the Shire. After exploring the Shire, he will go westwards, along the Zambesi. He wishes that he could leave as soon as poor Mary has been buried, but he will have to wait, until he is properly well. He wonders who will be chosen to read the funeral service; whether it will be himself or Charles.

'Boney fought the Prussians, way hay ya! And Boney fought the Russians, Jean Francois!'

At last, he falls asleep.

'What do you think?' Mina holds the flowers out to Miss Scrope. In the centre, she has mixed yellow primroses, pink orchids and bluebells. Around the edge, she has placed a border of white anemones.

'Very pretty,' says the governess. 'And what do you plan to do with it?'

Mina has not thought what she will do with her posy. She has picked the wild flowers on her morning walk, just because they are beautiful and she wants to celebrate the spring. There is a kind of quickness to the air that makes her want to skip with joy.

'I could put them in the schoolroom,' she says. 'Then Maggie can see them, when she gets back.'

Her sister has gone with the Camerons to visit the National Gallery of Scotland. Maggie had been greatly excited — she had spent days planning what to wear. With Mama's permission, she had taken her green velvet coat to the dressmaker's shop and she has set off for Edinburgh looking triumphant, with the sleeves re-cut and lined, in a way that even the sharpest of critics would consider absolutely *comme il faut*.

Miss Scrope stops walking and thoughtfully pokes at a small brown toadstool, with the point of her umbrella. 'It is kind of you to think of your sister,' she says, 'but Maggie is not due to return until Wednesday.'

'No,' says Mina, wondering why Miss Scrope should be so preoccupied. 'But they can still go in the schoolroom.'

The governess ceases her poking, and looks directly at Mina. 'I know of another place — a home in the city, where such country delights are rarely seen. A spring posy would, I think, be much appreciated.' She draws herself up to her full height. 'Especially so, if they could be delivered together with one of Cook's baskets. There was an accident last week, at the yard in Kelvinhaugh. A riveter called Jack Kent was injured, when a girder fell on him. He has returned to Dundee to be nursed by his sister — she is a member of the church that I attend. Such accidents are not infrequent at the Yard. A visit to the household would help you understand that the luxurious life that you enjoy, often comes at a considerable cost.'

Mina knows very well that life at the shipyard can be dangerous. All the Stephens children have been brought up to respect the Yard's workforce, and everyone in the family feels a sense of sorrow, when accidents occur. Al is particularly affected. Priding himself, as he does, on running the company efficiently, he views it as a personal failing if a worker gets hurt.

But Mina does not argue with her teacher, as they take the path home. She thinks about Jack Kent, lying in his sister's house, while she herself is out and about, enjoying the sunshine. Beside the gateway at Corona, she finds a cluster of sweet-smelling violets. She picks out the ones with longest stems, and adds them to her posy.

Mama and Papa have gone to visit John and Eliza; Winshaw has taken them in the Landau. When they go to the stables, Ben says he will not be able to take them to the town. The Phaeton is out of use, because the wheel rim has come loose.

'Never mind,' says Miss Scrope, 'We'll go by coach.'

Ben opens his mouth in surprise; the only public transport the Stephen women ever use is the railway train. Then he shrugs his shoulders, and slopes back to the horses.

Mina and Miss Scrope lunch together in the schoolroom; their simple meal is delivered by Katie, who wears a new frilled apron, and a matching cap.

'Hope it's all right, Miss,' she says, banging the hot serving dish down with a clatter. She stands back, with her arms folded. 'Will you be wanting wine?'

Miss Scrope shakes her head, impatiently. Katie should know that alcohol is never served in the schoolroom. The maid is not accustomed to serving at table; that role belongs to Neil, the footman, who has gone to Glasgow, to wait upon Mama.

At half past one, Mina and Miss Scrope set off for King Street. 'We must not dally,' says the governess. 'The coach will not delay for us. It is due to leave from outside the Eagle Inn, precisely at two.'

Mina walks briskly along the esplanade, with the basket on her arm. It weighs heavily, and bumps against her hip. She and Miss Scrope have had a peep under the cloth; Cook has supplied meat pies, pickles, an apple tart, a jar of peaches and a bottle of ginger wine. Mina has also tucked her flowers inside.

As a result of Miss Scrope's determination not to be late, they arrive too early. They stand together on the pavement, getting in the way of the passersby. A serving boy comes out of the front door. 'You can wait inside if you want. We have a small private room. There's sprung seats and a log fire. You don't have to buy anything — though we do a very nice cup of chocolate.'

To Mina's surprise, Miss Scrope gives a nod of acceptance, and they enter the building.

Mina sips her chocolate, and looks out into the busy street. She understands that Miss Scrope believes that her life should consist of more than piano playing and Petrarch. She feels grateful to the governess, for wanting to broaden her education. She wonders what kind of a future it is that Miss Scrope has in mind for her. But this is not a question that she feels she can ask.

* * *

The coach stops in the High Street. A fellow traveller, a man who looks like a farmer, lifts out the basket and hands it to

216

Mina. She follows Miss Scrope, who takes a road to the left. They weave through narrow side streets, taking various twists and turns, until they come to a row of tenements. A group of dirty-looking children are playing outside, kicking and fighting over a ball of rags tied up with string. Miss Scrope walks purposefully up the steps of the third terrace.

'This is a big house,' says Mina. 'Do Mr Kent's sister and her family live in the whole of it, or do they just have one floor?'

Miss Scrope knocks at the door. 'The Severs do not rent a floor. They do not have such wealth. They rent a single end.'

'A single end?'

'A single end is one room. That is all that many Dundee families can afford.'

The door is opened by a youngish woman, who is clearly with child. She supports the bulge under her dress with two hands and sighs heavily, as if she is finding her burden almost insupportable.

'Who d' yer want?'

When the woman opens her mouth, Mina can see that one of her front teeth is black and the two that should have been next to it, are completely missing.

'We have come to call on Mrs Severs, I believe she is expecting us.'

'Room on the left, third floor.' The woman eyes the basket with interest.

As she walks through the narrow corridor Mina is assailed by a sickly-sweet stench. It is a mixture of soured milk, urine and tobacco, together with other, unidentifiable things. Everywhere is dirty: the walls are covered in a layer of black grease and the steps are littered with dirty straw, discarded food wrappings, bits of crust and rags. Mina narrowly avoids putting her kidskin boot in a pile of dog excrement.

Mrs Severs is a tired-looking woman, who wears a faded

paisley dress and a darned wool shawl. 'It is very good of you to come,' she says. She takes the basket. 'Thank you so much. Please excuse our disorder...'

Stepping inside the room, Mina sees that the chaos results not so much from slovenly disregard, but more from the sheer number of people that occupy the space. Much of the floor is taken up with piles of bedding. There are at least six children of various ages and in various states of dress and undress. They clamber over one another, wailing and laughing. A baby cries, as his toddling sister takes his bottle and puts the teat in her own mouth. An older boy shouts out in irritation as his brother seizes the tract he is trying to read. An old lady is vacantly rocking herself in a corner of the room and under a narrow window a man with a bandaged face lies prone on a mattress.

The children gather round the basket, like piglets round a trough.

'Get away with you!' says Mrs Severs. She cuffs the elder boy on the ear and he runs for the door.

'Where are you going?'

'Outside.'

'Well don't get into mischief.' His mother reaches up, to place the basket safely out of reach, high on the top of a rickety shelf.

Mina thinks of her posy — the flowers should be in water — but it seems too late to say this.

'Please excuse Jack for not getting up,' says Mrs Severs, indicating the man on the floor. 'I'm sorry he cannot greet you properly. When the girder fell, he was knocked forwards so as well as bruising his back, he broke his cheekbone, and nose.'

'Good afternoon, Mr Kent.' Miss Scrope gets down to the floor, and Mina kneels beside her. 'May we shake hands?'

Jack lifts his right arm from under the bedcover. Miss Scrope puts her hand in his, and pumps the arm up and down.

'Pleased to meet you,' says Jack, in a quick, agitated voice, that contrasts with the stillness of his body.

'We're sorry to hear of your accident. We've come from St Mary's. We've brought meat pies and ginger wine. We hope you will get well soon.'

'Ginger wine. Ginger beer. Never fear.'

'I'm sorry,' says Mrs Severs. 'I don't think he's properly in this world. His friends at the shipyard had a collection for him. Some of it's paid for Dr Perry's visits. But most of the money's gone on cocaine. It costs more, but the doctor says it's better than laudanum. Jack seems to need more and more of the stuff.' She grabs the collar of a small boy, who is fighting his sister for the possession of a wooden clog, with a cloth wrapped round it. 'Jimmy! Will you stop it! That's Ada's doll!"

Jimmy lets go and his sister, who must be about two years old, falls back against Mina. The little girl looks up, wide-eyed. Her mouth turns down and she begins to cry.

Mina takes Ada in her arms, and gets to her feet. Seeking to distract the child, she points to a coloured print on the wall. The picture is of the baptism of Jesus. 'Look at the sky...' she says. 'What a beautiful blue... and there ... through the clouds you can see the face of an angel...' The girl ceases her crying, and gazes at the print. She takes her thumb from her mouth. 'Tree,' she says, pointing to a palm tree in the foreground.

'Good girl! Yes, tree,' says Mina. But her attention is no longer focused on the picture. She is looking instead at the surrounding wall. It bulges ominously in one corner, and there are forked cracks in other places. The paper is torn and has slipped down, from damp. But this is not what preoccupies her. She is looking at a dark patch — an area that she had taken to be a shadow. She realises, with horror, that the patch is moving. She is looking at many thousands of bugs, all gathered together, to form one heaving mass.

Mrs Severs follows her gaze. 'The building's infested,' she

says. 'All the tenements are. We try burning them off' — she indicates some smoke-blackened areas on the ceiling — 'but it doesn't work. They live behind the plaster. You get used to it. Excuse me...' She stops to scoop up the baby, who is determinedly crawling towards the fireplace.

The door is opened, and the elder boy comes back into the room. With him, is another boy of a similar age, and a young woman with painted cheeks who wears a red taffeta dress.

'I came to ask after Jack,' says the young woman. 'I hope he's gettin' better?'

'He's a bit better. But that's not why you're here.' Mrs Severs speaks without rancour. 'You've heard we have company. Well. I'd better introduce you. Mhairi, this is Miss Adeline Scrope. She's from St Mary's. And this young lady is...'

Mina gently puts Ada back down on the floor. 'My name is Mina Stephen. How do you do?' She holds out her hand.

Mhairi ignores her gesture. 'You're not one of Alexander Stephen's daughters are you? From Stephen's shipyard, where Jack works?'

'I am,' says Mina. 'And I am truly sorry about the accident.' She lowers her hand, it is clear that Mhairi has no intention of shaking it. The woman has curled her lip into an expression that combines hostility with contempt. 'I will speak directly to my brother,' Mina continues, uncertainly. 'To see what more can be done for Mr Kent...'

To Mina's alarm, Mhairi comes right up close and jabs a finger into her breastbone. The woman smells of stale sweat, and Eau de Cologne.

'Had a go at you, 'as he? Been dippin' 'is wick? Oh! We've read the notices, before they got tooked down! Been enjoyin hisself, 'as he, with you and yer sisters?'

Never before has Mina been in such a situation; she has no parameter, no reference point, no notion of how to respond.

Mhairi jabs at her again. Mina resolves not to cry — she

senses that the other woman would relish such an outcome. She steps back, just as Miss Scrope steps forward and slaps Mhairi across the face.

The governess takes Mina by the arm. 'Come,' she says. 'We are leaving. The company here is far from agreeable.'

Propelled by Miss Scrope, Mina walks briskly from the room and hurries down the filthy stairs. She can hear Mhairi calling after: 'I'll get yer'. I'll call the constable! It's assault, that's what it is!'

Mina follows Miss Scrope, as she twists her way along the side roads. She only starts to breathe more easily once they are standing back at the coach point in the busy High Street.

Miss Scrope readjusts her hat, fixing it through her hair with a jet-headed pin. 'I owe you an apology,' she says, 'for my misjudgement. I should never have taken you to such a place.'

Mina does not at first reply. She is thinking with dismay, of Mhairi's words. Her distress is mixed with shock at the governess's action, and sorrow for the poverty she has witnessed.

Out of politeness, she attempts a smile. 'It was interesting,' she says.

CHAPTER EIGHT

May 1863

 The Hygienic Laundry, Dundee, Scotland

Chrissy's days have fallen into a rhythm. For six days a week, she works for fourteen hours at Mr Galloway's Hygienic Laundry. Then, on the Sabbath, she walks twice to Constan, there and back, in order to attend both the morning and evening services. A cabinet-maker and his wife live not far from her lodgings, and they also attends St Dunstan's, but the couple do not offer to give her a lift in their carriage. Along with the rest of the congregation, they take the view that she is not a person with whom they wish to be associated.

The Reverend Willis takes a different stance from his flock. He shakes Chrissy's hand outside the church door, and asks after her welfare. He uses when speaking to her exactly the same exasperated tone that he does with everyone else. Chrissy would like to thank the Reverend for his support, but she is too shy to do so, and anyway, it is probably best not to remind him of the time when he took her in the blizzard to visit Constable Crieff. She wonders sometimes if the

Reverend's acceptance results from a lack of recognition — perhaps he has simply failed to make the link between herself and the girl who once bit his hand.

Chrissy goes to Constan because that is where she feels closest to Thomas. The knowledge that God did not directly provide her with a son, and instead chose to do so through the rough intervention of Andrew's brothers, has done nothing over the months to lessen her sense of wonder. She still counts it as a miracle that she was once gifted with a beautiful child; she still thinks lovingly of Thomas's sweet face and treasures the memory of his perfect, miniature body. During the services, while the Reverend recites the familiar words of the Bible and the *Book of Common Prayer*, she feels embraced by Love. The warmth that she feels, and the knowledge that the Reverend gave Thomas a proper burial, give reassurance to her; she knows that her son is safe. It does not matter that she is ignored by the rest of the congregation. At St Dunstan's, Chrissy can experience a sense of happiness. Every Sunday, she asks God to bless Mr Connor, for without his intervention she would still be in the asylum, unable to access such joy. She would like to stay near the village forever, but she knows she must follow God's plans. She pictures the sorrowful faces of Africa's children, turned away at Heaven's Gate, and wonders again if this could have been God's purpose, in giving her a son.

* * *

It is a Monday evening and Chrissy is leaving work. She has spent all her hours at the Laundry washing and ironing sheets. Her arms ache from using the dolly and her back hurts from hauling quantities of heavy wet linen. But it has been a good day. At noon, when she escaped the steam of the washroom, the sun had shone and when she sat on the wall with Maddie

223

and Jessie, to eat her lunch, the girls asked if she would go with them to Springthorpe's.

Chrissy thinks about this possible outing, as she closes the gate of the Laundry, and makes her way down the street. Jessie said it cost fourpence to see the waxworks, which is a reasonable price: the models move, they play musical instruments and wear fine clothes. She would like to go with the girls — she is very grateful to them, for wanting to include her. But on the other hand, she does not have the money. Everything she earns, apart from the sums she spends on food and lodging, must be put aside to pay the Asylum Trustees. She has paid off the amount that was originally owing for her dresses, but the chairman has written to say that more money is due, to pay the interest accrued.

Lost in her thoughts, Chrissy does not immediately notice that a startled horse has bolted, dragging his cart behind. The horse belongs to a rag and bone man, who chases after it, beating the animal's rump. The confused horse mounts the pavement — Chrissy fights to get out of the way. And then everything goes dark.

* * *

When she wakes up, her head hurts and when she tries to assemble her thoughts, they spin like spangled bobbins. She sits up and looks around. Opposite, she can see a row of beds but, to her alarm she cannot make out the faces of the beds' occupants. Something has happened to her vision. There is nothing, however, wrong with her hearing. With horrible clarity, she can hear a loud gargling sound. She lies back down and puts her hands over her ears. The sound is a death rattle. One of the bobbins spins, stops and dances anew, trailing a thread that shapes into words: 'Get out of here! Get out, or you die, too!'

224

Chrissy struggles to sit up. She lowers her feet to the ground, but the floor seems further away than it should be. She reaches for the support of the bed head. Everything is swimming. She fears she will faint, and closes her eyes.

She feels a gentle pressure on her shoulders. 'Please lie back down,' says a female voice. 'You are not yet well enough to walk. Let me make you comfortable…'

Chrissy is too weak to struggle. She does not protest as the covers are tucked firmly under the mattress, pinning her underneath. It is a relief to surrender responsibility. The woman attending to her wears what looks like a nun's habit. Her cap is like a wimple; it hides all her hair.

'Please tell me…' Chrissy says. 'I would like to know where I am.'

'You are in the Royal Infirmary. You were brought in here yesterday, suffering from a head injury. You were hit by a cart.'

A man — he must be a doctor — comes to stand beside the nurse. He takes Chrissy's pulse. 'We're pleased to see you're properly awake. You've been drifting in and out of consciousness. You are suffering from concussion.'

'I can't see properly…'

'You will, in time. You just need more rest.'

The nurse brings soup and bread. She fetches a white cloth, which she tucks under Chrissy's chin. 'You've had visitors,' she says, breaking the bread, to make it easier to manage. She holds out the steaming bowl and gives Chrissy a spoon. 'A girl called Jessie came — she said she works with you, at the Hygienic Laundry. And a reporter from the Courier. Apparently, after knocking into you, the horse — with the cart behind — went crashing through the window of Bonhams Bakery. Until the police came, people were helping themselves.'

Chrissy manages three spoonfuls of soup, but her head is hurting too much. 'I'm sorry,' she says, and pushes the bowl away.

She sleeps, on and off, for the next two days. The same woman always seems to be beside her, whenever she wakes. With efficiency and grace, the nurse provides meals and offers the use of a wheeled commode. To Chrissy's relief, she no longer hears the death rattle of her neighbour. The poor woman must have died. Although her head is still painful, she is relieved to find that her vision is almost back to normal. Large windows flood the ward with light and everything in sight is spotlessly clean. If it were not for her headache, she would believe herself to be in a kind of paradise.

But on the third day, the nurse says, 'I am afraid we will have to discharge you. We can only deal with acute cases here. But you will need further rest, to recover fully. Is there someone who can care for you?'

Chrissy thinks of her lodgings. In the crowded home of Mrs Horrocks' cousin, she occupies a little space under the stairs.

'Not really,' says Chrissy.

'I'll speak to the almoner. He'll see what he can do.'

When Chrissy wakes up that afternoon, there is a visitor beside her bed. It is Frank Barton. She blinks in surprise and wonders if she is dreaming. She has not seen the manager of the Tannery since his brief visit when she was in Bridewell. She thinks of all that has happened to her…Thomas's birth… her imprisonment.. her time in the Asylum. Frank is a person from a different, distant past.

Frank removes his hat, pulls out a chair from the central table and sits himself down. 'How's my prettiest girl?' he asks easily, just as if no time had passed at all. The nurse — who is hovering nearby — shoots him a warning look. 'Sorry. I'll start again… How are you, Miss Hogarth? I hear that you've been in an accident and that you need somewhere to recover. I've come to say that there's a spare room in my mother's house. She would be pleased to take care of you.'

Chrissy remembers an elderly, narrow-faced woman, with a permanently worried expression. She cannot imagine that Mrs Barton would readily have volunteered to offer her services as nurse. However, a room to herself sounds infinitely more appealing than her lodgings. 'Thank you,' she says, after a moment. 'I would be most obliged. But Mr Barton, how did you know I was here?'

'One of the men from the Tannery passed on a message from his sister. She'd been told by the almoner that you're in need of somewhere to rest. I had no idea you were working as a laundress. I thought you were still...' He stops himself, then goes on, 'mind you, I'd have found out anyway. Look at this...' From the pocket of his jacket, he produces a folded page taken from the Courier. He opens it out, and Chrissy reads:

Last Monday, an accident of an alarming nature occurred in Nethergate. Mr James McCready, a rag and bone merchant, had left his horse and cart stationary while he collected some waste matter from the Unicorn Public House. Startled by the noise of a barrel being unloaded, the animal ran amok down the street with Mr McCready following behind. The horse careered into the window of Bonhams Bakery. It is most regrettable to relate that certain passersby behaved most shamefully, in that they helped themselves to Mr Bonham's bread, buns and pies. They would have taken more, if a constable, who was nearby in Union Street, had not heard the commotion, and arrived promptly at the scene. A young woman, named Miss Chrissy Hogarth, was taken to the Royal Infirmary, having collided with the cart. Many of our esteemed readers will be familiar with Miss Hogarth's portrait. She is 'The Girl With The Lamp'; her smiling face adorns the cans of oil, processed by the Canadian Tannery, whose works occupy a large plot of land on the Marine Parade. The

aforementioned business is one of the most successful in
Dundee; its products are sold both in our fine city, and in
the furthest parts of the Empire. We wish Miss Hogarth a
speedy recovery, and hope that she will soon be able to
return to her work, as an employee of Mr Galloway's
Hygienic Laundry.

'See,' says Frank, 'I've made you famous.'

Chrissy hands the paper back. 'It's very nice to receive good wishes. But I wonder that you still use the picture, considering that … as I no longer work for you.'

'The partners did have a discussion at the time, I will admit. But they'd paid Mr Watt a lot of money, it's a lovely image and it's only in Dundee that your story is known. The cans were selling well and they still are. Our Arctic Oil outdoes all the competition. So in gratitude Miss Hogarth, allow me to take you to recuperate in my family home!'

Frank collects Chrissy later in the day. He takes her arm, as he leads her out of the hospital. Her head still spins, she sways on her feet and is glad of his support. He has borrowed the Tannery carriage and a man she recognises from the works sits on the dickey box, holding the horse's reins. Frank helps her up the steps, and they clatter through the busy streets until they reach his mother's house in William Street.

Chrissy feels nervous. She is uncertain what sort of reception she will receive. She has met Mrs Barton on two occasions, when Frank had invited both her and Mr Watt to take afternoon tea. The old lady had carefully inspected her features and her dress. Then, when Chrissy had accepted a second fairy cake, she had sniffed and frowned, so that Chrissy had felt embarrassed to have been caught out in what could have been taken as an act of greed.

The door is opened by a smiling maid, who wears a lace cap that is slightly askew.

'I've put some refreshment in the front room,' she says, 'I thought the young lady might be hungry.'

'Thank you, Gwen, that was thoughtful.' Frank smiles and runs his fingers through his rich dark hair. He wears a high collared shirt, with a blue check neckerchief. It occurs to Chrissy that there is a kind of lightness about him, that was not there before.

'Where is your mother?' she asks when seated in the front room. 'I feel I shall be putting her to such inconvenience. I trust she is well…'

'Ah,' says Frank. 'There is something I must tell you… My mother died a year ago. It was her heart. Her death was quick and she did not suffer. I am sorry to have deceived you. I thought you might not come if you knew she was not here. But truly, you have nothing to fear. You know I always valued your industry and skill. You were my best worker, as well as the prettiest. Mother told me not to visit you in Bridewell. I had to conceal from her the fact that I had disobeyed, and I didn't dare go again. Then we heard you were in the Asylum, and I thought you would be lost forever to the world.' He looks at Chrissy directly. 'I am pleased that our friendship has been given another chance.'

'And I am delighted to be here.' It is true. Chrissy sits in the prettily papered parlour, and sips the cordial provided by the maid. She is grateful to be in such civilised surroundings. 'But please, I wonder if I could be shown my room?' All the effort of moving has caused her the pain in her head to grow more severe.

The maid takes Chrissy upstairs and shows her the bedroom. The room has everything that she could want: a carpet on the floor, a washstand, frilled curtains and a neat iron bedstead, with a padded cover made from patchwork silk. She lies down, grateful to lose herself in the softness of the quilt.

That evening, Gwen brings upstairs a supper of shepherd's

229

pie and baked apples, served on a lacquered tray with an embroidered napkin placed beside. 'Thank you,' says Chrissy. She smiles. 'You are treating me like a queen.'

'I'm pleased to do so,' says Gwen. 'I understand you havna' got anyone else. An' if you're a friend of Mr Frank's, I'll treat you with respect, even if you are just a laundry girl. He's a good man, Mr Frank — though there's some who think that's a contradiction, being as what he is.'

Frank has a lodger, a young man who occupies the third bedroom of the terraced house. Chrissy meets him on her second day. Her head is feeling better, so that having spent the morning in bed she tells Gwen she is well enough to come downstairs. She is sitting quietly in the parlour, when the lodger returns.

'George Fairburn,' he says, advancing with his hand outstretched. 'To whom do I have the pleasure?' He is tall and blond, with a long nose and a sensitive face. 'Frank told me you were staying. He called you, 'The Girl With The Lamp', but I feel quite certain you must have a proper name, besides.'

'My name is Chrissy Hogarth.' George's grip is firm, and his smile radiates a kind of ethereal warmth. 'And I am pleased to meet you.'

'Can I fetch you anything? A glass of lemonade?'

'I want for nothing. I am grateful to have everything that I could possibly need.'

'In that case, please excuse me. I work as a clerk for Dryden's Solicitors. I am studying for my articles, and have twenty pages to get through before supper. I will like myself much better if I can get it done.'

He bounds from the room. Chrissy can hear him singing 'I dream of Jeanie with the light brown hair' as he goes upstairs.

Chrissy considers the odd position in which she finds herself, alone in a house with two young men. It is lucky, she thinks, that she has no reputation to lose. She might otherwise find it necessary to reject Frank's kindness and that would be a shame. For now, it is a good thing that no-one at the church will speak to her… because she is so comfortable in her chair. She picks up the book of Psalms she has picked from a shelf, but soon closes it and succumbs once more to the luxury of sleep.

She is awakened by Frank, who calls to her gently, telling her that it is time to eat. Places have been set for three, in the dining room.

Gwen brings in a plate of pig's pettitoes and a dish of stewed celery. Frank does not say Grace. Chrissy is about to question this, then remembers she is a guest, so she mutters her own prayer, and then starts to eat.

'I called in at the Hygienic laundry, on my way home,' Frank says. 'I spoke to Mr Galloway. He said he cannot hold your position beyond a week. He took you on as a favour to Mr Connor and although you are an excellent worker, there are some who know your story and choose to take their custom elsewhere.'

'It was good of you to talk with Mr Galloway. I will most certainly be well enough to work by the end of the week. And I have paid for my lodgings until the end of the month, so there should be no obstacle to my returning.'

Gwen removes the plates and brings a hasty pudding in from the kitchen, then fetches cream and jam. Chrissy mixes the jam with her tapioca. She thinks how delicious the combination tastes.

Frank watches her eat. 'You could stay here,' he says.

'I had better return.'

'You would be more comfortable, in this house. We are outsiders, me and George. And Chrissy, without wishing to seem harsh… you are an outsider, too.'

Chrissy says nothing, but thinks 'That is why I must leave'. She thinks of her perfect, innocent child. Others may choose to see her as a fallen woman, unfit to belong in society, but that is not how she can ever see herself.

When the meal is finished, George says he will play the piano.

'I should go to bed,' says Chrissy.

'Come and join us,' says Frank, steering her into the parlour. He leads her to the sofa and fetches cushions to make her comfortable.

George plays beautifully, and sings in a lovely tenor voice. When he finishes each song, Frank claps his hands and says, 'More please, more!' Every time he says this, George gets off his stool, and gets another set of song sheets, from out of the box underneath.

Chrissy stops thinking about her aching head, and loses herself in the music. Frank sits beside George, cupping his chin in his hand and looking across at him and smiling in admiration.

It grows dark outside, and still George sings.

'Let's have "A Good Time Coming".' There is a catch in his voice, as Frank makes his request.

George closes his eyes, as if gathering himself, and then starts to play. He knows the words off by heart: 'There's a good time coming, boys, a good time coming/ We may not live to see the day/ But earth shall glisten in the ray, of the good time coming.'

'To a better tomorrow,' Frank says.

Chrissy sees that there are tears in both men's eyes.

* * *

On her third day at Frank's house, Chrissy offers to help Gwen with her household tasks. Never before in her life has she sat around being waited on, and now that she is feeling better, she cannot bear to be idle.

232

'Well, I can't have you washing, or ironing,' says Gwen. 'And I can't have you beating the carpets, or blacking the grate…'

'Maybe I could dust the bookcases, and the figurines above the mantelpiece…'

'I have already done the dusting.'

'I would like to be useful. You have been so very good to me.'

'Let's see… I have some early rhubarb, bought yesterday from the market. I will bottle the best sticks, and make jam with the rest. If you like, you can help me prepare the jars.'

The jars have to be scrupulously clean, to prevent the bottled fruit from going mouldy. First, the range must be fired up, to ensure a supply of piping hot water. Gwen tips in a load of coal, opens up the flues, then sits herself down.

'Mr Frank said that you used to work at the Tannery. What did you do?'

'I was a seamstress. I sewed tippets and muffs.'

'So what made you leave? The Tannery pays well enough. Better than a laundry, I'm sure.'

Chrissy is saved from having to respond, by a knocking at the front door. Gwen goes to answer it. 'There's a young man,' she says doubtfully, when she returns. 'He is asking to see you. He would not give his name. I have shown him into the parlour, but I can turn him away if you wish. I will tell him that you are still unwell.'

'Don't do that,' says Chrissy. 'He may be bringing a message from Mr Galloway. I should hear what he has to say.'

Chrissy enters the parlour to find a man standing by the window. At first she does not recognise him. Then her hands grasp the back of a chair as she fears she will fall. The man is Sam Stephen, Andrew's brother. So many different emotions assault her that she is robbed both of speech and the power to move. Uppermost, is a rage that having done what he has, the man should dare to walk into a house where she has been offered kindness and shelter. But coupled with a desire to strike him, she feels drawn to study Sam's face. She seeks to find a likeness to her son. She also sees that although Sam is fair, while Andrew is dark, there is a similarity in the brothers' features. And so added to her anger, is a sharp sense of sorrow that life has denied her what she had been promised. If only she could have had a child, born in wedlock, whose birth could have been celebrated… A child who had lived… a child with warm cheeks, and sweet warm breath… She steadies herself, then turns to walk from the room.

'Don't go,' Sam pleads. 'Please don't go, until you have heard me out. I came here to say how sorry I am. I live in torment for the wrong that we did to you, my brothers and I.'

'How did you find me? How did you know that I was here?'

'I read about your accident in the Courier, and I recognised your picture. I went to Galloway's Laundry, and a girl called Jessie told me where you were staying. I hope you are completely recovered. Please, Chrissy … I cannot expect, and do not hope for, forgiveness. But I want to say if there is anything that I can do for you that is within my power, I will do it. I am no longer a student; I am an officer now, on one of my father's ships. I have a wage. I could make you an allowance.'

'It would shame me. I could never take your money.'

'There must be something I can do for you.'

'There is nothing.'

'So you have no dreams… no aspirations?'

Chrissy bridles. Sam has abused her most horribly, yet he dares to come to invade the peace of Frank's house and criticise her presumed limitations. She sees herself, as he must see her. A poor, broken laundry girl. She looks him in the eye. 'I do have a desire,' she says. 'I would like to travel to Africa, to help save the souls of innocent children, who do not yet know God. In the meantime, I will pray to Jesus and I will ask Him to save yours. As for me, you can have my forgiveness. I would do myself more of a disservice, were I to live a life dominated by bitterness and regret. Now, if you please, you will show yourself the door.'

She returns to the kitchen.

'Hope there's nothing wrong,' says Gwen.

'He brought a message,' says Chrissy. 'It was not important. Could you pass me the brush? I can start cleaning the jars.'

 **East Africa**

Lokim had hoped when he was purchased in the market place, that he would be put to work around his new owner's home. He had hoped that he would be set to planting crops and milking goats, he had dreamed that after a time he could steal away in the night. He would make the long journey back to his manyatta, living on what he could take from the land.

But the man who had bought him passed him swiftly on to another new owner, so that he once again found himself in a long line and chained by the neck, whilst carrying – as before – the thick end of a heavy ivory tusk. He heard someone say that this new coffle – like the previous one – was journeying to where they could sail across the Endless Water, to an island called Zanzibar. He no longer thought it possible that the slaves would be set free when they reached that place. But he tried not to succumb to despair. Whenever he was washed with self-pity, he concentrated intently on the physical process of putting one foot in front of the other.

'*Kuacha!*' shouts one of the traders, bringing down his whip. The line shuffles to a halt, and Lokim looks around him.

The slaves have reached a town where buildings made of brick and stone stand high next to straw-roofed huts. Birds caw and wheel in the sky, and the air smells oddly of salt. Lokim catches a glimpse of white sand and a stretch of greeny-blue that ripples in the breeze. With a sense of excitement mixed with foreboding, he understands that the coffle has arrived at the Endless Water.

The trader uses his whip to steer the line into an open square, in the middle of which lies a towering pile of ivory. Lokim would not have believed that there were so many elephants — alive or dead — in the world. The randomly heaped tusks remind him of a huge, unruly bird's nest. The trader points at the heap, and makes a lowering movement with his hand. When his turn comes, Lokim puts down his load, then stretches out his aching arms.

The man at the front of the line is pushed down into a kneeling position. Everyone jostles to see what is happening. From behind him, Lokim hears grunts of surprise and approval, as the other slaves realise that the man's chains are being cut through.

It is Lokim's turn to kneel. The trader sweats as he pushes the metal file to and fro, then he kicks Lokim in the chest to indicate that he has finished his work. Lokim gets up uncertainly. Without the chain, he feels strangely light. He is tempted to run, but his collar marks him out and, anyway, it would be fatal to try to escape. The traders all carry guns, which they have demonstrated their willingness to use.

The coffle snakes down a narrow road. '*Harakisha!*' calls a trader. 'Get a move on, will you!'

From behind him, Lokim hears a whistling sound. He moves quickly to one side, but the tip of the whip catches him on the back. He tries to move faster, but he finds himself treading on the heels of the man in front.

The trader stops outside a high-walled, almost windowless

236

building. '*Kupata katika!*' he shouts, 'Get inside!' A stench of faeces and urine makes Lokim want to cover his mouth and nose. He hesitates, and the trader kicks him hard on the shin then shoves him in the back, so that he stumbles through the open door. There is little light in the room, and for some moments, Lokim can see nothing at all. Once his eyes have adjusted, he becomes aware that against the filthy wall, a man lies dead. He must have been there for some days, because his body is swollen and puffed. More and more slaves are pushed into the room. The heat and the smell are appalling. Around him, people shriek and sob and cry.

Time passes. Lokim comforts himself with the thought that sooner or later, he will be given food and water. Once it has died, a goat or a cow has some value for its pelt. A slave when dead has no worth at all. Next to him, a woman is gibbering as if possessed. He manoeuvres himself to one side as she claws with hands, then reaches out, as if she would tear the flesh from his face. He sees that he was about to tread on a body; the small, broken thing must once have been her child.

A young, fine-featured woman is ill with dysentery. She leans against the wall for support, as she helplessly opens her bowels. The floor is awash with urine and ordure, while the air above buzzes with black flies.

Lokim tries to flick away the flies that crawl on his back; they gather to feed on the wound made by the whip. He reflects as he does so, on the strange capriciousness of pain. There were times in his previous life when a small splinter under his thumb could occupy all his attention but here in these terrible surroundings, the wet laceration he can feel with his hand hardly bothers him at all. It as if is protected by some big-hearted ancestor who will not allow him to suffer more than he can endure. Sustained by this thought, he works to create a further comforting image. He sees the strange woman leading him by the hand. He observes that in his imagining, he is not as he is now — weak and thin as a needle of gorse. Instead, he appears well-built and strong. He feels a rush of affection for the healthy, swift-running young herdsman, who was once himself.

The woman gives him a gourd of maize porridge, made creamy with milk; he savours each imaginary spoonful. Someone treads hard on his foot; someone else elbows him in the ribs. He holds himself straight and tall as a jackalberry tree on a windless afternoon. But then a man screams out with such intense despair that the sound pierces into him. The scream is impossible to ignore, and he opens his eyes.

The stench is terrible. Lokim longs to be near the door. It has a narrow gap below it, which allows some air to enter. The one window is too high and small to give much ventilation. Men, women and children continually call out in their distress. Beside him, a man with a lip plug is trying to hold up his wife, to prevent her from being trampled underfoot. Her eyes have rolled up, and her mouth has fallen open. Lokim can see that the man's efforts are in vain, for the woman has already died.

His back is more painful now; the spirit which had protected him, must have taken itself off elsewhere. With each heartbeat, the pain gets worse. A girl calls out frantically for water, and her cry is taken up by others. '*Maji, maji,*' she repeats until she grows hoarse.

When night comes, the exhausted slaves lie down, one by one, on the stinking floor. There is not sufficient space for each of them, so they lie on top of each other. The foot of a man rests heavily on Lokim's cheek, and two children lay themselves across his torso. 'In the morning, we will be fed,' Lokim tells himself. 'We will be fed, and given water.'

But all through the next day, the slaves are left parched and hungry. The eyes of the children who rested on Lokim are deeply sunken, and their breath is quick and shallow. By the time evening comes, both of them are dead. Lokim carries them to the corner of the room where the bodies have been heaped, to make more space for the living.

No-one attends to the slaves the following day, either. Those who remain alive are now too weak to cry out. Each man, woman or child, is locked in a silent struggle; each either fights to remain alive, or they are intent on dying as quickly as possible, in order to end their suffering.

Lokim wants to live. He pictures the blue clear sky of the world outside, and remembers the fresh water that sprang from the high hill, back home in Karamoja. He remembers the trusting eyes of his cow Pila, and the joy of running to give chase to an antelope, while holding high his spear. He suspects that the slaves are undergoing some kind of test. In the crudest possible way, the weak are being separated from the strong. On the third day, when the door is finally opened, he makes himself stand up. When he is told to move forwards, he tries to walk with firm steps.

Over half the slaves have died. Those that remain are made to gather in a shelter outside the building. They are handed calabashes of water which they pass from person to person. Anyone who is deemed to be holding the calabash for too long, is prodded with a sharp stick. Three big pots of porridge are brought out, and are placed in the middle of the floor, but the slaves are wary of starting to eat. They fear being punished, for greed. So they wait until they are kicked forward, to take their turn, then they eagerly scoop up the mess with their hands. A young boy is beyond hunger; he refuses the food. His mother frantically prises her fingers between his teeth, and pushes the food inside his mouth.

Lokim puts a hand behind his back and runs his fingers down his spine. His wound, though still painful, is scabbing over and he feels fortunate that it is healing. When he is handed the calabash, he resists the temptation to gulp down all the water it contains. He carefully watches the guard, waiting for a signal to stop. A breeze shakes the leaves of a nearby palm tree and the strange smell of the Endless Water signals a possibility of change. That night, he positions himself at the edge of the shelter, so that he can look out at the stars, before he falls asleep.

'*Amka! Amka!*'

A young trader in a dusty turban, kicks him with a sandalled foot. Lokim sees that most of the rest of the group are awake; they are already taking turns by the porridge pot. He quickly joins the queue.

At midday, when the sun is at its highest, the slaves are made to walk to the market place. Lokim endeavours to suppress his rage as men, women and children are separated and pushed into separate pens. He knows that his best hope is to be sold as soon as possible; he must do nothing to indicate that — if purchased — he would be anything other than biddable. When a pot of palm oil is handed round, he dutifully anoints himself. The oil makes the slaves' emaciated bodies gleam with an illusion of health.

Lokim is singled out by a pale-skinned man wearing a shati and cloths which cover each leg. He is clean shaven, but above his mouth he has allowed his hair to grow; he looks as if he has a large furry caterpillar attached to his upper lip. He pulls Lokim by the arm, and stares hard into his face. He seems to be unable to choose between Lokim and another man. He goes back and forth, between the two; he pinches Lokim's arm, then demands to see the soles of the other man's feet. He approaches one of the traders, who nods and lifts his whip.

Lokim groans silently. As the trader approaches, he wills his heart to slow its beating. He pictures the dream woman. He sees her wearing a cape of hide so soft and fine that it falls round her like water. The woman removes the cape and places it on his shoulders. When the whip falls, Lokim does not flinch.

240

The man with the caterpillar lip gives an approving nod. He talks with the trader, and after some negotiation, they settle on a price.

Lokim is led by his new owner along the shore. They stop at a stone building washed with white, which must be the man's home. A child is waiting at the front gate. She greets the man eagerly, tugging at his hand. He smiles, lifts his daughter in his arms and kisses her on both cheeks. Lokim lowers his head deferentially. His back is sore and aching from the beating. He prays that now he is one of the man's possessions, he will be spared such casual violence. He hopes that the man will prove to be a good slave master, as well as a caring father.

The man leads him through a sweet-smelling garden to a dusty, fenced off area. He points to a brick-built shelter, puts his two hands together, and rests his head. Lokim understands that the shelter is to be his sleeping-place.

* * *

The man's name is Pedro Almeida, and he is a trader in shells that are gathered from the Water, which he calls 'O Oceano'. Almeida's wife, who organises the household, has another name for the Water; she calls it 'The Sea'. The shells arrive and are taken away in large wooden boats, called 'dhows'. It is Lokim's job to carry the sacks of shells to and from the store house, where they are sorted, then stacked. One day, he is told that — if he behaves well and proves that he can be trusted — he will be allowed to travel in the dhow which is used by the Almeidas to collect the highest-quality shells from various ports further down the coast.

The person in charge of the store house, is a grizzled-haired man called Burro, who does little physical work, because it is his job to keep track of the bags. Burro does this by making marks on sheets of fibre, with a hollow metal tube, filled with pigment. Every morning, Lokim, Burro and the houseboy are summoned to the courtyard of the Almeidas' house. They are made to kneel, while Senhora Almeida recites words from a block of fibres, bound in black leather. She calls this 'reading from the Bible', and afterwards she expects everyone to put their hands together, and chant together a tuneless song, which she calls, 'The Lord's Prayer.'

Lokim notices that Burro is given status because of his ability to make sense of the squiggles he forms with his hollow tube. He watches Burro intently, and when Senhora Almeida recites her words, he carefully observes how her eyes follow the lines of shapes on the fibre sheets which she flips over using her thumb and forefinger. One day, he thinks, he himself will acquire these skills. Somehow, he will escape from slavery, and when he has done so, he will put his new-found knowledge to good use.

 Island of Mozambique

James steps from the bobbing rowing boat and slowly climbs the rope ladder, which has been thrown over the side of the *Gorgon*'s hull. By the time he reaches the top, he is exhausted. He is grateful for the assistance of a burly sailor, who reaches out his muscular arms to pull him onto the deck.

Wilson is standing with two junior officers, examining one of the paddles. Some of the casing has been removed from the wheel. Although the captain has his back to James, he is easily recognisable from his height, and from the gold rings on his cuffs. James approaches with his arm outstretched. But when Wilson turns round, he looks at him blankly, then frowns.

'Is there a problem?' James asks, indicating the paddle.

Wilson's face breaks into a smile. 'My dear chap!' he says.

'Not at all. Nothing that can't be sorted. I do sincerely apologise for my rudeness. Until I heard you speak, I didn't recognise you! Foolish of me — a messenger had brought your note, so I knew you would be coming. My poor friend — you are so very much changed.' He shakes James's hand, moving it briskly up and down as if pumping water. 'Let me show you to your berth, then we'll have lunch. You're clearly in need of nourishment. You're nothing but a bag of bones. And your red hair — it is nearly grey. Where's your luggage? I'll have it fetched for you.'

James indicates the small ditty bag, slung over his shoulder. 'This is all I possess. I have nothing left, except for my notebooks. Everything else has been traded — or lost in the river.'

Wilson continues to look James up and down, as if he still cannot quite believe his eyes. 'We'll have to find you some better clothes. Those rags you are wearing are fit only for a scarecrow. Now come with me. Our carpenter, Mr Milne, has vacated his bed for you.'

James follows Wilson to the quarter deck, then down the hatch. 'I would not wish to inconvenience anyone...'

'Don't trouble yourself. Mr Milne has agreed to bunk with the bos'n, and there's enough space for both in his cabin.'

James is not disposed to argue further. The carpenter's little room looks very inviting: the bed is equipped with a coverlet and pillow, and next to it there is a small table and a chair. A jug of water has been put out on a shelf, together with a plate of biscuits. It has been thoughtfully covered with a dome of fine netting, to protect it from flies.

'I'll see you at noon,' the Captain continues. 'I'll ask the cook to bring lunch up on deck. I'll get a sail rigged across the table to give some shade. I'm looking forward to an account of all your adventures.'

James has no belongings to unpack, and his new berth is

quickly explored. He slots himself into the bed, places his hands behind his head, and considers how lucky he is to be aboard the *Gorgon*. The frigate had steamed into port just at a point when he had despaired of ever being able to leave Mozambique. Livingstone, of course, would have believed that it was Providence, not Lady Luck, who had delivered up the good captain. And on this occasion, Livingstone might well have been right.

There is a knock on the door. James opens it to find a cabin boy holding a pile of clothes.

'The captain asked me to give you these,' says the boy. 'He said to tell you that he doesn't need them. He had them made by a tailor in Mombasa, but they don't fit.'

'Please convey my thanks to the captain. I am very grateful to him.'

James removes his torn and tattered garments, and puts on the trousers, shirt and jacket. Then he shaves, and combs and cuts his beard. By the time he goes up on deck, he is feeling much restored.

'So tell me,' says Wilson, as he pours James a glass of Madeira. 'However did you come to be marooned on the island?'

The two men are seated on padded leather chairs brought up from the map room. There is a clean white cloth on the table, and all around the sea glints and sparkles in the sunshine. 'It is my great good fortune to be here, and in receipt of your considerable kindness and hospitality.'

'Yes, well, never mind all that. I imagine that you might well do the same for me, were our situations reversed. How did you come to leave the expedition, and what in God's name have you been through? Little more than a year has passed since we were together. I have never seen a man so altered!'

James puts down his glass, then grasps it again as it slides. A breeze has caused the sea to swell.

'Livingstone,' he says carefully, 'has many good qualities.

But I feel that as a leader, he sometimes lacks focus. And, as you will remember, the *Pioneer*'s slow progress was a cause of considerable frustration to everyone. I knew that I could cover more ground — both literally and figuratively — were I to separate from the main party.'

'To say that he lacks focus is far too kind a way of putting it. The man's deluded, and when the real world stubbornly refuses to align itself with his imaginary version of the planet, other people suffer the consequences. Speaking of which, when I was in Cape Town, I heard that his wife had died, in April last year. Naturally, I was very sorry to hear the news. But I was also surprised... Mary seemed in good spirits when we took the ladies up the river to Quelimane.'

'She died suddenly of fever. Livingstone took it very badly.'

'And how did you take it?' Wilson looks across the table.

James is taken aback. Enter rumour painted full of tongues, he thinks to himself. So even Wilson cannot resist the lure of gossip.

'I lost a dear friend.' He looks directly back at the captain.

'Quite so,' says Wilson, muttering as if he rather regrets the question. 'Ah good! Here comes Mr Gifford, with our curried lamb. It is to be served with rice, fresh cucumber and tomatoes, purchased this morning from the local market. I sent a boat out first thing.'

The lamb is tender, cooked with coconut and not too highly spiced. The cucumber reminds James of crustless sandwiches served in drawing rooms back home. He eats eagerly at first, but then rests his knife and fork. After so much ill-health, his appetite has not returned.

Wilson picks up the wine bottle. 'Think of it as medicinal,' he says, when James hovers a protective hand over his glass. 'It will do you good. Where were we — oh yes — you had decided to separate from Livingstone. Did anyone from the party go with you?'

'I got my crew to row me up to Magomero. Proctor joined me there — one of the young men from the University mission. He had decided to leave the station as things were so bad. Starvation, dysentery, attacks by the Yao. It was all too much. Proctor finally made his mind up to go when he couldn't celebrate Communion, because the wine store had been raided. And when he went into the chapel, someone had stolen the altar cloth.'

'I wonder what they used it for? I hope it found a useful purpose.'

'Yes.' James thinks himself back to the enclosure next to the mission. Despite all their privations and the admonishments of the Christian missionaries, the villagers had exhibited a stubborn vitality. They had been singing and drumming, when he arrived, making as much noise as possible; they were hoping to induce a storm of rain. 'An outfit for a wedding perhaps... or a canopy for initiation ceremonies.'

'Well... maybe not initiation ceremonies.'

'Sorry. Wasn't thinking. Not initiation ceremonies. Most inappropriate.'

Both men remain silent. Then Wilson says: 'It gets to you, after a while, doesn't it? The African way of being.'

'Yes it does,' says James. He takes a sip of wine. 'And it is so much harder than I thought it would be, to impose a Christian — a British — morality. I'll give you an example. Proctor and I had a guide called Chinsora Chato, which means I am told 'Sorrow is over now'. I don't know what sorrow had thrown its dull shadow over his early life, but the man had eventually emerged from the gloom nothing-the-worse, with a great deal of sharpness, a wonderful shrewdness and an amazing humour. This fine chap, who could have held his own in any London club, turned around one day and casually offered to sell me some slaves.'

'How did you answer?'

'I was so taken aback by his matter-of-factness that I could only laugh and reply, 'No old fellow, I don't, but I wish I could prevent you selling them.' Then I got one of the paddlers to explain to him the English attitude to slavery, and the difference between the British and the Portuguese. No doubt he was at a loss to know if 'the English' were better than other men, or only fools.'

'Where did you go with Proctor? Did you learn anything useful?'

'We went up the Shire, then spent some weeks trying to navigate our way through the Elephant Marsh, where we were capsized by a hippopotamus, and mercilessly bitten by mosquitoes. We learned that slavery and warfare are rife in the area, and the one is the consequence of the other. It suits the Arabs and Portuguese for the local tribes to be constantly fighting each other. They feed local hostilities whichever way they can.'

'So where did you go next?'

'Back to Shupanga. We were there in time to help with the launch of the *Lady Nyassa*. Rae had finally agreed to assemble her. After much shoving, pushing, hauling, greasing and digging, we finally got her to float in the river, but she's no more fit for purpose than the *Pioneer*. Mind you, I think the navigation of the Zambesi would be a puzzle to any captain but the Yankee who could sail his steamer over the grass when the dew was upon it.'

'And then?'

'I went further up the Shire River, this time with Waller. The man is irrepressible. He finds comfort and joy in the most desperate of circumstances. I can picture him now, walking into a rancid, broken-down hut and pronouncing it to be a palace fit for a king. He declared a skinny flamingo we shot down and half-roasted to be the best meal he'd ever tasted. Sadly for me, Horace felt he had to get back, so we made our way back to the main expedition. We found the *Pioneer's* progress to be even slower. Now she was having to tow the *Lady Nyassa*.'

'I don't suppose that improved anyone's humour. How did Charles handle the situation? He always seemed to me to be a man on the edge of some sort of mental collapse.'

'I don't know which of the Livingstone brothers was the more moody or quarrelsome.'

'You must have been keen to relieve yourself of their company.' Wilson indicates James's plate, which is still half full. 'Don't let me stop you eating.' He spoons more curry onto his own plate.

James swallows a little rice before continuing: 'Yes. I took a boat with Thornton — the geologist — up to Tete. He had rejoined the expedition after Livingstone agreed to withdraw the charges he'd made against him. Livingstone still insisted on finding fault at every turn, so Thornton was pleased with the opportunity to get away. We spent Christmas Day digging out coal samples to send back to the University in Glasgow. Then we pushed on to Kebrabasa.' James shakes his head. 'The rapids were completely impassable, as Kirk had said they would be. But it was worth the journey, to see for myself. Then it was back again, to Shupanga. I kept being attacked by fever, and I was finding it harder and harder to carry on regardless. For a time, if I tried to stand up, I just fell over.'

'My poor friend...'

James acknowledges this interjection, then says: 'After a few weeks of lying prone on my bed, six fine natives rowed me to Quelimane, where I was received by a Portuguese gentleman called Nunes, whose uncle is a friend of Livingstone. Nunes showed me so much kindness, I probably owe him my life. But once I felt better, it was frustrating to be stuck in the town day after day. No-one would give me a passage out, until finally I got a lift in a schooner with some people from Goa. But to my frustration, they refused to take me any further than here. A trader saw me looking rather wretched on the beach and he allowed me to shelter in his warehouse, which was stacked full of cowrie shells. After a month, the Governor kindly sent for me, having heard word of my presence. He offered me a house. I have been much more comfortable but, of course still very keen to leave. None of the dhows I approached would allow me on board. The sailors thought I would report them for slaving. I cannot begin to tell you the extent of my relief when the Governor's servant reported that an English warship was coming in to port. And to find it was the *Gorgon*...' James is too overwhelmed to continue. He stoops to pick up his napkin, in order to conceal his emotion.

'Let's have another drink.' Wilson raises his refilled glass. 'Your good health. Now where is it you want to go? The *Gorgon* is at your disposal.'

'Surely not...'

'Well, within reason. I can't take you back to Scotland, but I can drop you anywhere along the coast. Shall we take you to Cape Town? My orders are to patrol the waters around Madagascar. I am free to interpret those orders quite broadly. This old ship is nearing the end of her life. She would count it as a privilege to do a good man a favour, before being ignominiously scrapped.'

James pauses, then says: 'Would it be too much of an inconvenience for you to take me to Algoa Bay? Before I left Scotland, I was given a list of mission stations in Kaffraria and a map of how to find them. I was asked to produce a report. If I could complete such a thing, I would have more to show for my time spent away. It has been nearly two years since I left home, and to be honest, I feel I have achieved precious little.'

On arrival at Port Elizabeth, James rather wishes that the voyage to Algoa Bay could have taken longer, he had been enjoying so much the companionship of Wilson and his officers. He watches as the sailors expertly uncoil the mooring rope, then lift the heavy anchor over the side.

Wilson orders the cabin boy to put two bolts of calico in the dinghy. The bo'sn steps forward, but the captain says that he himself will escort James to the shore. The sailors slice the oars briskly through the water, then pull the boat up on to the sand.

'Take them,' Wilson says, handing over the rolls of cloth. 'They belong to me personally, so you are not defrauding Her Majesty's Government. Exchange them for a good horse and make sure you eat properly. You look quite different from the haggard fellow we picked up from the Island. My crew and I would be mortified were you to undo our good work.'

They shake hands. But the gesture seems inadequate. James embraces his friend. He watches the dinghy until it has been hoisted back aboard the *Gorgon*, then waves a farewell to Wilson: he will have to find some way of repaying the captain's generosity. Carrying his bag on one shoulder and the heavy cloth on the other, he turns and walks inland.

The bustling streets of Port Elizabeth remind James of Cape Town. Europeans, Malays and Xhosas appear to be equably and peaceably going about their business. Outside a large hotel, he approaches a straw-hatted cab driver, who directs him to a farm on the edge of the town.

The owner of the farm is Scottish. When James comments on his accent, he explains that he is the son of one of the emigrants from the 1820s, who were given parcels of land by the Government, to encourage British settlement in the Colony. He takes James to an enclosure, where the earth has turned to mud after recent rain.

'This one will suit,' he says and catches a tall, ginger gelding. 'His name is Leopold.' He gives the animal an affectionate slap on the rump. 'I called him after the Queen's third son. Look after him, and I'll buy him back, on your return.'

'Thank you,' says James. 'But I intend to take a ship from East London, and so will part with him there. You don't happen to have an old saddle do you? And maybe some bread...?'

The farmer provides two panniers of water and a pack of biltong, as well as two loaves. Thus supplied, James sets off to begin his survey.

He rides slowly at first; he wants time to take in all that he sees. He is struck by how much more of the land is farmed compared with the area around the Zambesi. He passes orderly fields of maize and cassava, and acres of golden pumpkins. There are orange trees, lemon trees and avocados, while low on the ground, sweet-smelling pineapples sprout from fans of lance-like leaves. When he visits a Wesleyan mission, the minister enthuses about the beauty of the countryside, the productivity of the soil, and the diligence of his flock. The collection of huts that make up his settlement have all been newly whitewashed. In the centre stands a thatch-roofed church, whose walls have been made brilliant by blossoms of pink bougainvillea. Young boys in uniform trousers and shirts tend a vegetable garden where prize-size runner beans hang from a wooden frame.

'I am to undertake a marriage ceremony this afternoon,' says the minister. 'I am sure the happy couple would be honoured to welcome you as their guest.'

James is an object of considerable novelty and interest. Before the service, the congregation gather round, keen to greet him. He cannot respond in the people's own language, so he smiles broadly to indicate a general sense of bonhomie and nods enthusiastically, as he shakes a queue of hands. The bridegroom is dressed in a black frock coat, a shirt with a spotless turn-down collar, snowy white trousers and matching gloves. His bride wears a dress that is decorated with a flourish of coloured ribbons. Afterwards, the guests are provided with a generous supper of stewed goat. It is all most civilised, and most congenial.

He goes next to a German mission. James is glad that he can speak the language, because he finds the minister keen to unburden himself of his most understandable grief. The man wants to return to his own country, not because he is disheartened by his work, but because his wife and three daughters have recently drowned in the Kap. The river had risen and though their driver tried to cross at a place where the waters were at their lowest, he miscalculated the force of the flow and the heavy cart was washed away. That night, James finds himself sweating and turning in his bed; he is unsure whether this is because of the sadness of what he has heard, or because he is feeling the dregs of his old fever. At any rate, he is glad when morning comes, and it is time to saddle up Leopold, and continue on his way.

He travels to Grahamstown, where there is a new and very solidly built Anglican college, a purpose-built public library, an observatory and a museum. There is a cathedral, with a fine house next door: the bishop clearly lives in considerable style. Leopold snuffles at a neat strip of grass which runs down the centre of the driveway. James nudges him to move on, but the animal is unwilling to budge: he is in the process of copiously relieving himself. James sees that both horse and rider are being watched by two tittering black women. He doffs his hat to them, while he waits. When he glances back, he sees that the women are holding their hands over their mouths to conceal their laughter.

After several stops to ask directions, and a couple of wrong turns, he finds his way to the home of the Reverend and Mrs Knox, a Presbyterian couple who have lived in the Colony for the past thirty years. They have been recommended to him for their long service and their knowledge of the Xhosa language is said to be extensive. But when James finally arrives, he sees that their house looks as if it has been lifted by a hurricane and then abruptly abandoned. The walls are bulging and slipping, the glass windows are cracked and the thatch sticks out at all angles like Struwwelpeter's hair. He dismounts, ties Leopold to a hitching post, and knocks at the door.

The appearance of the Reverend Knox is as haphazard as his house; his beard is untrimmed, his hair is unruly and his coat is untidily patched. As soon as James steps inside, his nostrils are assailed. He feels something skim against his leg, and looking down, he sees a skinny domestic cat.

'We brought the first pair with us from Fife, and the naughty pussies will keep on having kittens,' says Mrs Knox. She is a hook-nosed little woman, with vaguely searching eyes.

James accepts some tea, which is served in a cracked and rather grubby cup. The room is crammed with elaborate native carvings and shelves of decorated ostrich eggs. Along one wall, six hollowed out elephants' feet stand in a row. The remaining floor space seethes with cats. They call out urgently and jump on the table to get at the milk jug.

'Get down puss,' says Knox, sweeping a striped tabby onto the floor. He sees James looking at the elephants' feet. 'They're for my nephew,' he says, with a nod. 'He has them converted to umbrella stands, and exported. These are awaiting collection, too.' He indicates the carvings. 'They sell in London or New York for relatively modest sums, but we acquire them for nothing, and so there are reasonable profits to be made.'

'I am sure that you put the money to good use.'

'The needs of our congregation are small, as indeed, are our own.' Knox jumps to his feet, and from a cupboard, he

253

fetches an album. He smoothes the watered silk cover and pushes the book into James's hands. 'My nephew uses the money to provide board and lodgings for young ladies who have been forced into prostitution by the American Civil War. He is kind enough to bring me pictures of those he has helped. As you can see, some have fallen into states of considerable degradation...'

James finds himself looking at a daguerreotype of a pouting woman. She is wearing nothing on her lower half except a swathe of muslin, and nothing on her top except for a feather boa. He hands the book back without comment: it would appear that the Reverend Knox has rather lost his way.

He declines the offer of a bed for the night, and apologises that he will not be there in the morning, to see the couple at their work. Then he climbs back into the saddle and sets off back along the dusty path.

His next destination is a place called Lovedale. His notes tell him that the mission was founded in the 1820s by a representative of the Glasgow Missionary Society. It is located near a small town called Alice, around fifty miles to the north of Grahamstown. James has no watch as the timepiece has been lost, having fallen out of his pocket. (It had anyway ceased to work properly, after suffering several unexpected immersions.) Using the height and position of the sun to gauge the time, he calculates that if the roads prove adequate, he should get there before nightfall.

His ride passes without incident, and on arrival, he is cheered by what he sees. His first impression is one of prosperity. Goats nibble in green fields, their clean white pelts shining in the gloaming. A young boy opens a set of imposing wrought iron gates. On either side of the driveway, plane trees have been planted. He hands over his horse, and goes up the sweeping staircase that leads to the front door of the main building. He knocks, and the door is opened by a wiry Scotsman, who introduces himself as Edward Govan.

Over supper, Govan explains his achievements and hopes. 'Christianity,' he says, 'cannot ever be enough. It is education that will transform the Colony for future generations. Education will be the key to unlock the boundless potential of Africa's people. Education is the thing, it will have to come before commerce. And we have here an institute that could rival any school in Scotland for the quality of its teaching, and the calibre of its pupils. We have white boys boarding here sent from as far as Johannesburg because of our good results. You'll see tomorrow how much we have achieved.'

The next morning, Govan shows James a bright, airy room, where black children and white children are sitting side by side, their heads bent over their desks as they work on complex mathematical calculations. Govan tells them to put down their pencils. He asks such questions as: 'If I multiply 123456 by 3, what do I get?' Every boy, after a few moments thought, is able to answer swiftly and accurately. There is absolutely no difference in ability between the black children and the white. In another class, a geography lesson is in progress. A small Xhosa boy called Samuel shows James a map of the world he has been working on; it is exquisitely and accurately drawn. James senses a growing excitement. He feels that before, he had merely been paying lip service to the principal of racial equality. Lovedale is demonstrating to him its actual truth. He thinks back to a young slave he had met on the island of Mozambique who had asked him in halting Swahili to show him the English alphabet. The young man had arrived by dhow to deliver a load of cowrie shells. James thinks about the urgency of the slave's request, and the disappointment on his face when he was pulled away from their lesson. Govan is right: education, not commerce, is the way forward. It is education that will defeat the traders; it is education that will release the slaves from their chains.

That afternoon, he asks Govan permission to preach at the local church.

'Of course,' says the teacher. 'I'll arrange an interpreter for you.'

The sight of James with his long limbs and strange hair draws a crowd; over a hundred people congregate to hear his words. He speaks for over an hour, trying to convey the radical nature of the New Testament. Jesus had been impatient with authority and had seen in everyone the possibility of change. James looks at the intent faces of the people in front of him. He recounts the parable of the talents: he tries to instil a sense of confidence and the excitement that comes from an acute awareness of potential. He is fired once more with the vision of an Africa made civilised and orderly. 'God has given to each of you both a powerful intellect and beautiful lands. You owe it to Him to make the best possible use of these gifts. By so doing, you can improve yourselves as individuals and radically change your society for the better.'

There is a murmur amongst the crowd. People are whispering to one another, and shaking their heads.

'What are they saying?' James asks.

'They say that their fate is not in their own hands. It is the white man who has control. Whenever a black man becomes powerful, the white man uses his guns.'

'It is wrong for them to do so,' says James. 'For the Xhosa were here before the Europeans. Believe in yourselves: there is so much that you can achieve. You are blessed to live in a rich and wonderful continent. You owe it to God and to yourselves to use all that you have been given.' He thinks of a map, beautifully drawn by an African child, with large areas painstakingly and unquestioningly painted pink. Feeling a sense of urgency, he spreads wide his arms. 'Africa: she belongs to you. She is your own country!'

Mina can hear her father cursing behind the half-shut door of his study. A drawer is opened then slammed abruptly shut. The process is repeated. Papa must have mislaid something that he considers important. 'Janet!' she hears him shout, 'Will you come here! Janet! Where are you girl! Come here at once!'

But Janet is not at home. She has gone with Maggie to visit the Rimes family. Since the sad death of the drawing master, his widow is reputed to have gone from bad to worse and as a consequence, the children are suffering. The little ones have been seen out in the street, barefoot and hungry. Mama has agreed that the household should offer some limited assistance and a basket is to be provided.

Mina gathers her courage, taps at the door, then enters the room. 'Can I be of help, Papa?' she asks. 'Have you lost something?'

'I am missing a receipt, from Kinnock, the rope maker. The damn fool says I haven't paid him for his last three spools. I know that I did... there's an entry in my ledger. Where's Janet?'

'Janet is in town. Let me help you look.'

'No. It can wait.' Papa seems deflated: looking all of his sixty-eight years, he slumps back in his leather-backed chair.

'Papa...'

'What is it?'

Mina had wanted to say something to indicate that she was aware of his grief. She wanted to add that it was a grief she shared. But her father's tone has crushed all possibility of any such intimacy. 'Would you like Parsons to bring you some tea?'

'Go away. Don't bother me.' He raises his voice to a shout: 'Leave me alone!'

Mina closes the door. Repressing the desire to cry, she takes herself off to the schoolroom. Suffering a rare indisposition,

Miss Scrope has remained at her lodgings, but the governess has sent a telegram with the summary instruction 'Horace, Odes 1.11. Then piecework. Be diligent!'

The Latin words dance meaninglessly before Mina's eyes, she finds it impossible to concentrate. She is distracted both by the concern she feels for her father and by her own sorrow. She plucks at the sleeve of her dress, and counts the days that have passed since she has worn any other colour than black. She does not consider it a sacrifice to wear mourning, she would gladly forgo the pleasure of ever wearing colour again if this would do anyone any good. But she cannot help reflecting that such dreariness seems an incongruous way of remembering her two sisters. In life, they had been as bright and cheerful as two springtime flowers.

She thinks back to the last time she saw Mary and Marjory together. It had been at a party given by Al at his house in Park Circus. Mary had been wearing burnt-orange satin and a necklace of moonstones, while Marjory had worn a dress of ruby red, with matching garnets that shone at her neck and in her hair. After dinner, Mary's husband had explained to Mama that he was worried about his wife's continual cough. For this reason, he had arranged to take a house by the seaside in Gibraltar. He hoped that a cure would be effected if she were to be removed for the winter to the warmer climate of the Mediterranean. Mama had given permission for Marjory to travel with Mary: it was decided that she would be a companion, and she could help with the care of the Templeton's two small children who would also make the journey.

On that crisp autumn evening, John Templeton's concerns had appeared misplaced. Mary had laughed and chatted: she had even demonstrated with Al a particular Highland dance, which was said to be popular at Balmoral.

It had been February when news was received at Corona

that Marjory, having developed a rash and high fever, had died suddenly, and that Mary's health had worsened. The awful news had thrown everyone into distress and confusion. John had wanted to leave straightaway. But then he said he was unable to leave the carpet factory: there were too many important orders to be fulfilled, and he had the welfare of his workforce to consider. Al had wanted to go, but he was needed at the Yard. And so it was Papa who sailed to Gibraltar to organise a headstone for Marjory and to be with Mary in what proved to be the last few weeks of her life.

He had returned more moody and irascible than ever. Now, in addition to his usual changes of mood, he suffered periods of apathy and bleak depression. Mina heard him tell Mama that he could accept the death of his daughters but when baby Mary, Mary's little daughter, died too, he had found himself questioning God's wisdom, and his own faith. 'She was innocent,' he kept repeating. 'She was a sweet, innocent child.' Mina cannot understand either, why a baby should have been brought into the world, only to die within a few short months. She tries to tell herself that little Mary is in heaven, and that Jesus has chosen her to be His companion, but this thought does not seem to provide the comfort that it should.

It had poured with rain on the day when Papa returned. He had got out of the coach without so much as looking at Mary's small son. The boy had stayed seated, looking white-faced and stricken. When Parsons fetched him down, and carried him into the house, the child had refused to speak: he had remained completely silent all the time he was at Corona. Mina's heart had melted with compassion. She felt that with time, she would have been able to earn the boy's trust, but after three days he was collected by his father, who took him off to stay with other relatives.

Mina thinks of the Rimes children, left bereft by their

father's death. Poor Rimes had carried on trying to teach until he could scarcely walk. Little was expected of him and Miss Scrope said that his visits should continue as long as possible as they were a way of supplementing the artist's income, which was much reduced since he no longer had the stamina to create his canvases. While Maggie and Mina worked at their easels, he would sit with his eyes closed, propping his head in his hands, until he was interrupted by another violent coughing fit. His whole body would shake as he fumbled for his handkerchief. Mina had wanted to go to his funeral, but Mama would not allow it, on account of Mrs Rimes and her scandalous behaviour.

There had been talk of a joint memorial service being held for Mary and Marjory, but in the end it never happened. There had been much discussion as to whether the event should take place in Broughty or Glasgow, until John Templeton finally said that he would find the whole occasion far too stressful. He was sure that an exposure to high emotion would have an adverse affect on his son: he would prefer to abandon the whole idea.

And so Mina wears black, in remembrance of people who were dear to her, to whom she has never had an opportunity to say goodbye. She thinks of Papa, alone in a strange country, holding a lonely vigil beside Mary until she breathed her last and then having to grieve afresh, for Mary's child. She wonders if a proper remedy will ever be found for consumption, something that would work better than the cold baths and plentiful fresh air that are currently prescribed. She has read in *The Times* of the Nursing School at St Thomas's Hospital. A part of her would very much like to run the gauntlet of her family's disapproval, and train there alongside Miss Nightingale. But in order to work as a nurse she would have to remain unmarried, and Mina is firmly of the belief that she would be happier with a husband. She dreams of a soul mate, someone kind with whom she could share her innermost thoughts. She thinks how fine it would be to be married to a clever doctor; she could help him in his work, she could support him when he applied the latest scientific knowledge in order to effectively heal and cure.

'You wouldn't believe the way Mrs Rimes keeps her house!'

Mina looks up: she had not heard her sister come into the room.

Maggie takes off her shawl, and continues: 'She paid the children no regard at all. And the place was in complete disarray. The table had not been cleared, and she had a pet parrot which was out of its cage. It kept squawking and its litter was all over the carpet.' She shudders and pulls off her hat. 'A man came to visit while we were there. He let himself in, just as if he had a right to belong.' Maggie blushes. 'He put his arm around Mrs Rimes's waist. She didn't object — she looked quite pleased. With poor Mr Rimes only two months dead!'

'Perhaps she thinks that the new man will be able to provide for her and the children.'

'Mina! A man should not touch a woman with such familiarity, unless they are married! There is such a thing as propriety!'

Mina picks up her copy of *The Odes* and pretends to study it. 'I suppose there is.' She cannot help thinking of the way Papa behaves with Hannah. He gazes sometimes at her bosom as if he would eat it: he seems to have no shame. She remembers Mhairi from the tenements in Dundee: the woman had inquired whether Papa had been 'dipping his wick'. There is no-one she feels she can ask but, having spent months thinking about it she has reached the uncomfortable conclusion that the phrase might refer to something other than candle wax. She loves Papa very much; she cares deeply about his welfare, and this idea is most distressing.

She pushes the book towards her sister. 'Please? I haven't been able to get very far.'

Maggie's eyes scan the verse. '*Carpe Diem* — seize the day.' She runs through her thumb and forefinger the black silk ribbon that trims her hat. 'I suppose I shouldn't be so quick to judge Mrs Rimes. That is probably what she is doing. Of course I'll help you. *Tu ne quaesieris...* Let's start from the beginning...'

That night, Mina sleeps only fitfully. At dawn, when woken by a chorus of blackbirds and sparrows, she cannot get back to sleep. She lies awake, grieving for Mary and Marjory. Then she begins to worry about Miss Scrope. Suppose that her illness develops further, into something more than slight? Mina does not like to think of the governess alone and suffering. Would Mama allow her to be nursed at Corona? Mina would do her best to ensure that she received the best possible care. And suppose that despite everyone's best efforts, Miss Scrope's illness grew yet worse?

In the morning, Mina is relieved to discover that her fears have been unfounded. For Miss Scrope appears in the hallway at her usual time. Briskly, she shakes her umbrella over the front door step. She snaps it closed and hangs up her coat.

'Come on girls! We have work to do! I have been thinking about the Underground Railway in London: what a marvellous thing it is! I read in Blackwood's about a Roman burial site that the engineers came upon, whilst tunnelling and this has led me to consider the Roman occupation of Britain. On reflection, I do not believe we have covered the period in sufficient attention; we have much to learn from that great empire, and from its decline...'

Mina and Maggie dutifully take themselves off to the schoolroom, and sit themselves down at the plain deal table. Miss Scrope hands each of them a copy of the first volume of Gibbon's *Decline and Fall of the Roman Empire.* 'I would like you to précis the first two sections, as concisely and accurately as possible. The skill is to recognise and retain the salient points and to discard anything that you find to be superfluous. Work with care, and I will ask permission to take you to see the Roman artefacts in the Royal Museum. Would you like that?'

'Of course, we would,' the girls reply in unison. They look at each other, then laugh.

'Miss Scrope?'

'What is it Mina?'

'I am glad to see that you are no longer indisposed.'

The governess pauses, before saying, 'to be truthful, I was not physically unwell. It was a crisis of a spiritual nature from which I suffered. I considered resigning my post. However, after a long night of prayer, I came to realise that God wishes me to remain as your tutor here at Corona, and I am happy to continue to be of service. God is generous in his forgiveness, whatever people's moral failings.'

''We would have missed you very much,' says Maggie. 'And whatever your misdemeanours, I am sure that they are very small and easy to forgive.'

'It is not myself who is in need of God's charity,' Miss Scrope flushes with a rush of unexpected anger.

'Has one of us done something wrong?' Maggie is distressed.

'No.'

'Then who has?'

The governess breathes out slowly, then says: 'I am grateful to Alexander Stephen, for the wages he pays me, and for the hospitality shown to me in this his house. I am sorry to be indiscreet, but sometimes the truth needs to be told.' She raises her head and looks into the distance, as if appealing to a higher authority. 'I know that I deserve to be given notice for saying so but as a man, your father has behaved with a lamentable lack of scruple, and as an elder of the Presbyterian church, I regret that he has laid himself open to an accusation of hypocrisy.'

Mina pinches together her finger and thumb. So Miss Scrope, too, has noticed the way Papa behaves when he is around Hannah. Miss Scrope, Mhairi from the tenements... Does everyone in the community regard her father with secret disgust? She pinches harder, and feels the blood drain from her face.

'Why Mina...you look quite faint. I am sorry to have upset you. But I cannot help my views. You know how strongly I disapprove of slavery.'

'Slavery... what has slavery got to do with anything? Papa does not keep slaves.'

'Of course he doesn't. But by trading directly with the Confederates, he supports their cause. There are two steamers being built at the Yard, for no other purpose than running the blockade. I cannot help my opinions: I believe that your father should be more circumspect when taking orders for his ships.'

CHAPTER NINE

September 1866

 Hygienic Laundry, Dundee, Scotland

'Chrissy, please! Listen to me...How long is it that you have been working here?'

'Four years, sir. If you remember, it is over four years since I started at your Laundry.'

'I know that, Chrissy! How could I have forgotten? The question was — so to speak —rhetorical. My point is, in all that time, have I treated you anything other than well?'

'You have always been a gentleman and generous, too. I am grateful to you, for your kindness. And I have never forgotten how you took me on when others would have turned me away.'

Mr Galloway puts a steadying hand on his chest: it is heaving in and out at an alarming rate, causing his shoulders to rise and fall like pistons. 'I repeat my question. Could you not find it in your heart to see me not as your employer, but as a humble suitor? I have the deepest admiration for you Chrissy, both for your beauty and your diligence. I would worship the ground that you walk on, if you would but allow me... Day after day, I have been maddened at the sight of you, as you go about your work... agitating the dolly... dashing away at the iron...'

'Mr Galloway, I think you confuse your emotions with those expressed in a popular song.'

'Don't mock me, Chrissy. It is cruel of you to do so. I am in torment... day after day, I have refrained from saying what I feel in case you could not find it in your heart to accept my plea. And then you might find it incumbent upon yourself to leave my service. I could not bear to be deprived of the daily delight of your presence. But I can keep silent no longer...' An excess of perspiration has caused two dark marks to appear under Mr Galloway's arms; the stains are speedily advancing towards the straining buttons of his waistcoat. He wipes his brow. 'Could we perhaps continue our dialogue inside my house? We could share a light supper in the dining room, and then you could help me to consider how I might have the front parlour redecorated. You could help me with the choice of a new paint colour for the walls... I have one of Templeton's catalogues... Together we could choose a new patterned carpet... Out of respect for my dear departed wife, I have kept things largely as they were. But it is many years now since she left us and my boys are quite grown up. Were you to do me the honour of accepting my hand, I would wish for you to feel entirely at home.' He slicks some loose strands of hair across the dome of his bald head, and gives an ingratiating smile.

Chrissy has no desire to encourage her employer. She is feeling thoroughly alarmed at his protestations. But neither does she wish to inflict the hurt that would inevitably result from an abrupt refusal. Mr Galloway is not a bad man, and it is entirely true that she is grateful to him. She is well aware that conditions in the Laundry are far better than many other work places in Dundee. She wipes her palms on her apron.

266

The fires have been closed down for the night, but the coppers are still bubbling under their covers and the air in the laundry hangs heavy with steam. The heat is adding to her mounting sense of panic. She longs not for the fustiness of the Galloways' house, but for fresh clean air. 'That is most kind of you sir. But I need to finish goffering these...' She seeks a suitable word — she cannot say 'smalls'. 'These *garments*, then afterwards, I have to lock up.' In an effort to deflect the conversation she adds, 'Mrs Morrell says that we should get a bar fitted to the outside door. There was a robbery in the street last Monday... perhaps you heard... Mr and Mrs Forster had just gone to bed when they heard a noise downstairs. Mr Forster found a man filling a sack with whatever he could lay his hands on. He threatened the thief with his grandfather's blunderbuss and he dropped the bag. But before he ran off, he must have pocketed Mrs Forster's purse, for it was missing, together with five gold sovereigns. She had been saving them to give to her grandson. He is hoping to buy his own fishing boat...'

Mr Galloway advances towards Chrissy. Taking her hand, he kisses it wetly. Chrissy is reminded of a slobbering lurcher that had scared her as a child. The dog had belonged to the local rat catcher, a bow legged man who had carried a basket of writhing ferrets on his back. It takes all her willpower not to pull away. 'I can tell,' he says, 'That you are not quite ready to make a decision. I will give you a week, then I will ask you again. In the meantime I will go about my business, and you will go about yours. Does that sound fair?'

'Oh indeed, sir. Indeed it does. Thank you for your understanding, and for your patience.'

* * *

In the following days, Chrissy goes about her tasks with fervour, scrubbing and pummelling, mangling and folding with an energy made more acute by anxiety. Thoughts flicker inside her head like darting swallows. She knows she should be grateful to Mr Galloway, for while he might be prepared to put her past to one side, she is certain that at St Michael's — the church where he goes every Sunday — his fellow-worshippers would show no such understanding. It is humbling that his devotion is such that he would suffer the congregation's disapproval and the whispered criticism of everyone else in the neighbourhood. She should be grateful, and to secure a future without the challenges and miseries of poverty, she would do well to accept his offer.

But it is lust that is driving Mr Galloway, pushing him to possess her, despite his own better interests. He wants her physically, and he knows that the only way he can achieve the union he so much desires and at the same time keep peace with his conscience, is to make her his wife. And when Chrissy imagines the reality of being married to her employer — sharing his bed, seeing his plump white body naked and exposed — she feels a pressure in her throat: it is as if someone is pressing on her windpipe: the panic she experiences, makes her retch...

He has implied that were she to refuse him, she could continue with her work. But would this, in reality, be the case? Rather, would he not feel that their relationship was too altered to be sustainable? And would she not find the same? But if she were to hand in her notice, would he be prepared to supply her with references, or would hurt pride cause him to refrain from doing so out of a desire to exact revenge? Even were she to be supplied with the most excellent letter of recommendation, it is doubtful that she would be given a job elsewhere. The Girl with the Lamp can still be seen everywhere about the town; there are many who know her story, and the image is a constant reminder of her fall from grace. If only Frank were still managing the Tannery! But he has left Scotland: George is now a singer in a Paris cafe, and Frank has followed him to France. Chrissy is flooded with a sense of frustration at her own powerlessness: she fervently wishes that she could fling off her vulcanised apron, and stride straight out of the Laundry without ever looking back. She longs for the opportunity to start her life again, somewhere altogether new.

 East London, Cape Colony

Dr Lawes remains seated at his desk. He smoothes out the single sheet, adjusts his spectacles, and studies it.

Lokim stands in front of him, tall and upright as one of the English naval officers he has seen walking around the town. He does his best to look impassive, while he waits anxiously for the doctor's reaction. He knows what the letter says because he has read it. Before the boat from Bagamoyo had docked in East London, he had removed the envelope from its keeping-place at the bottom of his bag, and scanned its contents. Humidity had rendered the flap easy to open; there was no seal, because Senhora Almeida had run out of wax. In the same way, she had exhausted her supplies of many other things, which she came in the end to count essential to her wellbeing. Letters are considered to be private: Lokim had struggled with his conscience before concluding that on balance it would be best for him to know what was being said about himself.

It was not that he did not trust Frances Almeida. She had been more than kind to him, and to her he owed his freedom. But it would, he felt, be imprudent to put the same faith in Dr Lawes, a man he had never met. The doctor might claim that bad things had been written about himself, as a way of exerting control. Or he might say that Senhora Almeida had

269

given orders for him to be sold, so that he could claim the money received in exchange. Lokim knows that the British do not in, in theory, traffic in slaves, but his experiences have led him to believe that there is a bad goat in every herd.

After what seems like a long time, Dr Lawes puts down the letter. 'My cousin Frances appears to have a high opinion of you,' he says. 'As she is returning to England, she has recommended that I should employ you as a servant.' He looks at Lokim, directly. 'What do you think? Would you like to work for me?'

Lokim gives a slight bow. 'I would be honoured to do so.' Silently, he adds: but treat me badly, and I will run away... And if necessary, I will kill you first. The savage cruelty he experienced during his chained and shuffling days still makes him smoulder: his memories can quickly fire him with a choking rage. He has inwardly resolved that whatever the cost, he will never again allow himself to be treated as another man's chattel.

'Frances — Mrs Almeida — says that you can read and write.'

Lokim nods. 'That is true.'

'How did you learn? It is unusual for a slave, I do beg your pardon, *ex*-slave, to have acquired such skills.'

I beg your pardon, ex-slave. Lokim warms to the doctor. 'Soon after I arrived to work at the warehouse, Senhor Almeida came to believe that the man he had put in charge was cheating him. But he needed proof. He thought that if I could read, I could catch him out, I could prove that he was doing wrong. I had learned the alphabet because I had asked the Almeidas' children to teach me. The Senhor asked the Senhora to help me make sense of what I knew. It was true that Burro was behaving dishonestly. He was listing one less sack in every other load.'

'So the man in charge of the sacks got the sack.' The doctor smiles as if he has made some kind of joke. Seeing the incomprehension on Lokim's face, he gives a little shake of his head. 'Frances says that you are originally from a village in Central Africa. Would you not like to go back there, now that you are free?'

The question is not one that Lokim has considered. He speaks slowly, wishing to give a truthful answer. 'In the years that have passed since I left, too much has happened.' He thinks of the manyatta, with its simple round huts. He thinks of the villagers, with their petty arguments and small celebrations. 'I am not sure that I would adjust. Besides... there is the journey to consider. Karamoja is far away. If you will have me, I would rather work for you here.'

'In that case, we'd better find something for you to do. Frances says you are good with animals, but I already have a boy who helps me with the horses and I have got rid of the cow. East London is well-supplied: we have a milk-cart that comes round every morning.'

'I could chop wood. Cook. Clean.' Lokim is concerned that he will not after all, be given the opportunity to work for the doctor. 'My English is good. Senhora Almeida lent me books from her library. I have read Dickens, and George Eliot. And of course, the King James Bible. I have learned to converse. After the sad death of the Senhor, the Senhora and I had many talks together, in the English language. She spoke of her plans for the garden, and for the church that she wished to build.'

'But now Frances has returned to Devon.' The doctor appears suddenly downcast; Lokim wonders if he once had a romantic attachment for his cousin. 'I kept thinking I would visit, but I kept putting it off... I could never get away from the practice...' For a short time, he seems lost in his thoughts. 'What was it that finally made her go?'

Lokim thinks of the gradual breaking down of hierarchy that occurred after the Senhor's death, which reflected a more general disintegration of the order which had previously

271

existed within the household. He wonders how best to respond. It is an odd experience, talking with a white man who addresses him as if he were an equal. He does not wish to sound disloyal. It was not the Senhora's fault that she could not keep control. The other traders did not respect her, because of her sex. She was too gentle, she would not threaten to use her gun. 'There were many reasons,' he says eventually.

'Sit down, won't you?' Doctor Lawes indicates the chair on the other side of his desk. 'Makes me uncomfortable, you looking down at me like that. I suppose she was naturally concerned for her safety, and that of the children, after what had happened.'

'For the first year after the robbery she wished only to make a success of the business. She saw it as a way of honouring her husband. He had died trying to protect the warehouse. But she grew tired. It is hard for a woman to be a trader in a place like Bagamoyo. People took advantage. She told me that she missed things more and more … little comforts… she talked of the sound of English church bells… And she worried about the children's education.'

'I can't blame her for giving up the fight.' Dr Lawes leans back in his chair and crosses his arms. 'So she's left Africa and she's sent you to me, as a kind of present.' He laughs. 'A gift that I'm expected to feed, clothe, shelter and wage. Oh well. I could do with some help in the dispensary. I'll show you how to make up some basic mixtures. And it would be helpful to have someone reliable who could deliver prescriptions around the town.'

 Glasgow, Scotland

James watches as Joseph Lister makes a midline excision, and then opens the abdominal cavity. He uses forceps of his own design to clamp the artery and cystic duct, before he ties them off and cuts them through.

'You can see how large the stone has become,' he says. 'It is almost the size of an apple. Must be causing considerable discomfort. No wonder the poor fellow's jaundiced. He glances across, to re-assess the patient's colour. The man lies on the table open-mouthed, having been rendered insensible with chloroform.

The surgeon lifts out the distended gall bladder and tosses it into the bucket. He fits a drain into the bile duct, then closes the cavity. Just as he finishes suturing, the patient gives a bellow of pain, and tries to sit up. Lister pushes him back down; he reacts mechanically, his expression is impassive. It is as if the man were inanimate, and had sprung unbidden from a jack-in-the box. 'Nearly finished, Mr Travis.' He turns to James. 'Would you mind putting some pressure on his shoulders? I've only got a couple of stitches left to do. It's not worth giving him another dose.'

James does as he is asked. Having completed his medical studies, he is spending a period of time working as Lister's dresser. James admires the surgeon's skill and believes that his revolutionary theories have logic in their favour. On Lister's orders, he applies a pad, dampened with carbolic acid to the wound. The surgeon thinks that the liquid could be effective in killing the micro-organisms which he believes to be the cause of infection, rather than miasma, or bad air, as is commonly supposed.

Bandaging Mr Travis takes rather longer than it should, because as well as suffering from the after-effects of chloroform, the man has drunk a quantity of whisky, before braving the operating theatre. The alcohol has made him belligerent. It is only by ducking judiciously that James avoids a black eye. By the time he has finished, he feels rather in need of refreshment himself.

He repairs to the Ale House, where he finds John Cowie seated in an armchair, ruminatively smoking a pipe.

'James! I could do with some company! Let me get you a beer.' John now works as an obstetrician. For two days a week, he volunteers at the Infirmary and the rest of his working week is spent building up a successful private practice. 'I have just delivered twins by Caesarean section. The mother lived, but it was touch and go...' He goes to the bar and returns with another glass, together with a foaming jug. He raises his own glass, before sitting back down. 'I'm glad to have seen you... I heard through the grapevine that you're off again to Africa. We'll miss you, if that's true.'

James savours the cool liquid. It has been a long afternoon. Thank you,' he says, 'but I'm not going until November ...'

'So we'll have the pleasure of your company for a few more weeks... but tell me, what's the attraction? Why not stay here? No-one can say that medicine isn't a worthwhile occupation. If you utilise your charm to good enough effect, you could make an excellent living.'

For John, success has always been measured on a monetary basis. 'We all have different motivations,' James says equably. 'Mine is to do my part in making Africa a better place.' He would like to say more; he would like to tell John about the excitement he had felt when he visited the school in Alice. But he does not think his friend would understand, nor would he be particularly interested.

John laughs. 'You want to be the equivalent of a prune: Going Into the Dark Interior and Doing Good. Well, as you say, each to his own.' He sucks at his pipe, then puts it down with a clatter. 'We should make the most of your company, while it is available!' What are you doing tonight? You could come to Dowanside Road... You'd be most welcome to join us for supper.'

'Regretfully, I must refuse. Though do please give my

regards to Violet.' John has recently married; his pretty young wife is sociable and charming. 'Sorry to say, I'm engaged elsewhere. I have promised to give a talk at the meeting rooms of the Reformed Church. It's been organised by The Ladies Association. They're a formidable group; they'd probably send a posse to hunt me out, were I to be late. I have to be there by seven.' He gets out his watch. 'So if you will excuse my rudeness, I must finish this drink, then take my leave.'

As he hurries down Castle Street, James considers what John has said. Medicine, it is true, is a worthwhile occupation. If Lister is right about germ theory, and his anti-septic techniques prove to be effective, then countless lives will be saved. If he were to remain in Glasgow, he would be able to help the surgeon to promulgate the findings of his invaluable work.

He swings open the wrought iron gate that leads into the small front garden of his lodgings. The paving stones are broken and cracked, but a few Michaelmas daisies are growing against the wall of the terraced house. He finds his key, opens the door and lets himself into his apartment. However tempting an option the life of a city doctor might appear to be, he will not abandon his missionary aspirations. He has asked if he can go back to Lovedale, the Elders of the Free Church have given permission for him to do so, and he has a duty to return.

When he takes off his coat, he sees that his shirt is spattered with the blood of Mr Travis. He rummages in a drawer and exchanges it for a clean one, laundered by his landlady. If he is honest with himself, it is not just duty that is calling him; he is also driven by ambition. He wants to achieve something great. Using Lovedale as a base, his dream is to create a university whose doors would be open to all races, creeds and colours, and which would rival the best colleges in the world in the quality of its teaching. Africans, he reflects, are mixed in their abilities, as are Europeans. And the brightest are as capable as their white brothers of achieving glittering academic success. Currently, they are deprived of the opportunity of doing so. The disappointment he endured as a result of the collapse of his Scheme has led him to be circumspect and he has not publicly discussed his desire, but privately he has decided to dedicate his life to putting right this inequality.

He searches round for his cufflinks. The advancement of female education is another cause to which he intends to apply his energies. He has already secured from The Ladies Association the promise of one hundred pounds per annum to provide secondary teaching for girl pupils at Lovedale. The Cape government has agreed to match this sum, and he has recruited a suitable teacher, a Miss Waterston, to act as headmistress. He fixes his tie, finds the things that he needs for his talk, puts his coat back on and sets off back up the road.

Turning left into Cathedral Street, he finds himself musing upon the character and person of Jane Waterston. She is a serious-minded young woman in her twenties with the courage to go against the wishes of her family, who have firmly stated that her place is at home. He met her while she was working as a nurse at the Infirmary, and was impressed by her practical skills and her intelligence. After he had introduced her to the Elders who funded the Free Church Mission, they tentatively inquired whether it was his intention to put his relationship with his future colleague on something other than a professional footing. It had been hinted that such an alliance would be not be looked upon unfavourably. In the normal way, a married woman would not be expected to work, but in circumstances rendered unusual by the South African bush, the rules could be relaxed. James had tried to make as clear as possible, without actually spelling it out, that he did not — he does not — look upon Miss Waterston as a prospective wife.

He stops to put sixpence into the hat of a former soldier, who sits at the corner of Taylor Street. A clumsily written card explains that the man has been reduced to begging because of wounds he had suffered in the Crimea War. James gives silent thanks for his own sound health, before continuing on his way. He hopes that when he does get back to Africa he is not revisited by fever.

There are scores of people milling outside the entrance of the Church. It is a source of surprise to James that he is still much in demand as a speaker, although it is three years since he returned from the Zambesi. His connection with Livingstone continues to exert a magnetic attraction, despite the pounding the explorer received from *The Times*, after the deaths of Mary, and of young Thornton. Livingstone was criticised for his poor leadership: he was considered to have put others to unnecessary risk, and the expedition was recalled. Rather than coming home, he had taken the *Lady Nyassa*, and sailed her, almost single-handedly, to Bombay, which was — James has no hesitation in admitting — a remarkable piece of seamanship.

He makes his way through the crowd, and is greeted by the minister, who ushers him through to the meeting room. It is already more than half full; by the time everyone has assembled, there will not be enough seats, so that some people will have to stand.

'We'll have prayers first of course,' the minister says. 'And there're one or two things I want to say about our appeal for the church roof. But I won't go on for long. It's you they've come to hear, not me. I hope you'll stay for some refreshment, and will make yourself available to answer some informal questions. People are curious to know about the personality of the doctor. Livingstone is a remarkable man. A truly remarkable man.'

James steps onto the platform. He begins by thanking the

members of The Ladies Association for their generous donation to Lovedale; he goes on to explain how valuable their contribution will be. 'You may have an idea,' he says, 'that the ground in Kaffraria is stony. That the seeds of learning will struggle to flourish. But this is not the case. In some ways, the native people who live in the vicinity of Alice, are more civilised than the British. If you will allow me, I will illustrate the truth of this.' From his satchel he takes a set of shackles, a thumbscrew, and a knuckleduster. He holds them up in turn. 'These objects were recently made in foundry not far from this building. Their purpose is to torture, oppress and to demean. By contrast...' he extracts from the bag a bible, a prayer book and some elaborate calling cards, bordered in gold. 'These instruments of Divine love and of civilised social intercourse, were printed in Africa, at the Lovedale Press. The Press also produces a newspaper...' he holds up a copy of *Indaba*, 'which has been circulated in the community for the last thirty years, and which is entirely self-funding. Its distribution is paid for by advertising...' He stops. He can tell that his words are having an effect, for his audience has ceased to fidget: an almost complete silence prevails in the room. For a moment he catches the eye of a young woman who is seated in the front row. She is regarding him with a thoughtful, steady gaze. She has fine, regular features and thick dark hair. Her brown eyes express compassion, while at the same time, they seem to dance with vitality. He feels himself grow hot with confusion. When she sees that he is looking at her, she gives a quick, shy smile.

At the reception afterwards, James finds it hard to concentrate. If he were not so sensible and rational a being, he would believe that with that one glance, he had fallen in love. He keeps looking across to the young woman; she is standing at the centre of what looks like a family group.

'Can I offer you more tea?' One of the members of The

Ladies Association — a Miss Adeline Scrope — is peering at him over her pince-nez.

'That would be most kind.'

She makes her way through the melee and returns not only with his refilled cup, but also a plate of sandwiches. 'I thought you might not have had an opportunity to eat,' she says, 'if you've had to come straight from the hospital.' James is touched by her thoughtfulness. He warms to Miss Scrope, although something seems to have robbed him of appetite; the food has no attraction. He feels at once both painfully incomplete and sharply aware of a beautiful and infinitely precious world. 'Tell me,' he asks, boldly, 'The people over there...' He indicates the group. 'Should I know who they are?'

'Oh,' says Miss Scrope. 'That's the Stephen family. Al and John are both shipbuilders; you'll have heard of Alexander Stephen, their father — he has yards in both Glasgow and Dundee. They're with their wives, Mary and Eliza. You should certainly get to know John. As well as being a wealthy man, he is most charitable in outlook. He is as keen as any of us, to put a final end to slavery.'

'And the young lady?' He has to ask.

Miss Scrope smiles. 'That lovely young woman is Williamina, Alexander Stephen's youngest daughter. She is staying with her brother Al, at his house in Park Circus. Before taking up my present post, I had the privilege of being employed as her governess. A sweeter child you could not wish to find.'

James is seized with a peculiar kind of panic: it is as if something he very much wants, is at risk of being snatched away. 'You call her a child, yet she looks quite grown up!'

'Mina is eighteen. As you say, really quite grown up. It is hard sometimes, for a teacher to adjust, when a pupil matures into adulthood. Come with me, I'll take you to meet them.'

James wishes that he had more time to prepare himself: he

should have combed his hair ... but at least he has changed his shirt. He fervently wishes that he were younger; he feels suddenly that he would give away all the challenges he has surmounted, all his hard won education, if he could lop ten off his thirty-five years. He puts his hand to his brow, in a useless attempt to smooth away the lines.

One of the Stephen men is telling the other some anecdote; the taller of the brothers leans in to listen and he half smiles in anticipation of the end of the tale.

Miss Scrope interrupts imperiously, just as the group dissolves into laughter. 'Ladies and gentlemen...' Her voice rings out as if she were addressing an unruly classroom: 'allow me to introduce the Reverend James Stewart!'

James shakes hands with the gentlemen and bows to the ladies. When he catches the young lady's — Williamina's — eye, he again experiences a sense of recognition. It is ridiculous, but he wants very much to take her in his arms.

John Stephen turns out to be well-informed on the subject of Central Africa. He says that he had considered signing up to the Scheme, but he had wanted more proof that there was sufficient infrastructure to support legitimate trade along the shores of the Zambesi. He proves to have considerable knowledge on the subject of education; he is on the governing board of two Glasgow schools, and has set up a programme of inducements and benefits to encourage the apprentices at the Stephen's Yard, which he personally supervises. After ten minutes conversation, he has promised to donate to Lovedale the sum of two hundred pounds.

'I give you my word,' says James, 'that your money will be well spent. Perhaps, at some future time, you yourself will be in a position to visit the settlement. You can see first-hand what has been achieved through the benefit of your generosity, and you will be able to provide me with the benefit of your invaluable advice.'

'I don't think so.' Eliza, his wife, gives a shudder. 'The privations of Africa — even in so-called civilised towns — would be too daunting for John. He has his health to consider.' She shakes her head. 'I myself could never travel to such a place.'

'I think it would be an adventure,' Williamina says, unexpectedly. 'I'd love to go, if I could.'

'And why would that be Mina?' Al regards her with the indulgence of an older sibling towards a favoured child.

'I have seen pictures in the copy of *Missionary Travels* …' Williamina looks at her erstwhile governess … 'which Miss Scrope lent me. There seems to be a lot of open space in Africa, and relatively few people. It would be wonderful for riding — I could do just as I pleased, because no-one would be watching.'

'Mina!' Miss Scrope sounds severe. 'Africa is not a place for the self-indulgent!'

'I'm sure Mina could make herself useful, wherever she put herself.' John intervenes kindly. 'She's very practical. Or rather, she always used to be. It is some months now since I married Eliza…' he takes his wife's hand… 'and left Broughty Ferry.'

'Mina could look after the sick,' Al says. 'Do you remember how she and Maggie had a dolls' hospital in the nursery? They took it fearfully seriously. I was summoned to visit; I had to play the part of a medical man. I ordered bread poultices, if I remember rightly, and afterwards, I got a wigging from Cook because the bread had been too liberally applied.'

'It wasn't your fault. We were determined to ensure a complete cure. But my best doll lost all the paint from her face.' Williamina gives a little frown, then blinks her long lashes, as she looks up at Al. 'It was kind of you to join in our game. You must have had much better things to do, than to play with us.'

James finds that he is irrationally envious. His emotions seem to be swooping up and down in a curious way; it is as if his heart has attached itself to a bandalore. He wishes that he — rather than Al — were the happy object of the enchanting young woman's attention, and he is acutely aware that the evening will shortly draw to a close. He must speak before the possibility of further acquaintance is lost. He feels daunted: it is as if he is about to jump naked into untested water in rare sunshine on a winter's day. He gathers his courage and plunges in: 'I hope, Miss Stephen, that you are spending an agreeable time in Glasgow, and that my talk this evening has not diverted you from more pleasurable activities.' He does his best to look winning, then worries that he has produced a grimace instead of a smile.

Williamina regards him levelly, then lowers her eyes. 'I asked if I could stay at Park Circus especially because I wanted to hear you speak.'

'I am flattered, Miss Stephen.'

'Please call me Mina — everyone else does. There are four of us in the family who can correctly be addressed as Miss Stephen. Too often, this causes confusion.'

Miss Scrope shoots a warning look. Her sharp glance is noticed by Al: he, in turn, regards the ex-governess with folded arms. 'Too late, Miss Scrope, I regret to say. My sister has outgrown your care. The degree of decorum with which she conducts herself, is no longer your responsibility. Within reason, Mina can be called what she wishes, and can do as she pleases.' Al Stephen shakes his head, then raises his hands in pretend dismay.

Miss Scrope responds severely; 'I believe that I know your sister well enough to attest that she is a young woman who will always choose the better way; she will never be tempted by the other path, simply because it appears to be the easier to tread.'

'Tell me, Mr Stewart,' says Eliza Stephen, 'what was it like to travel with so great a man as Livingstone? Did you not feel privileged to be in his company? He has achieved so much. I understand that the native people hold him in the highest esteem.'

'That is undoubtedly so,' James replies. 'Livingstone treats every man as his brother.'

Eliza looks at him quizzically. 'What of his wife?' she asks. 'It was such a sad business, her dying like that, so far from home. The papers said that he should have paid more regard to his children. He should not have demanded that their mother should join him in such an inhospitable place.'

Inwardly, James groans. He wonders what has motivated the question: has Eliza Stephen heard the gossip, too? Is his name forever to be associated with whispered scandal? He decides to speak no more than — and no less than — the truth. 'The Livingstones were devoted to one another,' he tells her. 'Mary gained much happiness from being reunited with her husband.'

John Stephen produces a notebook from his jacket pocket. 'I'd like to know a little more about this newspaper — the *Indaba* did you call it? What kind of a circulation does it reach?'

John asks more pertinent questions, carefully recording James's responses, until the minister claps his hands for silence and asks everyone for quiet. After a short prayer, and a request for any further donations to be put in the box by the door, the meeting is drawn to a close.

James returns to his lodgings. He gets out a dictionary and phrase book of Afrikaans and sits at his desk until midnight, but he cannot concentrate: he is too much distracted by his meeting with Williamina Stephen. He retires to bed, but finds it impossible to sleep. Images come to him of Mina's sweet smile, her sparkling eyes, her pure complexion and her perfect nose. He would like to softly kiss her face and draw her to him, pressing her youthful body against his own. But it is not for her beauty that he wants Mina. It is because for some wonderful and unfathomable reason, he is sure that the two of them would complete each other — it is as if they are two halves of just one soul. He is shocked at himself for thinking such thoughts. Since his liaison with Mary, he had set his heart against romance. He has considered marriage in a theoretical kind of way and has vaguely assumed that at some point he will settle down with a suitable woman, who will bear him children, organise the groceries and read the bible out loud. He has never anticipated being felled by what can only be described as Love. And he has never imagined that Love would present him with someone so delightful... so innocent... so young! But realistically, could Mina ever want him? Someone duty bound to leave Scotland for rural Africa... someone older... someone serious... someone dull?

In the morning, he dresses swiftly. He is glad to have the distraction of the Infirmary. He helps Lister with his operating list, until midday, when the professor leaves for London. James eats a tasteless lunch in the Ale House. He intends going back to the hospital, to spend the afternoon in the medical library, but on impulse, he takes himself instead to Dowanside Road. He runs up the steps of the Cowie's town house, two at a time and knocks loudly at the front door.

'Is Mrs Cowie in?' he asks the maid. 'Please let her know that I wish to see her. I will take up only a few minutes of her time.'

He is ushered upstairs to the drawing room, where he is greeted by Violet, who rises from her writing desk and shakes his hand warmly. 'Your visit is as welcome as it is unexpected,' she says. 'To what do I owe the pleasure?'

James comes straight to the point. 'I need advice,' he says. 'I need guidance from a feminine perspective.' He recounts the events of the previous night. 'I would not wish to cause embarrassment to the young lady. Perhaps I am impossibly arrogant to believe that she might consider my suit.' He looks at his shoes as if they might provide inspiration. 'Do you think that I have the slightest hope?'

Violet looks at him solemnly, then bursts into a peel of laughter.

'I'm sorry,' says James. 'I should not have troubled you.' He tries to smile, but finds that he has lost control of his lower lip. 'She is beautiful, vibrant and young. Whereas I... I don't... I haven't...' He cannot finish the sentence. He is choked by tears.

'Oh my poor friend,' says Violet. 'You are properly smitten. Here. Take my handkerchief.' She holds out a tiny linen square. 'Dry your eyes. You read me wrongly. It is true that you are behaving as a fool, but only because you cannot see what is set before you. You reported that Mina told you she came to Glasgow for the sole purpose of hearing you speak. She said she would like to go to Africa. What more could she do, in order to signal her availability?'

'You really think that she might consider me?'

'Of course. You should not be so surprised. You are quite famous in Scotland for your Africa adventures, your abilities as an orator, and — amongst the ladies — you are known for your good looks. She would be the envy of many a young woman were she to secure your hand. Tomorrow you must go to her father; you must seek his permission to call.'

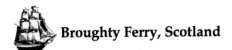 **Broughty Ferry, Scotland**

On the train journey back from Glasgow, Mina is aglow with excitement. Ever since she had first seen James Stewart's exploits reported in the *Courier*, she had longed to meet the missionary. His adventures had seemed so courageous, his aspirations so noble and from a sketch she had seen of him, his looks so striking, that he had seemed to exemplify all that was best, and all that might be desirable, in a person of the opposite sex.

Her sister Janet had heard him speak in Edinburgh. She had spoken enthusiastically of the Reverend Stewart's quick wits: when the gas lighting had failed, he had straightaway turned the situation to advantage, by comparing the resulting darkness to the current lack of enlightenment in many parts of Africa. Overhearing Janet's report, Moira had interrupted to say that her cousin had been treated by the Reverend at the Infirmary and had been full of praise for the doctor's skills. Moira had gone on to whisper that there were rumours that Stewart's relationship with Mary Livingstone had been closer than was proper. For Mina, this hint of impropriety had simply added to Stewart's appeal, by adding a layer of intrigue.

At the Glasgow meeting, James had succeeded in outshining Mina's highest expectations. Certainly, he was handsome, but had seemed unaware of the fact or, if he were aware, he seemed to consider his looks to be an irrelevance. He had displayed a kind of humility, a gentleness, that had made him seem touchingly accessible: at the same time, he had emanated a quiet strength that came from his sense of total conviction. As the train approaches Dundee, Mina reflects, with a bittersweet tug to her heart, that she had previously fallen for the idea of the man: now she has fallen for the man himself.

Seated next to Al, in the cab they have taken to Broughty, she is tempted to ask her brother how soon she can return to his house in Park Circus: she would like so much to have a further opportunity of meeting James. 'I am flattered,' the missionary had said, as he had regarded her with his extraordinary grey-green eyes. But nearing home, she wonders if James were merely being polite: could a man of such greatness care for the opinion of someone as foolish and inexperienced as herself? She could weep with frustration. She will have no opportunity of finding out: James will soon be on his way to Africa, and forever out of reach.

* * *

She realises that something is wrong at Corona, as soon as Neil has opened the heavy front door. Normally, Al is warmly greeted when he returns to Corona. He is a favourite of the servants because of his affability and because, despite not being the eldest, he is seen as Papa's natural successor at the shipyard.

But the footman remains expressionless, as he takes Al's hat and coat. 'I hope you have had a good journey, Sir.' He speaks without the expectation of response.

Moira comes down the staircase. She gives the briefest of smiles, and says, 'I have put your flowered chintz dress out, for you to wear at dinner. I will be along to lace it, and I will unpack your things, after I have seen to your mother. Now, if you will excuse me, I must attend to Mrs Stephen.'

'Moira, is Mama unwell?'

'No. She is distressed.' The lady's maid adds quietly, 'As well she might be.'

'Whatever has happened?'

'Forgive me, Miss Mina. I do not believe that it is my place to say.'

Mina goes quickly to seek out Maggie; she finds her in her bedroom, embroidering a coverlet for Anne's new baby.

Maggie tosses her sewing aside, and the two sisters embrace.

'Where to begin...,' says Maggie. 'I have so much to tell you! So much has happened in so short a time.' Mina is puzzled; Maggie sounds quite cheerful.

'Begin at the beginning,' Mina says.

287

'It is Hannah! Oh Mina! It is so romantic! Hannah has eloped! On Tuesday, she did not appear at breakfast, and when Moira went to her room, she found a note on the bed. It explained everything! For months, she has been corresponding with an accountant whom she met by chance at Waverley Station. His name is William Adams and he's from Australia! That's where they've gone. They travelled overnight to reach the Docks. He had already purchased tickets for their passage. They are aboard the *Earl of Dalhousie*, and it's as if they wanted to cause more upset as the steamer is one of Papa's ships!'

'Will Papa not try to stop them?'

'He says there is no point.' Maggie's voice falters. 'He says Hannah could never again be welcome here. She has been disgraced.'

Both girls remain silent as they take in the significance of the statement.

'Poor Hannah,' says Mina, after a while. 'I am sad for her, and for us, that we shall not see her, but happy that she has found love. Let us hope that Mama at least, will find it in her heart to forgive.'

'But I have more news... News that concerns you! James Stewart was here today — he arrived just after lunch. He asked to see Papa, and they went into the library. Then afterwards I heard Papa talking to Mama and he kept saying your name. Suppose the Reverend Stewart wants to court you and to ask for your hand in marriage! Whatever would you say?'

Mina thinks of James Stewart, a man who is all that she could ever want and thinks of how life would be at Corona with only Janet at home — for Maggie is betrothed to Robert Mudie. 'I should say yes,' she replies. 'I should say yes, with all my heart.'

'But you would have to go with him to Africa... and live in a hut! However would you cope? And whatever would you do?'

'I would care for the sick and needy... I would keep house...' Mina pauses, then gives a rueful smile, '...I would prefer to live in a house, rather than a hut.' She opens wide her eyes. 'I would do whatever James asked of me, to help him in his work.'

CHAPTER TEN

November 1866

 Hygienic Laundry, Dundee, Scotland

Chrissy is thinking about Mr Galloway. Her employer had reluctantly accepted that she did not want to marry him, but now he is saying that he will have to cut down on his staff and in the new year, she will have to start looking for another post. She pushes hard on the dolly to sink a quantity of sheets under the bubbling water.

She hears the sound of tapping at the laundry window and turns to see a young boy in a brown-check cap. He is pointing to indicate that she should open the door. She looks to check on the whereabouts of Mrs Morrell. The older woman is out of sight, with Maddie in the ironing room.

'I'm looking for a Miss Chrissy Hogarth,' the boy says. 'I've been told to bring her this.' He extracts an envelope from his pocket, looks at it doubtfully, then wipes it on his jacket in an attempt to remove a sooty black mark.

'I am Miss Hogarth.' Chrissy takes the envelope. She

shakes her head. 'I am sorry. I have nothing to give you.'

'That's all right. The gentleman's paid. He says I'm to wait, and you're to give me a reply.'

Chrissy breaks the seal and reads:

Dear Chrissy,

Three years have passed since I visited you to express my sorrow for the events that occurred in the summer of 1860. In all that time, not a day has gone by during which I have not regretted what I did to you. I asked you then if there was anything I could offer that would help to make amends.

You told me then that you wished to go to Africa, in order to help save children's souls. At that time, it seemed impossible that I should be able to help you to achieve your desire. But a circumstance has arisen which has changed matters.

I ask that you hear me out! If you are willing, I will come in a cab at the end of your working day, and will instruct the driver to take you to your lodgings. In this way, I can talk to you discreetly, without compromising your position or my own, for I am engaged now; I am to be married to a Miss Euphemia Baxter.

Please tell the boy from what time I should be waiting.

Yours faithfully, and forever in remorse,

Samuel Stephen

Chrissy replaces the letter in the envelope. 'Seven o'clock,' she says. 'Tell him that I should finish at seven o'clock.'

* * *

It is a dark winter's evening, but there is a small paraffin lamp hanging on the inside of the cab, which enables Chrissy to see Sam's face. His years at sea have given him a weathered complexion, but there is still a fragility about him; he looks more suited to a profession in law than a life on the open sea.

'Am I right that it is still your heart's desire to go to Africa?' Sam looks at her searchingly.

'It is. Most certainly, it is.'

'Then I have found a way… My sister Mina is engaged to marry a missionary called the Reverend James Stewart, and just as soon as the wedding is over, they are to travel together to the port of East London, in the Cape Colony. They will go to place called Lovedale, where there is a church, and a school. I have told Mina a little about you, and she has asked her future husband if he would allow you to travel with them, as one of the party. On Wednesday they are to have a meeting with the Foreign Mission Board. They will need your decision before then.'

'But why has she agreed to this? And what would I do?'

'She has agreed because she cares for me and once she has met you, she will care for you, too. As for what you would do… Stewart intends to open a secondary school for girls. He would like to prepare them to be secretaries or articled clerks, but he says that to begin with, he must temper his ambitions. Realistically, the girls are only likely to find employment as domestic workers. Laundering, cleaning, sewing whole garments… these are skills of which my sister knows nothing. He has employed a Miss Waterston, who will act as headmistress, but she is a gentlewoman… She too, is ignorant of such tasks.'

Chrissy is stunned by the implication of Sam's words. Her first contact with Sam, James Stewart's lecture at the Asylum, her work at the Hygienic laundry, her refusal of Mr Galloway — all these events have been carefully planned and organised. She should never, for an instant, have doubted. Nothing has occurred without His Foresight. Every pain that she has suffered — every sorrow that has made her weep — it has all been well-intentioned. Everything that has happened … it has all been brought about through the Agency of Love. She opens her mouth to reply to Sam, but she can find no words: she is dumbfounded with awe.

 East London, Cape Colony

Lokim is in the dispensary, working under Dr Lawes's instruction, as he assembles the ingredients needed to make an ointment for rheumatism.

'Mix the powders together first,' says the doctor. 'Give them all a good grinding with the pestle, before adding the hog's grease. Did I say to add two scruples of wormwood? I didn't? Well add some now.'

Lokim pulls out the appropriate drawer, extracts the right measure and adds it to the mortar. He enjoys learning from the doctor, but he is finding it hard to concentrate. A cockerel in the garden next door had woken him early and he had found it impossible to get back to sleep.

He is relieved when Dr Lawes says that they are running out of wax: he will have to send him to Choudhary's, to purchase some more. 'There are a few other things we need,' the doctor adds. 'I'll give you the list, and you can get them at the same time. We'll stop for today and start afresh first thing tomorrow. If you do the shopping now, it will save Blossom having to do the carrying. She's been complaining again about her knees.' Blossom is the maid. She is a wide-hipped, laughing woman who, to Lawes's mild irritation, insists on painting her face red with ochre, in the firm belief that the application will protect her from disease.

As he walks to Choudhary's, Lokim resists the temptation to take off his shoes. He is accustomed to wearing the fine clothes that have been provided for him, but the sensation of

293

having his feet encased seems wrong — just now, he would like to be able to spread out his toes, which are feeling uncomfortably warm. But, he reminds himself, the wearing of shoes is a trifling price to pay for the benefits that he enjoys as a servant of so generous a man as the doctor. Lawes is something called a Quaker. He says that Quakers believe in equality, and that if everyone is equal, then everyone should be treated equally well. Lokim has been given a room to sleep in, all of his own, with a wooden slatted bed made soft with a mattress stuffed with kapok. He is fed with bread, meat, cheese and vegetables, and once his allotted work has finished, he is allowed to rest.

At the end of his first month, Dr Lawes had given him some coins. He had explained that they were due to him: they were his wages, no more and no less. Lokim had thought he would use the money to buy his new master a present, but when he asked Blossom what he should get, the maid had laughed so much that she had to wipe her eyes with the corner of her apron. She had said that wages were not given simply to be handed back, and if Lokim felt that he wanted for nothing, surely there were members of his family who would benefit from his change in fortune.

Lokim had been on the point of telling Blossom that such family as he had, lived far, far away. He nearly shared with her his life in the manyatta, with Niampa and Amuarkar, but he had stopped himself from doing so. He feared that if he allowed himself to talk of his old life, everything in the past would become more vivid, including those experiences which were dreadful to remember. It was best to live entirely in the present. So he had simply nodded to Blossom, while he suppressed an image of himself jerking and gasping, rendered as helpless in his new environment as a flailing fish, stranded in mud.

At the front of Choudhary's crowded shop, sacks of

coloured spices are stacked side by side. Stalls are piled high with fruit and vegetables. Lokim consults his list: *Packet of Wax. Household soap. Half a dozen apples. Two pounds of onions. One pound of tomatoes. A dozen oranges. Four lemons. Sugar. Flour.* He savours the differing scents of bunched green herbs and sweet ripe pineapples and looks with curiosity at the soft, furred skin of a round pink fruit. He moves inside. He will buy the fresh foodstuffs last, so that they can go on top of his canvas carrier.

Lokim goes to the counter and orders sugar and flour.

'All on account, for Dr Lawes?'

Lokim assents and Young Mr Choudhary opens the tally book. He has slicked his hair, and resembles a canary in his yellow sarong.

'And eight ounces of wax.'

'Sealing wax?'

'No, plain wax. The best quality. It is for medicine.'

Mr Choudhary disappears into the store and emerges with the required packet. 'What else can I get you?'

'Soap,' Lokim reads. 'A bar of household soap.'

The shopkeeper disappears again, and returns with the packet. 'We have a new shipment,' he says. 'It is the same price as that from our previous supplier, but it is said to remove stains more cleanly. ...' He stops. 'You are looking concerned. Tell Doctor Lawes to try it. I am sure that it will prove to be acceptable.'

'Please. Yes. Please add it to my bag.'

Lokim returns, in a daze, to Dr Lawes's house. He lets himself in with the key that is kept under a stone slab and unpacks the shopping on the kitchen table. Then he sits himself down so that he can look properly at the soap — or rather, at the label which has been glued to its wrapper.

'Canadian Tannery,' he reads. 'Made From Best Whale Oil.' But it is not the words that have seized his attention. It is the picture above the words. He sees the woman, as he had seen her image on his captors' boat. Her strange colouring... her haunting smile... His mind whirls. He cups his head in his two hands. He feels a need to tether himself. He sits back, closes his eyes and recalls the pleasure and delight he had experienced when he had drunk Atum's potion. Then a picture comes to him of a man with a knotted whip. He shudders and opens his eyes. The awful memory causes him to break out into a sweat. He stretches out his hand and touches the woman's face with his forefinger. As he does so, his racing heart slows and he is suffused with a sense of peace. '*Alakara*,' he says. 'Thank you.' He tries to make sense of what has happened. It seems that, through some magic, the image that sustained and comforted him throughout his years of enslavement, has again been captured and transferred to paper. '*Alakara*,' he says again. He would like to peel off the label and keep it safe in his room, but the soap is not his property; it belongs to Dr Lawes. 'I could buy my own soap,' he thinks, excitedly. 'I have money. I can use my wages.'

'What you doin', boy?' Blossom is standing in the doorway regarding him with puzzlement. 'You done the shopping?'

Lokim indicates the sugar and the flour.

'Where's my onions? Where's my tomatoes?' Blossom shakes her head in disbelief. 'You forgot? You din't get them? You'd best get yourself back to Choudhary's! You'd best do that quick!'

 Dundee, Scotland

James hears a whistle and the rhythmic sound of wheels clattering on the tracks. He smells the burning coal from the firebox and sees puffs of blackened smoke rising from the funnel. The sight is thrilling. There is a magnificence about the engine which, through the ingenuity of its design, has steadfastly pulled many times its own weight through fields, towns and villages. Now it has arrived at Ward Street, right on time. When with a long squeal of the brakes the train finally comes to a halt, he is tempted to jump up onto the running board, so that he can congratulate the driver on being in charge of so splendid a machine.

Despite the cold of the winter's day, he is aglow with wellbeing; he feels he would like to embrace the whole world. There, descending from the second carriage, is his old friend Waller: he has come all the way from London, in order to act as witness at his marriage to Mina, which is to take place the following day.

'My dear chap!' Horace lifts a battered leather case from out of the compartment, and bumps it onto the platform. 'My dear, dear Stewart! I thought I would be deprived of an opportunity of seeing you, before you leave. Instead of which, I am doubly blessed: not only will I have the pleasure of personally wishing you well, tomorrow I will have the happiness of meeting the young lady who is to be your wife!'

James claps Horace on the shoulder. His current, joyful circumstances are so much of a contrast to the sufferings they endured when exploring the Zambesi that he is, for a moment, quite overwhelmed. He shakes Waller's hand. 'I am so very pleased that you are here,' he says. 'It is too good of you to come.' He signals to the driver of a Hansom. 'The Eagle Inn, Broughty, if you would be so kind.'

* * *

Both men are seated in the saloon of the Eagle; each is equipped with a glass. 'We have so much to catch up on!' says James. He takes a warming sip of spiced wine. 'You must tell me of your plans … And what of Livingstone? Are there any more reports which might help establish his whereabouts?

Agnes is to be at the celebrations tomorrow, I am pleased to say. She's just back from Paris, where she has been at school. It must be a worrying time for her.'

'No news at present, but Agnes should feel reassured. If any man can keep himself safe in Africa, that man is her father. He will turn up again, I am sure of it. I am less sanguine about her brother.' Horace's face clouds. 'You heard that Robert went to America, and enlisted for the Unionists, under an assumed name?'

'I did hear a rumour.'

'Before he returned, Livingstone received a letter to say that his eldest son had been wounded and taken prisoner by the Confederates. He was going by the name of Rupert Vincent since he said he didn't want the Livingstone name to be dishonoured. That was two years ago, and there's been no word since. I can only assume the worst.'

'One shouldn't give up hope. It is just as likely that he recovered, and now the war is over, he has chosen to make a completely new life for himself.' James thinks of the headstrong, sensitive fourteen year old, who had crept out of the house in Glasgow, driven by a compulsion to gamble. He remembers Mary's words 'Robert needs his father'. He wishes that he himself had done more for the boy. He remains silent, then says, 'I hope that you will find the Eagle sufficiently comfortable. We were offered hospitality with some rather grand friends of the Stephens, but I politely declined.'

'There is an advantage to being here: I will be able to buy you a reviving whisky, should you suffer a bout of last minute nerves.' Horace looks carefully at James. 'Though I must say, you seem pretty well contented.'

'Horace, I am truly happy!'

'From your demeanour, I would have believed nothing less. So tell me, what is she like, Miss Mina Stephen... the future Mrs Stewart?'

298

'There is a sweetness about her, a grace, a lightness. Mina is in possession of all the qualities that I lack. I feel so glad… so immeasurably grateful, that she has agreed to become my wife.'

'I am delighted for you. Before I forget… I have brought you a present!' Waller retrieves a package from beside his chair and puts it in the table.

'Why, thank you. Should I open it?'

'Of course.'

James unwraps a swathe of tissue paper and looks with confusion at a pair of lavender-coloured gloves, elegantly sewn from the softest doeskin. 'That's very kind of you Horace… most kind… but I'm not sure that these are quite my sort of thing.'

'I thought you'd say that, but honestly, you should accept them…' Lavender is *de rigueur* for a groom these days. The colour signifies new love.'

'This isn't one of your japes?'

'My good friend, I would not joke about such an important matter.'

'Then I thank you again for your kindness, and also for your generosity. I will, of course, wear them. For Mina, I would dye my hair bright purple, were it to be considered the proper thing to do.'

 Broughty Ferry, Scotland

When Mina awakes, she is puzzled to find that Maggie is lying next to her, fast asleep. After a moment, she remembers: Maggie has vacated her own bed, to make way for Helen and her husband. Along with Sam, William and his wife, and the Croudaces, the Logans have stayed the night at Corona, because today is the day that she is to be married: the ceremony is to take place at noon.

She considers with a mixture of elation and trepidation the implications of this momentous fact. First, there will the ceremony itself. She hopes that James will find her appearance pleasing, dressed as she will be in the white taffeta dress that is filling the whole space of Mama's second wardrobe. A lunch party is to follow, for close family and friends. Al and Mary are coming from Glasgow; they are to share a carriage with John Templeton. And, of course, her brother John will bring Eliza. Anne will come, with Duncan Wilkie… Mina tries not to think too much about those who will not be there… Andrew has not been invited, because he is still feuding with Al and Papa. Hannah is on her way to New South Wales, and Papa has forbidden any mention of her name… Mary and Marjory lie in their graves on the island of Gibraltar, and James lies buried in the churchyard at Moffat. Her dashing, high-living brother had suffered a sudden fatal fever. Al would have gone to him, but the news of his illness had come too late.

In the evening, there will be a further celebration, for a larger party. The library is to be emptied, to make space for dancing. Then afterwards… afterwards, she will sleep in the best spare bedroom, with James Stewart… and she will be his wife.

As soon as it is morning, Winshaw will take her and James to the railway station and they will get the first train to Glasgow, where they will board the steamer which is to take them to the Cape. Their many containers have been sent on ahead, and have already been stowed aboard the ship. Mama has organised clothing, cutlery, crockery, pots, pans, table linen, bedding, tins of food, sacks of sugar, sacks of flour, equipment for washing, equipment for cleaning and assorted pieces of furniture. She has added a couple of paintings, one of the Clyde and one of Highland cattle — she has said that the pictures will serve as a reminder of home. Mina could think of little that she wanted for herself until, on an impulse, she had asked if she could take a piano. Papa agreed that she could have one as a wedding gift, and so a new upright has been purchased from Broadwoods; it has been packed by the manufacturers in a specially padded box. Mina has also chosen a small collection of books. For Miss Scrope's sake, she has included the poems of Petrarch, along with Shakespeare's complete works, and the novels of Dickens.

Maggie is still sleeping. Mina tiptoes up to the window and pulls back the curtain. It is early – Katie has not yet been up to light the fire — and she can see little outside, for it is still dark. She lies back down and tries to sleep, but there is too much to think about. She wonders about life aboard ship: what will the food be like? Will she suffer from seasickness… and how cramped will her quarters be? She wonders what she will do to occupy herself on the long journey and how she will find the company of Miss Waterston, who has been appointed to be Girls' Headmistress at Lovedale. Jane Waterston seems rather intense and not a little severe. Mina is glad that there will be another woman in their group: a Miss Chrissy Hogarth, will also travel to Africa. Sam introduced the young lady to her and then to James — he explained that Chrissy possessed an unshakeable conviction that her purpose in life was to help save African souls. As her knowledge of domestic work would be of undoubted value, the Foreign Mission Board had agreed — without meeting her — that she could travel, too.

Mina had been curious to know exactly how Sam had first met Chrissy, but something told her it would be better not to ask. She wondered if Sam had made some sort of romantic connection, which he had broken off when he became engaged to Euphemia. Chrissy is certainly pretty, and with her red hair and large blue eyes, she bears a striking resemblance to The Girl with a Lamp, whose ubiquitous image is used to advertise products from the Canadian Tannery.

Maggie stirs, and opens her eyes. 'Mina…' she says, 'it is

today... you are to be married!' She sits up, and sleepily examines one of her plaits, which has lost its ribbon, and is coming undone.

Mina feels a kind of lurching in the region of her heart. Maggie has been her constant companion; she has never gone for more than a week without her sister's presence. So how will she feel in the morning, when she sets off in the Landau, to live away from Maggie, away from Corona, and away from all that she has ever held dear? 'I know,' she says. 'I know that it is.'

* * *

It is ten o'clock, and Mina is in Mama's bedroom: the time has come to put on her wedding dress. Moira laces her corsets even more tightly than usual. 'A bride must look her very best,' the maid says, as she yanks firmly at the ribbons.

Slowly, for it is not easy to move, Mina steps inside the hoops of her crinoline and lifts it up to her middle. The maid does more pulling and tugging, as she ties the skirt around her waist. Two petticoats follow, one of cambric, the other of muslin, copiously tucked and extravagantly flounced. Moira stands on a chair to lift the dress itself over her head. Mina slides her arms into the wide sleeves, which have been ruched with a pink satin trim. The vast quantities of taffeta fall heavily around her. Moira gets down from the chair, smoothes the skirts and pulls the dress tight, in order to fasten a row of tiny buttons, which secure the bodice at the back.

'There,' says the maid. 'I just need to pin up your hair, then fix your circlet and veil. I'll fetch your brush.'

Mina looks at dressing table, where the circlet is resting on a papier mache tray. It is made up of lily of the valley. The delicate, bell-shape blooms are so perfect that they look artificial, but they are real; they were delivered the previous

302

day, having been ordered from a large hothouse in Edinburgh, along with a dozen crates of assorted white flowers. The dining room has been decorated with huge globe chrysanthemums, which are filling the house with their scent. Mama seems determined that her marriage to James should be celebrated in style, despite the short notice that she is has been given for the preparations. Mina wonders if this to make up in some way for Hannah's elopement and is some sort of revenge upon her sister, but then she thinks that this is unfair, for — despite being Presbyterians — her parents have never been averse to spending money when it comes to entertaining. At the launch of the Eastern Monarch, Papa gave a huge banquet, with eighteen toasts, and at the ball that followed, a quadrille was danced, to a tune that he had especially commissioned from the celebrated composer, Mr Thomson.

'No bride could look lovelier,' says Moira, who has returned holding a brush and comb set, and a pot of hairpins. But then she drops the pot, and the pins scatter on the carpet. She stoops to collect them, and when she gets to her feet, Mina sees that the maid's eyes are full of tears. 'What is it?' she asks. She takes her hand. 'Come, sit down. Tell me… what is the matter?'

Moira covers her face, then looks up. 'Mina dear… I cannot help myself. I will speak frankly… I have known you since you were born. I was *there* when you were born… a bonnier baby never existed, and a sweeter child would be hard to find. My dearest Mina, Mr Stewart is so much older… so well travelled… and there have been rumours … It is not too late to change your mind! I took the liberty of speaking to Parsons; we would help you, if you cannot face your father and mother. We have talked… we would look after you… Parsons has a sister who is married to a clergyman and lives in some style — you could stay with her until enough time has passed for your parents to have come to terms with your change of plan.'

Ignoring the inconvenience of her vast skirts, Mina kneels at Moira's feet. She is immeasurably touched at the maid's concern and even more so to hear that the butler should also have been prepared to put his job at risk, in order to protect her welfare. But her mind is made up… 'Do not be concerned for me,' she says, gently. 'I love James. He is all I have ever dreamed of.'

'My dear, you do not know him…' Moira strokes the hair that she had been going to comb.

'I *do* know him! I have met him four times.'

'Four times is a slight acquaintance on which to base a new life. You will be away from your family… Your home will be an uncivilised and inhospitable land. You will not be able to return to us, here at Corona, where you would find true friends.' Moira bites her lip. 'In the circumstances, I do not understand your father. How could he allow such a union!'

'Papa was opposed to my marrying. It was Al who persuaded him to give permission. Al knows that it is what I want and he has the greatest respect for James. Moira, it is kind of you to want to help me… Of course it will be hard, leaving you all! But James is all that I could ever want. He is kind and noble and true. He has the courage to dream and he has the industry to fulfil those dreams… it will be a privilege to be at his side. As for any future privations I might endure, we have choices in how we approach matters. And I will have to make the best of things.'

Mina gets to her feet; the hoops spring up, spreading wide her skirt. She takes the silver brush from the dressing table, and hands it across. In silence, the maid brushes Mina's chestnut hair.

CHAPTER ELEVEN

January 1867

 East London, Cape Colony

A day and a night have passed since the boat has docked, and the four members of the missionary party have walked across a narrow, springing gang plank, and onto the muddy shore. After so many weeks, Chrissy suffers the uncomfortable sensation that she is still at sea. Although she stands on solid land, the earth seems to rock and swell beneath her. She ceases trying to organise her belongings and sits down on a little chair that is placed beside her bed. She does this so abruptly that the seat creaks noisily, causing Miss Waterston to look up from her cross stitch.

'Are you all right?' she asks. 'You are looking pale. I hope to goodness that you are not going down with fever. We have four days' journey ahead of us. I have never travelled by ox cart, but I am not disposed to believe that it is the most comfortable form of transport.'

'I am quite well, thank you', Chrissy replies, primly. 'A little giddy from the voyage, that's all. Please don't be concerned.'

The two women have shared a cabin, and now a room, since Cape Town. Little intimacy has grown up between them. On the journey south, Miss Waterston had paid extra from her own funds so that she could travel first class. She explained that it was not luxury that she craved; she needed space to herself, as from time to time, she suffered from migrainous headaches. There were no single berths available in the small ex-whaler which took them up the coast, and so she had no choice but to sleep on a lower bunk, with Chrissy up above. The box-like space had been little bigger than one of the packing crates that were stacked high on the deck, one upon the other. To be fair to Miss Waterston, she had not complained. Perhaps this was because without actually saying so, the Reverend Stewart had made it clear that whatever social differences that might have been applicable in Scotland, he would think the less of Jane Waterston were she to behave towards Chrissy as if she were anything other than an equal. He had stated that both women will have different, but important, parts to play at Lovedale: Jane will educate the girls in the three Rs, while Chrissy will help with the school's laundry, and will share her skills with the older pupils.

Miss Waterston bends her head, and continues with her sewing. Since Glasgow, she has been sporadically working on a sampler which is to have the words 'Thou oh Lord seeest everything,' emblazoned across it. Chrissy privately thinks that Miss Waterston is not really cut out for embroidery; she tends to be impatient, and she fails to count the stitches with accuracy, so that she ends up unpicking more than she sews.

Chrissy looks out of the window, where she can see a patch of green lawn. The missionary party are staying in a guest house, which is attached to St George's Presbyterian Church. A rose is climbing up a white-painted pergola. To the right of the pergola is a palm tree with a strange kind of nest hanging from its branches, it looks like a basket carefully woven from grass. The sun is shining brightly. It seems extraordinary that back home, people are shivering and hurrying to keep warm; it may even be snowing, 'Do you think the Minister would allow me to read in his garden?' she says. 'It looks so lovely outside.'

'I cannot imagine that Mr Lavery would object. We are his guests, after all, and by tomorrow, the wagons will have been packed, and we will be gone. But you should apply a deterrent, to put off the mosquitoes. There is a bottle of rosemary and turpentine on the washstand; you should use it.'

Chrissy sits on a wooden bench. As she lifts her head to enjoy a slight, welcoming breeze, and listens to the whirring of crickets, the feeling of continuous motion lessens, then ceases. She tips some of the mixture onto her hands. It pours too quickly; some runs through her fingers and a splash of the liquid stains her dress. She rubs her face and neck; the smell of the turpentine reminds her of Mr Watt and his paintbrushes. She considers how far she has travelled — both literally and metaphorically — since she sat for the artist, and wonders whether it is the past or the present, which feels most unreal.

She watches a small yellow bird flit past the basket, then settle on a branch. It occurs to her that before she left Scotland, she would probably not have asked herself such a question. She had felt secure in the knowledge that a Higher Being had carefully planned every single event that had occurred in her life, she had firmly believed that in travelling with the Stewarts, she was fulfilling God's purpose. Her own history, her own feelings were largely an irrelevance. She had considered herself no more than a vessel, a means of transporting God's Truth.

She does not regret what has happened; she is not sorry

that she was admitted to the Royal Lunatic Asylum, where she was able to hear the Reverend Stewart's rousing sermon. She is glad to have left the Hygienic Laundry, and although the voyage was sometimes alarming and it is very odd to be in Africa, she is quite prepared to go to Lovedale, and to see what happens there. But her faith, which had always been unshakeable, is no longer as firm as it was. There are two reasons for her doubts. The first is a book, given to her on the voyage, and which is now resting on her lap.

Vestiges of the Natural History of Creation was presented to her by a rich young adventurer from Galashiels. He was travelling to the Colony to relieve his boredom; he was to join up with a cousin, and together they would search for gold. He said that he had read it, he himself had no further use for it, she was welcome to have it, and to make of it what she would. He brought it to her when she was seated up on the deck. She did not notice him at first, and had started when she saw him since her view had been blocked by a shawl, which she had strung up to protect her face from the sun. She had accepted the gift in some confusion.

The man had given her the book because, providing that the weather was not too inclement, it was the custom for the passengers to organise for themselves some sort of afternoon entertainment, up on the foredeck. Two weeks out from port, the activity had been a session of 'Show and Tell'; everyone present had to bring an object, then explain its significance to the rest of the group. Chrissy had fetched from her cabin her piece of lucky coal and she had pointed to where God had decorated it, with the clear outline of a fern. The adventurer had admired the coal, turning it in his hands and running his forefinger along the impression of the leaves. But he had disputed her version of its origin.

'God did not carve this,' he said. 'He did not make the world all at once, like some divine craftsman. Creation did not happen in a week. It took place over millions of years. This sample is most interesting. It is from the carboniferous period, when terrestrial vegetation became transmuted by pressure. Sometimes, a plant can still be seen, crushed between the layers. This is such a case.'

Chrissy had been a member of the lending library in Dundee, but she had never possessed a book of her own before aside from her little Bible, passed onto her by her mother. She had opened the covers of *Vestiges* reverentially and turned the pages with care. The writer was anonymous, but whoever he was he seemed very sure of his facts. He stated that the world was at first very hot. Gradually, it cooled down, and over vast lengths of time, vegetable and animal life developed. The evidence for this could be demonstrated by the existence of plants and extinct animals, which had been fossilised in layers of rock. The arrival of mankind, the anonymous writer maintained, was a comparatively recent event. The proof of this was the lack of human remains, 'except in deposits obviously of very modern date.'

If all this was true, Chrissy thought, then the story of Genesis must be a representation of the truth, rather than the truth itself. But, she reasoned, if Creation did not happen in the space of six days, what other stories in the Bible might be illustrations, rather than accurate accounts of real events?

Perhaps God had planned to test her faith by presenting her with the book: he had placed fossils in the ground for a similar reason. But if this were the case, how could a humble believer distinguish between a trick and the truth? She thought of Jesus, up in heaven, surrounded by angels, holding the hands of innocent children. He was surely too noble and pure to tempt a worshipper from the path of true belief. But perhaps the Holy Spirit was less praiseworthy; maybe He delighted in causing confusion. Chrissy is dismayed by this notion, and wishes it had not occurred to her.

She has to hide her book from Miss Waterston, who would be angry if she saw it. When another of the passengers had mentioned Mr Darwin and his theory of Evolution, she had made a disgusted 'Phth!' noise; it had sounded almost as if she were spitting. This is another conundrum. If God plans and foresees everything, and has given His Blessing to the expedition, how does it serve His purpose to introduce the possibility of dissention within the party?

The second reason why Chrissy no longer feels quite as sure of her faith as she did, is the attitude of James Stewart. She had been certain that her purpose was to ensure that the innocent were enabled to enter Heaven's Gates. But when the Reverend talks of Lovedale, his plans are all about education. He has two main themes: education as a means to ending slavery, and the need for Africans to have a college with standards as high as any British university. The saving of souls seems to him to be almost inconsequential. Does God have a different purpose for Stewart, than He has for herself? Yet it is Stewart who is the ordained missionary, while she herself is no more than a laundry girl.

It is all most unsettling.

The words dance too brightly in the sunshine. Chrissy moves the book into the shadow, and learns that near Weymouth, traces of a petrified forest can be found. There are roots and trunks of trees, buried in something called a dirt-bed. She tries to picture the scene, but the thought of Weymouth makes her homesick. She knows that it is a place by the sea, and she imagines it to be a city like Dundee. She looks up, and watches the yellow bird; it is now hanging upside down from the woven basket, calling out and fluttering its wings.

Her mind turns again to James Stewart. He seems different from the powerful preacher, whose sermon in the chapel had made such an impression on the asylum inmates. He is gentler, and when he is with his wife, it is clear that he is a man who is very much in love. With Mina, he smiles a lot, and laughs easily; she seems to lift him from himself. Mina, in turn, delights in his company. Without him, she sometimes looks very young and rather lost, but when he is there, her face lights up. It is as if the discomforts of the journey and separation from her family are nothing compared to the joy that she feels at being in her husband's presence.

Chrissy is dismayed to realise that she feels an unaccustomed envy towards the newlyweds: she is jealous of the happiness that they derive from being with one another. Seated in the minister's strange garden, she is washed with an unaccustomed loneliness. She wishes she were able to share the book's troublesome revelations with someone… Someone who would refrain from judgement and would seek nothing in return. She shudders as an image comes to her of Mr Galloway, licking his lips and rubbing his hands.

The yellow bird is making a chick sound in response to the arrival of a grey-brown bird with a curious crest on its head. Chrissy thinks, as she has not done for a long time, of Andrew and his broken promises. She remembers the fantasy that sustained her in the asylum: the happy family that might have been, if Andrew had not left her, and if Thomas had not died. How would Mina react, she wonders, were she to learn that Chrissy had once been engaged to her brother? Sam had explained nothing of the circumstances that had brought them together, instead he had told the Stewarts that he learned of Chrissy's missionary ambitions through a person who attended Euphemia's church. Although it is understandable for him to have lied, Chrissy would prefer that he had been more truthful: he has left her with an unnecessary weight of guilt. She tries to comfort herself with the memory of Thomas's sweet face, but now she is troubled by a new voice, one which whispers that a more real comfort could be obtained from holding another baby, one that was quick with life who would grow big enough to laugh. She feels her arms ache in the same painful way as they used to. She longs, with all her being, to hold a healthy child of her own.

It will not happen. Not while she is in Africa. And it could not have happened, back in Dundee, certainly not while Mr Galloway was her suitor.

She returns to her book, but a page which refers to a Mr Weekes of Sandwich causing insects to appear from potash charged with a voltaic battery, leaves her too perplexed to carry on. She is about to go back inside, when she hears the sound of a horse and trap. She turns the book over, to hide its title.

Mina pushes open the garden gate; she is accompanied by the minister's wife. The two women make a contrasting pair. Mina is dressed in a cream-coloured gown and a little straw boater decorated with streamers, while her stout, middle-aged companion is dressed in brown, with a black-veiled bonnet.

'The wagons have arrived!' says Mina. 'I have been with James, down at the dock. It's such a sight, you would not believe! Nearly fifty oxen — they're such patient, noble-looking beasts. I have come to ask for your help. We must oversee the packing of the kitchen things. But first, there are some supplies to be fetched from the town. Mrs Lavery has kindly agreed to lend her trap and to show us where to go.' She smiles warmly at the stout woman, who nods briefly in return. 'Will you come, Chrissy?'

'With pleasure.'

'I would have asked Jane, too, but there isn't room, and she would probably prefer to stay inside, where it's cool. We need medicines from the pharmacy, to replace those that were used on the voyage, and we could do with some eggs, fresh vegetables and a large round of cheese. If there are any personal items you require, we will add them to the list.'

'I have had a message from John Harvey,' says Dr Lawes. 'His gout is worse and he would like some more of those pills we made up for him. Here's the recipe, can you roll them in the machine, then take them round?'

'I will do so.' Lokim lowers his eyes in respect, then, remembering that expressions of humility served only to irritate his master, he looks directly at the doctor.

'Thank you, Lokim. You are quick to learn and you work hard. I have written to Frances to let her know of your good progress.'

'Please send Senhora Almeida my kind regards. I hope that she, and her children, are in good health. I send a thousand thanks to her, for giving me to such a considerate master.'

'She didn't *give* you to me. She recommended you... Now, where's my bag? The Bowker child is ill again — I had better get started on my visits.'

Lokim stirs the powders, binds them together with chalk and water, makes the tablets and leaves them to dry while he tidies the dispensary. Then he counts out the little round pills, wraps them in paper, locks up and sets off to make his delivery.

John Harvey lives in a large house on the High Street, which is built of iron and wood. He owns a flour mill, which is used by many of the local farmers to grind their corn. He is one of the town's wealthier inhabitants. His door is opened by a white maid, who politely receives the package. Lokim has been told by Dr Lawes that in the Colony, white and black servants, and ex-slaves, all have equal status under the law, but it is strange, nevertheless, to be treated with respect by a white person of lower class.

Walking back, he catches sight of himself in the glass window of a dressmaker's shop. His image shimmers as if it were being reflected in a glimmering pool. He sees a tall, elegant-looking young man, who looks entirely at ease in his surroundings. Wearing drilled cotton trousers and a matching jacket — made for him by one of Blossom's brothers who works as a tailor, and is the proud possessor of a Singer sewing machine — he could pass for one of the traders, who meet outside the Standard Bank to chat and smoke cheroots.

East London, he considers, is a strange place. On the surface, its mixed races get on well together, but there has been much bad history between the Xhosa, the British and the Boers, and as a result, there is little trust. The British have taken more and more of the Xhosa's land. Whenever the Xhosa have tried to fight back, their homes and their crops have been fired and the native people have been left to starve. The Boers' are worse: they steal African children to use as labour on their homesteads. The Boers are firmly of the belief that they have a right to keep slaves. Many of them have trekked north, to escape British jurisdiction and the Slavery Abolition Act.

It is Blossom who has told Lokim these things. Since the incident with his wages, when he wanted to give them away, she has appointed herself as his teacher, as well as his friend. She has told him where in town it is safe to go and which places are best avoided. She has also shared with Lokim a tragic episode involving her own people. She wept when she spoke of it, for many of her own family had died. What happened was this: ten years before, her tribe had rebelled against the British, and had been forced to accept defeat. Later, a young girl called Nongkawuse reported that, while fetching water from a well, she had met a stranger who had told her that the tribe should kill all their fat cattle. If they did this, other cows would come, more beautiful and perfect than those they replaced. Fields of ripe corn would appear, and the dead would rise to do battle and triumph over the white oppressors. Urged on by the chief of the tribe, great kraals were prepared for the promised animals, and huge skin sacks, to hold the milk, that would plentifully flow. The appointed day came, and the cattle were slaughtered. But no new cows appeared, and the dead stayed resolutely underground. In the resulting famine, thousands died and those that remained were forced to turn to the British for help.

Walking along Settler's Way, Lokim considers the tragic consequences of the tribe's eagerness to trust in the words of the child. He thinks of Frances Almeida, who believed firmly in the resurrection of Jesus Christ: she had explained that Christianity was a religion, and true, while African beliefs were no more than superstition. The second Sunday after he had arrived in East London, he had taken himself off to the nearest church, in deference to Frances, but he had never gone back. He had been put off by a large painted carving of Jesus nailed to a cross; it had seemed a grim thing to choose to worship. What was the difference between the belief that Jesus had been dead, then come back to life, and the Xhosa people's faith that their ancestors would rise up from their graves?

He thinks of the slavers who would stop the line, while they bowed their heads to the ground and prayed. Their religion did not seem to have made them any happier. He wonders about the faith of his own tribe, who spoke of a sky god, Didigwari, who was said to have lowered the first Ik to earth, on a long length of vine.

Lokim is approaching the doctor's house. Superstition and religious belief he concludes, are one and the same, and hold little benefit. But he cannot completely dismiss the spirit world. He thinks of Atum, who taught him to respect the ancestors, and fed him his special potion: in so doing, he had gifted him with the wonderful image which had enabled him to survive. He smiles, and shakes his head in amazement — it still seems extraordinary that the strange woman's picture should have appeared on a can of oil, and then on a bar of soap. He has bought his own soap, and has fixed the circle of paper with the woman's image on it, above his bed.

Lokim quickens his step. A trap has been parked outside the house, he must get back to the dispensary. He must hurry to serve the waiting customers.

 East London, Cape Colony

One of the ox wagons has been sent from the mission, along with two drivers, and a cook boy. Its canvas has been made more waterproof with linseed oil, its woodwork has been freshly painted and its wheels have recently been fitted with new iron rims. The wagon's drivers are called Matthew and Mark. They are smartly dressed, keen to oblige and solicitous to their animals. The cook boy is called Joshua; he has brewed a canister of fresh coffee on a portable charcoal stove. He pours the liquid into a long-handled pot, and places it on a brass tray along with a china cup and saucer. He presents it to James, and regards him expectantly.

'Thank you,' says James, He seats himself on a folding chair, which has been carefully positioned in the shade. 'Delicious.'

'Would you like anything else, Mr Stewart? I can cook you some lamb chops.'

'Thank you, but no. I had a good breakfast at the guest house.'

The two other wagons have been hired from a local entrepreneur called John Harvey. They are not in a good state of repair. There is a spoke missing from the wheels of one, and there is a large tear in the hood of the other. But of more immediate concern to James is the condition of the wagons' drivers. They had arrived late and when they did eventually appear, they were bleary-eyed and indolent; up close, they smelled of beer. He had asked them to begin loading the larger cases — those that contain items of furniture — but after a brief attempt at moving the box containing Mina's piano, they announced that it was too heavy. They outspanned their oxen, and retreated to the shade of a tree fern. Now, they are asleep, or pretending to be, with their feet stretched out. They lie equally spaced, like four points of a compass, while their animals lie near them, snorting at the buzzing flies, and occasionally flicking their tails.

James sips his coffee. He will have to have some sort of confrontation, otherwise the party will never get moving. He is aware that his actions, or lack of them, are being scrutinised by the Lovedale drivers, who have already loaded their wagon with the food supplies, and the camping equipment. He is glad that Mina is not present, if there are to be any difficulties, he would rather she were not there to witness the scene. Mrs Lavery has taken her to the town — they have gone to purchase more quinine from the local pharmacy.

Darling Mina… She is so trusting, and so determined to keep cheerful. At one point on the journey, she had suffered miserably from seasickness. After she had slept, and washed her face, she had declared that it had almost been worth it, because it was so nice to feel well again. The only time that her courage had failed her was when she had said that she would adjust to life in Africa, so long as he remained at her side. 'You will never leave me, will you, James?' she had entreated, 'I do not believe I could bear to be apart from you — not even for one night!' As gently as possible, he had explained that he would have to spend time away; he would need to explore the area, to find for himself the best places to expand the mission; he would have to go to Cape Town, from time to time, and to Port Elizabeth… he might even need to return to Scotland, if funds for his ambitious schemes were not sufficiently forthcoming. Mina's role would be to stay at Lovedale,

317

ensuring that everything ran smoothly, whilst leading by example and making a happy home. 'You will have Jane for company,' he had said, 'and Chrissy will be there, too.' Mina had wept; she had looked so pitiful that he had felt his own heart would break. She had only stopped when he kissed the tears from her eyes in such a clumsy way that his tongue had tangled in her hair. They had both smiled, then laughed, before tumbling back down on the padded platform that formed their cabin bed.

'Mr Stewart...' The cook boy is holding out the coffee pot. 'Can I please fill up your cup?'

'No thank you, Joshua.' James gets up, and advances towards the resting men. 'Come,' he says to them. Going down on one knee, he pulls the leader to his feet. 'Time to get moving. I'll help with the bigger boxes, and we'll ask Mark and Matthew to give a hand, too. We'll get as much done as we can before lunch, then we'll stop for something to eat. Gentlemen, I require your co-operation; without it, I shall be forced to ask your employer for a different crew.'

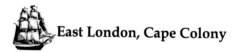 **East London, Cape Colony**

The trap rattles noisily as it rolls over the ruts of the packed dirt road. The three women sit crammed together, with Mrs Lavery in the centre. A guard stands on the footboard behind them. Mina had been confused to see that he carried a primitive bow and arrow instead of a gun. He wears a stove-pipe hat with no top to it, and tucked into his belt, is a ladies' fan. Observing his getup, she had been reminded of a strange little book Al had given her, after a trip to London. It had featured a girl called Alice, who fell down a rabbit hole, and into a place called Wonderland.

As they dip in and out of a pot hole, Mina holds onto her

hat. 'I'm so sorry,' she says to the minister's wife, as her arm makes contact with the other woman's chin.

'Couldn't be helped,' says Mrs Lavery. 'Hold tight — there's a sharp corner coming.'

They swing to the right. Mina looks to the kerb, and stifles a scream: she has spotted a snake lying coiled on the verge. As she watches, the snake's wide head rises from the ground, and its tongue emerges from its mouth. It makes a loud hissing sound. The trap rattles on. Mina refrains from looking back. She will have to get used to such things. The night before, when she went to fetch water from the kitchen, a score of brown cockroaches were milling around the floor, and that morning while they were waiting for breakfast to be served a family of monkeys had run through the room. The largest had swung from a chair to land on the table. It had pillaged a bread roll, before exiting through the window.

They travel down the main street; there is a Standard bank, a grocer's store, a dressmaker's and a shop selling farm implements. People stop and stare. Mina realises that three white women together must be a novelty in the town. She feels Mrs Lavery's elbow digging into her ribs as the driver turns into a track.

There are four houses in the road, each with a verandah, roofed with corrugated iron. They stop outside the fourth house. As soon as her feet touch the ground, her patent leather boots become covered in dry dust and lose all their shine. She would be better off in workers' clogs. She realises how hot she is and she envies the guard, who has opened his fan and is languidly flapping it across his face. She stands, waiting with Chrissy beside her, while Mrs Lavery knocks authoritatively at the door.

'Lawes must be out, on his visits,' the minister's wife says. 'There's usually someone here though — the room they use for the pharmacy, is to the side.' She disappears round a corner, then re-emerges, shaking her head.

'Shall we get the eggs and cheese first,' Mina asks, and then come back?'

'We could do — but if it's left out too long, the butter will turn to ghee.'

Just then, a tall young African comes hurrying towards them. 'Excuse me ladies,' he calls, 'I will open the pharmacy, if it is medicines you require.' He speaks in an odd, educated kind of accent. He gets out a key, opens the door, and leads them into the shop.

'We need quinine,' says Mina, as she stands at the counter. 'And some grains of salicylic acid.'

'How much would you like?'

'Five packets, and forty grains of the acid. Is there anything you need Chrissy? Would you like any laudanum?'

Chrissy steps forward, out of the shadow. And then something strange happens. 'I am Lokim,' the man says, speaking urgently. 'My name is Lokim.' He fetches the medicine, without saying anything more.

* * *

Mina has returned with Chrissy to the docks, where James is helping to load the second wagon. He has unbuttoned the collar of his shirt, and rolled up his sleeves. A large wooden container stands on the ground, with ropes fixed beneath it. He hauls and pulls with the hired drivers, while the Lovedale men lift and heave from below. Eventually, the box is manoeuvred into place. James jumps down, and comes towards her, smiling in welcome. 'I am lucky,' Mina thinks. 'Whatever problems may lie ahead, I am lucky to be cherished by so beautiful a man.' When he takes her hand, she melts with the remembrance of past pleasure, and with the anticipation of pleasure to come.

'Excuse me, madam.' The cook boy, is holding up a kettle, and a frying pan. 'Where will I put these items?'

Mina kisses James quickly on the cheek, then steps away. 'Come, Chrissy,' she says. We have work to do. And I am not sure how best to begin.'

 East London, Cape Colony

When she came forward, and Lokim saw that under her bonnet, her face was framed with red curls and that her eyes were blue, he wondered if he was in some kind of trance; she so closely resembled the dream-woman who had protected him, and whose image he had so strangely been able to buy. He had tried to introduce himself, feeling that he must — by some means — communicate. He had quickly fallen silent, not knowing what more to say.

The girl in the ribboned hat had addressed the woman as Chrissy. As he works in the pharmacy, Lokim repeats the name, over and again. 'Chrrrrisy...' he says, 'Chrissy.' He takes a bunch of dried arnica down from its hanging place. 'Chrisssy... Cccchrisssy.' He separates the flowers, and one by one, he pulls off their petals. 'Chrissy,' he repeats, dropping the petals into the mortar. He had thought that she must be an illusion, a thing of magic, but when she had stepped in front of the counter, he knew for certain that she was real. Her dress was the colour of a loerie bird, and there was a small stain on her skirt. Beads of sweat had caused her hair to cling to her forehead, and her cheeks were fired pink by the heat. He had been tempted to get down on his knees, he wanted to plead with her, to explain how they were connected with one another. He had watched, helpless, as she walked out through the door.

At noon, he goes to the kitchen, where his lunch has been put out on a plate. Blossom is rolling pastry; she is making mince pies for Lawes. The doctor always says how much he likes them, because they remind him of home.

Lokim begins to eat, then puts down his bread and cheese. 'We had some new customers today. Mrs Lavery brought two other white women in her trap. I had not seen them before. Do you know if they are to settle in the town?'

'I expect they are the missionaries who are on their way to Lovedale.' Blossom presses a metal ring into the pastry to make a circle.

'Isn't there a school there?'

'And a press. It is where the *Indaba* is printed.'

'When will they leave?'

Blossom pushes the metal ring down again, lifts it up and another circle of pastry falls onto the board. 'How should I know? They were at the docks, when I went to buy fish. Why you asking?' She looks at him, carefully. 'Now just because you've got fine new clothes, don't you be getting ideas. Don't think you can go after no white woman. It's time got yourself a nice black girl. There's plenty that would want you.' She picks up a little canister with holes in the top and shakes it energetically, sprinkling Lokim, as well as the table, with dots of white flour.

That afternoon, Lokim's work is to cut the grass. He gets the heavy shearing machine from the outhouse. Although the work is hard, it is a simple task to form the neat stripes, which are so much prized by the doctor. His mind is left free to think and to plan. His life is intertwined with that of the red-haired woman. He feels compelled to follow her. But he also knows how lucky he is to be in his current situation. He has much to be thankful for and much to lose. There are days when memories of the starvation he has endured, the thrashings he suffered, and the acts of random cruelty he has witnessed, all crowd and cut into him; he has to beat the thoughts away, as if they are sharp-thorned briers. On such days, he feels he could be a garment, only loosely held together. The slightest tug, would cause him to fall apart.

He waits for a week before he approaches the doctor. He finds Lawes sitting with his pipe, watching as the evening sun slips below the horizon. 'May I speak with you?' he asks.

'Of course. But first, look at the sunset.'

Lokim looks at the sky, which is a glorious mix of gold and pink and red. 'It is very beautiful.'

'It is, Lokim. It is. Now what can I do for you?'

'I have heard of a place called Lovedale. I would be interested to go there.' His attachment to the red-haired woman sounds too odd and complex to explain. He continues: 'They have printing presses, which I would like to learn how to use. I feel it would be...'

'An advancement?'

'Yes. An advancement.'

'I can understand the attraction of such a place.'

'Are they kind there, like you? Do they treat black people fairly?' Lokim has broken out into a sweat.

'There is nowhere in the Colony that indigenous people are more valued. Govan, who runs the mission, takes seriously the Cape's policy of being 'colour blind'. And I have heard that the new fellow, James Stewart, is even more committed to the native cause. You would like it. The only thing...'

'Yes?'

'Well, it is mission. You would be expected to worship Christ.'

Lokim is silent. He is thinking of the cross in the church he visited and the painted blood that had dripped from a crown of metal thorns.

'Don't let that stop you. Do as I do: just take the good parts from Christianity, and don't get too preoccupied with what you do or don't believe.'

'How far away is Lovedale? Could I walk there?'

'It is around sixty miles. You could do it in two days. But I'd rather you didn't leave until I have found someone to replace you.' The doctor stands up, and claps him on the shoulder. 'You're a good man, Lokim. I shall be sorry to see you go.'

CHAPTER TWELVE

February 1873

 **Lovedale**

In the six years that Chrissy has been at Lovedale, she has learned not to look back to Dundee, in the way that she used to. Feeling homesick for things that were familiar, she would turn it in her mind's eye to a place of comfort, in a way that it never truly was. She still wishes that she were not so far from Thomas's grave, but she knows that she is far better off in Africa than she could ever be in Scotland. At Lovedale, no-one treats her with disdain (except, sometimes, for Jane Waterston, who cannot resist asserting her own intellectual superiority). If Mina, or James, have discovered from Sam the truth about her past, they give no intimation of having done so.

On the whole, she is content. Her greatest joy comes from being with the little ones: she is happiest when they clamber on her lap, put their arms around her neck, and try to rub the freckles from her nose.

She works hard at the mission. Everyone does. James Stewart believes in leading by example, and he himself does the work of ten. During the day, he builds roads, digs the gardens, manages the farm, oversees the press, sees patients, takes services and teaches science to the older boys. At night, the lamp in his study burns till the early hours. He is producing a Xhosa phrasebook and dictionary, and he is constantly writing papers and fund-raising letters. He is determined to build a hospital at Alice and to expand the training college. His dearest and most repeated goal is for Lovedale to grow into a university, with standards as high as Edinburgh or London. Chrissy feels sympathy for Mina. Whenever his wife begs James to rest, he smiles and says, 'It suits me to keep busy.'

Chrissy's days are spent instructing the older girls in sewing and laundry work. She also works at the primary school, where she reads out stories and holds up cards to teach the youngest their letters and numbers. She has learned to speak Xhosa, having mastered, with difficulty, the necessary clicks of the tongue. At the school, pupils are encouraged to converse in both their own language and in English. But they no longer have to learn Latin and Greek; despite considerable opposition, James has discontinued their teaching. He says that the Classics hark back to the past; it is English that will be the universal language of the future. Chrissy is glad of this; she had felt disadvantaged, never having learned Latin herself.

She is reading from Mother Goose, pausing at every line, to offer an approximate translation, when the bell sounds for eleven o'clock. It is Tuesday, so she must go over to the main school to help Jane, who has recently introduced a physical education session for the older girls. She hands the book over to Letty, one of the other teachers. 'Work hard,' she tells the pupils. 'I will see you tomorrow.'

The children straggle to their feet. 'Goodbye Miss Hogarth,' they chant. 'We wish you a good morning.'

The tables and chairs in the hall have already been cleared

and stacked. Chrissy apologises to Jane for being late: she explains that she had stopped to ask after the welfare of one of the boarders, who was back in school, after two weeks in the infirmary. 'There is nowhere a patient could have received better treatment,' she says. 'It is amazing to see him so well.'

The teacher frowns to indicate the inappropriateness of such chatter. She claps her hands.

'Quiet girls! Quiet! We will start with some marching. Elijah! Play us that new hymn, that I gave you. Have you got the sheet? The one we were sent in that parcel from London. If you know the words, you can sing as you march.'

'Onward Christian Soldiers', the girls sing as they parade, and Elijah's bow works up and down. 'Forward into ba-a-attle do his banners go.' When they have got through all the verses, Miss Waterston again claps her hands. 'And now you will perform a Scottish dance. Each of you must find a partner. You will have to decide between you, who will play the part of the gentleman. Miss Hogarth, you will be the caller. Assemble yourselves into groups of six. Elijah! Play the piece you have prepared... The Dashing White Sergeant, if you please!'

Elijah fiddles, and the dance begins. Chrissy instructs the girls while they circle, turn, advance, arch their hands and tunnel through. She is reminded of another time she heard the familiar reel; she remembers the asylum, when she danced with Deborah beside her, and came face to face with the Duke of Dunoon. She tries to concentrate on her task, but the music from the violin becomes louder and louder. Perhaps Jane's abrupt manner has put her out of sorts; the tune uncomfortably fills her ears. She backs away, and leans for support against the nearest wall. She ceases to call out instructions, for she can see her friend again, dancing in her maharani outfit. She sees poor Deborah lying dead, having collapsed in the thin man's arms. Elijah is playing faster and faster. The girls dance with abandon: one girl trips over, and lies laughing on the floor.

Elijah lowers his violin. Jane advances towards the girl. 'This is disgraceful. Get up at once!'

The girl is still laughing, and does not instantly respond. The teacher seizes her by the arm and pulls her to her feet. 'Don't you dare be so impertinent,' she says, in a low voice.

Something inside Chrissy goes snap. 'Leave Sana alone,' she says. 'It was an accident; she did not mean to fall.' The girls have assembled themselves into two lines. Chrissy walks straight down the middle of them, and out of the room.

She does not care what kind of an impression she has made. She will not go back to the hall until she is ready. It occurs to her how little she has allowed herself to grieve for Deborah, who had been a true and beloved friend. She thinks of Deborah's coronet of paper flowers and her hope that she would be fetched from the asylum, and would be welcomed back home. Sweet Deborah... who had been so cruelly deprived of her liberty: her only madness had been to have liked pretty things.

When Chrissy thinks of the fine funeral that Deborah's husband held for her, she rages at the hypocrisy of the man, and at the hypocrisy of the society that allowed Mr Buchanan to lock his wife away. She needs space for herself; she walks quickly away from the school, and down the road that leads to the farm. She keeps on walking until she comes to a field where a score of oxen are nudging gently at the grass. She leans on a gate and tries to find solace in watching the gentle animals.

A man is walking in her direction. It is Lokim the printer, who is always kind and who charms the girls with his easy smile. She wipes her eyes and blows her nose. She does not want sympathy; her grief is her own. She clings to the top bar of the gate. She would like to stop crying, but something inside has become unstopped.

 **Lovedale**

The *Indaba* is now printed on a rotary press which was sent from America, after Dr Stewart had made one of his appeals. It consists of a table and a complicated system of cylinders, levers, cogs and wheels. It is so large that it requires three men to work it and it is so heavy that it arrived in Alice in many different parts. The complicated machinery was finally assembled after a week of discussion and head-scratching. Lokim enjoys being in charge of 'The Roller' as it is affectionately called, but he likes using the old hand presses, too. The Stanhope is his favourite, because of its solid structure and logical design.

He had come to Lovedale with a letter of recommendation and the clothes he stood up in, together with an extra shirt and a pair of trousers donated to him by Dr Lawes. He had also brought the soap wrapping, with Chrissy's image stamped upon the label.

When he took his letter to James Stewart and Lokim saw his red hair, he realised that he was the person who had tried, until the overseer had abruptly ended their session, to teach him to read on the Island of Mozambique. The white man was much thinner then, but he was the same person. And when Stewart, in turn, remembered where they had previously met, he had been delighted. He himself had shown Lokim how to fill a galley with a composing stick and how to accurately place a paper sheet between the frisket and the tympan.

Now Lokim can typeset quicker than anyone. Recently, he has begun to produce articles for the *Indaba*. He avoids anything that might be considered controversial; he knows he is still a novice. But once he has mastered the craft, he will record his experiences. The world must learn the truth about slavery. The Abolition Act may have been passed in England, but the awful practice continues elsewhere. People must not be able to plead ignorance as an excuse.

Stewart believes that it benefits a man to have variety in his work, and so one morning a week, Lokim helps out on the Lovedale farm. On this Tuesday he is to milk the goats, but first, he has been asked to check on an ox who has been seen limping. He is known to have a way with animals; he can sometimes tell what is amiss, at just one glance.

He is approaching the oxen field, when he stops. He has seen Chrissy leaning on the gate, with her hands covering her face. He thinks she must want privacy... why else would she be there? But in order to look at the animal, he must pass through the gate. And if she is unhappy, he would like very much to make her better. But suppose he says something wrong? He has never expressed his devotion, nor has he told her how her image protected him when he walked in a collar and chains. It is enough that he lives near her, and is able to see her, every day.

For all Stewart's talk of racial equality, there is no denying that Chrissy is white and he is black. He wants to bring comfort, but he risks appearing over-familiar. He fears creating a tension between them that did not exist before. If she takes offence, he will lose the thing that he treasures most in the world... He is about to turn away, when she looks up. Now that she has seen him, he must approach.

He comes to stand beside her. Patiently, he waits for her to acknowledge that he is there.

'I'm sorry,' she says, indicating the gate, 'I am blocking your way.'

'I cannot pass and leave you in distress. Tell me what it is that is troubling you. A sorrow is often better shared.'

Chrissy hides her face. She is crying afresh. 'I'm sorry,' she says, after a time. 'I'm sorry.'

'Has someone hurt you?' He remonstrates with himself: his hand is tingling to hold a spear.

'Not here. It was some time ago. A dear friend died, back

in Dundee… she was treated very badly by her husband. Men back home can be cruel to their women.'

Lokim realises that he knows little of Chrissy's country. He stays silent, then says: 'So all men in Scotland are not like Dr Stewart?'

Chrissy shakes her head. Tear drops cling to her lashes and fall down her cheeks. Her lips are red and swollen from crying. She looks as if she has been eating the plums that drop in autumn from Mrs Stewart's tree. 'No,' she whispers, 'they are not.'

He guesses, from the way she has spoken, that Chrissy has herself been wronged by a man. He is concerned that if she goes on to say more, she will feel she has revealed too much, so that afterwards, she will be embarrassed, and will want to keep her distance. Not wishing to lose the intimacy that is between them, he decides to share some of his own suffering. 'Our experiences can turn to memories which are sometimes hard to bear,' he says. 'I was a slave before I came to East London, and to the home of Dr Lawes. I met bad men and one good man, who was driven to a bad place. I was made to walk as part of a line, carrying ivory, until we came to the coast. I count myself lucky to be here at Lovedale.'

Chrissy's eyes are wide. 'That must have been terrible for you.'

Lokim nods. Now that the real woman is standing beside him, rather than her likeness, he feels driven to share more. 'For me, and for many others. I saw men beaten, I saw women killed, I saw men kicked to death, when they were too weak to walk. I saw a brave woman shot for trying to look after her child.'

For some reason, Chrissy looks away.

'One of the traders took her little girl and killed her, by dashing her head against a stone.' Lokim speaks urgently. The incident with Luma had been the worst thing. He ignores

331

Chrissy's own distress. He needs her to express some sympathy.

She stays silent, her face set.

'It is hard for you to understand... you have not experienced a mother's devotion. A mother can be like a lioness, when...'

He does not get to finish his sentence, because Chrissy is raining blows upon his chest. He tries to catch her flying fists, but she fights like one possessed. It is as if all the anger she has ever felt, is being vented upon his upper body.

'I had a child,' she sobs, 'I had a son.'

Lokim ceases trying to defend himself. Tears from Chrissy's blue eyes stream down her face while she hits out, and then suddenly she stops. Her shoulders drop. She lowers her head, and when at last she looks up, he sees in her face an expression which mixes yearning with the deepest sorrow.

Tentatively, Lokim stretches out his hand. Gently, he wipes the tears from under her eyes. She offers no resistance as he takes her in her arms. 'Then you have been loved,' he says. 'You have been loved, as well as hurt.' He strokes her red hair over and again. 'And you will be loved once more.'

 Fingoland, Cape Province

The appointed meeting place is not easy to find. James has been told to look out for an umbrella thorn on a piece of level ground between two streams, but he has seen many umbrella thorns on his journey and an overnight downpour has filled the shallow gullies that run down from the hills. He swats at the flies which buzz around his head, while he wonders whether or not he should follow a foaming rivulet. He is annoyed with himself for not having accepted the Fingoes' offer of a guide.

His horse is steaming from the heat, and perspiration is causing his shirt to cling uncomfortably to his back. He dismounts to let the horse drink, then he takes a swill of water from his pannier. He straightens himself and stretches. He removes the crude map supplied to him by Captain Blyth from his pack and unfolds it. After studying it, he realises that he should be further west; he needs to go a couple of miles further before he can pick up the stream, then follow it to the point where it splits into two.

He continues on his way. He passes a settlement, where the rough path widens into something like a road. His horse travels more purposefully. Bucket is a bay gelding, seventeen hands high, bought from a breeder in Alice. It was Little Mina who named him, because of the way the horse had galloped, on his first morning at Lovedale, from the other side of the field to be fed. James smiles at the thought of his daughter. As well as sharing her mother's name, Little Mina has a similar personality. She mixes a sweet concern for others with intelligence and good humour.

He remembers the day when he became a father. 'What shall we call her?' Mina had asked, when she lay with the new baby in a crib beside her. He had held out a finger, which the little one had firmly grasped. 'Horace,' he had replied, high on happiness. 'We'll call her Horace, after good old Waller.' Mina had been unusually firm. 'No James. We can't give her a boy's name. It would be too confusing.' And so they had agreed on Williamina, with Waller as a middle name. And now, to their delight, five year old Williamina has a sister. When he had left, Mina had been nursing little Florence in her arms. She had kissed him goodbye and the baby had waved her hand. James reflects that there are advantages to living in rural Africa. The bond between himself and his family is all the stronger because he had delivered the girls himself. When Florence was born, he had to ligate the cord, before she could be born, for it was wrapped around her neck. Mina had been so brave.

Passing a flame tree, he is reminded of Mary. He thinks of her love of Africa, her stoic courage and her unexpected frailties. He had told Mina of their relationship, of course. He would not have her hearing gossip from other people, without herself knowing the truth. 'Poor Mary,' was all Mina had said. 'Poor Mary, to have been parted from her children.'

Ahead of him, he sees a stream. He takes the path that runs alongside it then, having passed through a thicket of trees, he comes to a flat area of ground. He experiences a frisson of nerves when he sees a group of people gathered in the shade of a large umbrella thorn.

It is James who has called the meeting. Observing the success of the mission since he had taken over from Govan as principal, a group of elders from the Nqamakwe district had come to him for help. They had asked him to build 'a Child of Lovedale,' as they poetically put it. James had explained that a lot of money would be required. He had challenged them to raise a thousand pounds from their own people. He had added that if they succeeded, he would obtain a matching sum from Scotland.

Captain Blyth, representative of the government of the Cape Colony, is already there; James can see his scarlet jacket. He is standing next to the Reverend Ross, from Toleni, who is dressed in a dark gown. James touches his open-necked shirt. He should have thought to dress more formally.

A young boy takes Bucket's rein and leads him to a place where he can graze. James walks over to greet the company.

'I hope your optimism does not prove unfounded,' says the Captain. 'You are expecting uneducated farmers to give most generously. I am not sure that they possess such funds.'

'Africans, here in the Cape, have learned to prize learning. And the Mfengu have proved themselves to be consummate traders. My faith will not prove misplaced.' He speaks with much more confidence than he actually feels.

A table has been set up and chairs provided for the three white men. Word has been sent out that each residential area should deliver a separate contribution. After two hours' wait, a horseman arrives wearing sailcloth trousers, a bone necklace and a cheetah skin cloak. He throws a small bag of coins down upon the table, then leaves, without saying a word. No-one else comes for a long time. Even in the shade, it is far too hot. Blyth sighs heavily from time to time, while the Reverend Ross frets that he will not be back in time to take the evening service.

When James says, 'Don't feel you have to wait,' Ross looks at him in an odd way, so that James wonders if he is altogether trusted by the clergyman.

Then, in late afternoon, four horsemen canter down from the hill. Each hands over a bulging bag of money. James looks up and sees that dozens more horsemen have appeared on the skyline. The Mfengu are subsistence farmers; they have waited until their day's work is done. The tribesmen make their deliveries, and it is not long before the makeshift table is in danger of collapsing under the weight of over one hundred bags.

Together, James and Blyth count out the contributions: the Mfengu have donated over fifteen hundred pounds. One of the elders sweeps an arm over the piles of coins. 'These are the stones,' he tells James. 'Now build.'

 **Lovedale**

The baby is asleep, and Little Mina is in the front room, enjoying a game of tiddlywinks with Letty. Mina goes to the study and begins to write a reply to the last letter she had received from Broughty Ferry.

Dear Janet, she begins…

I am very sorry to hear that life has become so difficult for you. I suppose it is only natural that Papa should become more short-tempered as his health worsens. You say that he is breathless at times, and suffers pains in his chest if he exerts himself too much. It must be frustrating for him not to be able to take an active part in the running of the Yard, although it will be compensation to him that Al and John are both so competent.

Mina thinks of poor Janet, left behind at Corona, putting up with Papa's cruelty and with no-one to turn to for support. She goes on:

But that is no excuse for Papa to treat you as he does, and for him to humiliate you in front of others. Would it be possible for you to spend more time with John and Eliza? John's charitable causes are so many that I am sure he would benefit from some help in their administration.

As for the matter of Andrew, and his threats to reveal the contents of the casket he possesses, unless he receives three thousand pounds

Mina puts down her pen. She was going to say '*I do not believe that any papers the box contains can possibly be so damaging as to justify the payment of such a large amount*' but this would not be true. If Andrew's allegations were to come to Court, his evidence would become public knowledge. In all likelihood, her father would be financially as well as personally ruined — the Yard's customers would choose to buy their ships elsewhere. She thinks of Hannah's sudden flight to New South Wales, and a letter she had received, soon after she married, from her eldest sister Anne. '*You will be missed by those you love,*' Anne had written, *but you will also benefit from being in Africa. Papa's behaviour can be illiterate'* It had been such a strange word to choose: *illiterate*. Papa could read a book in a day, and he could turn a sentence as elegantly as Mr Trollope.

She wishes that Janet had not confided in her. The letter has been a reminder of her trip to the tenements with Miss Scrope. For a long time afterwards, she had not been able to make proper sense of the rough woman's words. Now that she is married, she fully understands what Mhairi meant and the accusation makes her feel quite sick. If it were any other matter, she would wait and discuss with James — on his return from Fingoland — how best to reply to her sister. But she has never told him of Andrew's awful claims and the posters that her brother put up around Dundee. It is not that James would be shocked. He has often said that after his years spent working in Glasgow Infirmary, there is nothing of human nature that could surprise him. But she does not want the image that he has of her to become tainted by compassion, and she would loathe for him to consider her in any way unclean.

She gets up and spends some moments looking out of the window, then sits back down and writes: *'it is a vast amount of money. Has Papa taken legal advice from anyone other than DWP?'* She will say no more on the subject; it is too wretched to think about.

'How fortunate,' she continues, *that you met Miss Scrope at the monthly bazaar after you had spoken to John. I am sure she will be a splendid addition to the Orphans' Welfare Committee. I am glad to hear that she is enjoying her work as Latin Mistress at the Ladies College.'*

Once more, she puts down her pen. She can hear Florence stirring in the next room. She is making little 'whaaa' sounds; Mina can picture her turning from side to side, and pushing her fists in her mouth. She goes to the baby and lifts her from her crib; she smells her daughter's sweet baby scent and feels the satisfying weight of her sturdy little body. She changes her cloth, then dresses her in a fine lace gown, sent out by the Templetons in their Christmas parcel. There is no point in keeping it for best when Florrie is growing so fast. She unties her bodice, and offers her full breast. She feeds her baby, whilst rocking in her chair.

 ## Lovedale

Chrissy is in her room in the teachers' quarters. It is soon after six, but it is still hot; she has just heard the chapel bell. She tips some water from the ewer into her washbowl, and splashes her face and hands.

In half an hour, it will be time for supper, and she will see Lokim again; at Lovedale everyone is expected to eat together in the large dining hall. Lokim has said that he will do whatever she wishes. If she prefers to pretend that the events of the morning never took place, he will do the same. He will even leave Lovedale, if that is what she wants. He desires only to make her happy.

Chrissy looks at her reflection in a small round mirror. Her years at Lovedale have benefited her, she does not look so very different from the smiling girl who had sat for Mr Watt. Lokim had told her that he had seen her picture on the label of an oil drum, when he was a prisoner on a boat. He had seen her image again on a bar of soap, when he was a free man in East London. She had not believed Frank's boast that the Tannery's products were sold in the farthest parts of the Empire, but now she realises that he spoke the truth.

She had told Lokim how the picture had been created to advertise the Canadian Tannery, where she had worked as a seamstress. He had said that her image was so beautiful that it had helped him to survive. When he saw her in the pharmacy, he had thought at first he must be dreaming. After she had gone, he had asked Dr Lawes's cook how he could find her. He had made the journey to Lovedale, knowing that she would be there.

Chrissy takes off her work dress, and lies down on her bed. She remembers Lokim's past deference to her, and the way he would rush to be helpful if she needed any worksheets printed for the school. When he saw her, he would start as if surprised, then slowly smile. While he seemed immune to the charms of the other female teachers, he had on occasions brought her flowers. Once, he had given her a wooden case that he had carved, saying that she needed somewhere to keep her pens and pencils. It seems obvious now, that he had always cared for her.

He said that he had not declared his love, because he thought she would reject him. She would have considered the differences between them to be too great. Up until the point when he took her in his arms, he would have been right. Chrissy closes her eyes, and remembers the sensation of being held. She had felt that at last, she no longer had to bear her grief alone. She had told him about Thomas, explaining — between her tears — the circumstances of his conception. Lokim had said little; instead, he had held her more closely. Gently, he had stroked her hair. She had felt no shame as she spoke of what had happened; she had relaxed in a sense of complete acceptance.

Chrissy feels her cheeks go red... Amidst her sorrow for Thomas, her distress for Deborah and her anger at the cruel slaver who had so casually killed a child, she had experienced another, entirely selfish emotion. It had been a gladness — a joy in being alive. For she had enjoyed Lokim's embrace. She had not been able to help herself. She had moved closer to him.

Pressed against his chest, she had been able to hear his beating heart; she had thrilled to hear the sound. She had felt pleasure at the muscles of his arms, and the taut strength of his long legs. She blushes more; she has remembered her interest in the half-naked Hottentot, whose picture Mr Connor had brought to the asylum.

She gets up and washes her face again. She puts on a newly laundered dress, and steps outside. She walks purposefully down the path, across the well-tended gardens and enters the dining hall.

CHAPTER THIRTEEN

July 1874

 **Lovedale**

It is late. Normally, once the girls are asleep, and the supper has been cleared, Mina does some sewing or letter-writing and then retires, to be followed much later by James. Tonight, she has delayed her bedtime. James has just returned from a trip to Britain. He has been away for five months, and there is much to talk about.

They are seated together in the study of the principal's house, and they are belatedly celebrating Mina's birthday by sharing some chocolates that he had bought for her in Fortnum's. James steals a glance across at his wife. Childbirth and hard work have done nothing to diminish her beauty. Her profile still brings a lump to his throat. He counts himself extraordinarily lucky to have found not only a wife and a mistress, but also a colleague and a soul mate. Unstintingly, she supports his schemes and projects. Although she would much prefer for him to remain always at her side, when he does go away, she wastes no time in lamenting her loneliness.

Instead, she makes sure that Lovedale continues to operate harmoniously. The locals call her 'Nowaka,' which means 'mother of the people'. She settles any disputes that arise, offers encouragement where it is needed, answers enquiries and acts as hostess to the many visitors who come to witness the mission's success.

'I forgot to tell you,' he says, 'Bartle Frere will be arriving tomorrow, with a couple of his men. Can we find them a room, and something for supper? There was a telegram from him, waiting in Alice. He's the ex-Governor of Bombay. He's decided to do a short tour of Southern Africa, before going on to Zanzibar. I met him at the Geographical Society.'

'We'd better let him have our bedroom and the nursery. We'll sleep in the study, and Little Mina can stay with Letty and John. They make such a fuss of her, she always counts it a treat. Such elevated company you've been keeping, James. I'll do my best to ensure that we impress.'

'Don't try too hard. He should take us as he finds us, like everyone else.' James gets up and extracts a copy of the *Illustrated London News* from his Gladstone bag. 'I brought you this: it's an account of the funeral. You can't imagine the fuss that was made. It was as if every family in the kingdom had lost a much-loved personal friend, who also happened to be a saint. Apparently, there hadn't been such an outpouring of national grief since Nelson was brought back from Trafalgar. Miss Nightingale added to the general lamentation; she said that the greatest man of his generation has been lost.'

Mina reads how Livingstone's body had arrived from Africa in a ship called the *Malwa*. The mayor had been there to receive the coffin, which was transferred to a hearse drawn by four horses. A procession of dignitaries had followed the hearse to Southampton railway station, and a military band had played the 'Dead March' from Handel's Saul. A special train had brought the coffin to London. The body had lain in state at The Royal Geographical Society, and Queen Victoria had sent an elaborate arrangement of flowers.

She hands back the newspaper. 'Are they sure that it really was Livingstone?

'Oh yes. Sir William Fergusson examined the remains. He found that the humerus — the upper bone of the arm — had a false joint from an old injury, where Livingstone had been mauled by a lion. It was definitely him. Waller and Kirk were there in the room. They said there wasn't much else to recognise. The embalming process had — of necessity — been crude. The journey took nine months. His servants had to make detours around various pockets of fighting.'

'It must be a great distance, from Ilala to Bagamoyo.'

'About fifteen hundred miles. Susi, Chuma and Jacob were greeted like heroes when they got to England. Their story was made to fit the public mood. The newspapers said they travelled all that way because they were inspired by love and a deep respect for their master.'

'Was that not the case?'

'Jacob told me they were worried that if they didn't bring back proof of Livingstone's death, they would have been accused of abandoning him. They are the elite of caravanners; they wanted to ensure that they were in a position to secure future work. Jacob did put on a good show though, when it came to the actual burial. He hurled a large palm leaf into the grave, then made as if to dive in after it. Stanley leaped from the pews to stop him. It could have been a scene from *East Lynne*.'

Mina smiles. 'Don't be cynical James. You shouldn't judge.'

'I don't. We're all mere players, with our exits and entrances. I'm no different. It's just that I'm not given to displays of emotion...' He reaches across, and kisses her hand. 'Except where you're concerned. My role is to get things done. This is what I want to talk to you about: you

343

should have seen how packed the Abbey was, and the vast crowds that had congregated on the road to Westminster. I know you got my letter, but I'll explain again: during the service it occurred to me that this was an opportunity. I could utilise all that goodwill and raise more funds. Young was there — he acted as a pall bearer — Gunner Young, as we called him, when we were together on the Zambesi. I talked to him afterwards. As long as he can be assured of getting his job back — he's now a Coastguard in Deal — he'll agree to take a steamer to Lake Nyassa. I can't go myself because I'm committed to overseeing all the new building work here and in Mfenguland. Of course, the steamer will have to be transported overland, in small parts — it will require some clever engineering, for each piece will have to weigh no more than the amount one man can easily carry. The distance to be travelled is over a thousand miles. Once there is full access, the Lake can be opened up to legitimate trade.' James is aware that in his eagerness, he is gabbling. He takes a breath and makes an effort to slow his speech. 'Believe me, Mina, we can make a direct difference to ending the slave trade. You know that Kirk is now consul in Zanzibar? He's been doing his best to put pressure on the Sultan, and I think he may prove effective. He's offered his support to my plan. We'll call the steamer the *Ilala*, after the village where Livingstone died. We'll build a town, with a college, and if we call the settlement Livingstonia, the people who have donated money in their hero's memory can feel well served.'

'Such a lot to be achieved... but if anyone can do it, you can. Did you see Agnes? How was she?'

'She was overwhelmed by the reception. I think that her sadness was outweighed by a sense of relief that there was a finality to things. After David had been found by Stanley, and had refused to go back with him to the coast, there could be no happy outcome. His health was increasingly compromised. In his last letter to Horace, he confessed to being terribly knocked up.'

James watches the flickering flame of the paraffin lamp. David Livingstone may have been feted in death, but in the last months of his life he was ill, without physical comfort, and with no family around him. James wonders how different things might have been, had Mary lived. If she had been alive to welcome him home, would he have been happy to accompany the reporter back to England? Or would he still have refused, his desire to discover the source of the Nile having by then become a deranged obsession?

He watches a moth batter itself at the glass column that surrounds the flame of the lamp. 'Agnes did ask after you,' he says. 'She sent her good wishes. She was with Anna — who's now quite grown up. Tom and Oswell were there of course.' He frowns. 'There was sad news of Robert. Agnes told me his death has been confirmed. He died in a Confederate prisoner-of-war camp in North Carolina. I wish I could have done more for him... I should have tried harder.'

'You did your best. I know how fond of him you were. But that news is indeed very sad.'

James remembers the passionate youth, who had accused him of laughing at his mother. Robert had been right to protest at his own lack of manners. He changes the subject, and asks, 'Did you hear from John and Eliza? They agreed to host the first meeting of our new mission to the Lake. They are always so hospitable at Shieldhall. John has offered to make and donate the *Ilala*'s sails.'

'John did write to me. He said that the meeting went on till after midnight. By turns, you charmed, then lectured. He also said that Papa's health is no better.'

'Mina, I must tell you that before I left, I saw your father for a second time. He does seem to be becoming increasingly frail — but then, he is getting on for eighty. In many ways, he is doing well. His mind is completely alert.'

'I thought you would have been too busy to return to Broughty Ferry.'

'When Alexander heard I was in Edinburgh, he asked me to come. He wanted me to act as an intermediary in a rather difficult matter.'

'What matter?'

'Your brother Andrew was asking for money.'

'He received his due many years ago.'

James hears the agitation in Mina's voice. He sees that she is pressing her thumb and forefinger together in a way that she used to do, when something had upset her. His instinct is to protect. 'Do not be concerned. Do you know, even Andrew has offered his help. He said he'll donate a harmonium to the expedition. He has connections with the admiralty; there are strings he can pull. And he can put me in touch with a well-connected wholesaler; he says the man can supply anything from a flea to an elephant. A harmonium is not one of the things I would previously have considered essential to the exploration of a largely unmapped lake, but who am I to judge? Let's have another chocolate.'

 **Lovedale**

With a flood of happiness, Lokim realises that it is Chrissy whom he lies beside. He opens his eyes. She is sleeping peacefully, with her red hair tumbling onto the pillow. Her pretty lips are softly parted and inside her nightdress, her breast gently rises and falls.

He had been dreaming that he was back in Bagamoyo. He was being forced to eat porridge, but his arm was shackled, so that he found it impossible to lift his hand. He knew that time

346

was running short. The man standing near him was holding up a panga, and would slice at his neck if he did not move. He woke up feeling chilled, with his heart thumping, and his breath coming in quick short gasps. When he found someone next to him, he had wondered for a moment who the person was.

The reason he is cold is because he has kicked off a patchwork coverlet, carefully sewn by Chrissy into a colourful pattern of diamonds and squares. He has rolled onto his hand, squashing his fingers under his thigh. It is this sensation that has given rise to his nightmare. He exults in the joyful reality of his situation. Not only is he a free man, he is married to Chrissy, and for the past six months, they have contentedly shared a home.

It is a Sunday, so the printing press will stay shut down, and no teaching will take place at the school. He stretches out luxuriously. He does not have to get up just yet; Sunday is officially a day of rest. Later on, he will go with Chrissy to the dining hall, where they will help Mrs Stewart serve a meal to the elderly of the district. In the evening, they will attend the service in Lovedale's chapel, where they will pray, sing hymns, and listen to John Bokwe preach. Lokim is not at all convinced that Jesus is still alive, and he suspects that prayers directed to the figure on the cross are a waste of time. But he very much likes the music — especially when the congregation is accompanied by the Lovedale band of schoolboy musicians — and it will be interesting to hear John's address. Like himself, John is a man determined to self-advance. He is training for the ministry; he is hoping to find a sponsor, who will enable him to attend one of the Scottish Universities.

Chrissy stirs. He rolls further onto his side, so that he can see her face. She has long golden lashes and a dusting of freckles on her nose. He still finds it extraordinary that she had agreed to marry him. Before their wedding, she had explained

347

that she did not care for the opinion of Jane Waterston, who would doubtless disapprove. She said that when she was with him she felt safe; he was different in every way from the white men who had ill-used her.

For months — after he had taken her in his arms at the gate by the oxen field — they had sought each other out at every opportunity. He had hesitated to ask the question, until he had been sure that her answer would be 'yes.' One summer's day, they had walked hand in hand to find James Stewart. He had been in the office, looking at some building plans. Hesitantly, they had asked if he would be prepared to conduct the ceremony. He had promptly rolled up the drawings and offered his congratulations. He had hunted round for a calendar, so that he could find a suitable date. 'You will have to decide,' he said, 'whether you want the service to take place as soon as the banns have been read, or whether you would prefer to wait until my return from overseas.'

Neither of them wanted to wait. So they had married in December, on the longest day. Mrs Stewart had, with a team of girls, decorated the chapel with hibiscus and frangipani. She had also provided yards and yards of muslin, which Chrissy had secretly sewn into a fine dress. The material had been meant for curtains — Lokim had been worried when he found this out. He said that he would pay, using his wages. Mrs Stewart had laughed and said there was no need; there were far more important things to life than window drapes. And anyway, she had already asked Eliza to send out some more bolts of the cloth.

Dr Lawes had accepted an invitation to come with Blossom from East London. He had sat in the front pew as Chrissy had walked down the aisle on John Bokwe's arm. In her white dress, wearing a circle of fresh flowers in her hair, she had looked like an angel — she could have stepped from the pages of one of the illustrated books, available on loan from the mission library. The children had jumped up from their seats, and had spontaneously clapped their hands. Miss Waterston had attended the ceremony and she had even brought a present of some silver spoons. Lokim had thought she might find an excuse not to come. He had overheard the teacher telling Dr Stewart how unsuitable she thought it was for a white woman to marry a black man. Stewart had replied that the whole basis of Lovedale was equality, which must logically include an acceptance of mixed marriage. If Jane found that a problem, it would be better for her to go elsewhere.

Lokim gets out of bed. He will surprise Chrissy by having breakfast prepared, before she wakes. As he puts on his clothes, he looks with satisfaction at their home. It is a rectangular building with a thatched roof. The Stewarts had offered two rooms in the teachers' quarters, but Chrissy had wanted more privacy and a small piece of ground. She said she wanted to grow the raspberries and cabbages that were native to her Scotland. The older boys had put up the posts for the frame of the house, and the younger pupils had gathered sticks and reeds to weave in between the struts. Lokim had borrowed a handcart from the farm, which he had used to fetch fine soil from termite mounds, so that he could pack the walls.

In time, the house will have running water, but for the moment, he needs to fill the kettle from the tap in the staff kitchen, before he lights their spirit stove. He turns to tuck the cover over Chrissy's naked foot. He is glad that she is still asleep. He thinks back to the words of the wedding service: *'Marriage is ordained for the procreation of children'*. Chrissy needs to rest. The night before, she had shared with him her excitement; her monthly loss is overdue. Lokim knows how much she longs for a baby, and he too would love to have a child. He picks up the kettle. As he steps outside, he hums the tune to one of his favourite hymns. He feels immensely blessed. 'All things bright and beautiful,' he sings, under his breath. He is tempted to get down on his knees; he would like to give thanks to Didigwari, the Ancestors and the Holy Ghost.

 **Lovedale**

For the weekly lunch, a score of chickens have been cooked with tomatoes, beans and herbs. Mina has added turmeric, cardamom and cumin until the flavour has achieved just the right piquancy. She has welcomed a hundred elderly people into the dining hall, greeting each individual by name. Once a seat has been found for everyone, a huge pot of the prepared stew has been wheeled into the room, together with a great vat of rice. After James has said grace and the helpers have distributed the food, Mina has moved between the trestle tables, ensuring that each person has enough to eat. For pudding, sweet mealie cakes have been served, and a milk tart, baked with raisins.

Now the guests have gone, the plates have been washed, and the clearing up completed. Mina has fed Florence, before retreating to the quiet of the study. She has just picked up her sewing, when Little Mina comes to her, and pulls her by the hand. 'Come and hear me at the piano,' she says. 'I've learned to play 'Home Sweet Home'.'

Mina gets up and follows her daughter into the front room. Little Mina is hesitant at first, but she grows more confident, and eventually produces a creditable version of the tune. Mina applauds. 'Well done, darling! Well done.'

Little Mina plays again. Mina thinks of a day soon after she had arrived in Lovedale, when she had sat at the piano and played the same melody. It had seemed unbearably poignant. Tears had streamed down her face as she had remembered her family and friends. John Bokwe had been a shy youth then. She had observed him watching through an open door, so she had dried her tears and beckoned for him to come inside. Then she had pulled herself together and asked if he knew the best source of clean water.

So much has changed in the seven years that have passed since. As soon as Govan retired, and James became Principal, he had begun the ongoing process of expanding the mission. With so much to do, and the children to look after, there has been no time for homesickness. Besides, Lovedale is home now.

'Shall I practise my scales?'

'Yes darling, do.'

Mina has given up wishing that James would restrict his activities, so that he could spend more time with her and the children. He would not be the man she loves, were he to limit his ambition. It is boundless, and his energy is indefatigable. The local people call him Longstrider, because of his seeming ability to be in so many different places at once. James is not ambitious for himself — he is genuinely disinterested in the praise of other men. All his ambition is for Africa. Work has already begun on the mission in Mfenguland, plans are advancing for the Victoria Hospital, and he has begun to lobby parliament about the building of a University at Fort Hare.

And now he has a new scheme, to set a steamer on Lake Nyassa. Mina considers the conversation of the night before; it is typical of James that he did not even mention the slight that was done to him at Livingstone's funeral. For why had he not been asked to carry the coffin, alongside Kirk, Waller and Young? She suspects that for some people, his reputation is irredeemably damaged by the rumours of what happened between himself and Mary. Gossip, she reflects, can be more insidious and damaging than poison.

'Shall I try playing the sharps?'

'Please do.'

'You won't mind if I get them wrong?'

'Not at all. That's how we learn.' Mina watches her small daughter. She looks so small and purposeful, seated as she is, on two extra cushions, so that she can reach the keys. She corrects her thoughts: words are but words, they cannot harm like stones. Mina will teach her children that people should be judged by their actions, and not by hearsay.

She thinks of Chrissy who, with her husband Lokim, had given up part of her rest day, in order to help out at the lunch. After they had arrived at Lovedale, her brother Sam had sent a letter, in which he stated the true circumstances of his request that Chrissy should travel with them to Africa. Sam had written because he was tormented by guilt. He wanted reassurance that she was not unhappy at the mission. Mina had been appalled by what she read; her heart had gone out to Chrissy, when she considered the extent of her suffering. She had discussed the letter with James, who had been equally outraged. But he added that what was done was done, and it could not be undone. Her reply had said simply that Chrissy had adjusted well to her new life. She had sent her good wishes both to Sam and to Euphemia.

She pictures Chrissy as she had been earlier in the day, happily handing out bowls of rice, with Lokim at her side. Having had a child out of wedlock, she must have been the object of much unpleasant scrutiny. At the same time, she had suffered the awful, aching pain of having lost her child. Now Chrissy has ignored the tongue-wagging of the other missionary wives: she has married a handsome African, who was a once a slave.

Mina will take courage from Chrissy's example. She is tired of living with the fear of James learning the full truth about her family. How much had Papa shared with him, when he asked him to come to Corona? She will confront him directly, and ask him what he knows.

She waits until Little Mina has ceased her playing. 'Let's go and find Letty, shall we?' she says.

* * *

She finds James in the office, seated at his big work table, with Florence asleep in her basket. 'I heard her wake up,' he says. 'She was crying, and I didn't want to disturb you. I took her out her out to see the goats, she soon settled down.'

'I want to talk to you, James.'

'You're looking very serious — did you hear about the window? I found that people have been using it as a short-cut into the office. In order to stop it happening, I said I'd operate a system of fines. I'm afraid that twice today, I've had to fine myself.'

'Don't joke.'

'Sorry. It's true though. John will tell you, and I've put it in my notebook. I have fined myself half a shilling.'

'Well don't expect my sympathy.' She sits down next to him. 'James, I want to talk to you about your second visit to Corona. What was Papa's business with Andrew? Don't try to be evasive. I want to know the truth. I don't want there to be any secrets between us. I know that Andrew has in the past made allegations of incest.' There. She has said it. 'I myself have never been a victim of any unwelcome attentions from Papa. But I cannot speak for all of my sisters...' She had tried to level her words, but her voice emerged sounding high and strained.

James takes her hand. All trace of his previous flippancy has gone. 'I don't want there to be any secrets either. I would have said, but I didn't want to distress you.'

'I would be more distressed now, were you to keep silent.'

'Then I'll tell you. There was a meeting at the house. John came, DWP, Al, Anne, Janet and Andrew. And of course your father was there. Andrew had brought a casket. Your father wouldn't let the others go through the contents, but he asked me to have a look, before we all gathered in the library. He felt I needed to be informed, if I were to mediate successfully. He had invited me to chair the meeting, as a kind of neutral party.'

'So what was inside?'

'There were witness statements from servants and trades' people. And some letters.'

'Who were the letters from?'

'I cannot tell you; your father swore me to secrecy. He maintained that they were forgeries and I had no means of telling whether or not the hand was the purported writer's. And the witness statements could have been purchased or produced under some sort of duress. Whatever the real truth of the matter, Andrew was insistent that your father had horribly abused his position. Eventually, Alexander gave him a money order for three thousand pounds, and Al took the casket to throw into the Clyde. Hopefully, the matter is now at an end.'

Mina bites her lower lip. She is wondering what James really thinks of her family. Andrew had promised to marry Chrissy, and then he had abandoned her. James and Sam had abused the poor girl. Now her father has paid an enormous sum of money to destroy evidence that he had molested one or more of his daughters. It is all so horrible and so very much the antithesis of how decent people should, and do, behave.

She struggles to speak. 'Do you think Papa is guilty, as Andrew says?'

'I know only this: I have every reason to be grateful to him. You were eighteen years old, and he let me bring you here.'

'You don't feel that I am somehow tainted?'

'My dearest darling Mina, I am the luckiest man alive to

have you! Nothing — and I mean *nothing* — could ever change my opinion about that.'

But Mina is not so easily reassured. She is remembering the fight that took place, when Papa had his coat torn, and Andrew was held by Neil the footman, in a tight headlock. 'There are medical men,' Andrew had said, 'who can treat such perversions as you are gripped by.' Andrew had seemed to genuinely want to help Papa. She turns away, and slowly rubs her forehead, with her forefinger.

James takes her in his arms, and holds her close. He speaks quietly, but with urgency: 'Whatever may, or may not have happened, we must not allow it to come between us.' He kisses her lips. 'We are so lucky to have one another. We should seize the moment. We should make the most of our joy. Come with me to the bedroom.'

Mina feels too agitated; she thinks she will refuse. But she is touched by James's unshakeable love and she knows the happiness that can be achieved through complete union. Compared with that pleasure, there is nothing that can give her such peace.

* * *

They undress hurriedly. Time is short because the baby might wake, and anyway, they cannot wait. James kisses her from top to toe, pushing his tongue in the softest place. He enters her gently; she relaxes completely, content to feel the weight of him on top of her, and the fullness of him inside. He thrusts with increasing urgency, while she lies back, and then she tightens, and moves rhythmically, while he stays still. They climax at the same time; the pleasure seems to go on and on. Mina cannot contain herself: she cries out in her delight.

Both of them look at one another: through the window, they have heard the sound of people treading on the gravel path. They hear a very English voice: 'Do you know where I can find the Principal? I'm told his house is here.'

Both Mina and James cover their mouths. They had completely forgotten the incipient arrival of Her Imperial Majesty's ex-Governor of Bombay, Order of the Bath and Star of India, Sir Bartle Frere. 'I said he should take us as he finds us,' whispers James. 'But perhaps we should put on some clothes.'

 Lovedale

After the evening service, Chrissy and Lokim linger to chat with others from the congregation. They spend some time talking to a couple from Alice who are planning to set up a tailor's shop. Then Lokim leaves Chrissy to go to the printing room. There is a new order for a thousand hymn sheets, and before he comes home, he wants to check that the big press is primed, so that it will be ready first thing in the morning, to start its rolling.

Chrissy takes the path from the chapel. While she walks, she wonders what the Stewarts' three bewhiskered guests will have made of the sermon. Given by John Bokwe, the address had been an expansion of the text, 'And God created man in His own image.' John had stated that all men — and women — of any colour, are capable of limitless improvement. He had himself begun as a carpenter at the mission, and now he is in training for the ministry.

Lokim — Chrissy reflects — has the same kind of ambition; he hopes to become a journalist, as well as a printer. As for herself, she is not sure that she has the will to do anything more than she does already. Today, it feels enough that she can speak Xhosa, and can manage a class. Perhaps she will feel better once she has got over the disappointment of the afternoon. For as she was preparing to go out, she had felt a familiar pain. She knew instantly, that her menses had come. She did not tell Lokim, because he would have wanted to look after her, and really, she was only a little late. There was no need to fuss. She should not have shared her excitement — it had been too soon. As she walked to the chapel, she had forced herself to hold her head up high.

A group of young people are returning to their village. 'Good evening, Miss Hogarth,' they say, as they overtake her on the path. They are dressed in their Sunday best, and they are all smiles, as they greet her. She makes herself smile in return. Perhaps she will conceive again soon, or perhaps she will never have another child. In either case — she tells herself — she will have been blessed. She has experienced the joy of being a mother, albeit briefly. In Lokim, she has a clever and devoted husband who, she is sure, will continue to love her, whatever the future does, or does not, bring. And she is blessed to have the Stewarts as friends. James's high intelligence and energy would be off-putting, were he not so generous, and if he did not have such a capacity for laughter. No-one could ever be daunted by Mina; she is all care and kindness. Chrissy thinks back to her wedding, when Mina had decorated the chapel with hibiscus and frangipani, and had given her yards of material to make a white dress. At first she had refused the muslin. With burning cheeks, she had explained that it would not be becoming for her to wear white. Mina had silenced her stammerings. She said that she knew from Sam why Chrissy might think that this was the case. Sam was very sorry for what had happened and she, Mina, would like to offer her deepest and sincerest apologies for the appalling way her brothers had behaved. But Chrissy herself was innocent. She had been ill-used, but this had done nothing to change the purity of her soul. It would distress Mina very much if Chrissy should refuse her gift.

As Chrissy turns towards her house, she is thinking how she should make a present for Mina. She is planning how she will embroider a tablecloth that will be ready in time for Christmas, when she is surprised by the smell of tobacco. She slows her step; one of the Stewarts' guests is smoking a cigarette. He is standing next to her garden fence.

'I hope you don't mind my being here,' the man says. 'Our host, the Reverend Stewart, has the curious notion that inhaled smoke is bad for his children. He has banished me from his house. Such nonsense. He should know better; I understand he is a medical man.'

He holds out his hand. 'Allow me to introduce myself: Captain Stuart Jameson. I am accompanying Sir Bartle on his journey to Zanzibar.'

'And my name, sir, is Chrissy Hogarth.'

'Do you mind if I sit down?' Jameson points over the fence to a double seat, made by Lokim in the carpentry room. Without waiting for permission, he pushes open the wicker gate.

Chrissy is in a quandary: she wants to tell the man to leave, but she has no wish to seem rude. She would tell Jameson that it is too cold to sit outside, but then he might suggest going into her home. With his fleshy white face, drooping moustache and arrogant manner, he repels her. She stays motionless, unsure what next to say or do.

Jameson throws down his cigarette: he grinds it under his heel. He turns, leering, towards her, then of a sudden, he seizes her round the waist and pulls her through the gate and into the garden. For a moment or two, Chrissy is too stunned to respond. 'You're a pretty thing; you remind me of the girl on my soap packet,' he says. 'Let's go inside; we will be more private there.'

Chrissy struggles, then exhales in relief: She can see Lokim hurrying towards her. In her panic, she had not observed his approach. Lokim runs forward and seizes Jameson by the collar, just as Chrissy pulls herself free.

'Leave. Her. Alone.' For good measure, Lokim gives Jameson a shove in the chest.

Jameson turns to Chrissy. 'Surely,' he says, 'you are not going to let this Kaffir manhandle me!'

'This Kaffir is my husband.' Chrissy savours the shock on Jameson's face. Then she stands on tiptoe, and kisses Lokim long and full, directly on the mouth.

POSTSCRIPT

December 1875

Lokim is printing a set of posters, but he is finding it too hard to concentrate; Chrissy is very near her time. Before he left, she had said that she was well, but she wanted to rest; it was just that she felt too hot and heavy to go into the school.

Lokim wants above all else, for Chrissy to give birth to a healthy child. When, after a year of marriage, she had failed to conceive, he had gone up into the hills, where he had prayed for Atum's help. His uncle had not appeared to him, but while sheltering in a cave from a shower of rain, Lokim had remembered that back in the manyatta, cassava had been used to aid fertility. So he had stopped on his way home at the market in Alice, where he had bought three roots of the yam. Chrissy had said that she was content to be childless, it was enough that she could spend time with the smallest pupils. But as she spoke, there had been a haunting sadness in her eyes, and she had gratefully eaten the porridge that he made her.

Whether it was the cassava, good timing or the offices of the Holy Ghost, no-one could say, but soon, Chrissy's menses stopped, and her belly had begun to swell. After four months, she had felt the quickening of new life inside her.

Lokim looks at the sheet he has printed; it is an advertisement for a sale of agricultural equipment. Someone else had done the type-setting, and 'plough' has been misspelt 'plow.' He crumples the paper, throws it into the bin, and sets off home.

* * *

Chrissy cannot get comfortable. She wonders if she is in labour, but the pains should be spasmodic, and the discomfort that she feels in her lower back is almost continuous. She tries to remember what it had felt like when she gave birth before, but the circumstances had been so different. Then, she had been entirely alone. This time, she has the loving support of Lokim, and the Stewarts have said that they, too, would like to look after her. They plan for her to stay in the Principal's house, until her strength is recovered and the baby is feeding properly. Mina will act as a midwife; having helped several other women, she says she knows just what to do.

Chrissy goes outside and walks up and down the path. Under her instruction, Lokim has created a typical cottage garden; snap dragons and nasturtiums grow amongst lettuces and peas, and a froth of sweet-smelling alyssum grows beside her raspberry canes. She stands in the dappled shade of a peach tree and shoos away a red-chested bird, which is about to thieve a thimble of bright fruit. She breathes in the scent of the flowers and stretches out her naked arms. It is a glorious summer's day, and the sky is azure blue. As she does so, she feels a different type of tightening, and knows she is truly in labour.

* * *

361

Lokim finds her back in bed. She is lying on her side, and she is experiencing a long episode of pain. She makes no sound, but her face is wet with perspiration. She has closed her eyes, and pulled up her knees. He strokes her back, moving his fingers in long sweeps, until the episode has passed.

'I think it's time to fetch Mina.'

Lokim brings water, and a cloth which he moistens in a bowl. He wipes her face, then hands her the cloth. 'Bite on this the next time the pain comes. It can help to be distracted, when you are suffering. I will come back very soon.'

He runs to the Principal's house, but Mina is not there. He finds her in the sanatorium, with Florence beside her. She is helping a young boy to eat; his arm has been broken, and set in a splint. 'It is Chrissy,' he says. 'Her time has come.'

Mina gets to her feet. 'Go to the school. Ask Letty to come. She can take over here, and she can also look after Florrie.'

* * *

Mina knows something is wrong, as soon as she has lifted Chrissy's gown, and palpated her abdomen. On one side, above the hip, she can feel something round and hard. The baby's head should be down in the pelvis, ready to progress down the birth canal. But it is in the wrong place. The pains are coming fast, one upon the other, and Chrissy's waters have gone. Mina wishes that she could call Jane — she is more experienced as a midwife than herself. But Jane Waterston has left for England. She has developed such an interest in medicine that she has gone to train as a doctor, with Elizabeth Garrett Anderson.

Mina tucks her hair behind her ear, lowers her head and listens. She can hear a sound like the rapid beating of hooves. 'I am going to get James,' Mina says. 'Your baby is well — but not in the correct position. And James will know what to do.'

362

* * *

James is miles away. He has taken his sextant, and has gone in the direction of Fort Willshier where there have been several carting accidents, and he wants to straighten out the road. Mina will have ride fast, or it will be too late.

Wolf — her horse — comes eagerly towards her. She fetches from the stable not her own side-saddle, but a spare one, which they use for guests. She buckles it on, and adjusts the stirrups. She pulls up her skirt, and holds it in her teeth as she tries to mount — but the swathes of material are too much in the way. She tears off the skirt; it is much easier to manage, now that she is attired in nothing but her pantaloons.

Astride Wolf, she gallops recklessly along the track. She will do all that she can to ensure that the baby arrives safely into the world.

* * *

James is stretching out a length of tape when Mina finds him. As soon as he sees her curious dress and hears her say 'Chrissy…' he understands that there is an emergency; by the time she has finished explaining, his measuring equipment has been packed away.

Galloping back to Lovedale, he considers what he will do. First, he will attempt a manual rotation. If that fails to work, he will perform a Caesarean section. The operation carries considerable risk, but if the baby remains in the transverse position, so that the labour is obstructed, the uterus will rupture: both Chrissy and her baby will die. He visualises the cupboard in the treatment room of the sanatorium where he keeps his knives, saws, forceps and sutures. Everything is in order, and it is all kept scrupulously clean. But his instruments will be of no use unless he gets back in time. Bucket is doing his best. He presses forward, with Mina and Wolf coming along behind.

* * *

Lokim fights an increasing sense of panic. He wants to have a child — of course he does — but the baby is a person whom he does not know. Whereas Chrissy — his most precious friend, his lover and wife, is someone he knows very well. All his concern is for her. In Africa, it is commonplace for a woman to die in labour; his own mother had died that way, when he was a small child.

On the surface, he keeps calm. He strokes Chrissy's back, cools her brow and puts the kettle on the stove, so that he will be able to offer tea to the Stewarts, when they return. Silently, desperately, he prays that Chrissy will live. Whether it was luck, a miracle or magic that had brought them together, he does not know; he knows only that he loves her. They are forever linked: they have each struggled through darkness, out into the light.

* * *

Chrissy sees James's tall frame appear in the doorway. She wonders if she is hallucinating — when Mina follows him inside, she is wearing only her pantaloons. Then she is racked by a pain so powerful that there is no further possibility of thought. She bites on the wet cloth that Lokim has given her, to stop herself from screaming.

James scrubs his hands at the basin. 'I'm going to examine you,' he says. 'And I'm going to try to turn the baby from inside. If that doesn't work, I will give you some chloroform — so that you will know nothing — and I will remove the baby through a cut. Before I begin, can I give you some opium to dull the pain?'

Chrissy shakes her head. She will take nothing that might affect the baby.

The pain is so bad that James's hand cannot make it worse.

'The cervix is fully dilated,' he says. 'And I can feel the baby's ear. I'll just pull it down... like so... Now Mina, if you can apply pressure on the abdomen, and Chrissy, a few more contractions... I think we can get the little one to move across, and into the right position.'

James asks her sit at the edge of the bed — he says that the force of gravity will help to correct the baby's lie. Chrissy puts her arms around Lokim's neck; with his support, she stays upright, as she endures each long pain.

After what feels a long time, she feels a kind of grinding and a burning. She looks at Lokim wide-eyed.

'Let me examine you again,' says James. He removes his hand with a look of elation. 'The baby's head is crowning. All is now as it should be.'

'Can I move back on the bed and really push?'

'Go ahead. Start now. One, two, three...'

* * *

Lokim has never seen anything more extraordinary. First, there is a round of black hair, and a furrowed little face raises itself up. The head turns, and it is followed by a shoulder. Then an entire perfect body slides out of Chrissy and into James's waiting hands.

'Congratulations!' says Mina, who seems to have mislaid her skirt. 'Dearest Chrissy, Dearest Lokim, you have a fine, healthy daughter!'

James ties off the cord, cuts it and hands the baby — who is now crying lustily — over to Lokim. He looks with amazement at his child. She has the thick black curls of an African, and Chrissy's large blue eyes. Her skin is the colour

365

of dark, warm honey. She is spectacularly, wonderfully, beautiful.

Mina is holding out a little sheet, embroidered with rabbits. He hands the baby over. Mina wraps her in the sheet, and passes the warm bundle to Chrissy. 'You will have to think what to call her.'

Chrissy loosens her gown, for the little one is rooting with her mouth and tongue. She looks up expectantly.

'We've already decided,' Lokim says. He nods in affirmation, then puts out a hand to gently stroke the baby's still-damp hair. 'Her name is Thomasina.'

PLACES IN AFRICA MENTIONED IN
DAPPLED LIGHT

AFRICA

Lake Victoria

Karamoja Region

(Huge Pool)

Equator

Bagamoyo

Zanzibar

Lake Nyassa

Madagascar

ATLANTIC

Zambesi River

Shupanga

AFRICA

Cape Town

Lovedale

East London

SELECT BIBLIOGRAPHY

The main source I used for information about James was '*The Life of James Stewart*' by James Wells D.D. (Hodder and Stoughton 1908). For Mina's family, I referred to *Shared Lives* by Maureen Borland (published by Maureen Borland 2006) and *A Shipbuilding History* (printed for Alexander Stephen and Sons Ltd by ED Burrows in 1932). *Clydebuilt* by Eric J Graham (Birlinn 2006) provided information about the three ships that were built by the Stephen's Yard to see service as blockade-runners in the American Civil War. I used Colin Turnbull's *The Mountain People* (Simon and Schuster 1987) for information about Lokim's tribe, the Ik. Elaine Showalter's *The Female Malady: Women Madness and English Culture 1830 – 1980* (Virago 1987) provided background for Chrissy's experiences in the Royal Lunatic Asylum. For details of domestic life, I referred to Judith Flanders '*The Victorian House*' (Harper Perrenial 2004.) A N Wilson's *The Victorians* (Arrow Books 2003) gave me an overview of the Victorian era. Edna Healey's *Wives of Fame* (Sidgwick and Jackson 1980) provided information about the life of Mary Livingstone, as did Margaret Forster's *Good Wives? Mary, Fanny, Jennie and Me, 1985-2001* (Chatto and Windus 2001). I gained further knowledge of the Zambesi Expedition and the character of David Livingstone from Oliver Ransford's *David Livingstone: The Dark Interior* (Camelot Press,

1978) and Tim Jeal's *Explorers of the Nile* (Faber and Faber 2011). Alastair Hazell's volume *The Last Slave Market: Dr John Kirk And The Struggle To End The African Slave Trade* (Constable and Robinson 2011) gave an insight into the slave trade in the African interior. Original sources used were A *Popular Account of Missionary Travels and researches in Southern Africa* by David Livingstone (reprinted General Books 2010), Richard Burton's *First Footsteps in East Africa* (reprinted by Dover in 1987), *Vestiges of the Natural History of Creation* by Robert Chambers (reprinted University of Chicago 1994), *The Zambesi Journal of James Stewart 1862 - 1863* edited by JPR Wallis (Chatto and Windus 1952), and *The Letters of Jane Elizabeth Waterston 1866 - 1905.* (Van Riebeek Society 1983).

SPELLING

Some place names appear as they did in Livingstone's journals, rather than in their current spelling. Hence the Zambesi rather than the Zambezi, Lake Nyassa, rather than Nyasa, and Shupanga rather than Chupanga.

THE STEPHEN FAMILY

Mina's father, Alexander Stephen, was a successful shipbuilder, with yards in Glasgow and Dundee, and a large house in Broughty Ferry. The firm Alexander Stephen and sons went on to build many notable ships, including the Terra Nova, which was used by Scott to explore the Antarctic, and the Sir Galahad, which was lost in the Falklands war.

Two of Mina's brothers — Andrew and James — gave up stakes in the family firm in exchange for compensatory payments, but afterwards they felt that the money they had been given was insufficient and a court case began. Mina's sister Anne was married to the family lawyer, Duncan Wilkie Paterson, who kept papers about the case in a wicker box. I inherited the box from my mother, because he and Anne were my great great grandparents. Going through its contents one wet afternoon, I found letters from Andrew, which record the hold that Hannah Stephen had over her father, and the dislike that Alexander felt towards his youngest son Sam. They also mention a Miss Chrissy Hogarth for whom Andrew expressed a passionate attachment, and with whom James also seems to have been involved. A pencil written note which Alexander sent to Anne in 1874 reads: 'I present you herewith as a free and absolute gift the sum of two thousand pounds sterling,' In a shaking hand, he had added the single word 'Free?'

The implication was that Alexander was being blackmailed. When I found out more about my Stephen ancestors, I learned that Andrew had publicly accused his father of incest, by putting up posters around Dundee.

The children of Alexander Stephen travelled the world at a time when many people did not venture further than their home village. While Mina made her home in Africa, her brothers and sisters travelled to America, China, Australia, and Europe.

Here are the names and occupations of 'The Eighteen':

Elspeth Murray b 1824, m William Croudace, shipbuilder
William b 1826, shipbuilder m 1st Jane Henderson, 2nd
   Elizabeth Henderson
Anne b 1827, m Duncan W Paterson, lawyer
James b 1828, m 1st Williamina Grant, 2nd Eliza
   McCorquadale
Helen b 1830, m Revd John Logan
Alexander (Al) b 1832, shipbuilder m Mary Templeton
Andrew b 1833, medical doctor m Eleanor Stuart

John b 1835, shipbuilder and philanthropist m Elizabeth
(Eliza) Wilson
Mary b 1836, m John Templeton carpet manufacturer
Elizabeth b 1837, died aged 4 in an accident
Mary-Ann b 1838, m William Wright, tea-merchant
Hannah b 1839, m William Adams accountant from
Newcastle Australia
Janet b 1840
Marjory b 1841, died of typhoid in Gibralter age 22
Ruth b 1842, died age 1
Samuel b 1844, sea captain, m Euphemia Baxter
Margaret b 1847, m Robert Mudie shipbuilder
Williamina (Mina) b 1848 m James Stewart medical
missionary

JAMES STEWART

James Stewart was born in Edinburgh in 1831. He died at
Lovedale in 1905, having worked tirelessly for the cause of
racial equality in Southern Africa. He harnessed logic and
reason to change things for the better, listing — for example
— the professions of past students when fund-raising for the
mission; he recorded that 768 graduates had become teachers,
while 112 were employed as interpreters, magistrates clerks,
postmen or telegraph workers.

His dream was that Southern Africa should have its own
university, which would be open to all, and where the teaching
would be of the highest quality. He skilfully lobbied
parliament to secure a site at Fort Hare, and a week after his
death, 130 delegates met at Lovedale, where they agreed to
raise the astonishing sum of £50,000 to further the
establishment of the proposed institute. From his sick bed, he
had organised accommodation for all the attendees.

A story recorded by his biographer illustrates how persistently he challenged prejudice. He was travelling with an African friend called Mr Mzimba when it became necessary for the two travellers to stop at a wayside inn. James was offered a bedroom, while his companion was shown a space above the stable. James insisted to the landlady that if there was only one proper room available, his friend should be given the better place to stay, while he himself would sleep above the animals. The upshot was that Mr Mzimba was also given a comfortable room inside the main building.

He had devoted forty years to furthering the cause of African education, yet his last words to his friend John Bokwe were 'I wish I could have done more for your people.' A tall column fashioned to resemble a lighthouse was constructed as his memorial; it stands high on Sandilis Kop near Lovedale, and can be seen for miles around.

But James's reputation has continually suffered because of his relationship with Mary Livingstone. Mary's biographer, Edna Healey described him as self-regarding; she said that he used Mary to gain access to her famous husband. We will never know the truth of what happened between them, but Mary was a sensual person. Her husband was away, and she had lost any religious certainty that she may once have had. What was there to stop her from taking advantage of the presence in her home of a young man who was dependent on her to help him achieve his goal of reaching Africa? James had good looks and charisma — he was a tempting prospect. It is perfectly possible — if not probable — that if anyone was a victim in their liaison, it was he, rather than she.

James Stewart was kind, and funny. He was a linguist, a political negotiator, a doctor, an engineer, a road-builder, a botanist, a hospital administrator, an industrialist, as well as being a minister in the Free Church of Scotland. I hope that *Dappled Light* will go some small way to celebrating the life of this gifted man, who deserves to be remembered as far more than a footnote in the biography of the wife of David Livingstone.

ORIGINAL SOURCES

David's Livingstone's letters and journals are available to view on the wonderful *Livingstone online* internet site. They make good reading. The explorer's style is vivid and his writing is often peppered with humour. But his journals were heavily edited by his friend Horace Waller, who was keen to place the explorer in the best possible light, so the truth is sometimes obfuscated. It is recorded in Livingstone's *Narrative of an expedition to the Zambesi and its tributaries* that James Stewart arrived in the Gorgon in April 1862, which gives the impression that James arrived later than Mary. In fact, they had travelled out from Scotland together, and had spent months in each other's company.

Extract from letter: David Livingstone to Captain Washington
(with kind permission of Livingstone online)

March 1862

'A gentleman has been sent out by the free church of Scotland to obtain information with a view to a mission on Nyassa. As this will not interfere with the bishop, I invited him to come up and see the country and people for himself. His name is Revd James Stewart. There is room for all that in the region, and it is questionable whether the bishop has not blocked up his own way Northwards by attacking the Ajawa, who now possess all the East bank of Shire from the cataracts up to the Lake. His sister, <u>a confirmed invalid,</u> came up to him. Captain Wilson seeing how slowly we got up — (3 weeks to Shupanga! Last year 2 days only!) acceded to her request to be taken with M<u>rs</u> Burrup (another of the missionaries) forward to the Ruo in his gig. The bishop engaged to be there but did not appear & Captain Wilson pushed on to Chibisa's the invalid being more dead than alive. We expect him daily on his return, and when he does so I shall give you the latest intelligence.

I feel it rather too much to have to give passages to all the missionaries I was willing and anxious to do all I could for them & am still willing, but it is a serious draw back to our own success. Rev M<u>r</u> Proctor wanted to come down for a wife, & the bishop proposed to come too. I had to tell them that the Pioneer was not a passenger vessel. It is a serious tax on our stores. M<u>r</u> Stewart offers payment for everything has calico to buy his own provisions and works at whatever he can do. Some of the bishop's people believe that they have a right to everything here, and on board the men of war which causes grumbling among the officers.'

Extract from letter: David Livingstone to James Stewart
(with kind permission of University of Cape Town Library)

1864

'Whatever may be said or written no variation so far as I was conscious was made in my conduct either to the dead or the living.

I do not consider myself above being deceived but unless led to foolish conduct I do not feel that I have been befooled generally. I can forgive and I prefer not to take forwards unkind feelings towards anyone along the path of life.

If we carry sunshine in our own bosoms why should we allow silly sayings or the past to come back to cloud our joy.'

Eliza Stephen writing to James in 1875
(with kind permission of University of Cape Town Library)

'Poor little Mrs Hoare

She would be quite overpowered by your gallantry.

My cousin, when he came down told me he had asked you to dine at his club.

I assume you never suggested such a thing. He seems to have come under the spell that most people come under. They see you are worth knowing and would like to see a little more of you.'

Extract from letter; Mina Stewart to her sister Maggie 1903
(University of Cape Town Library)

Mina had been given Johnston's *Life of Livingstone* by a Mr Bruce. She wrote; 'I don't like it. He should not have spoken of Mrs L as he has.'

ACKNOWLEDGEMENTS

I would like to thank the staff of the University of Glasgow Archives Services who produced for me diaries kept by John and Al Stephen, the staff of the University of Cape Town Libraries, Manuscripts and Archives Division who showed me the papers of James Stewart, and the assistant at our local library in Newtown, who acquired for me James Stewart's Zambesi Journal. I would also like to thank David Robertson of St Peter's Free Church in Dundee for his prompt and helpful response to my enquiry about nineteenth century attitudes to babies born out of wedlock. I am indebted to Sandy Stephen for the detailed genealogy he produced of 'The Eighteen'. Thank you also to Ann McCay for her pictures and map. In writing *Dappled Light*, I have mixed fact with fiction. I sincerely hope that by doing so, I have not caused offence to anyone. My desire has been to entertain, whilst celebrating the lives of two remarkable people.